GREAT AMERICAN GHOST STORIES

GREAT AMERICAN GHOST STORIES
Chilling Tales by Poe, Bierce, Hawthorne and Others

Edited by
MIKE ASHLEY

DOVER PUBLICATIONS, INC.
MINEOLA, NEW YORK

Acknowledgments

"Call Me From the Valley" by Manly Wade Wellman: Copyright © 1954 by Fantasy House, Inc. Originally published in the March 1954 issue of *The Magazine of Fantasy & Science Fiction*.

"The Fire When It Comes" © 1981 by Parke Godwin. First appeared in *The Magazine of Fantasy & Science Fiction*, May 1981.

Copyright

Bibliographical Note

Great American Ghost Stories: Chilling Tales by Poe, Bierce, Hawthorne and Others, first published by Dover Publications, Inc., in 2008, is a new anthology of sixteen stories reprinted from standard sources. A new Introduction, written by Mike Ashley, has been specially prepared for the present edition.

Library of Congress Cataloging-in-Publication Data

Great American ghost stories : chilling tales by Poe, Bierce, Hawthorne, and others / edited by Mike Ashley.
    p. cm.
  ISBN-13: 978-0-486-46602-6
  ISBN-10: 0-486-46602-7
   1. Ghost stories, American. 2. Horror tales, American. I. Ashley, Michael.

PS648.G48G73 2008
813'.0873308—dc22

2008010000

Manufactured in the United States of America
Dover Publications, Inc., 31 East 2nd Street, Mineola, N.Y. 11501

Contents

Contents

Introduction

WHEN ANY discussion turns to ghost stories it is almost certain that the examples given and the authors mentioned are invariably English—from Charles Dickens to Algernon Blackwood, and from Bulwer Lytton to M. R. James. The word "English" may be used, rather broadly, to include Welsh (Arthur Machen), Irish (Sheridan Le Fanu), and Scottish (Margaret Oliphant), but it rarely incorporates any American writers. By adoption, Henry James is sometimes included in the discussion. Yet, though James may have settled in England in 1876, he only took on British citizenship in 1915, a year before his death.

The question arises as to whether a distinct school of American ghostly fiction emerged during the nineteenth century and, if so, how it differed from the English. Despite such leviathans of the literature as Hawthorne, Ambrose Bierce, and that presiding genius Edgar Allan Poe, the full scale of the American ghost story is seldom considered in detail. Much of Poe's work is categorized as "horror," an unhelpful phrase dealing more with mood than content, but as a consequence the great legacy of America's ghostly fiction is all too easily bypassed. Writing in *American Supernatural Fiction* (Garland, 1996), Benjamin Fisher noted the belief that "there is not in America any very great tradition of the macabre."

Yet the simple truth is that the ghost story has as full and independent a history in America as it does in Britain. Though both the English and American ghost story owe their origins to the broader strand of European fiction, especially German and Italian, which had given rise to the fascination with gothic fiction, and though similarities remained between the two developing strands, the American ghost story soon acquired its own character and more style, as the stories reprinted here show.

The gothic influence had been imported to America, to some degree, in the early works of Charles Brockden Brown, such as *Wieland* (1798) and *Arthur Mervyn* (1799). Washington Irving's early supernatural tales, such as "The Spectre Bridegroom" (1819) and "The Adventure of the German Student" (1824) are firmly rooted in the gothic tradition, and Irving's travels throughout Europe inspired many stories based on folktales collected in *Tales of a Traveller* (1824) and *The Alhambra* (1832). America's first popular ghost story, "Peter Rugg, The Missing Man" by William Austin, published in the *New England Galaxy* for 10 September 1824, owes much to the European legends of the Flying Dutchman and Wandering Jew, reworked into the style of Washington Irving's "Rip Van Winkle" (1819).

These early tales, drawing from the universal memory of folktale and myth, gradually gave way to stories drawing from the American experience, and that is where this collection of classic American ghost stories begins. Two authors in particular— Edgar Allan Poe (1809–1849) and Nathaniel Hawthorne (1804– 1864)—shaped the medium, transplanting the gothic from the decadence and desolation of central Europe to New England and the American South.

Poe's early work was heavily influenced by the gothic. His first published story, "Metzengerstein" (1832), is pure gothic, right down to the castle battlements. He transferred the gothic mood to American soil in probably his best known story, "The Fall of the House of Usher" (1839), which is imbued with all the potency of Poe's fears of death, decline, and doom. Unlike the early gothic writers, who produced their work on a grand scale, Poe was able to personalize it, and in so doing brought the real horror of death and decay into the individual consciousness. Poe's whole life was tragic. It was a life of loss—abandoned by his father soon after his birth, his mother dying of tuberculosis before he was three, and his wife Virginia developing tuberculosis when she was nineteen. She was an invalid for her remaining five years, her decline matched by Poe's increasing reliance on drugs and alcohol. Poe was devoted to his wife, whom he had married when she was only thirteen in September 1835. He dreaded losing her and that feeling saturates the story included here, "Ligeia," first published in the *American Museum* for 18 September 1838. Poe believed it was one of his best stories and it has long been regarded as a classic of American literature.

Although Hawthorne, like Poe, lost his father at an early age, and spent much of his early life in dreamlike isolation ("I have not lived, but only dreamed about living," he later wrote), his life was not so full of tortured anguish. Yet some of his fiction reflects the concerns, fears, and worries of the early colonial life. Hawthorne was descended from William Hathorne who settled in Massachusetts in 1630 and whose son, John Hathorne, was one of the judges who oversaw the infamous Salem witch trials of the 1690s. It has been suggested that Hawthorne added the "w" to his name in order to distance himself from his notorious ancestor. Many of his early stories drew upon the uncertainty and dilemmas of the early Puritan settlers, such as in "The Hollow of the Three Hills" (1830) and "Young Goodman Brown" (1835). These dilemmas are perhaps best demonstrated in the story reprinted here, "The Gray Champion" (*New England Magazine,* January 1835), which goes to the very roots of freedom and justice.

William Gilmore Simms (1806–1870) is not a name one immediately associates with Poe and Hawthorne, and yet Poe regarded Simms as the best novelist America had yet produced. Like Poe, Simms lost his mother in infancy and, though he studied law, took to a life of journalism and literature in his beloved South Carolina, achieving fame first as a poet. Irish by descent, Simms was remarkably prolific for his day, producing over eighty works including poetry, novels, stories, and historical studies. Amongst them is a gothic novel of a haunted mansion with the delightful title *Castle Dismal* (1844). Simms' work has long fallen out of favor, possibly in part because of his pro-slavery views, though his novel, *The Yemassee* (1835), was supportive of the American Indians. In his day, Poe rated his story "Grayling; or 'Murder Will Out'" (*The Gift*, Christmas 1842) as "one of the best defined ghost stories we have ever read." Once frequently reprinted, "Grayling" is pretty much forgotten today. The ghost element is only a small part of the story and yet is crucial to the plot, no matter how much the author seeks to rationalize it at the end. In fact one can see in the story the start of a more realistic treatment of the supernatural.

Henry James (1843–1916) was one of the godfathers of the realist movement. Like Simms, he was Irish by descent, and he also studied law but was more attracted to literature, selling his first story, "A Tragedy of Error," in 1864. James was initially influenced by Nathaniel Hawthorne, setting his first ghost story, "The Romance of Certain Old Clothes" (1868), in eighteenth-century Massachusetts, though this story of revenge from the grave owes as much to Poe. James traveled extensively through Europe and settled in England in 1876. His classic story, "The Turn of the Screw" (1898) undeniably betrays the atmosphere of the English ghost story. It may seem strange for a master of modern realism to explore the ghost story, so closely attached to the romantic movement, and James regarded his work on "The Turn of the Screw" and similar stories as an "excursion into chaos." By applying his outlook to the supernatural, he was able to transform the ghost story from the more direct, physical haunting, to an unsettling psychological invasion. "The Real Right Thing" (*Collier's Weekly*, 16 December 1899), which was the ghost story he wrote after "The Turn of the Screw," has all the elements of a haunting which is no less real without a ghost. It was an approach that had its roots in the work of Poe, whose horrors were as much of the mind as of the body.

James's contemporary, Sarah Orne Jewett (1849–1909), from South Berwick, Maine, also liked the uncertain, ambiguous ghost story as is evident from "Lady Ferry." She had problems selling the story to the periodicals and so published it in her collection *Old Friends and New* in 1879. There will be those who regard this as a story of immortality rather than a ghost story, but that is deliberate on Jewett's part, because no one really knows who, or what, Lady Ferry was. Jewett's career spanned nearly forty years, from her first story, "Jenny Garrow's Lovers" in 1868 to her last, "A Spring Sunday," in 1904, by which time she had been incapacitated by an accident and could no longer write. She produced a number of ghost stories though no individual collection appeared in her lifetime and they were only assembled recently by Jessica Amanda Salmonson as *Lady Ferry and Other Uncanny People* (1998). Yet during her lifetime her work was admired widely by the likes of Rudyard Kipling, Harriet Beecher Stowe, and Rebecca West. Willa Cather, who also features in this anthology, met her in her final year, and was inspired by her work. She regarded Jewett's novel *The Country of the Pointed Firs* (1896) as an American classic, ranking alongside Hawthorne's *The Scarlet Letter* and Twain's *Huckleberry Finn*.

Mark Twain (1835–1910) is not especially remembered for his supernatural fiction, and when he did on occasion, turn to matters metaphysical, it tended to be for reasons of satire or humor, such as in "A Ghost Story" (1888) and *Extracts from Captain Stormfield's Visit to Heaven* (1909). But just once or twice he treated the matter seriously and, when he did, the results were very effective. "My Platonic Sweetheart" was written in 1898 but not published until after Twain's death (*Harper's Magazine*, December 1912). It bears comparison to Jewett's "Lady Ferry" because, once again, we are uncertain as to the nature of the haunting. Is it simply a girl of the narrator's dreams, or memories of another existence, or an astral influence? One of the delights of the ghost story is just how ambiguous they can become.

Like Mark Twain, Frank R. Stockton (1834–1902) had a reputation as a humorist and he produced several amusing ghost stories such as his spoof on Dickens's *A Christmas Carol*, "Stephen Skarridge's Christmas" (1872) and "The Transferred Ghost" (1882), which is often reprinted, even though it lacks any spectral atmosphere. At the start of his career, he was best known for his children's stories and fairy tales, many written for *St. Nicholas Magazine* of which he was, from 1874 to 1878, an assistant editor. The best are collected in *The Bee-Man of Orn* (1887) and most recently in *Fairy Tales of Frank Stockton* (1990). Stockton delighted in challenging dilemmas and this resulted in his best known story, the classic "The Lady or the

Tiger?" (1882), in which the protagonist has to make a choice and the reader is left uncertain which one (if either) was right. He brought that same creative questioning to what many regard as his best ghost story, "The Philosophy of Relative Existences" (*Century Magazine,* August 1892), which is collected here, and which introduces a highly original concept on the nature of ghosts.

For a more sinister ghost, indeed a malign one, with a powerful presence, one can do no better than turn to "The Upper Berth" (*Unwin's Annual,* 1886) by F. Marion Crawford (1854–1909). At one time this story appeared in just about every ghost story collection and perhaps for that reason it has been neglected in recent years and thus needs another outing. Everett Bleiler called it "one of the best material-horror stories, convincing and strong." Although Crawford was American by descent—his aunt was the poet Julia Ward Howe—and was educated partly in America, he was born and lived most of his life in Italy and thus, like Henry James, had a wider, more cosmopolitan outlook. Yet most of his works are forgotten today, and it is only his supernatural fiction, issued posthumously as *Wandering Ghosts* (1911), that keeps his name alive.

The exotic, and the grasp of European culture and literature, was also evident in the work of Emma Frances Dawson (1839–1926). She had been born in Maine, as were so many writers of ghost stories, and moved with her mother to California after the American Civil War. A poet, journalist, and music teacher, she became one of the major writers on the San Francisco scene in the 1880s and her work was admired by Ambrose Bierce. She was a trained musician and singer and also fluent in several European languages, and most of her income—when she wasn't teaching music—came from translating stories for the San Francisco papers. Her own stories, mostly weird and unusual, were collected as *An Itinerant House* in 1896, copies of which are now exceedingly scarce as many were destroyed in the San Francisco earthquake. A second volume, *A Gracious Visitation,* for which Bierce wrote an introduction, remained unpublished until 1921. "An Itinerant House" first appeared in *The Argonaut* for 20 April 1878 and utilizes the fact that at that time in San Francisco homes were often mobile and transported from place to place. Her knowledge of music and delight in poetry is perhaps something of a distraction in what is otherwise a most unusual and original story.

Dawson's mentor, Ambrose Bierce (1842–1914?) is perhaps the best known of the San Francisco school of writers of weird fiction, though he had been born in Ohio and raised in Indiana. He fought throughout the Civil War and was seriously wounded at the Battle of Kennesaw Mountain in June 1864. His experiences during the war, which embittered an already cynical outlook on life, later earning him the nickname "Bitter Bierce," formed the basis of many of his stories, especially those collected in *Tales of Soldiers and Civilians* (1891). Bierce is perhaps best remembered today for *The Devil's Dictionary* (1911), which includes his own cynical definitions of words and phrases, but he was a prolific journalist and writer and a surprising amount of his output still remains uncollected from the original newspapers. He was interested in strange phenomena, in some ways presaging Charles Fort in his reporting of unusual events, and his story here, "The Moonlit Road" (*Cosmopolitan,* January 1907) is an interesting example of how a haunting appeared to different individuals, not all of them living.

Another Maine author was Harriet Prescott Spofford (1835–1921). She established her reputation as an author of imaginative gothic romance with her early novel, *Sir Rohan's Ghost* (1860) and her story collection *The Amber Gods* (1860). Henry James, though recognizing the author's talent, saw in her work more of the romantic than the realist and remarked in his review of *The Amber Gods* that its content was "morbid and unhealthful." Spofford's writing career lasted for over sixty years, from 1856 to 1920, and in that time she produced scores of weird tales, the best of which have recently been reassembled as *The Moonstone Mass and Others* (1920). Her story included here, "The Conquering Will," first appeared in *The Smart Set* for June 1901.

Mary Eleanor Wilkins (1852–1930) already had a substantial literary career before she married Dr. Charles Freeman in 1902, but she is generally remembered today under her married

name, as Mary E. Wilkins Freeman. She was born in
Massachusetts, living there and in Vermont for many years,
though later settling in New Jersey. She wrote over twenty
books and also served as private secretary to Oliver Wendell
Holmes. The majority of her books reflect New England life
without any recourse to the supernatural, but on those occasions
when she introduced a ghostly element, the results were
extremely effective. Her ghost stories, some of which were collected in *The Wind in the Rose-Bush* (1903), with more included
in the posthumous collection *Collected Ghost Stories* (1974), are
highly regarded for their atmosphere and characterization. "The
Shadows on the Wall" first appeared in *Everybody's Magazine*
for March 1903.

Though born in New York, and traveling with her family
throughout Europe in her childhood, Edith Wharton (1862–
1937) lived in Massachusetts from 1901 to 1911, after which she
settled in France for the remainder of her life. She came from a
fabulously wealthy family—her maiden name was Jones, and it
has been suggested that her parents were the original socialites
about whom the phrase "keeping up with the Joneses" was
coined. Her original interests were in landscape gardening and
interior design and she designed and had built her home in
Lenox, Massachusetts. Her fame, though, rests on her fiction,
particularly *The Age of Innocence* (1920), with which she
became the first woman to win a Pulitzer Prize. Her supernatural stories are spread throughout her career, from "The Fullness
of Life" in 1893 to her very last story, "All Souls," written a few
months before her death; but by far the majority of them were
written after she settled in France. There were, though, a cluster written during her years in Massachusetts, most of which
reflect life in New York and New England amongst the upper
crust of society. Of these, "The Eyes" (*Scribner's Magazine*,
June 1910) is especially haunting. Her ghost stories are generally held in high regard and at the time of her death a collection
was being assembled which appeared as *Ghosts* (1937) and
remains an essential volume for any devotee of the outré.

Like Wharton, Willa Cather (1873–1947) was initially influenced by Henry James, as evidenced by her first novel,

Alexander's Bridge (1912). However, in 1908 she met Sarah
Orne Jewett, who encouraged Cather to look to her roots, particularly her upbringing in Nebraska, and this led to Cather
producing *O Pioneers!* (1913), the first of her prairie trilogy.
Her regional work would eventually win her the Pulitzer Prize
in 1923 for her novel *One of Ours*. Like Jewett, Cather was fascinated with the potential of the ghost story, and though she
wrote few, "Consequences" stands out for its originality and
approach. It bears comparison both with the work of Henry
James and with Stockton's story included here. It first appeared
in the November 1915 *McClure's Magazine*, of which Cather
had been Managing Editor from 1908 to 1911.

Manly Wade Wellman (1903–1986) was a prolific writer of a
wide variety of genre fiction, including mystery, fantasy, supernatural, and science fiction—winning awards in most of the
fields in which he dabbled. He was born in Angola, or Portuguese
West Africa, as it was then known, where his father was a medical officer. After returning to the United States, and completing
his studies, Wellman became a journalist but soon found he was
earning more selling stories to the pulp magazines, and these
became his major market for the next thirty years. He was a
well-known contributor to the two leading magazines of weird
fiction, *Weird Tales* and *Unknown,* and with the change in
magazines in the fifties he became a regular at *The Magazine of
Fantasy & Science Fiction*. It was this magazine that published
Wellman's series featuring John the Balladeer, a backwoods
wanderer in the Appalachians, around Wellman's home in
North Carolina, whose guitar has silver strings and its tunes help
John out of the problems he encounters. "Call Me From the
Valley" appeared in the March 1954 issue. The stories were
subsequently collected as *Who Fears the Devil?* (1963). They
are based on local folklore and legend and thus bring us back
full circle to the early writers, such as Nathaniel Hawthorne and
William Gilmore Simms, who drew upon American tradition for
their tales.

Parke Godwin (b. 1929) is the author of the most recent story
in this collection, "The Fire When It Comes," which also
appeared in *The Magazine of Fantasy & Science Fiction* (May

1981). It won the World Fantasy Award for Best Novella in 1982. Godwin has worked for some years as a professional actor, but is probably best known for his historical fantasies. These include *Firelord* (1980) about King Arthur, *Beloved Exile* (1984) about Guinevere, *The Last Rainbow* (1985) about St. Patrick, and *Sherwood* (1991) about Robin Hood. Godwin returned to the supernatural with the powerful novel, *A Cold Blue Light* (1983), written with Marvin Kaye.

All these stories clearly bear the stamp of their American roots, whether from folktales, local settings, authors' experiences, or, most distinctly, an original American approach, bringing new thinking to the ghost story. Some of these stories may be comparable to their English cousins in basic content, but their realistic approach and characterization makes them distinctly American. That the stories have stood the test of time and read as well today as when they were first written shows that the authors have created something worthy of celebrating.

MIKE ASHLEY

Ligeia

Edgar Allan Poe

And the will therein lieth, which dieth not. Who knoweth the
mysteries of the will, with its vigor? For God is but a great will
pervading all things by nature of its intentness. Man doth not
yield him to the angels, nor unto death utterly, save only through
the weakness of his feeble will. —*Joseph Glanvill.*

I cannot, for my soul, remember how, when or even precisely
where, I first became acquainted with the lady Ligeia. Long
years have since elapsed, and my memory is feeble through
much suffering. Or, perhaps, I cannot *now* bring these points to
mind, because, in truth, the character of my beloved, her rare
learning, her singular yet placid cast of beauty, and the thrilling
and enthralling eloquence of her low musical language, made
their way into my heart by paces so steadily and stealthily pro-
gressive that they have been unnoticed and unknown. Yet I
believe that I met her first and most frequently in some large,
old, decaying city near the Rhine. Of her family—I have surely
heard her speak. That it is of a remotely ancient date cannot be
doubted. Ligeia! Ligeia! Buried in studies of a nature more than
all else adapted to deaden impressions of the outward world, it
is by that sweet word alone—by Ligeia—that I bring before
mine eyes in fancy the image of her who is no more. And now,
while I write, a recollection flashes upon me that I have *never
known* the paternal name of her who was my friend and my
betrothed, and who became the partner of my studies, and
finally the wife of my bosom. Was it a playful charge on the part

of my Ligeia? or was it a test of my strength of affection, that I should institute no inquiries upon this point? or was it rather a caprice of my own—a wildly romantic offering on the shrine of the most passionate devotion? I but indistinctly recall the fact itself—what wonder that I have utterly forgotten the circumstances which originated or attended it? And, indeed, if ever that spirit which is entitled *Romance*—if ever she, the wan and the misty-winged *Ashtophet* of idolatrous Egypt, presided, as they tell, over marriages ill-omened, then most surely she presided over mine.

There is one dear topic, however, on which my memory fails me not. It is the *person* of Ligeia. In stature she was tall, somewhat slender, and, in her latter days, even emaciated. I would in vain attempt to portray the majesty, the quiet ease, of her demeanor, or the incomprehensible lightness and elasticity of her footfall. She came and departed as a shadow. I was never made aware of her entrance into my closed study save by the dear music of her low sweet voice, as she placed her marble hand upon my shoulder. In beauty of face no maiden ever equalled her. It was the radiance of an opium-dream—an airy and spirit-lifting vision more wildly divine than the phantasies which hovered about the slumbering souls of the daughters of Delos. Yet her features were not of that regular mould which we have been falsely taught to worship in the classical labors of the heathen. "There is no exquisite beauty," says Bacon, Lord Verulam, speaking truly of all the forms and *genera* of beauty, "without some *strangeness* in the proportion." Yet, although I saw that the features of Ligeia were not of a classic regularity— although I perceived that her loveliness was indeed "exquisite," and felt that there was much of "strangeness" pervading it, yet I have tried in vain to detect the irregularity and to trace home my own perception of "the strange." I examined the contour of the lofty and pale forehead—it was faultless—how cold indeed that word when applied to a majesty so divine!—the skin rivalling the purest ivory, the commanding extent and repose, the gentle prominence of the regions above the temples; and then the raven-black, the glossy, the luxuriant and naturally-curling tresses, setting forth the full force of the Homeric epithet, "hyacinthine!" I looked at the delicate outlines of the nose—and nowhere but in the graceful medallions of the Hebrews had I beheld a similar perfection. There were the same luxurious smoothness of surface, the same scarcely perceptible tendency to the aquiline, the same harmoniously curved nostrils speaking the free spirit. I regarded the sweet mouth. Here was indeed the triumph of all things heavenly—the magnificent turn of the short upper lip—the soft, voluptuous slumber of the under— the dimples which sported, and the color which spoke—the teeth glancing back, with a brilliancy almost startling, every ray of the holy light which fell upon them in her serene and placid, yet most exultingly radiant of all smiles. I scrutinized the formation of the chin—and here, too, I found the gentleness of breadth, the softness and the majesty, the fullness and the spirituality, of the Greek—the contour which the god Apollo revealed but in a dream, to Cleomenes, the son of the Athenian. And then I peered into the large eyes of Ligeia.

For eyes we have no models in the remotely antique. It might have been, too, that in these eyes of my beloved lay the secret to which Lord Verulam alludes. They were, I must believe, far larger than the ordinary eyes of our own race. They were even fuller than the fullest of the gazelle eyes of the tribe of the valley of Nourjahad. Yet it was only at intervals—in moments of intense excitement—that this peculiarity became more than slightly noticeable in Ligeia. And at such moments was her beauty—in my heated fancy thus it appeared perhaps—the beauty of beings either above or apart from the earth— the beauty of the fabulous Houri of the Turk. The hue of the orbs was the most brilliant of black, and, far over them, hung jetty lashes of great length. The brows, slightly irregular in outline, had the same tint. The "strangeness", however, which I found in the eyes, was of a nature distinct from the formation, or the color, or the brilliancy of the features, and must, after all, be referred to the *expression*. Ah, word of no meaning! behind whose vast latitude of mere sound we intrench our ignorance of so much of the spiritual. The expression of the eyes of Ligeia! How for long hours have I pondered upon it! How have I, through the whole of a mid-summer night, struggled to fathom it! What was it—that something more profound than the well of Democritus—which lay far within the pupils of my beloved? What *was* it? I was possessed with a passion to discover. Those eyes! those large, those shining, those divine orbs! They became to me twin stars of Leda, and I to them devoutest of astrologers.

There is no point, among the many incomprehensible anomalies of the science of mind, more thrillingly exciting than the fact—never, I believe, noticed in the schools—that, in our endeavors to recall to memory something long forgotten, we often find ourselves *upon the very verge* of remembrance, without being able, in the end, to remember. And thus how frequently, in my intense scrutiny of Ligeia's eyes, have I felt approaching the full knowledge of their expression—felt it approaching—yet not quite be mine—and so at length entirely depart! And (strange, oh strangest mystery of all!) I found, in the commonest objects of the universe, a circle of analogies to that expression. I mean to say that, subsequently to the period when Ligeia's beauty passed into my spirit, there dwelling as in a shrine, I derived, from many existences in the material world, a sentiment such as I felt always aroused within me by her large and luminous orbs. Yet not the more could I define that sentiment, or analyze, or even steadily view it. I recognized it, let me repeat, sometimes in the survey of a rapidly-growing vine—in the contemplation of a moth, a butterfly, a chrysalis, a stream of running water. I have felt it in the ocean; in the falling of a meteor. I have felt it in the glances of unusually aged people. And there are one or two stars in heaven—(one especially, a star of the sixth magnitude, double and changeable, to be found near the large star in Lyra) in a telescopic scrutiny of which I have been made aware of the feeling. I have been filled with it by certain sounds from stringed instruments, and not unfrequently by passages from books. Among innumerable other instances, I well remember something in a volume of Joseph Glanvill, which (perhaps merely from its quaintness—who shall say?) never failed to inspire me with the sentiment;—"And the will therein lieth, which dieth not. Who knoweth the mysteries of the will, with its vigor? For God is but a great will pervading all things by nature of its intentness. Man doth not yield him to the angels, nor unto death utterly, save only through the weakness of his feeble will."

Length of years, and subsequent reflection, have enabled me to trace, indeed, some remote connection between this passage in the English moralist and a portion of the character of Ligeia. An *intensity* in thought, action, or speech, was possibly, in her, a result, or at least an index, of that gigantic volition which, during our long intercourse, failed to give other and more immediate evidence of its existence. Of all the women whom I have ever known, she, the outwardly calm, the ever-placid Ligeia, was the most violently a prey to the tumultuous vultures of stern passion. And of such passion I could form no estimate, save by the miraculous expansion of those eyes which at once so delighted and appalled me—by the almost magical melody, modulation, distinctness and placidity of her very low voice—and by the fierce energy (rendered doubly effective by contrast with her manner of utterance) of the wild words which she habitually uttered.

I have spoken of the learning of Ligeia; it was immense—such as I have never known in woman. In the classical tongues was she deeply proficient, and as far as my own acquaintance extended in regard to the modern dialects of Europe, I have never known her at fault. Indeed upon any theme of the most admired, because simply the most abstruse of the boasted erudition of the academy, have I *ever* found Ligeia at fault? How singularly—how thrillingly, this one point in the nature of my wife has forced itself, at this late period only, upon my attention! I said her knowledge was such as I have never known in woman—but where breathes the man who has traversed, and successfully, *all* the wide areas of moral, physical, and mathematical science? I saw not then what I now clearly perceive, that the acquisitions of Ligeia were gigantic, were astounding; yet I was sufficiently aware of her infinite supremacy to resign myself, with a child-like confidence, to her guidance through the chaotic world of metaphysical investigation at which I was most busily occupied during the earlier years of our marriage. With how vast a triumph—with how vivid a delight—with how much of all that is ethereal in hope—did I *feel,* as she bent over me in studies but little sought—but less known—that delicious vista by slow degrees expanding before me, down whose long, gorgeous, and all untrodden path, I might at length pass onward to the goal of a wisdom too divinely precious not to be forbidden!

How poignant, then, must have been the grief with which, after some years, I beheld my well-grounded expectations take wings to themselves and fly away! Without Ligeia I was but as a child groping benighted. Her presence, her readings alone, rendered vividly luminous the many mysteries of the transcendentalism in which we were immersed. Wanting the radiant lustre of her eyes, letters, lambent and golden, grew duller than Saturnian lead. And now those eyes shone less and less frequently upon the pages over which I pored. Ligeia grew ill. The wild eyes blazed with a too—too glorious effulgence; the pale fingers became of the transparent waxen hue of the grave, and the blue veins upon the lofty forehead swelled and sank impetuously with the tides of the most gentle emotion. I saw that she must die—and I struggled desperately in spirit with the grim Azrael. And the struggles of the passionate wife were, to my astonishment, even more energetic than my own. There had been much in her stern nature to impress me with the belief that, to her, death would have come without its terrors;—but not so. Words are impotent to convey any just idea of the fierceness of resistance with which she wrestled with the Shadow. I groaned in anguish at the pitiable spectacle. I would have soothed—I would have reasoned; but, in the intensity of her wild desire for life—for life—*but* for life—solace and reason were alike the uttermost of folly. Yet not until the last instance, amid the most convulsive writhings of her fierce spirit, was shaken the external placidity of her demeanor. Her voice grew more gentle—grew more low—yet I would not wish to dwell upon the wild meaning of the quietly uttered words. My brain reeled as I hearkened entranced, to a melody more than mortal—to assumptions and aspirations which mortality had never before known.

That she loved me I should not have doubted; and I might have been easily aware that, in a bosom such as hers, love would

have reigned no ordinary passion. But in death only, was I fully
impressed with the strength of her affection. For long hours,
detaining my hand, would she pour out before me the overflow-
ing of a heart whose more than passionate devotion amounted
to idolatry. How had I deserved to be so blessed by such
confessions?—how had I deserved to be so cursed with the
removal of my beloved in the hour of her making them? But
upon this subject I cannot bear to dilate. Let me say only, that
in Ligeia's more than womanly abandonment to a love, alas! all
unmerited, all unworthily bestowed, I at length recognized the
principle of her longing with so wildly earnest a desire for the
life which was now fleeing so rapidly away. It is this wild longing—it is this eager vehemence of desire for life—*but* for life—
that I have no power to portray—no utterance capable of
expressing.

At high noon of the night in which she departed, beckoning
me, peremptorily, to her side, she bade me repeat certain verses
composed by herself not many days before. I obeyed her.—
They were these:

> Lo! 't is a gala night
>   Within the lonesome latter years!
> An angel throng, bewinged, bedight
>   In veils, and drowned in tears,
> Sit in a theatre, to see
>   A play of hopes and fears,
> While the orchestra breathes fitfully
>   The music of the spheres.
>
> Mimes, in the form of God on high,
>   Mutter and mumble low,
> And hither and thither fly—
>   Mere puppets they, who come and go
> At bidding of vast formless things
>   That shift the scenery to and fro,
> Flapping from out their Condor wings
>   Invisible Wo!
>
> That motley drama!—oh, be sure
>   It shall not be forgot!
> With its Phantom chased forever more,

By a crowd that seize it not,
    Through a circle that ever returneth in
        To the self-same spot,
    And much of Madness and more of Sin
        And Horror the soul of the plot.

But see, amid the mimic rout,
    A crawling shape intrude!
A blood-red thing that writhes from out
    The scenic solitude!
It writhes!—it writhes!—with mortal pangs
    The mimes become its food,
And the seraphs sob at vermin fangs
    In human gore imbued.

Out—out are the lights—out all!
    And over each quivering form,
The curtain, a funeral pall,
    Comes down with the rush of a storm,
And the angels, all pallid and wan,
    Uprising, unveiling, affirm
That the play is the tragedy, "Man,"
    And its hero the Conqueror Worm.

"O God!" half shrieked Ligeia, leaping to her feet and extending her arms aloft with a spasmodic movement, as I made an end of these lines—"O God! O Divine Father!—shall these things be undeviatingly so?—shall this Conqueror be not once conquered? Are we not part and parcel in Thee? Who—who knoweth the mysteries of the will with its vigor? Man doth not yield him to the angels, *nor unto death utterly*, save only through the weakness of his feeble will."

And now, as if exhausted with emotion, she suffered her white arms to fall, and returned solemnly to her bed of death. And as she breathed her last sighs, there came mingled with them a low murmur from her lips. I bent to them my ear and distinguished, again, the concluding words of the passage in Glanvill—"*Man doth not yield him to the angels, nor unto death utterly, save only through the weakness of his feeble will.*"

She died;—and I, crushed into the very dust with sorrow, could no longer endure the lonely desolation of my dwelling in

the dim and decaying city by the Rhine. I had no lack of what
the world calls wealth. Ligeia had brought me far more, very far
more than ordinarily falls to the lot of mortals. After a few
months, therefore, of weary and aimless wandering, I pur-
chased, and put in some repair, an abbey, which I shall not
name, in one of the wildest and least frequented portions of fair
England. The gloomy and dreary grandeur of the building, the
almost savage aspect of the domain, the many melancholy and
time-honored memories connected with both, had much in uni-
son with the feelings of utter abandonment which had driven
me into that remote and unsocial region of the country. Yet
although the external abbey, with its verdant decay hanging
about it, suffered but little alteration, I gave way, with a child-
like perversity, and perchance with a faint hope of alleviating my
sorrows, to a display of more than regal magnificence within.—
For such follies, even in childhood, I had imbibed a taste and
now they came back to me as if in the dotage of grief. Alas, I feel
how much even of incipient madness might have been discovered in the gorgeous and fantastic draperies, in the solemn carvings of Egypt, in the wild cornices and furniture, in the Bedlam
patterns of the carpets of tufted gold! I had become a bounden
slave in the trammels of opium, and my labors and my orders
had taken a coloring from my dreams. But these absurdities I
must not pause to detail. Let me speak only of that one chamber, ever accursed, whither in a moment of mental alienation,
I led from the altar as my bride—as the successor of the unfor-
gotten Ligeia—the fair-haired and blue-eyed Lady Rowena
Trevanion, of Tremaine.

There is no individual portion of the architecture and decora-
tion of that bridal chamber which is not now visibly before me.
Where were the souls of the haughty family of the bride, when,
through thirst of gold, they permitted to pass the threshold of an
apartment *so* bedecked, a maiden and a daughter so beloved?
I have said that I minutely remember the details of the chamber—yet I am sadly forgetful on topics of deep moment—and
here there was no system, no keeping, in the fantastic display, to
take hold upon the memory. The room lay in a high turret of the
castellated abbey, was pentagonal in shape, and of capacious

size. Occupying the whole southern face of the pentagon was the sole window—an immense sheet of unbroken glass from Venice—a single pane, and tinted of a leaden hue, so that the rays of either the sun or moon, passing through it, fell with a ghastly lustre on the objects within. Over the upper portion of this huge window, extended the trellice-work of an aged vine, which clambered up the massy walls of the turret. The ceiling, of gloomy-looking oak, was excessively lofty, vaulted, and elaborately fretted with the wildest and most grotesque specimens of a semi-Gothic, semi-Druidical device. From out the most central recess of this melancholy vaulting, depended, by a single chain of gold with long links, a huge censer of the same metal, Saracenic in pattern, and with many perforations so contrived that there writhed in and out of them, as if endued with a serpent vitality, a continual succession of parti-colored fires.

Some few ottomans and golden candelabra, of Eastern figure, were in various stations about—and there was the couch, too— the bridal couch—of an Indian model, and low, and sculptured of solid ebony, with a pall-like canopy above. In each of the angles of the chamber stood on end a gigantic sarcophagus of black granite, from the tombs of the kings over against Luxor, with their aged lids full of immemorial sculpture. But in the draping of the apartment lay, alas! the chief phantasy of all. The lofty walls, gigantic in height—even unproportionably so—were hung from summit to foot, in vast folds, with a heavy and massive-looking tapestry—tapestry of a material which was found alike as a carpet on the floor, as a covering for the ottomans and the ebony bed, as a canopy for the bed, and as the gorgeous volutes of the curtains which partially shaded the window. The material was the richest cloth of gold. It was spotted all over, at irregular intervals, with arabesque figures, about a foot in diameter, and wrought upon the cloth in patterns of the most jetty black. But these figures partook of the true character of the arabesque only when regarded from a single point of view. By a contrivance now common, and indeed traceable to a very remote period of antiquity, they were made changeable in aspect. To one entering the room, they bore the appearance of simple monstrosities; but upon a farther advance, this appearance gradually departed; and step by step, as the visitor moved his station in the chamber, he saw himself surrounded by an endless succession of the ghastly forms which belong to the superstition of the Norman, or arise in the guilty slumbers of the monk. The phantasmagoric effect was vastly heightened by the artificial introduction of a strong continual current of wind behind the draperies—giving a hideous and uneasy animation to the whole.

In halls such as these—in a bridal chamber such as this—I passed, with the Lady of Tremaine, the unhallowed hours of the first month of our marriage—passed them with but little disquietude. That my wife dreaded the fierce moodiness of my temper—that she shunned me and loved me but little—I could not help perceiving; but it gave me rather pleasure than otherwise. I loathed her with a hatred belonging more to demon than to man. My memory flew back, (oh, with what intensity of regret!) to Ligeia, the beloved, the august, the beautiful, the entombed. I revelled in recollections of her purity, of her wisdom, of her lofty, her ethereal nature, of her passionate, her idolatrous love. Now, then, did my spirit fully and freely burn with more than all the fires of her own. In the excitement of my opium dreams (for I was habitually fettered in the shackles of the drug) I would call aloud upon her name, during the silence of the night, or among the sheltered recesses of the glens by day, as if, through the wild eagerness, the solemn passion, the consuming ardor of my longing for the departed, I could restore her to the pathway she had abandoned—ah, *could* it be forever?—upon the earth.

About the commencement of the second month of the marriage, the Lady Rowena was attacked with sudden illness, from which her recovery was slow. The fever which consumed her rendered her nights uneasy; and in her perturbed state of half-slumber, she spoke of sounds, and of motions, in and about the chamber of the turret, which I concluded had no origin save in the distemper of her fancy, or perhaps in the phantasmagoric influences of the chamber itself. She became at length convalescent—finally well. Yet but a brief period elapsed, ere a second more violent disorder again threw her upon a bed of suffering; and from this attack her frame, at all times feeble, never alto-

gether recovered. Her illnesses were, after this epoch, of alarming character, and of more alarming recurrence, defying alike
the knowledge and the great exertions of her physicians. With
the increase of the chronic disease which had thus, apparently,
taken too sure hold upon her constitution to be eradicated by
human means, I could not fail to observe a similar increase in
the nervous irritation of her temperament, and in her excitabil-
ity by trivial causes of fear. She spoke again, and now more
frequently and pertinaciously of the sounds—of the slight
sounds—and of the unusual motions among the tapestries, to
which she had formerly alluded.

One night, near the closing in of September, she pressed this
distressing subject with more than usual emphasis upon my
attention. She had just awakened from an unquiet slumber and
I had been watching, with feelings half of anxiety, half of vague
terror, the workings of her emaciated countenance. I sat by the
side of her ebony bed, upon one of the ottomans of India. She
partly arose, and spoke, in an earnest low whisper, of sounds
which she *then* heard, but which I could not hear—of motions
which she *then* saw, but which I could not perceive. The wind
was rushing hurriedly behind the tapestries, and I wished to
show her (what, let me confess it, I could not *all* believe) that
those almost inarticulate breathings, and those very gentle
variations of the figures upon the wall, were but the natural
effects of that customary rushing of the wind. But a deadly pallor, overspreading her face, had proved to me that my exertion
to reassure her would be fruitless. She appeared to be fainting,
and no attendants were within call. I remembered where was
deposited a decanter of light wine which had been ordered by
her physicians, and hastened across the chamber to procure it.
But, as I stepped beneath the light of the censer, two circumstances of a startling nature attracted my attention. I had felt
that some palpable although invisible object had passed lightly
by my person; and I saw that there lay upon the golden carpet,
in the very middle of the rich lustre thrown from the censer, a
shadow—a faint, indefinite shadow of angelic aspect—such as
might be fancied for the shadow of a shade. But I was wild with
the excitement of an immoderate dose of opium, and heeded

these things but little, nor spoke of them to Rowena. Having found the wine, I recrossed the chamber, and poured out a goblet-ful, which I held to the lips of the fainting lady. She had now partially recovered, however, and took the vessel herself, while I sank upon an ottoman near me, with my eyes fastened upon her person. It was then that I became distinctly aware of a gentle foot-fall upon the carpet, and near the couch; and in a second thereafter, as Rowena was in the act of raising the wine to her lips, I saw, or may have dreamed that I saw, fall within the goblet, as if from some invisible spring in the atmosphere of the room, three or four large drops of a brilliant and ruby colored fluid. If this I saw—not so Rowena. She swallowed the wine unhesitatingly, and I forbore to speak to her of a circumstance which must, after all, I considered, have been but the suggestion of a vivid imagination, rendered morbidly active by the terror of the lady, by the opium, and by the hour.

Yet I cannot conceal it from my own perception that, imme-diately subsequent to the fall of the ruby-drops, a rapid change for the worse took place in the disorder of my wife; so that, on the third subsequent night, the hands of her menials prepared her for the tomb, and on the fourth, I sat alone, with her shroud-ed body, in that fantastic chamber which had received her as my bride.—Wild visions, opium-engendered, flitted, shadow-like, before me. I gazed with unquiet eye upon the sarcophagi in the angles of the room, upon the varying figures of the drapery, and upon the writhing of the parti-colored fires in the censer over-head. My eyes then fell, as I called to mind the circumstances of a former night, to the spot beneath the glare of the censer where I had seen the faint traces of the shadow. It was there, however, no longer; and breathing with greater freedom, I turned my glances to the pallid and rigid figure upon the bed. Then rushed upon me a thousand memories of Ligeia—and then came back upon my heart, with the turbulent violence of a flood, the whole of that unutterable wo with which I had regarded *her* thus enshrouded. The night waned; and still, with a bosom full of bitter thoughts of the one only and supremely beloved, I remained gazing upon the body of Rowena.

It might have been midnight, or perhaps earlier, or later, for

I had taken no note of time, when a sob, low, gentle, but very distinct, startled me from my revery.—I *felt* that it came from the bed of ebony—the bed of death. I listened in an agony of superstitious terror—but there was no repetition of the sound. I strained my vision to detect any motion in the corpse—but there was not the slightest perceptible. Yet I could not have been deceived. I *had* heard the noise, however faint, and my soul was awakened within me. I resolutely and perseveringly kept my attention riveted upon the body. Many minutes elapsed before any circumstance occurred tending to throw light upon the mystery. At length it became evident that a slight, a very feeble, and barely noticeable tinge of color had flushed up within the cheeks, and along the sunken small veins of the eyelids. Through a species of unutterable horror and awe, for which the language of mortality has no sufficiently energetic expression, I felt my heart cease to beat, my limbs grow rigid where I sat. Yet a sense of duty finally operated to restore my self-possession. I could no longer doubt that we had been precipitate in our preparations—that Rowena still lived. It was necessary that some immediate exertion be made; yet the turret was altogether apart from the portion of the abbey tenanted by the servants—there were none within call—I had no means of summoning them to my aid without leaving the room for many minutes—and this I could not venture to do. I therefore struggled alone in my endeavors to call back the spirit still hovering. In a short period it was certain, however, that a relapse had taken place; the color disappeared from both eyelid and cheek, leaving a wanness even more than that of marble; the lips became doubly shrivelled and pinched up in the ghastly expression of death; a repulsive clamminess and coldness overspread rapidly the surface of the body; and all the usual rigorous stiffness immediately supervened. I fell back with a shudder upon the couch from which I had been so startlingly aroused, and again gave myself up to passionate waking visions of Ligeia.

An hour thus elapsed when (could it be possible?) I was a second time aware of some vague sound issuing from the region of the bed. I listened—in extremity of horror. The sound came again—it was a sigh. Rushing to the corpse, I saw—distinctly saw—a tremor upon the lips. In a minute afterward they relaxed, disclosing a bright line of the pearly teeth. Amazement now struggled in my bosom with the profound awe which had hitherto reigned there alone. I felt that my vision grew dim, that my reason wandered; and it was only by a violent effort that I at length succeeded in nerving myself to the task which duty thus once more had pointed out. There was now a partial glow upon the forehead and upon the cheek and throat; a perceptible warmth pervaded the whole frame; there was even a slight pulsation at the heart. The lady *lived;* and with redoubled ardor I betook myself to the task of restoration. I chafed and bathed the temples and the hands, and used every exertion which experience, and no little medical reading, could suggest. But in vain. Suddenly, the color fled, the pulsation ceased, the lips resumed the expression of the dead, and, in an instant afterward, the whole body took upon itself the icy chilliness, the livid hue, the intense rigidity, the sunken outline, and all the loathsome peculiarities of that which has been, for many days, a tenant of the tomb.

And again I sunk into visions of Ligeia—and again, (what marvel that I shudder while I write?) *again* there reached my ears a low sob from the region of the ebony bed. But why shall I minutely detail the unspeakable horrors of that night? Why shall I pause to relate how, time after time, until near the period of the gray dawn, this hideous drama of revivification was repeated; how each terrific relapse was only into a sterner and apparently more irredeemable death; how each agony wore the aspect of a struggle with some invisible foe; and how each struggle was succeeded by I know not what of wild change in the personal appearance of the corpse? Let me hurry to a conclusion.

The greater part of the fearful night had worn away, and she who had been dead, once again stirred—and now more vigorously than hitherto, although arousing from a dissolution more appalling in its utter hopelessness than any. I had long ceased to struggle or to move, and remained sitting rigidly upon the ottoman, a helpless prey to a whirl of violent emotions, of which extreme awe was perhaps the least terrible, the least consuming.

The corpse, I repeat, stirred, and now more vigorously than before. The hues of life flushed up with unwonted energy into the countenance—the limbs relaxed—and, save that the eyelids were yet pressed heavily together, and that the bandages and draperies of the grave still imparted their charnel character to the figure, I might have dreamed that Rowena had indeed shaken off, utterly, the fetters of Death. But if this idea was not, even then, altogether adopted, I could at least doubt no longer, when, arising from the bed, tottering, with feeble steps, with closed eyes, and with the manner of one bewildered in a dream, the thing that was enshrouded advanced boldly and palpably into the middle of the apartment.

I trembled not—I stirred not—for a crowd of unutterable fancies connected with the air, the stature, the demeanor of the figure, rushing hurriedly through my brain, had paralyzed—had chilled me into stone. I stirred not—but gazed upon the apparition. There was a mad disorder in my thoughts—a tumult unappeasable. Could it, indeed, be the *living* Rowena who confronted me? Could it indeed be Rowena *at all*—the fair-haired, the blue-eyed Lady Rowena Trevanion of Tremaine? Why, *why* should I doubt it? The bandage lay heavily about the mouth— but then might it not be the mouth of the breathing Lady of Tremaine? And the cheeks—there were the roses as in her noon of life—yes, these might indeed be the fair cheeks of the living Lady of Tremaine. And the chin, with its dimples, as in health, might it not be hers?—but *had she then grown taller since her malady?* What inexpressible madness seized me with that thought? One bound, and I had reached her feet! Shrinking from my touch, she let fall from her head, unloosened, the ghastly cerements which had confined it, and there streamed forth, into the rushing atmosphere of the chamber, huge masses of long and dishevelled hair; *it was blacker than the raven wings of midnight!* And now slowly opened *the eyes* of the figure which stood before me. "Here then, at least," I shrieked aloud, "can I never—can I never be mistaken—these are the full, and the black, and the wild eyes—of my lost love—of the lady—of the LADY LIGEIA."

The Gray Champion

Nathaniel Hawthorne

There was once a time, when New England groaned under the actual pressure of heavier wrongs, than those threatened ones which brought on the Revolution. James II, the bigoted successor of Charles the Voluptuous, had annulled the charters of all the colonies, and sent a harsh and unprincipled soldier to take away our liberties and endanger our religion. The administration of Sir Edmund Andros lacked scarcely a single characteristic of tyranny: a Governor and Council, holding office from the King, and wholly independent of the country; laws made and taxes levied without concurrence of the people, immediate or by their representatives; the rights of private citizens violated, and the titles of all landed property declared void; the voice of complaint stifled by restrictions on the press; and, finally, disaffection overawed by the first band of mercenary troops that ever marched on our free soil. For two years, our ancestors were kept in sullen submission, by that filial love which had invariably secured their allegiance to the mother country, whether its head chanced to be a Parliament, Protector, or popish Monarch. Till these evil times, however, such allegiance had been merely nominal, and the colonists had ruled themselves, enjoying far more freedom, than is even yet the privilege of the native subjects of Great Britain.

At length, a rumor reached our shores, that the Prince of Orange had ventured on an enterprise, the success of which would be the triumph of civil and religious rights and the salvation of New England. It was but a doubtful whisper; it might be

17

false, or the attempt might fail; and, in either case, the man, that stirred against King James, would lose his head. Still the intelligence produced a marked effect. The people smiled mysteriously in the streets, and threw bold glances at their oppressors; while, far and wide, there was a subdued and silent agitation, as if the slightest signal would rouse the whole land from its sluggish despondency. Aware of their danger, the rulers resolved to avert it by an imposing display of strength, and perhaps to confirm their despotism by yet harsher measures. One afternoon in April, 1689, Sir Edmund Andros and his favorite councillors, being warm with wine, assembled the red-coats of the Governor's Guard, and made their appearance in the streets of Boston. The sun was near setting when the march commenced.

The roll of the drum, at that unquiet crisis, seemed to go through the streets, less as the martial music of the soldiers, than as a muster-call to the inhabitants themselves. A multitude, by various avenues, assembled in King Street, which was destined to be the scene, nearly a century afterwards, of another encounter between the troops of Britain, and a people struggling against her tyranny. Though more than sixty years had elapsed, since the pilgrims came, this crowd of their descendants still showed the strong and sombre features of their character, perhaps more strikingly in such a stern emergency than on happier occasions. There was the sober garb, the general severity of mien, the gloomy but undismayed expression, the scriptural forms of speech, and the confidence in Heaven's blessing on a righteous cause, which would have marked a band of the original Puritans, when threatened by some peril of the wilderness. Indeed, it was not yet time for the old spirit to be extinct; since there were men in the street, that day, who had worshipped there beneath the trees, before a house was reared to the God, for whom they had become exiles. Old soldiers of the Parliament were here, too, smiling grimly at the thought, that their aged arms might strike another blow against the house of Stuart. Here also, were the veterans of King Philip's war, who had burnt villages and slaughtered young and old, with pious fierceness, while the godly souls throughout the land were helping them with prayer. Several ministers were scattered among the crowd, which, unlike all other mobs, regarded them with such reverence, as if there were sanctity in their very garments. These holy men exerted their influence to quiet the people, but not to disperse them. Meantime, the purpose of the Governor, in disturbing the peace of the town, at a period when the slightest commotion might throw the country into a ferment, was almost the universal subject of inquiry, and variously explained.

"Satan will strike his master-stroke presently," cried some, "because he knoweth that his time is short. All our godly pastors are to be dragged to prison! We shall see them at a Smithfield fire in King Street!"

Hereupon, the people of each parish gathered closer round their minister, who looked calmly upwards and assumed a more apostolic dignity, as well befitted a candidate for the highest honor of his profession, the crown of martyrdom. It was actually fancied, at that period, that New England might have a John Rogers of her own, to take the place of that worthy in the Primer.

"The Pope of Rome has given orders for a new St. Bartholomew!" cried others. "We are to be massacred, man and male child!"

Neither was this rumor wholly discredited, although the wiser class believed the Governor's object somewhat less atrocious. His predecessor under the old charter, Bradstreet, a venerable companion of the first settlers, was known to be in town. There were grounds for conjecturing, that Sir Edmund Andros intended, at once, to strike terror, by a parade of military force, and to confound the opposite faction, by possessing himself of their chief.

"Stand firm for the old charter Governor!" shouted the crowd, seizing upon the idea. "The good old Governor Bradstreet!"

While this cry was at the loudest, the people were surprised by the well-known figure of Governor Bradstreet himself, a patriarch of nearly ninety, who appeared on the elevated steps of a door, and, with characteristic mildness, besought them to submit to the constituted authorities.

"My children," concluded this venerable person, "do nothing

rashly. Cry not aloud, but pray for the welfare of New England, and expect patiently what the Lord will do in this matter!"

The event was soon to be decided. All this time, the roll of the drum had been approaching through Cornhill, louder and deeper, till, with reverberations from house to house, and the regular tramp of martial footsteps, it burst into the street. A double rank of soldiers made their appearance, occupying the whole breadth of the passage, with shouldered matchlocks, and matches burning, so as to present a row of fires in the dusk. Their steady march was like the progress of a machine, that would roll irresistibly over everything in its way. Next, moving slowly, with a confused clatter of hoofs on the pavement, rode a party of mounted gentlemen, the central figure being Sir Edmund Andros, elderly, but erect and soldier-like. Those around him were his favorite councillors, and the bitterest foes of New England. At his right hand rode Edward Randolph, our arch enemy, that "blasted wretch," as Cotton Mather calls him, who achieved the downfall of our ancient government, and was followed with a sensible curse, through life and to his grave. On the other side was Bullivant, scattering jests and mockery as he rode along. Dudley came behind, with a downcast look, dreading, as well he might, to meet the indignant gaze of the people, who beheld him, their only countryman by birth, among the oppressors of his native land. The captain of a frigate in the harbor, and two or three civil officers under the Crown, were also there. But the figure which most attracted the public eye, and stirred up the deepest feeling, was the Episcopal clergyman of King's Chapel, riding haughtily among the magistrates in his priestly vestments, the fitting representative of prelacy and persecution, the union of church and state, and all those abominations which had driven the Puritans to the wilderness. Another guard of soldiers, in double rank, brought up the rear.

The whole scene was a picture of the condition of New England, and its moral, the deformity of any government that does not grow out of the nature of things and the character of the people. On one side the religious multitude, with their sad visages and dark attire, and on the other, the group of despotic rulers, with the high churchman in the midst, and here and there a crucifix at their bosoms, all magnificently clad, flushed with wine, proud of unjust authority, and scoffing at the universal groan. And the mercenary soldiers, waiting but the word to deluge the street with blood, shewed the only means by which obedience could be secured.

"Oh! Lord of Hosts," cried a voice among the crowd, "provide a Champion for thy people!"

This ejaculation was loudly uttered, and served as a herald's cry, to introduce a remarkable personage. The crowd had rolled back, and were now huddled together nearly at the extremity of the street, while the soldiers had advanced no more than a third of its length. The intervening space was empty—a paved solitude, between lofty edifices, which threw almost a twilight shadow over it. Suddenly, there was seen the figure of an ancient man, who seemed to have emerged from among the people, and was walking by himself along the centre of the street, to confront the armed band. He wore the old Puritan dress, a dark cloak and a steeple-crowned hat, in the fashion of at least fifty years before, with a heavy sword upon his thigh, but a staff in his hand, to assist the tremulous gait of age.

When at some distance from the multitude, the old man turned slowly round, displaying a face of antique majesty, rendered doubly venerable by the hoary beard that descended on his breast. He made a gesture at once of encouragement and warning, then turned again, and resumed his way.

"Who is this gray patriarch?" asked the young men of their sires.

"Who is this venerable brother?" asked the old men among themselves.

But none could make reply. The fathers of the people, those of four-score years and upwards, were disturbed, deeming it strange that they should forget one of such evident authority, whom they must have known in their early days, the associate of Winthrop and all the old Councillors, giving laws, and making prayers, and leading them against the savage. The elderly men ought to have remembered him, too, with locks as gray in their youth, as their own were now. And the young! How could he have passed so utterly from their memories—that hoary sire, the relic of long departed times, whose awful benediction had surely been bestowed on their uncovered heads, in childhood?

"Whence did he come? What is his purpose? Who can this old man be?" whispered the wondering crowd.

Meanwhile, the venerable stranger, staff in hand, was pursuing his solitary walk along the centre of the street. As he drew near the advancing soldiers, and as the roll of their drum came full upon his ear, the old man raised himself to a loftier mien, while the decrepitude of age seemed to fall from his shoulders, leaving him in gray, but unbroken dignity. Now, he marched onward with a warrior's step, keeping time to the military music. Thus the aged form advanced on one side, and the whole parade of soldiers and magistrates on the other, till, when scarcely twenty yards remained between, the old man grasped his staff by the middle, and held it before him like a leader's truncheon.

"Stand!" cried he.

The eye, the face, and attitude of command; the solemn, yet warlike peal of that voice, fit either to rule a host in the battle-field or be raised to God in prayer, were irresistible. At the old man's word and outstretched arm, the roll of the drum was hushed at once, and the advancing line stood still. A tremulous enthusiasm seized upon the multitude. That stately form, combining the leader and the saint, so gray, so dimly seen, in such an ancient garb, could only belong to some old champion of the righteous cause, whom the oppressor's drum had summoned from his grave. They raised a shout of awe and exultation, and looked for the deliverance of New England.

The Governor, and the gentlemen of his party, perceiving themselves brought to an unexpected stand, rode hastily forward, as if they would have pressed their snorting and affrighted horses right against the hoary apparition. He, however, blenched not a step, but glancing his severe eye round the group, which half encompassed him, at last bent it sternly on Sir Edmund Andros. One would have thought that the dark old man was chief ruler there, and that the Governor and Council, with soldiers at their back, representing the whole power and authority of the Crown, had no alternative but obedience.

"What does this old fellow here?" cried Edward Randolph, fiercely. "On, Sir Edmund! Bid the soldiers forward, and give the dotard the same choice that you give all his countrymen—to stand aside or be trampled on!"

"Nay, nay, let us show respect to the good grandsire," said Bullivant, laughing. "See you not, he is some old round-headed dignitary, who hath lain asleep these thirty years, and knows nothing of the change of times? Doubtless, he thinks to put us down with a proclamation in Old Noll's name!"

"Are you mad, old man?" demanded Sir Edmund Andros, in loud and harsh tones. "How dare you stay the march of King James's Governor?"

"I have staid the march of a King himself, ere now," replied the gray figure, with stern composure. "I am here, Sir Governor, because the cry of an oppressed people hath disturbed me in my secret place; and beseeching this favor earnestly of the Lord, it was vouchsafed me to appear once again on earth, in the good old cause of his saints. And what speak ye of James? There is no longer a popish tyrant on the throne of England, and by to-morrow noon, his name shall be a byword in this very street, where ye would make it a word of terror. Back, thou that wast a Governor, back! With this night, thy power is ended—to-morrow, the prison!—back, lest I foretell the scaffold!"

The people had been drawing nearer and nearer, and drinking in the words of their champion, who spoke in accents long disused, like one unaccustomed to converse, except with the dead of many years ago. But his voice stirred their souls. They confronted the soldiers, not wholly without arms, and ready to convert the very stones of the street into deadly weapons. Sir Edmund Andros looked at the old man; then he cast his hard and cruel eye over the multitude, and beheld them burning with that lurid wrath, so difficult to kindle or to quench; and again he fixed his gaze on the aged form, which stood obscurely in an open space, where neither friend nor foe had thrust himself. What were his thoughts, he uttered no word which might discover. But whether the oppressor were overawed by the Gray Champion's look, or perceived his peril in the threatening attitude of the people, it is certain that he gave back, and ordered his soldiers to commence a slow and guarded retreat. Before another sunset, the Governor, and all that rode so proudly with him, were prisoners, and long ere it was known that James had abdicated, King William was proclaimed throughout New England.

But where was the Gray Champion? Some reported, that when the troops had gone from King Street, and the people were thronging tumultuously in their rear, Bradstreet, the aged Governor, was seen to embrace a form more aged than his own. Others soberly affirmed, that while they marvelled at the venerable grandeur of his aspect, the old man had faded from their eyes, melting slowly into the hues of twilight, till, where he stood, there was an empty space. But all agreed, that the hoary shape was gone. The men of that generation watched for his reappearance, in sunshine and in twilight, but never saw him more, nor knew when his funeral passed, nor where his gravestone was.

And who was the Gray Champion? Perhaps his name might be found in the records of that stern Court of Justice, which passed a sentence, too mighty for the age, but glorious in all after times, for its humbling lesson to the monarch and its high example to the subject. I have heard, that, whenever the descendants of the Puritans are to show the spirit of their sires, the old man appears again. When eighty years had passed, he walked once more in King Street. Five years later, in the twilight of an April morning, he stood on the green, beside the meeting-house, at Lexington, where now the obelisk of granite, with a slab of slate inlaid, commemorates the first fallen of the Revolution. And when our fathers were toiling at the breastwork on Bunker's Hill, all through that night, the old warrior walked his rounds. Long, long may it be, ere he comes again! His hour is one of darkness, and adversity, and peril. But should domestic tyranny oppress us, or the invader's step pollute our soil, still may the Gray Champion come; for he is the type of New England's hereditary spirit; and his shadowy march, on the eve of danger, must ever be the pledge, that New England's sons will vindicate their ancestry.

Grayling; or, "Murder Will Out"

William Gilmore Simms

CHAPTER I

The world has become monstrous matter-of-fact in latter days. We can no longer get a ghost story, either for love or money. The materialists have it all their own way; and even the little urchin, eight years old, instead of deferring with decent reverence to the opinions of his grandmamma, now stands up stoutly for his own. He believes in every "ology" but pneumatology. "Faust" and the "Old Woman of Berkeley" move his derision only, and he would laugh incredulously, if he dared, at the Witch of Endor. The whole armoury of modern reasoning is on his side; and, however he may admit at seasons that belief can scarcely be counted a matter of will, he yet puts his veto on all sorts of credulity. That cold-blooded demon called Science has taken the place of all the other demons. He has certainly cast out innumerable devils, however he may still spare the principal. Whether we are the better for his intervention is another question. There is reason to apprehend that in disturbing our human faith in shadows, we have lost some of those wholesome moral restraints which might have kept many of us virtuous, where the laws could not.

The effect, however, is much the more seriously evil in all that concerns the romantic. Our story-tellers are so resolute to deal in the real, the actual only, that they venture on no subjects the details of which are not equally vulgar and susceptible of proof. With this end in view, indeed, they too commonly choose their subjects among convicted felons, in order that they may avail themselves of the evidence which led to their conviction; and, to prove more conclusively their devoted adherence to nature and the truth, they depict the former not only in her condition of nakedness, but long before she has found out the springs of running water. It is to be feared that some of the coarseness of modern taste arises from the too great lack of that veneration which belonged to, and elevated to dignity, even the errors of preceding ages. A love of the marvelous belongs, it appears to me, to all those who love and cultivate either of the fine arts. I very much doubt whether the poet, the painter, the sculptor, or the romancer, ever yet lived, who had not some strong bias—a leaning, at least—to a belief in the wonders of the invisible world. Certainly, the higher orders of poets and painters, those who create and invent, must have a strong taint of the superstitious in their composition. But this is digressive, and leads us from our purpose.

It is so long since we have been suffered to see or hear of a ghost, that a visitation at this time may have the effect of novelty, and I propose to narrate a story which I heard more than once in my boyhood, from the lips of an aged relative, who succeeded, at the time, in making me believe every word of it; perhaps, for the simple reason that she convinced me she believed every word of it herself. My grandmother was an old lady who had been a resident of the seat of most frequent war in Carolina during the Revolution. She had fortunately survived the numberless atrocities which she was yet compelled to witness; and, a keen observer, with a strong memory, she had in store a thousand legends of that stirring period, which served to beguile me from sleep many and many a long winter night. The story which I propose to tell was one of these; and when I say that she not only devoutly believed it herself, but that it was believed by sundry of her contemporaries, who were themselves privy to such of the circumstances as could be known to third parties, the gravity with which I repeat the legend will not be considered very astonishing.

The revolutionary war had but a little while been concluded. The British had left the country; but peace did not imply repose. The community was still in that state of ferment which was natural enough to passions, not yet at rest, which had been brought into exercise and action during the protracted seven years' struggle through which the nation had just passed. The state was overrun by idlers, adventurers, profligates, and criminals. Disbanded soldiers, half-starved and reckless, occupied the highways,—outlaws, emerging from their hiding-places, skulked about the settlements with an equal sentiment of hate and fear in their hearts;—patriots were clamouring for justice upon the tories, and sometimes anticipating its course by judgments of their own; while the tories, those against whom the proofs were too strong for denial or evasion, buckled on their armour for a renewal of the struggle. Such being the condition of the country, it may easily be supposed that life and property lacked many of their necessary securities. Men generally travelled with weapons which were displayed on the smallest provocation: and few who could provide themselves with an escort ventured to travel any distance without one.

There was, about this time, said my grandmother, and while such was the condition of the country, a family of the name of Grayling, that lived somewhere upon the skirts of "Ninety-six" district. Old Grayling, the head of the family, was dead. He was killed in Buford's massacre. His wife was a fine woman, not so very old, who had an only son named James, and a little girl, only five years of age, named Lucy. James was but fourteen when his father was killed, and that event made a man of him. He went out with his rifle in company with Joel Sparkman, who was his mother's brother, and joined himself to Pickens's Brigade. Here he made as good a soldier as the best. He had no sort of fear. He was always the first to go forward; and his rifle was always good for his enemy's button at a long hundred yards. He was in several fights both with the British and tories; and just before the war was ended he had a famous brush with the Cherokees, when Pickens took their country from them. But though he had no fear, and never knew when to stop killing while the fight was going on, he was the most bashful of boys that I ever knew; and so kind-hearted that it was almost impossible to believe all we

heard of his fierce doings when he was in battle. But they were
nevertheless quite true for all his bashfulness.

Well, when the war was over, Joel Sparkman, who lived with
his sister Grayling, persuaded her that it would be better to
move down into the low country. I don't know what reason he
had for it, or what they proposed to do there. They had very
little property, but Sparkman was a knowing man, who could
turn his hand to a hundred things; and as he was a bachelor, and
loved his sister and her children just as if they had been his own,
it was natural that she should go with him wherever he wished.
James, too, who was restless by nature—and the taste he had
enjoyed of the wars had made him more so—he was full of it;
and so, one sunny morning in April, their waggon started for the
city. The waggon was only a small one, with two horses, scarcely
larger than those that are employed to carry chickens and fruit
to the market from the Wassamaws and thereabouts. It was
driven by a negro fellow named Clytus, and carried Mrs.
Grayling and Lucy. James and his uncle loved the saddle too
well to shut themselves up in such a vehicle; and both of them
were mounted on fine horses which they had won from the
enemy. The saddle that James rode on—and he was very proud
of it—was one that he had taken at the battle of Cowpens from
one of Tarleton's own dragoons, after he had tumbled the
owner. The roads at that season were excessively bad, for the
rains of March had been frequent and heavy, the track was very
much cut up, and the red clay gullies of the hills of "Ninety-six"
were so washed that it required all shoulders, twenty times a
day, to get the waggon-wheels out of the bog. This made them
travel very slowly—perhaps not more than fifteen miles a day.
Another cause for slow travelling was, the necessity of great caution, and a constant look-out for enemies both up and down the
road. James and his uncle took it by turns to ride a-head, precisely as they did when scouting in war, but one of them always
kept along with the waggon. They had gone on this way for two
days, and saw nothing to trouble and alarm them. There were
few persons on the high road, and these seemed to the full as
shy of them as they probably were of strangers. But just as they
were about to camp, the evening of the second day, while they

were splitting light-wood, and getting out the kettles and the frying-pan, a person rode up and joined them without much ceremony. He was a short thick-set man, somewhere between forty and fifty: had on very coarse and common garments, though he rode a fine black horse of remarkable strength and vigour. He was very civil of speech, though he had but little to say, and that little showed him to be a person without much education and with no refinement. He begged permission to make one of the encampment, and his manner was very respectful and even humble; but there was something dark and sullen in his face—his eyes, which were of a light gray colour, were very restless, and his nose turned up sharply, and was very red. His forehead was excessively broad, and his eyebrows thick and shaggy—white hairs being freely mingled with the dark, both in them and upon his head. Mrs. Grayling did not like the man's looks, and whispered her dislike to her son; but James, who felt himself equal to any man said promptly—

"What of that, mother? we can't turn the stranger off and say 'no'; and if he means any mischief, there's two of us, you know."

The man had no weapons—none, at least, which were then visible; and deported himself in so humble a manner, that the prejudice which the party had formed against him when he first appeared, if it was not dissipated while he remained, at least failed to gain any increase. He was very quiet, did not mention an unnecessary word, and seldom permitted his eyes to rest upon those of any of the party, the females not excepted. This, perhaps, was the only circumstance that, in the mind of Mrs. Grayling, tended to confirm the hostile impression which his coming had originally occasioned. In a little while the temporary encampment was put in a state equally social and warlike. The waggon was wheeled a little way into the woods, and off the road; the horses fastened behind it in such a manner that any attempt to steal them would be difficult of success, even were the watch neglectful which was yet to be maintained upon them. Extra guns, concealed in the straw at the bottom of the waggon, were kept well loaded. In the foreground, and between the waggon and the highway, a fire was soon blazing with a wild but cheerful gleam; and the worthy dame, Mrs. Grayling, assisted by the little girl, Lucy, lost no time in setting on the frying-pan, and cutting into slices the haunch of bacon, which they had provided at leaving home. James Grayling patrolled the woods, meanwhile for a mile or two round the encampment, while his uncle, Joel Sparkman, foot to foot with the stranger seemed—if the absence of all care constitutes the supreme of human felicity— to realize the most perfect conception of mortal happiness. But Joel was very far from being the careless person that he seemed. Like an old soldier, he simply hung out false colours, and concealed his real timidity by an extra show of confidence and courage. He did not relish the stranger from the first, any more than his sister; and having subjected him to a searching examination, such as was considered, in those days of peril and suspicion, by no means inconsistent with becoming courtesy, he came rapidly to the conclusion that he was no better than he should be.

"You are a Scotchman, stranger," said Joel, suddenly drawing up his feet, and bending forward to the other with an eye like that of a hawk stooping over a covey of partridges. It was a wonder that he had not made the discovery before. The broad dialect of the stranger was not to be subdued; but Joel made slow stages and short progress in his mental journeyings. The answer was given with evident hesitation, but it was affirmative.

"Well, now, it's mighty strange that you should ha' fou't with us and not agin us," responded Joel Sparkman. "There was a precious few of the Scotch, and none that I knows on, saving yourself, perhaps,—that didn't go dead agin us, and for the tories, through thick and thin. That 'Cross Creek settlement' was a mighty ugly thorn in the sides of us whigs. It turned out a raal bad stock of varmints. I hope—I reckon, stranger—you ain't from that part."

"No," said the other; "oh, no! I'm from over the other quarter. I'm from the Duncan settlement above."

"I've hearn tell of that other settlement, but I never know'd as any of the men fou't with us. What giniral did you fight under? What Carolina giniral?"

"I was at Gum Swamp when General Gates was defeated;" was still the hesitating reply of the other.

"Well, I thank God, I warn't there, though I reckon things wouldn't ha' turned out quite so bad, if there had been a leetle sprinkling of Sumter's, or Pickens's, or Marion's men, among them two-legged critters that run that day. They did tell that some of the regiments went off without ever once emptying their rifles. Now, stranger, I hope you warn't among them fellows."

"I was not," said the other, with something more of promptness.

"I don't blame a chap for dodging a bullet if he can, or being too quick for a bagnet, because, I'm thinking, a live man is always a better man than a dead one, or he can become so; but to run without taking a single crack at the inimy, is downright cowardice. There's no two ways about it, stranger."

This opinion, delivered with considerable emphasis, met with the ready assent of the Scotchman, but Joel Sparkman was not to be diverted, even by his own eloquence, from the object of his inquiry.

"But you ain't said," he continued, "who was your Carolina gineral. Gates was from Virginny, and he stayed a mighty short time when he come. You didn't run far at Camden, I reckon, and you joined the army ag'in, and come in with Greene? Was that the how?"

To this the stranger assented, though with evident disinclination.

"Then, mou't be, we sometimes went into the same scratch together? I was at Cowpens and Ninety-Six, and seen sarvice at other odds and eends, where there was more fighting than fun. I reckon you must have been at 'Ninety-Six,'—perhaps at Cowpens, too, if you went with Morgan?"

The unwillingness of the stranger to respond to these questions appeared to increase. He admitted, however, that he had been at "Ninety-Six," though, as Sparkman afterwards remembered, in this case, as in that of the defeat of Gates at Gum Swamp, he had not said on which side he had fought.—Joel, as he discovered the reluctance of his guest to answer his questions, and perceived his growing doggedness, forbore to annoy him, but mentally resolved to keep a sharper look-out than ever upon his motions. His examination concluded with an inquiry, which, in the plain-dealing regions of the south and south-west, is not unfrequently put first.

"And what mout be your name, stranger?"

"Macnab," was the ready response, "Sandy Macnab."

"Well, Mr. Macnab, I see that my sister's got supper ready for us; so we mou't as well fall to upon the hoecake and bacon."

Sparkman rose while speaking, and led the way to the spot, near the waggon, where Mrs. Grayling had spread the feast.— "We're pretty nigh on the main road here, but I reckon there's no great danger now. Besides, Jim Grayling keeps watch for us, and he's got two as good eyes in his head as any scout in the country, and a rifle that, after you once know how it shoots, 'twould do your heart good to hear its crack, if so be that twa'n't your heart that he drawed sight on. He's a perdigious fine shot, and as ready to shoot and fight as if he had a nateral calling that way."

"Shall we wait for him before we eat?" demanded Macnab, anxiously.

"By no sort o' reason, stranger," answered Sparkman.—"He'll watch for us while we're eating, and after that I'll change shoes with him. So fall to, and don't mind what's a coming."

Sparkman had just broken the hoecake, when a distant whistle was heard.

"Ha! that's the lad now!" he exclaimed, rising to his feet. "He's on trail. He's got sight of an inimy's fire, I reckon.— 'Twon't be onreasonable, friend Macnab, to get our we'pons in readiness"; and, so speaking, Sparkman bid his sister get into the waggon, where the little Lucy had already placed herself, while he threw open the pan of his rifle, and turned the priming over with his finger. Macnab, meanwhile, had taken from his holsters, which he had before been sitting upon, a pair of horseman's pistols, richly mounted with figures in silver. These were large and long, and had evidently seen service. Unlike his companion, his proceedings occasioned no comment. What he did seemed a matter of habit, of which he himself was scarcely conscious. Having looked at his priming, he laid the instruments beside him without a word, and resumed the bit of hoecake which he had just before received from Sparkman. Meanwhile, the signal whistle, supposed to come from James Grayling, was repeated. Silence then ensued for a brief space, which Sparkman employed in perambulating the grounds immediately contiguous. At length, just as he had returned to the fire, the sound of a horse's feet was heard, and a sharp, quick halloo from Grayling informed his uncle that all was right. The youth made his appearance a moment after, accompanied by a stranger on horseback, a tall, fine-looking young man, with a keen, flashing eye, and a voice whose lively, clear tones, as he was heard approaching, sounded cheerily like those of a trumpet after victory. James Grayling kept along on foot beside the newcomer; and his hearty laugh, and free, glib, garrulous tones, betrayed to his uncle, long ere he drew nigh enough to declare the fact, that he had met unexpectedly with a friend, or, at least, an old acquaintance.

"Why, who have you got there, James?" was the demand of Sparkman, as he dropped the butt of his rifle upon the ground.

"Why, who do you think, uncle? Who but Major Spencer— our own major?"

"You don't say so!—what!—well! Li'nel Spencer, for sartin! Lord bless you, major, who'd ha' thought to see you in these parts; and jest mounted too, for all natur, as if the war was to be fou't over ag'in. Well, I'm raal glad to see you.—I am, that's sartin!"

"And I'm very glad to see you, Sparkman," said the other, as he alighted from his steed, and yielded his hand to the cordial grasp of the other.

"Well, I knows that, major, without you saying it. But you've jest come in the right time. The bacon's frying, and here's the bread;—let's down upon our haunches, in right good airnest, camp fashion, and make the most of what God gives us in the way of blessings. I reckon you don't mean to ride any further to-night, major?"

"No," said the person addressed, "not if you'll let me lay my heels at your fire. But who's in your waggon? My old friend, Mrs. Grayling, I suppose?"

"That's a true word, major," said the lady herself, making her way out of the vehicle with good-humoured agility, and coming forward with extended hand.

"Really, Mrs. Graylin, I'm very glad to see you." And the stranger, with the blandness of a gentleman and the hearty warmth of an old neighbour, expressed his satisfaction at once more finding himself in the company of an old acquaintance. Their greetings once over, Major Spencer readily joined the group about the fire, while James Grayling—though with some reluctance—disappeared to resume his toils of the scout while the supper proceeded.

"And who have you here?" demanded Spencer, as his eye rested on the dark, hard features of the Scotchman. Sparkman told him all that he himself had learned of the name and character of the stranger, in a brief whisper, and in a moment after formally introduced the parties in this fashion—

"Mr. Macnab, Major Spencer. Mr. Macnab says he's true blue, major, and fou't at Camden, when General Gates run so hard to 'bring the d—d militia back.' He also fou't at Ninety-Six, and Cowpen—so I reckon we had as good as count him one of us."

Major Spencer scrutinized the Scotchman keenly—a scrutiny which the latter seemed very ill to relish. He put a few questions to him on the subject of the war, and some of the actions in which he allowed himself to have been concerned; but his evident reluctance to unfold himself—a reluctance so unnatural to the brave soldier who has gone through his toils honourably—had the natural effect of discouraging the young officer, whose sense of delicacy had not been materially impaired amid the rude jostlings of military life. But, though he forbore to propose any other questions to Macnab, his eyes continued to survey the features of his sullen countenance with curiosity and a strangely increasing interest. This he subsequently explained to Sparkman, when, at the close of supper, James Grayling came in, and the former assumed the duties of the scout.

"I have seen that Scotchman's face somewhere, Sparkman, and I'm convinced at some interesting moment: but where, when, or how, I cannot call to mind. The sight of it is even associated in my mind with something painful and unpleasant; where could I have seen him?"

"I don't somehow like his looks myself," said Sparkman, "and I mislists he's been rether more of a tory than a whig; but that's nothing to the purpose now; and he's at our fire, and we've broken hoecake together; so we cannot rake up the old ashes to make a dust with."

"No, surely not," was the reply of Spencer. "Even though we know him to be a tory, that cause of former quarrel should occasion none now. But it should produce watchfulness and caution. I'm glad to see that you have not forgot your old business of scouting in the swamp."

"Kin I forget it, major?" demanded Sparkman, in tones which, though whispered, were full of emphasis, as he laid his ear to the earth to listen.

"James has finished supper, major—that's his whistle to tell me so; and I'll jest step back to make it cl'ar to him how we're to keep up the watch to-night."

"Count me in your arrangements, Sparkman, as I am one of you for the night," said the major.

"By what sort of means," was the reply. "The night must be shared between James and myself. If so you wants to keep company with one or t'other of us, why, that's another thing, and, of course, you can do as you please."

"We'll have no quarrel on the subject, Joel," said the officer, good-naturedly, as they returned to the camp together.

CHAPTER II

The arrangements of the party were soon made. Spencer renewed his offer at the fire to take his part in the watch; and the Scotchman, Macnab, volunteered his services also; but the offer of the latter was another reason why that of the former should be declined. Sparkman was resolute to have everything his own way; and while James Grayling went out upon his lonely rounds, he busied himself in cutting bushes and making a sort of tent for the use of his late commander. Mrs. Grayling and Lucy slept in the waggon. The Scotchman stretched himself with little effort before the fire; while Joel Sparkman, wrapping himself up in his cloak, crouched under the waggon body, with his back resting partly against one of the wheels. From time to time he rose and thrust additional brands into the fire, looked up at the night, and round upon the encampment, then sunk back into his perch and stole a few moments, at intervals, of uneasy sleep. The first two hours of the watch were over, and James Grayling was relieved. The youth, however, felt in no mood for sleep, and taking his seat by the fire, he drew from his pocket a little volume of Easy Reading Lessons, and by the fitful flame of the resinous light-wood, he prepared, in this rude manner, to make up for the precious time which his youth had lost of its legitimate employments, in the stirring events of the preceding seven years consumed in war. He was surprised at this employment by his late commander, who, himself sleepless, now emerged from the bushes and joined Grayling at the fire. The youth had been rather a favourite with Spencer. They had both been reared in the same neighbourhood, and the first military achievements of James had taken place under the eye, and had met the approbation of his officer. The difference of their ages was just such as to permit of the warm attachment of the lad without diminishing any of the reverence which should be felt by the inferior. Grayling was not more than seventeen, and Spencer was perhaps thirty-four—the very prime of manhood. They sat by the fire and talked of olden times and told old stories with the hearty glee and good nature of the young. Their mutual inquiries led to the revelation of their several objects in pursuing the present journey. Those of James Grayling were scarcely, indeed, to be considered his own. They were plans and purposes of his uncle, and it does not concern this narrative that we should know more of their nature than has already been revealed. But whatever they were, they were as freely unfolded to his hearer as if the parties had been brothers, and Spencer was quite as frank in his revelations as his companion. He, too, was on his way to Charleston, from whence he was to take passage for England.

"I am rather in a hurry to reach town," he said, "as I learn that the Falmouth packet is preparing to sail for England in a few days, and I must go in her."

"For England, major!" exclaimed the youth with unaffected astonishment.

"Yes, James, for England. But why—what astonishes you?"

"Why, lord!" exclaimed the simple youth, "if they only knew there, as I do, what a cutting and slashing you did use to make among their red coats, I reckon they'd hang you to the first hickory."

"Oh, no! scarcely," said the other, with a smile.

"But I reckon you'll change your name, major?" continued the youth.

"No," responded Spencer, "if I did that, I should lose the object of my voyage. You must know, James, that an old relative has left me a good deal of money in England, and I can only get it by proving that I am Lionel Spencer; so you see I must carry my own name, whatever may be the risk."

"Well, major, you know best; but I do think if they could only have a guess of what you did among their sodgers at Hobkirk's and Cowpens, and Eutaw, and a dozen other places, they'd find some means of hanging you up, peace or no peace. But I don't see what occasion you have to be going cl'ar away to England for money, when you've got a sight of your own already."

"Not so much as you think for," replied the major, giving an involuntary and uneasy glance at the Scotchman, who was seemingly sound asleep on the opposite side of the fire. "There is, you know, but little money in the country at any time, and I must get what I want for my expenses when I reach Charleston. I have just enough to carry me there."

"Well, now, major, that's mighty strange. I always thought that you was about the best off of any man in our parts; but if you're strained so close, I'm thinking, major,—if so be you wouldn't think me too presumptuous,—you'd better let me lend you a guinea or so that I've got to spare and you can pay me back when you get the English money."

And the youth fumbled in his bosom for a little cotton wallet, which, with its limited contents, was displayed in another instant to the eyes of the officer.

"No, no, James," said the other, putting back the generous tribute; "I have quite enough to carry me to Charleston, and when there I can easily get a supply from the merchants. But I thank you, my good fellow, for your offer. You *are* a good fellow, James, and I will remember you."

It is needless to pursue the conversation farther. The night passed away without any alarms, and at dawn of the next day the whole party was engaged in making preparation for a start. Mrs. Grayling was soon busy in getting breakfast in readiness. Major Spencer consented to remain with them until it was over; but the Scotchman, after returning thanks very civilly for his accommodation of the night, at once resumed his journey. His course seemed, like their own, to lie below; but he neither declared his route nor betrayed the least desire to know that of Spencer. The latter had no disposition to renew those inquiries from which the stranger seemed to shrink the night before, and he accordingly suffered him to depart with a quiet farewell, and the utterance of a good-natured wish, in which all the parties joined, that he might have a pleasant journey. When he was fairly out of sight, Spencer said to Sparkman,

"Had I liked that fellow's looks, nay, had I not positively disliked them, I should have gone with him. As it is, I will remain and share your breakfast."

The repast being over, all parties set forward; but Spencer, after keeping along with them for a mile, took his leave also. The slow waggon-pace at which the family travelled, did not suit the high-spirited cavalier; and it was necessary, as he assured them, that he should reach the city in two nights more. They parted with many regrets, as truly felt as they were warmly expressed; and James Grayling never felt the tedium of waggon travelling to be so severe as throughout the whole of that day when he separated from his favourite captain. But he was too stout-hearted a lad to make any complaint; and his dissatisfaction only showed itself in his unwonted silence, and an over-anxiety, which his steed seemed to feel in common with himself, to go rapidly ahead. Thus the day passed, and the wayfarers at its close had made a progress of some twenty miles from sun to sun. The same precautions marked their encampment this night as the last, and they rose in better spirits with the next morning, the dawn of which was very bright and pleasant, and encouraging. A similar journey of twenty miles brought them to a place of bivouac as the sun went down; and they prepared as usual for their securities and supper. They found themselves on the edge of a very dense forest of pines and scrubby oaks, a portion of which was swallowed up in a deep bay—so called in the dialect of the country—a swamp-bottom, the growth of which consisted of mingled cypresses and bay-trees, with tupola, gum, and dense thickets of low stunted shrubbery, cane grass, and dwarf willows, which filled up every interval between the trees, and to the eye most effectually barred out every human intruder. This bay was chosen as the background for the camping party. Their waggon was wheeled into an area on a gently rising ground in front, under a pleasant shade of oaks and hickories, with a lonely pine rising loftily in occasional spots among them. Here the horses were taken out, and James Grayling prepared to kindle up a fire; but, looking for his axe, it was unaccountably missing, and after a fruitless search of half an hour, the party came to the conclusion that it had been left on the spot where they had slept last night. This was a disaster, and, while they meditated in what manner to repair it, a negro boy appeared in sight, passing along the road at their feet, and driving before him a small herd of cattle. From him they learned that they were only a mile or two from a farmstead where an axe might be borrowed; and James, leaping on his horse, rode forward in the hope to obtain one. He found no difficulty in his quest; and, having obtained it from the farmer, who was also a tavern-keeper, he casually asked if Major Spencer had not stayed with him the night before. He was somewhat surprised when told that he had not.

"There was one man stayed with me last night," said the farmer, "but he didn't call himself a major, and didn't much look like one."

"He rode a fine sorrel horse,—tall, bright colour, with white fore foot, didn't he?" asked James.

"No, that he didn't! He rode a powerful black, coal black, and not a bit of white about him."

"That was the Scotchman! But I wonder the major didn't stop with you. He must have rode on. Isn't there another house near you, below?"

"Not one. There's ne'er a house either above or below for a matter of fifteen miles. I'm the only man in all that distance that's living on this road; and I don't think your friend could have gone below, as I should have seen him pass. I've been all day out there in that field before your eyes, clearing up the brush."

Chapter III

Somewhat wondering that the major should have turned aside from the track, though without attaching to it any importance at that particular moment, James Grayling took up the borrowed axe and hurried back to the encampment, where the toil of cutting an extra supply of light-wood to meet the exigencies of the ensuing night, sufficiently exercised his mind as well as his body, to prevent him from meditating upon the seeming strangeness of the circumstance. But when he sat down to his supper over the fire that he had kindled, his fancies crowded thickly upon him, and he felt a confused doubt and suspicion that something was to happen, he knew not what. His conjectures and apprehensions were without form, though not altogether void; and he felt a strange sickness and a sinking at the heart which was very unusual with him. He had, in short, that lowness of spirits, that cloudy apprehensiveness of soul which takes the form of presentiment, and makes us look out for danger even when the skies are without a cloud, and the breeze is laden, equally and only, with balm and music. His moodiness found no sympathy among his companions. Joel Sparkman was in the best of humours, and his mother was so cheery and happy, that when the thoughtful boy went off into the woods to watch, he could hear her at every moment breaking out into little catches of a country ditty, which the gloomy events of the late war had not yet obliterated from her memory.

"It's very strange!" soliloquized the youth, as he wandered along the edges of the dense bay or swamp-bottom, which we have passingly referred to,—"it's very strange what troubles me so! I feel almost frightened, and yet I know I'm not to be fright-

ened easily, and I don't see anything in the woods to frighten
me. It's strange the major didn't come along this road! Maybe
he took another higher up that leads by a different settlement. I
wish I had asked the man at the house if there's such another
road. I reckon there must be, however, for where could the
major have gone?"

The unphilosophical mind of James Grayling did not, in his
farther meditations, carry him much beyond this starting point;
and with its continual recurrence in soliloquy, he proceeded to
traverse the margin of the bay, until he came to its junction
with, and termination at, the high road. The youth turned into
this, and, involuntarily departing from it a moment after, soon
found himself on the opposite side of the bay thicket. He wandered on and on, as he himself described it, without any power
to restrain himself. He knew not how far he went; but, instead
of maintaining his watch for two hours only, he was gone more
than four; and, at length, a sense of weariness which overpowered him all of a sudden, caused him to seat himself at the foot
of a tree, and snatch a few moments of rest. He denied that he
slept in this time. He insisted to the last moment of his life that
sleep never visited his eyelids that night,—that he was conscious
of fatigue and exhaustion, but not drowsiness,—and that this
fatigue was so numbing as to be painful, and effectually kept
him from any sleep. While he sat thus beneath the tree, with a
body weak and nerveless, but a mind excited, he knew not how
or why, to the most acute degree of expectation and attention,
he heard his name called by the well-known voice of his friend,
Major Spencer. The voice called him three times,—"James
Grayling!—James!—James Grayling!" before he could muster
strength enough to answer. It was not courage he wanted,—of
that he was positive, for he felt sure, as he said, that something
had gone wrong, and he was never more ready to fight in his life
than at that moment, could he have commanded the physical
capacity; but his throat seemed dry to suffocation—his lips
effectually sealed up as if with wax, and when he did answer, the
sounds seemed as fine and soft as the whisper of some child just
born.

"Oh! major, is it you?"

Such, he thinks, were the very words he made use of in reply; and the answer that he received was instantaneous, though the voice came from some little distance in the bay, and his own voice he did not hear. He only knows what he meant to say. The answer was to this effect.

"It is, James!—It is your own friend, Lionel Spencer, that speaks to you; do not be alarmed when you see me! I have been shockingly murdered!"

James asserts that he tried to tell him that he would not be frightened, but his own voice was still a whisper, which he himself could scarcely hear. A moment after he had spoken, he heard something like a sudden breeze that rustled through the bay bushes at his feet, and his eyes were closed without his effort, and indeed in spite of himself. When he opened them, he saw Major Spencer standing at the edge of the bay, about twenty steps from him. Though he stood in the shade of a thicket, and there was no light in the heavens save that of the stars, he was yet enabled to distinguish perfectly, and with great ease, every lineament of his friend's face.

He looked very pale, and his garments were covered with blood; and James said that he strove very much to rise from the place where he sat and approach him;—"for in truth," said the lad, "so far from feeling any fear, I felt nothing but fury in my heart; but I could not move a limb. My feet were fastened to the ground; my hands to my sides; and I could only bend forward and gasp. I felt as if I should have died with vexation that I could not rise; but a power which I could not resist, made me motionless, and almost speechless. I could only say, 'Murdered!'—and that one word I believe I must have repeated a dozen times.

"'Yes, murdered! Murdered by the Scotchman who slept with us at the fire the night before last. James, I look to you to have the murderer brought to justice! James!—do you hear me, James?'"

"These," said James, "I think were the very words, or near about the very words, that I heard; and I tried to ask the major to tell me how it was, and how I could do what he required; but I didn't hear myself speak, though it would appear that he did, for almost immediately after I had tried to speak what I wished to say, he answered me just as if I had said it. He told me that the Scotchman had waylaid, killed, and hidden him in that very bay; that his murderer had gone to Charleston; and that if I made haste to town, I would find him in the Falmouth packet, which was then lying in the harbour and ready to sail for England. He farther said that everything depended on my making haste,—that I must reach town by to-morrow night if I wanted to be in season, and go right on board the vessel and charge the criminal with the deed. 'Do not be afraid,' said he, when he had finished; 'be afraid of nothing, James, for God will help and strengthen you to the end.' When I heard all I burst into a flood of tears, and then I felt strong. I felt that I could talk, or fight, or do almost anything; and I jumped up to my feet, and was just about to run down to where the major stood, but, with the first step which I made forward, he was gone. I stopped and looked all around me, but I could see nothing; and the bay was just as black as midnight. But I went down to it, and tried to press in where I thought the major had been standing; but I couldn't get far, the brush and bay leaves were so close and thick. I was now bold and strong enough, and I called out, loud enough to be heard half a mile. I didn't exactly know what I called for, or what I wanted to learn, or I have forgotten. But I heard nothing more. Then I remembered the camp, and began to fear that something might have happened to mother and uncle, for I now felt, what I had not thought of before, that I had gone too far round the bay to be of much assistance, or indeed, to be in time for any, had they been suddenly attacked. Besides, I could not think how long I had been gone; but it now seemed very late. The stars were shining their brightest, and the thin white clouds of morning were beginning to rise and run towards the west. Well, I bethought me of my course, for I was a little bewildered and doubtful where I was; but, after a little thinking, I took the back track, and soon got a glimpse of the camp-fire, which was nearly burnt down; and by this I reckoned I was gone considerably longer than my two hours. When I got back into the camp, I looked under the waggon, and found uncle in a sweet sleep, and though my heart was full almost to bursting with what I had heard, and the cruel sight I had seen, yet I wouldn't waken him; and I beat about and mended the fire, and watched, and waited, until near daylight, when mother called to me out of the waggon, and asked who it was. This wakened my uncle, and then I up and told all that had happened, for if it had been to save my life, I couldn't have kept it in much longer. But though mother said it was very strange, Uncle Sparkman considered that I had been only dreaming; but he couldn't persuade me of it; and when I told him I intended to be off at daylight, just as the major had told me to do, and ride my best all the way to Charleston, he laughed, and said I was a fool. But I felt that I was no fool, and I was solemn certain that I hadn't been dreaming; and though both mother and he tried their hardest to make me put off going, yet I made up my mind to it, and they had to give up. For, wouldn't I have been a pretty sort of a friend to the major, if, after what he had told me, I could have stayed behind, and gone on only at a waggon-pace to look after the murderer! I don't think if I had done so that I should ever have been able to look a white man in the face again. Soon as the peep of day, I was on horse-back. Mother was mighty sad, and begged me not to go, but Uncle Sparkman was mighty sulky, and kept calling me fool upon fool, until I was almost angry enough to forget that we were of blood kin. But all his talking did not stop me, and I reckon I was five miles on my way before he had his team in traces for a start. I rode as briskly as I could get on without hurting my nag. I had a smart ride of more than forty miles before me, and the road was very heavy. But it was a good two hours from sunset when I got into town, and the first question I asked of the people I met was, to show me where the ships were kept. When I got to the wharf they showed me the Falmouth packet, where she lay in the stream, ready to sail as soon as the wind should favour."

CHAPTER IV

James Grayling, with the same eager impatience which he has been suffered to describe in his own language, had already hired a boat to go on board the British packet, when he remembered that he had neglected all those means, legal and otherwise, by which alone his purpose might be properly effected. He did not know much about legal process, but he had common sense enough, the moment that he began to reflect on the subject, to know that some such process was necessary. This conviction produced another difficulty; he knew not in which quarter to turn for counsel and assistance; but here the boatman who saw his bewilderment, and knew by his dialect and dress that he was a back-countryman, came to his relief, and from him he got directions where to find the merchants with whom his uncle, Sparkman, had done business in former years. To them he went, and without circumlocution, told the whole story of his ghostly visitation. Even as a dream, which these gentlemen at once conjectured it to be, the story of James Grayling was equally clear and curious; and his intense warmth and the entire absorption, which the subject had effected, of his mind and soul, was such that they judged it not improper, at least to carry out the search of the vessel which he contemplated. It would certainly, they thought, be a curious coincidence—believing James to be a veracious youth— if the Scotchman should be found on board. But another test of his narrative was proposed by one of the firm. It so happened that the business agents of Major Spencer, who was well known in Charleston, kept their office but a few rods distant from their own; and to them all parties at once proceeded. But here the story of James was encountered by a circumstance that made somewhat against it. These gentlemen produced a letter from Major Spencer, intimating the utter impossibility of his coming to town for the space of a month, and expressing his regret that he should be unable to avail himself of the opportunity of the foreign vessel, of whose arrival in Charleston, and proposed time of departure, they had themselves advised him. They read the letter aloud to James and their brother merchants, and with difficulty suppressed their smiles at the gravity with which the former related and insisted upon the particulars of his vision.

"He has changed his mind," returned the impetuous youth; "he was on his way down, I tell you,—a hundred miles on his way,—when he camped with us. I know him well, I tell you, and talked with him myself half the night."

"At least," remarked the gentlemen who had gone with James, "it can do no harm to look into the business. We can procure a warrant for searching the vessel after this man, Macnab; and should he be found on board the packet, it will be a sufficient circumstance to justify the magistrates in detaining him, until we can ascertain where Major Spencer really is."

The measure was accordingly adopted, and it was nearly sunset before the warrant was procured, and the proper officer in readiness. The impatience of a spirit so eager and so devoted as James Grayling, under these delays, may be imagined; and when in the boat, and on his way to the packet where the criminal was to be sought, his blood became so excited that it was with much ado he could be kept in his seat. His quick, eager action continually disturbed the trim of the boat, and one of his mercantile friends, who had accompanied him, with that interest in the affair which curiosity alone inspired, was under constant apprehension lest he would plunge overboard in his impatient desire to shorten the space which lay between. The same impatience enabled the youth, though never on shipboard before, to grasp the rope which had been flung at their approach, and to mount her sides with catlike agility. Without waiting to declare himself or his purpose, he ran from one side of the deck to the other, greedily staring, to the surprise of officers, passengers, and seamen, in the faces of all of them, and surveying them with an almost offensive scrutiny. He turned away from the search with disappointment. There was no face like that of the suspected man among them. By this time, his friend, the merchant, with the sheriff's officer, had entered the vessel, and were in conference with the captain. Grayling drew nigh in time to hear the latter affirm that there was no man of the name of Macnab, as stated in the warrant, among his passengers or crew.

"He is—he must be!" exclaimed the impetuous youth. "The major never lied in his life, and couldn't lie after he was dead. Macnab is here—he is a Scotchman—"

The captain interrupted him—

"We have, young gentleman, several Scotchmen on board, and one of them is named Macleod—"

"Let me see him—which is he?" demanded the youth.

By this time, the passengers and a goodly portion of the crew were collected about the little party. The captain turned his eyes upon the group, and asked,

"Where is Mr. Macleod?"

"He is gone below—he's sick!" replied one of the passengers.

"That's he! That must be the man!" exclaimed the youth. "I'll lay my life that's no other than Macnab. He's only taken a false name."

It was now remembered by one of the passengers, and remarked, that Macleod had expressed himself as unwell, but a few moments before, and had gone below even while the boat was rapidly approaching the vessel. At this statement, the captain led the way into the cabin, closely followed by James Grayling and the rest.

"Mr. Macleod," he said with a voice somewhat elevated, as he approached the berth of that person, "you are wanted on deck for a few moments."

"I am really too unwell, captain," replied a feeble voice from behind the curtain of the berth.

"It will be necessary," was the reply of the captain. "There is a warrant from the authorities of the town, to look after a fugitive from justice."

Macleod had already begun a second speech declaring his feebleness, when the fearless youth, Grayling, bounded before the captain and tore away, with a single grasp of his hand, the curtain which concealed the suspected man from their sight.

"It is he!" was the instant exclamation of the youth, as he beheld him. "It is he—Macnab, the Scotchman—the man that murdered Major Spencer!"

Macnab,—for it was he,—was deadly pale. He trembled like an aspen. His eyes were dilated with more than mortal apprehension, and his lips were perfectly livid. Still, he found strength to speak, and to deny the accusation. He knew nothing of the

youth before him—nothing of Major Spencer—his name was
Macleod, and he had never called himself by any other. He
denied, but with great incoherence, everything which was urged
against him.

"You must get up, Mr. Macleod," said the captain; "the circumstances are very much against you. You must go with the
officer!"

"Will you give me up to my enemies?" demanded the culprit.
"You are a countryman—a Briton. I have fought for the king,
our master, against these rebels, and for this they seek my life.
Do not deliver me into their bloody hands!"

"Liar!" exclaimed James Grayling—"Didn't you tell us at our
own camp-fire that you were with us? that you were at Gates's
defeat, and Ninety-Six?"

"But I didn't tell you," said the Scotchman, with a grin, "which
side I was on!"

"Ha! remember that!" said the sheriff's officer. "He denied,
just a moment ago, that he knew this young man at all; now, he
confesses that he did see and camp with him."

The Scotchman was aghast at the strong point which, in his
inadvertence, he had made against himself; and his efforts to
excuse himself, stammering and contradictory, served only to
involve him more deeply in the meshes of his difficulty. Still he
continued his urgent appeals to the captain of the vessel, and his
fellow-passengers, as citizens of the same country, subjects to
the same monarch, to protect him from those who equally hated
and would destroy them all. In order to move their national
prejudices in his behalf, he boasted of the immense injury which
he had done, as a tory, to the rebel cause; and still insisted that
the murder was only a pretext of the youth before him, by which
to gain possession of his person, and wreak upon him the
revenge which his own fierce performances during the war had
naturally enough provoked. One or two of the passengers,
indeed, joined with him in entreating the captain to set the
accusers adrift and make sail at once; but the stout Englishman,
who was in command, rejected instantly the unworthy counsel.
Besides, he was better aware of the dangers which would follow
any such rash proceeding. Fort Moultrie, on Sullivan's Island,

had been already refitted and prepared for an enemy; and he was lying, at that moment, under the formidable range of grinning teeth, which would have opened upon him, at the first movement, from the jaws of Castle Pinckney.

"No, gentlemen," said he, "you mistake your man. God forbid that I should give shelter to a murderer, though he were from my own parish."

"But I am no murderer," said the Scotchman.

"You look cursedly like one, however," was the reply of the captain. "Sheriff, take your prisoner."

The base creature threw himself at the feet of the Englishman, and clung, with piteous entreaties, to his knees. The latter shook him off, and turned away in disgust.

"Steward," he cried, "bring up this man's luggage."

He was obeyed. The luggage was brought up from the cabin and delivered to the sheriff's officer, by whom it was examined in the presence of all, and an inventory made of its contents. It consisted of a small new trunk, which, it afterwards appeared, he had bought in Charleston, soon after his arrival. This contained a few changes of raiment, twenty-six guineas in money, a gold watch, not in repair, and the two pistols which he had shown while at Joel Sparkman's camp fire; but, with this difference, that the stock of one was broken off short just above the grasp, and the butt was entirely gone. It was not found among his chattels. A careful examination of the articles in his trunk did not result in anything calculated to strengthen the charge of his criminality; but there was not a single person present who did not feel as morally certain of his guilt as if the jury had already declared the fact. That night he slept—if he slept at all—in the common jail of the city.

CHAPTER V

His accuser, the warm-hearted and resolute James Grayling, did not sleep. The excitement, arising from mingling and contradictory emotions,—sorrow for his brave young commander's fate, and the natural exultation of a generous spirit at the conscious-

ness of having performed, with signal success, an arduous and
painful task combined to drive all pleasant slumbers from his
eyes; and with the dawn he was again up and stirring, with his
mind still full of the awful business in which he had been
engaged. We do not care to pursue his course in the ordinary
walks of the city, nor account for his employments during the
few days which ensued, until, in consequence of a legal examination into the circumstances which anticipated the regular
work of the sessions, the extreme excitement of the young
accuser had been renewed. Macnab or Macleod,—and it is possible that both names were fictitious,—as soon as he recovered
from his first terrors, sought the aid of an attorney—one of
those acute, small, chopping lawyers, to be found in almost
every community, who are willing to serve with equal zeal the
sinner and the saint, provided that they can pay with equal lib-
erality. The prisoner was brought before the court under *habeas
corpus*, and several grounds submitted by his counsel with the
view to obtaining his discharge. It became necessary to ascertain, among the first duties of the state, whether Major Spencer,
the alleged victim, was really dead. Until it could be established
that a man should be imprisoned, tried, and punished for a
crime, it was first necessary to show that a crime had been committed, and the attorney made himself exceedingly merry with
the ghost story of young Grayling. In those days, however, the
ancient Superstition was not so feeble as she has subsequently
become. The venerable judge was one of those good men who
had a decent respect for the faith and opinions of his ancestors;
and though he certainly would not have consented to the hanging of Macleod under the sort of testimony which had been
adduced, he yet saw enough, in all the circumstances, to justify
his present detention. In the meantime, efforts were to be
made, to ascertain the whereabouts of Major Spencer; though,
were he even missing,—so the counsel for Macleod contended,—
his death could be by no means assumed in consequence. To
this the judge shook his head doubtfully. "'Fore God!" said he,
"I would not have you to be too sure of that." He was an
Irishman, and proceeded after the fashion of his country. The
reader will therefore *bear* with his *bull*. "A man may properly be

hung for murdering another, though the murdered man be not dead; ay, before God, even though he be actually unhurt and uninjured, while the murderer is swinging by the neck for the bloody deed!"

The judge,—who it must be understood was a real existence, and who had no small reputation in his day in the south,—proceeded to establish the correctness of his opinions by authorities and argument, with all of which, doubtlessly, the bar were exceedingly delighted; but, to provide them in this place would only be to interfere with our own progress. James Grayling, however, was not satisfied to wait the slow processes which were suggested for coming at the truth. Even the wisdom of the judge was lost upon him, possibly, for the simple reason that he did not comprehend it. But the ridicule of the culprit's lawyer stung him to the quick, and he muttered to himself, more than once, a determination "to lick the life out of that impudent chap's leather." But this was not his only resolve. There was one which he proceeded to put into instant execution, and that was to seek the body of his murdered friend in the spot where he fancied it might be found—namely, the dark and dismal bay where the spectre had made its appearance to his eyes.

The suggestion was approved—though he did not need this to prompt his resolution—by his mother and uncle, Sparkman. The latter determined to be his companion, and he was farther accompanied by the sheriff's officer who had arrested the suspected felon. Before daylight, on the morning after the examination before the judge had taken place, and when Macleod had been remanded to prison, James Grayling started on his journey. His fiery zeal received additional force at every added moment of delay, and his eager spurring brought him at an early hour after noon, to the neighbourhood of the spot through which his search was to be made. When his companions and himself drew nigh, they were all at a loss in which direction first to proceed. The bay was one of those massed forests, whose wall of thorns, vines, and close tenacious shrubs, seemed to defy invasion. To the eye of the townsman it was so forbidding that he pronounced it absolutely impenetrable. But James was not to be baffled. He led them round it, taking the very course which he had pursued the night when the revelation was made him; he showed them the very tree at whose foot he had sunk when the supernatural torpor—as he himself esteemed it—began to fall upon him; he then pointed out the spot, some twenty steps distant, at which the spectre made his appearance. To this spot they then proceeded in a body, and essayed an entrance, but were so discouraged by the difficulties at the outset that all, James not excepted, concluded that neither the murderer nor his victim could possibly have found entrance there.

But, lo! a marvel! Such it seemed, at the first blush, to all the party. While they stood confounded and indecisive, undetermined in which way to move, a sudden flight of wings was heard, even from the centre of the bay, at a little distance above the spot where they had striven for entrance. They looked up, and beheld about fifty buzzards—those notorious domestic vultures of the south—ascending from the interior of the bay, and perching along upon the branches of the loftier trees by which it was overhung. Even were the character of these birds less known, the particular business in which they had just then been engaged, was betrayed by huge gobbets of flesh which some of them had borne aloft in their flight, and still continued to rend with beak and bill, as they tottered upon the branches where they stood. A piercing scream issued from the lips of James Grayling as he beheld this sight, and strove to scare the offensive birds from their repast.

"The poor major! the poor major!" was the involuntary and agonized exclamation of the youth. "Did I ever think he would come to this!"

The search, thus guided and encouraged, was pressed with renewed diligence and spirit; and, at length, an opening was found through which it was evident that a body of considerable size had but recently gone. The branches were broken from the small shrub trees, and the undergrowth trodden into the earth. They followed this path, and, as is the case commonly with waste tracts of this description, the density of the growth diminished sensibly at every step they took, till they reached a little pond, which, though circumscribed in area, and full of cypresses, yet proved to be singularly deep. Indeed, it was an alligator-hole, where, in all probability, a numerous tribe of these reptiles had their dwelling. Here, on the edge of the pond, they discovered the object which had drawn the keen-sighted vultures to their feast, in the body of a horse, which James Grayling at once identified as that of Major Spencer. The carcass of the animal was already very much torn and lacerated. The eyes were plucked out, and the animal completely disembowelled. Yet, on examination, it was not difficult to discover the manner of his death. This had been effected by fire-arms. Two bullets had passed through his skull, just above the eyes, either of which must have been fatal. The murderer had led the horse to the spot, and committed the cruel deed where his body was found. The search was now continued for that of the owner, but for some time it proved ineffectual. At length, the keen eyes of James Grayling detected, amidst a heap of moss and green sedge that rested beside an overthrown tree, whose branches jutted into the pond, a whitish, but discoloured object, that did not seem native to the place. Bestriding the fallen tree, he was enabled to reach this object, which, with a burst of grief, he announced to the distant party was the hand and arm of his unfortunate friend, the wristband of the shirt being the conspicuous object which had first caught his eye. Grasping this, he drew the corpse, which had been thrust beneath the branches of the tree, to the surface; and, with the assistance of his uncle, it was finally brought to the dry land. Here it underwent a careful examination. The head was very much disfigured; the skull was fractured in several places by repeated blows of some hard instrument, inflicted chiefly from behind. A closer inspection revealed a bullet-hole in the abdomen, the first wound, in all probability, which the unfortunate gentleman received, and by which he was, perhaps, tumbled from his horse. The blows on the head would seem to have been unnecessary, unless the murderer—whose proceedings appeared to have been singularly deliberate,—was resolved upon making "assurance doubly sure." But, as if the watchful Providence had meant that nothing should be left doubtful which might tend to the complete conviction of the criminal, the constable stumbled upon the butt of the broken pistol which had been found in Macleod's trunk.

This he picked up on the edge of the pond in which the corpse had been discovered, and while James Grayling and his uncle, Sparkman, were engaged in drawing it from the water. The place where the fragment was discovered at once denoted the pistol as the instrument by which the final blows were inflicted. "'Fore God," said the judge to the criminal, as these proofs were submitted on the trial, "you may be a very innocent man after all, as, by my faith, I do think there have been many murderers before you; but you ought, nevertheless, to be hung as an example to all other persons who suffer such strong proofs of guilt to follow their innocent misdoings. Gentlemen of the jury, if this person, Macleod or Macnab, didn't murder Major Spencer, either you or I did; and you must now decide which of us it is! I say, gentlemen of the jury, either you, or I, or the prisoner at the bar, murdered this man; and if you have any doubts which of us it was, it is but justice and mercy that you should give the prisoner the benefit of your doubts; and so find your verdict. But, before God, should you find him not guilty, Mr. Attorney, there, can scarcely do anything wiser than to put us all upon trial for the deed."

The jury, it may be scarcely necessary to add, perhaps under certain becoming fears of an alternative such as his honour had suggested, brought in a verdict of "Guilty," without leaving the panel; and Macnab, *alias* Macleod, was hung at White Point, Charleston, somewhere about the year 178–.

"And here," said my grandmother, devoutly, "you behold a proof of God's watchfulness to see that murder should not be hidden, and that the murderer should not escape. You see that he sent the spirit of the murdered man—since, by no other mode could the truth have been revealed—to declare the crime, and to discover the criminal. But for that ghost, Macnab would have got off to Scotland, and probably have been living to this very day on the money that he took from the person of the poor major."

As the old lady finished the ghost story, which, by the way, she had been tempted to relate for the fiftieth time in order to combat my father's ridicule of such superstitions, the latter took up the thread of the narrative.

"Now, my son," said he, "as you have heard all that your grandmother has to say on this subject, I will proceed to show you what you have to believe, and what not. It is true that Macnab murdered Spencer in the manner related; that James Grayling made the discovery and prosecuted the pursuit; found the body and brought the felon to justice; that Macnab suffered death, and confessed the crime: alleging that he was moved to do so, as well because of the money that he suspected Spencer to have in his possession, as because of the hate which he felt for a man who had been particularly bold and active in cutting up a party of Scotch loyalists to which he belonged, on the borders of North Carolina. But the appearance of the spectre was nothing more than the work of a quick imagination, added to a shrewd and correct judgment. James Grayling saw no ghost, in fact, but such as was in his own mind; and, though the instance was one of a most remarkable character, one of singular combination, and well depending circumstances, still, I think it is to be accounted for by natural and very simple laws."

The old lady was indignant.

"And how could he see the ghost just on the edge of the same bay where the murder had been committed, and where the body of the murdered man even then was lying?"

My father did not directly answer the demand, but proceeded thus:

"James Grayling, as we know, mother, was a very ardent, impetuous, sagacious man. He had the sanguine, the race-horse temperament. He was generous, always prompt and ready, and one who never went backward. What he did, he did quickly, boldly, and thoroughly! He never shrank from trouble of any kind: nay, he rejoiced in the constant encounter with difficulty and trial; and his was the temper which commands and enthrals mankind. He felt deeply and intensely whatever occupied his mind, and when he parted from his friend he brooded over little else than their past communion and the great distance by which they were to be separated. The dull travelling waggon-gait at which he himself was compelled to go, was a source of annoyance to him; and he became sullen, all the day, after the departure of his friend. When, on the evening of the next day, he came to the house where it was natural to expect that Major Spencer would have slept the night before, and he learned the fact that no one stopped there but the Scotchman, Macnab, we see that he was struck with the circumstance. He mutters it over to himself, 'Strange, where the Major could have gone!' His mind then naturally reverts to the character of the Scotchman; to the opinions and suspicions which had been already expressed of him by his uncle, and felt by himself. They had all, previously, come to the full conviction that Macnab was, and had always been, a tory, in spite of his protestations. His mind next, and very naturally, reverted to the insecurity of the highways: the general dangers of travelling at that period; the frequency of crime, and the number of desperate men who were everywhere to be met with. The very employment in which he was then engaged, in scouting the woods for the protection of the camp, was calculated to bring such reflections to his mind. If these precautions were considered necessary for the safety of persons so poor, so wanting in those possessions which might prompt cupidity to crime, how much more necessary were precautions in the case of a wealthy gentleman like Major Spencer! He then remembered the conversation with the major at the camp fire, when they fancied that the Scotchman was sleeping. How natural to think then, that he was all the while awake; and, if awake, he must have heard him speak of the wealth of his companion. True, the major, with more prudence than himself, denied that he had any money about him, more than would bear his expenses to the city; but such an assurance was natural enough to the lips of a traveller who knew the dangers of the country. That the man, Macnab, was not a person to be trusted, was the equal impression of Joel Sparkman and his nephew from the first. The probabilities were strong that he would rob and perhaps murder, if he might hope to do so with impunity; and as the youth made the circuit of the bay in the darkness and solemn stillness of the night, its gloomy depths and mournful shadows, naturally gave rise to such reflections as would be equally active in the mind of a youth, and of one somewhat familiar with the arts and usages of strife. He would see that the spot was just the one in which a practised partizan would delight to set an ambush for an unwary foe. There ran the public road, with a little sweep, around two-thirds of the extent of its dense and impenetrable thickets. The ambush could lie concealed, and at ten steps command the bosom of its victim. Here, then, you perceive that the mind of James Grayling, stimulated by an active and sagacious judgment, had by gradual and reasonable stages come to these conclusions: that Major Spencer was an object to tempt a robber; that the country was full of robbers; that Macnab was one of them; that this was the very spot in which a deed of blood could be most easily committed, and most easily concealed; and, one important fact, that gave strength and coherence to the whole, that Major Spencer had not reached a well-known point of destination, while Macnab had.

"With these thoughts, thus closely linked together, the youth forgets the limits of his watch and his circuit. This fact, alone, proves how active his imagination had become. It leads him forward, brooding more and more upon the subject, until, in the very exhaustion of his body, he sinks down beneath a tree. He sinks down and falls asleep; and in his sleep, what before was plausible conjecture, becomes fact, and the creative properties of his imagination give form and vitality to all his fancies. These forms are bold, broad, and deeply coloured, in due proportion with the degree of force which they receive from probability. Here, he sees the image of his friend; but, you will remark—and this should almost conclusively satisfy any mind that all that he sees is the work of his imagination,—that, though Spencer tells him that he is murdered, and by Macnab, he does not tell him how, in what manner, or with what weapons. Though he sees him pale and ghostlike, he does not see, nor can he say, where his wounds are! He sees his pale features distinctly, and his garments are bloody. Now, had he seen the spectre in the true appearances of death, as he was subsequently found, he would not have been able to discern his features, which were battered, according to his own account, almost out of all shape of humanity, and covered with mud; while his clothes would have streamed with mud and water, rather than with blood."

"Ah!" exclaimed the old lady, my grandmother, "it's hard to make you believe anything that you don't see; you are like St.

Thomas in the Scriptures; but how do you propose to account for his knowing that the Scotchman was on board the Falmouth packet? Answer to that!"

"That is not a more difficult matter than any of the rest.—You forget that in the dialogue which took place between James and Major Spencer at the camp, the latter told him that he was about to take passage for Europe in the Falmouth packet, which then lay in Charleston harbour, and was about to sail. Macnab heard all that."

"True enough, and likely enough," returned the old lady; "but, though you show that it was Major Spencer's intention to go to Europe in the Falmouth packet, that will not show that it was also the intention of the murderer."

"Yet, what more probable, and how natural for James Grayling to imagine such a thing! In the first place, he knew that Macnab was a Briton; he felt convinced that he was a tory; and the inference was immediate, that such a person would scarcely have remained long in a country where such characters laboured under so much odium, disfranchisement, and constant danger from popular tumults. The fact that Macnab was compelled to disguise his true sentiments, and affect those of the people against whom he fought so vindictively, shows what was his sense of the danger which he incurred. Now, it is not unlikely that Macnab was quite as well aware that the Falmouth packet was in Charleston, and about to sail, as Major Spencer. No doubt he was pursuing the same journey, with the same object, and had he not murdered Spencer, they would, very likely, have been fellow-passengers together to Europe. But, whether he knew the fact before or not, he probably heard it stated by Spencer, while he seemed to be sleeping; and, even supposing that he did not then know, it was enough that he found this to be the fact on reaching the city. It was an after-thought to fly to Europe with his ill-gotten spoils; and whatever may have appeared a politic course to the criminal, would be a probable conjecture in the mind of him by whom he was suspected. The whole story is one of strong probabilities, which happened to be verified; and, if proving anything, proves only that which we know, that James Grayling was a man of remarkably sagacious judgment, and quick, daring imagination. This quality of imagination, by the way, when possessed very strongly in connection with shrewd common sense, and well-balanced general faculties, makes that particular kind of intellect which, because of its promptness and powers of creation and combination, we call genius. It is genius only which can make ghosts, and James Grayling was a genius. He never, my son, saw any other ghosts than those of his own making!"

I heard my father with great patience to the end, though he seemed very tedious. He had taken a great deal of pains to destroy one of my greatest sources of pleasure. I need not add that I continued to believe in the ghost, and, with my grandmother, to reject the philosophy. It was more easy to believe the one than to comprehend the other.

The Real Right Thing

Henry James

1

When, after the death of Ashton Doyne—but three months after—George Withermore was approached, as the phrase is, on the subject of a "volume," the communication came straight from his publishers, who had been, and indeed much more, Doyne's own; but he was not surprised to learn, on the occurrence of the interview they next suggested, that a certain pressure as to the early issue of a Life had been brought to bear upon them by their late client's widow. Doyne's relations with his wife had been, to Withermore's knowledge, a very special chapter—which would present itself, by the way, as a delicate one for the biographer; but a sense of what she had lost, and even of what she had lacked, had betrayed itself, on the poor woman's part, from the first days of her bereavement, sufficiently to prepare an observer at all initiated for some attitude of reparation, some espousal even exaggerated of the interests of a distinguished name. George Withermore was, as he felt, initiated; yet what he had not expected was to hear that she had mentioned him as the person in whose hands she would most promptly place the materials for a book.

These materials—diaries, letters, memoranda, notes, documents of many sorts—were her property, and wholly in her control, no conditions at all attaching to any portion of her heritage; so that she was free at present to do as she liked—free, in particular, to do nothing. What Doyne would have arranged had he had time to arrange could be but supposition and guess.

Death had taken him too soon and too suddenly, and there was all the pity that the only wishes he was known to have expressed were wishes that put it positively out of account. He had broken short off—that was the way of it; and the end was ragged and needed trimming. Withermore was conscious, abundantly, how close he had stood to him, but he was not less aware of his comparative obscurity. He was young, a journalist, a critic, a hand-to-mouth character, with little, as yet, as was vulgarly said, to show. His writings were few and small, his relations scant and vague. Doyne, on the other hand, had lived long enough—above all had had talent enough—to become great, and among his many friends gilded also with greatness were several to whom his wife would have struck those who knew her as much more likely to appeal.

The preference she had, at all events, uttered—and uttered in a roundabout, considerate way that left him a measure of freedom—made our young man feel that he must at least see her and that there would be in any case a good deal to talk about. He immediately wrote to her, she as promptly named an hour, and they had it out. But he came away with his particular idea immensely strengthened. She was a strange woman, and he had never thought her an agreeable one; only there was something that touched him now in her bustling, blundering impatience. She wanted the book to make up, and the individual whom, of her husband's set, she probably believed she might most manipulate was in every way to help it to make up. She had not taken Doyne seriously enough in life, but the biography should be a solid reply to every imputation on herself. She had scantly known how such books were constructed, but she had been looking and had learned something. It alarmed Withermore a little from the first to see that she would wish to go in for quantity. She talked of "volumes"—but he had his notion of that.

"My thought went straight to *you*, as his own would have done," she had said almost as soon as she rose before him there in her large array of mourning—with her big black eyes, her big black wig, her big black fan and gloves, her general gaunt, ugly, tragic, but striking and, as might have been thought from a certain point of view, "elegant" presence. "You're the one he liked

most; oh, *much!*"—and it had been quite enough to turn
Withermore's head. It little mattered that he could afterward
wonder if she had known Doyne enough, when it came to that,
to be sure. He would have said for himself indeed that her testimony on such a point would scarcely have counted. Still, there
was no smoke without fire; she knew at least what she meant,
and he was not a person she could have an interest in flattering.
They went up together, without delay, to the great man's vacant
study, which was at the back of the house and looked over the
large green garden—a beautiful and inspiring scene, to poor
Withermore's view—common to the expensive row.

"You can perfectly work here, you know," said Mrs. Doyne;
"you shall have the place quite to yourself—I'll give it all up to
you; so that in the evenings, in particular, don't you see? for
quiet and privacy, it will be perfection."

Perfection indeed, the young man felt as he looked about—
having explained that, as his actual occupation was an evening
paper and his earlier hours, for a long time yet, regularly taken
up, he would have to come always at night. The place was full
of their lost friend; everything in it had belonged to him; everything they touched had been part of his life. It was for the
moment too much for Withermore—too great an honour and
even too great a care; memories still recent came back to him,
and, while his heart beat faster and his eyes filled with tears,
the pressure of his loyalty seemed almost more than he could
carry. At the sight of his tears Mrs. Doyne's own rose to her
lids, and the two, for a minute, only looked at each other. He
half expected her to break out: "Oh, help me to feel as I know
you know I want to feel!" And after a little one of them said,
with the other's deep assent—it didn't matter which: "It's here
that we're *with* him." But it was definitely the young man who
put it, before they left the room, that it was there he was with
them.

The young man began to come as soon as he could arrange it,
and then it was, on the spot, in the charmed stillness, between
the lamp and the fire and with the curtains drawn, that a certain
intenser consciousness crept over him. He turned in out of the
black London November; he passed through the large, hushed

house and up the red-carpeted staircase where he only found in his path the whisk of a soundless, trained maid, or the reach, out of a doorway, of Mrs. Doyne's queenly weeds and approving tragic face; and then, by a mere touch of the well-made door that gave so sharp and pleasant a click, shut himself in for three or four warm hours with the spirit—as he had always distinctly declared it—of his master. He was not a little frightened when, even the first night, it came over him that he had really been most affected, in the whole matter, by the prospect, the privilege, and the luxury, of his sensation. He had not, he could now reflect, definitely considered the question of the book—as to which there was here, even already, much to consider: he had simply let his affection and admiration—to say nothing of his gratified pride—meet, to the full, the temptation Mrs. Doyne had offered them.

How did he know, without more thought, he might begin to ask himself, that the book was, on the whole, to be desired? What warrant had he ever received from Ashton Doyne himself for so direct and, as it were, so familiar an approach? Great was the art of biography, but there were lives and lives, there were subjects and subjects. He confusedly recalled, so far as that went, old words dropped by Doyne over contemporary compilations, suggestions of how he himself discriminated as to other heroes and other panoramas. He even remembered how his friend, at moments, would have seemed to show himself as holding that the "literary" career might—save in the case of a Johnson and a Scott, with a Boswell and a Lockhart to help—best content itself to be represented. The artist was what he *did*—he was nothing else. Yet how, on the other hand, was not *he*, George Withermore, poor devil, to have jumped at the chance of spending his winter in an intimacy so rich? It had been simply dazzling—that was the fact. It hadn't been the "terms," from the publishers—though these were, as they said at the office, all right; it had been Doyne himself, his company and contact and presence—it had been just what it was turning out, the possibility of an intercourse closer than that of life. Strange that death, of the two things, should have the fewer mysteries and secrets! The first night our young man was alone in the room it seemed to him that his master and he were really for the first time together.

2

Mrs. Doyne had for the most part let him expressively alone, but she had on two or three occasions looked in to see if his needs had been met, and he had had the opportunity of thanking her on the spot for the judgment and zeal with which she had smoothed his way. She had to some extent herself been looking things over and had been able already to muster several groups of letters; all the keys of drawers and cabinets she had, moreover, from the first placed in his hands, with helpful information as to the apparent whereabouts of different matters. She had put him, in a word, in the fullest possible possession, and whether or no her husband had trusted her, she at least, it was clear, trusted her husband's friend. There grew upon Withermore, nevertheless, the impression that, in spite of all these offices, she was not yet at peace, and that a certain unappeasable anxiety continued even to keep step with her confidence. Though he was full of consideration, she was at the same time perceptibly *there:* he felt her, through a supersubtle sixth sense that the whole connection had already brought into play, hover, in the still hours, at the top of landings and on the other side of the doors, gathered from the soundless brush of her skirts the hint of her watchings and waitings. One evening when, at his friend's table, he had lost himself in the depths of correspondence, he was made to start and turn by the suggestion that some one was behind him. Mrs. Doyne had come in without his hearing the door, and she gave a strained smile as he sprang to his feet. "I hope," she said, "I haven't frightened you."

"Just a little—I was so absorbed. It was as if, for the instant," the young man explained, "it had been himself."

The oddity of her face increased in her wonder. "Ashton?"

"He does seem so near," said Withermore.

"To you too?"

This naturally struck him. "He does then to you?"

She hesitated, not moving from the spot where she had first stood, but looking round the room as if to penetrate its duskier angles. She had a way of raising to the level of her nose the big black fan which she apparently never laid aside and with which she thus covered the lower half of her face, her rather hard eyes, above it, becoming the more ambiguous. "Sometimes."

"Here," Withermore went on, "it's as if he might at any moment come in. That's why I jumped just now. The time is so short since he really used to—it only *was* yesterday. I sit in his chair, I turn his books, I use his pens, I stir his fire, exactly as if, learning he would presently be back from a walk, I had come up here contentedly to wait. It's delightful—but it's strange."

Mrs. Doyne, still with her fan up, listened with interest. "Does it worry you?"

"No—I like it."

She hesitated again. "Do you ever feel as if he were—a—quite—a—personally in the room?"

"Well, as I said just now," her companion laughed, "on hearing you behind me I seemed to take it so. What do we want, after all," he asked, "but that he shall be with us?"

"Yes, as you said he would be—that first time." She stared in full assent. "He *is* with us."

She was rather portentous, but Withermore took it smiling. "Then we must keep him. We must do only what he would like."

"Oh, only that, of course—only. But if he *is* here—?" And her sombre eyes seemed to throw it out, in vague distress, over her fan.

"It shows that he's pleased and wants only to help? Yes, surely; it must show that."

She gave a light gasp and looked again round the room. "Well," she said as she took leave of him, "remember that I too want only to help." On which, when she had gone, he felt sufficiently—that she had come in simply to see he was all right.

He was all right more and more, it struck him after this, for as he began to get into his work he moved, as it appeared to him, but the closer to the idea of Doyne's personal presence. When once this fancy had begun to hang about him he welcomed it, persuaded it, encouraged it, quite cherished it, looking forward all day to feeling it renew itself in the evening, and waiting for the evening very much as one of a pair of lovers might wait for the hour of their appointment. The smallest accidents humoured and confirmed it, and by the end of three or four weeks he had come quite to regard it as the consecration of his enterprise. Wasn't it what settled the question of what Doyne would have thought of what they were doing? What they were doing was what he wanted done, and they could go on, from step to step, without scruple or doubt. Withermore rejoiced indeed at moments to feel this certitude: there were times of dipping deep into some of Doyne's secrets when it was particularly pleasant to be able to hold that Doyne desired him, as it were, to know them. He was learning many things that he had not suspected, drawing many curtains, forcing many doors, reading many riddles, going, in general, as they said, behind almost everything. It was at an occasional sharp turn of some of the duskier of these wanderings "behind" that he really, of a sudden, most felt himself, in the intimate, sensible way, face to face with his friend; so that he could scarcely have told, for the instant, if their meeting occurred in the narrow passage and tight squeeze of the past, or at the hour and in the place that actually held him. Was it '67, or was it but the other side of the table?

Happily, at any rate, even in the vulgarest light publicity could ever shed, there would be the great fact of the way Doyne was "coming out." He was coming out too beautifully—better yet than such a partisan as Withermore could have supposed. Yet, all the while, as well, how would this partisan have represented to any one else the special state of his own consciousness? It wasn't a thing to talk about—it was only a thing to feel. There were moments, for instance, when, as he bent over his papers, the light breath of his dead host was as distinctly in his hair as his own elbows were on the table before him. There were moments when, had he been able to look up, the other side of the table would have shown him this companion as vividly as the shaded lamplight showed him his page. That he couldn't at such a juncture look up was his own affair, for the situation was ruled—that was but natural—by deep delicacies and fine timidities, the dread of too sudden or too rude an advance. What was intensely in the air was that if Doyne *was* there it was not nearly so much for himself as for the young priest of his altar. He hovered and lingered, he came and went, he might almost have been, among the books and the papers, a hushed, discreet librarian, doing the particular things, rendering the quiet aid, liked by men of letters.

Withermore himself, meanwhile, came and went, changed his place, wandered on quests either definite or vague; and more than once, when, taking a book down from a shelf and finding in it marks of Doyne's pencil, he got drawn on and lost, he had heard documents on the table behind him gently shifted and stirred, had literally, on his return, found some letter he had mislaid pushed again into view, some wilderness cleared by the opening of an old journal at the very date he wanted. How should he have gone so, on occasion, to the special box or drawer, out of fifty receptacles, that would help him, had not his mystic assistant happened, in fine prevision, to tilt its lid, or to pull it half open, in just the manner that would catch his eye?— in spite, after all, of the fact of lapses and intervals in which, *could* one have really looked, one would have seen somebody standing before the fire a trifle detached and over-erect—somebody fixing one the least bit harder than in life.

3

That this auspicious relation had in fact existed, had continued, for two or three weeks, was sufficiently proved by the dawn of the distress with which our young man found himself aware that he had, for some reason, from a certain evening, begun to miss it. The sign of that was an abrupt, surprised sense—on the occasion of his mislaying a marvellous unpublished page which, hunt where he would, remained stupidly, irrecoverably lost—that his protected state was, after all, exposed to some confusion and even to some depression. If, for the joy of the business, Doyne and he had, from the start, been together, the situation had, within a few days of his first new suspicion of it, suffered the odd change of their ceasing to be so. That was what was the matter, he said to himself, from the moment an impression of mere mass and quantity struck him as taking, in his happy outlook at his material, the place of his pleasant assumption of a clear course and a lively pace. For five nights he struggled; then never at his table, wandering about the room, taking up his references only to lay them down, looking out of the window, poking the fire, thinking strange thoughts, and listening for signs and sounds not as he suspected or imagined, but as he vainly desired and invoked them, he made up his mind that he was, for the time at least, forsaken.

The extraordinary thing thus became that it made him not only sad not to feel Doyne's presence, but in a high degree uneasy. It was stranger, somehow, that he shouldn't be there than it had ever been that he *was*—so strange, indeed, at last that Withermore's nerves found themselves quite inconsequently affected. They had taken kindly enough to what was of an order impossible to explain, perversely reserving their sharpest state for the return to the normal, the supersession of the false. They were remarkably beyond control when, finally, one night, after resisting an hour or two, he simply edged out of the room. It had only now, for the first time, become impossible to him to remain there. Without design, but panting a little and positively as a man scared, he passed along his usual corridor and reached the top of the staircase. From this point he saw Mrs. Doyne looking up at him from the bottom quite as if she had known he would come; and the most singular thing of all was that, though he had been conscious of no notion to resort to her, had only been prompted to relieve himself by escape, the sight of her position made him recognize it as just, quickly feel it as a part of some monstrous oppression that was closing over both of them. It was wonderful how, in the mere modern London hall, between the Tottenham Court Road rugs and the electric light, it came up to him from the tall black lady, and went again from him down to her, that he knew what she meant by looking as if he would know. He descended straight, she turned into her own little lower room, and there, the next thing, with the door shut, they were, still in silence and with queer faces, confronted over confessions that had taken sudden life from these two or three movements. Withermore gasped as it came to him why he had lost his friend. "He has been with *you?*"

With this it was all out—out so far that neither had to explain and that, when "What do you suppose is the matter?" quickly passed between them, one appeared to have said it as much as the other. Withermore looked about at the small, bright room in which, night after night, she had been living her life as he had been living his own upstairs. It was pretty, cosy, rosy; but she had by turns felt in it what he had felt and heard in it what he had heard. Her effect there—fantastic black, plumed and extravagant, upon deep pink—was that of some "decadent" coloured print, some poster of the newest school. "You understood he had left me?" he asked.

She markedly wished to make it clear. "This evening—yes. I've made things out."

"You knew—before—that he was with me?"

She hesitated again. "I felt he wasn't with *me*. But on the stairs—"

"Yes?"

"Well—he passed, more than once. He was in the house. And at your door—"

"Well?" he went on as she once more faltered.

"If I stopped I could sometimes tell. And from your face," she added, "to-night, at any rate, I knew your state."

"And that was why you came out?"

"I thought you'd come to me."

He put out to her, on this, his hand, and they thus, for a minute, in silence, held each other clasped. There was no peculiar presence for either, now—nothing more peculiar than that of each for the other. But the place had suddenly become as if consecrated, and Withermore turned over it again his anxiety. "What *is* then the matter?"

"I only want to do the real right thing," she replied after a moment.

"And are we not doing it?"

"I wonder. Are *you* not? "

He wondered too. "To the best of my belief. But we must think."

"We must think," she echoed. And they did think—thought, with intensity, the rest of that evening together, and thought, independently—Withermore at least could answer for himself—during many days that followed. He intermitted for a little his visits and his work, trying, in meditation, to catch himself in the act of some mistake that might have accounted for their disturbance. Had he taken, on some important point—or looked as if he might take—some wrong line or wrong view? had he somewhere benightedly falsified or inadequately insisted? He went back at last with the idea of having guessed two or three questions he might have been on the way to muddle; after which he had, above stairs, another period of agitation, presently followed by another interview, below, with Mrs. Doyne, who was still troubled and flushed.

"He's there?"

"He's there."

"I knew it!" she returned in an odd gloom of triumph. Then as to make it clear: "He has not been again with *me*."

"Nor with me again to help," said Withermore.

She considered. "Not to help?"

"I can't make it out—I'm at sea. Do what I will, I feel I'm wrong."

She covered him a moment with her pompous pain. "How do you feel it?"

"Why, by things that happen. The strangest things. I can't describe them—and you wouldn't believe them."

"Oh yes, I would!" Mrs. Doyne murmured.

"Well, he intervenes." Withermore tried to explain. "However I turn, I find him."

She earnestly followed. "'Find' him?"

"I meet him. He seems to rise there before me."

Mrs. Doyne, staring, waited a little. "Do you mean you see him?"

"I feel as if at any moment I may. I'm baffled. I'm checked." Then he added: "I'm afraid."

"Of *him*?" asked Mrs. Doyne.

He thought. "Well—of what I'm doing."

"Then what, that's so awful, *are* you doing?"

"What you proposed to me. Going into his life."

She showed, in her gravity, now a new alarm. "And don't you *like* that?"

"Doesn't *he?* That's the question. We lay him bare. We serve him up. What is it called? We give him to the world."

Poor Mrs. Doyne, as if on a menace to her hard atonement, glared at this for an instant in deeper gloom. "And why shouldn't we?"

"Because we don't know. There are natures, there are lives, that shrink. He mayn't wish it," said Withermore. "We never asked him."

"How *could* we?"

He was silent a little. "Well, we ask him now. That's, after all, what our start has, so far, represented. We've put it to him."

"Then—if he has been with us—we've had his answer."

Withermore spoke now as if he knew what to believe. "He hasn't been 'with' us—he has been against us."

"Then why did you think—"

"What I *did* think, at first—that what he wishes to make us feel is his sympathy? Because, in my original simplicity, I was mistaken. I was—I don't know what to call it—so excited and charmed that I didn't understand. But I understand at last. He only wanted to communicate. He strains forward out of his darkness; he reaches toward us out of his mystery; he makes us dim signs out of his horror."

"'Horror'?" Mrs. Doyne gasped with her fan up to her mouth.

"At what we're doing." He could by this time piece it all together. "I see now that at first—"

"Well, what?"

"One had simply to feel he was there, and therefore not indifferent. And the beauty of that misled me. But he's there as a protest."

"Against *my* Life?" Mrs. Doyne wailed.

"Against *any* Life. He's there to *save* his Life. He's there to be let alone."

"So you give up?" she almost shrieked.

He could only meet her. "He's there as a warning."

For a moment, on this, they looked at each other deep. "You *are* afraid!" she at last brought out.

It affected him, but he insisted. "He's there as a curse!"

With that they parted, but only for two or three days; her last word to him continuing to sound so in his ears that, between his need really to satisfy her and another need presently to be noted, he felt that he might not yet take up his stake. He finally went back at his usual hour and found her in her usual place. "Yes, I *am* afraid," he announced as if he had turned that well over and knew now all it meant. "But I gather that you're not."

She faltered, reserving her word. "What is it you fear?"

"Well, that if I go on I *shall* see him."

"And then—?"

"Oh, then," said George Withermore, "I *should* give up!"

She weighed it with her lofty but earnest air. "I think, you know, we must have a clear sign."

"You wish me to try again?"

She hesitated. "You see what it means—for me—to give up."

"Ah, but *you* needn't," Withermore said.

She seemed to wonder, but in a moment she went on. "It would mean that he won't take from me—" But she dropped for despair.

"Well, what?"

"Anything," said poor Mrs. Doyne.

He faced her a moment more. "I've thought myself of the clear sign. I'll try again."

As he was leaving her, however, she remembered. "I'm only afraid that to-night there's nothing ready—no lamp and no fire."

"Never mind," he said from the foot of the stairs; "I'll find things."

To which she answered that the door of the room would probably, at any rate, be open; and retired again as if to wait for him. She had not long to wait; though, with her own door wide and her attention fixed, she may not have taken the time quite as it appeared to her visitor. She heard him, after an interval, on the stair, and he presently stood at her entrance, where, if he had not been precipitate, but rather, as to step and sound, backward and vague, he showed at least as livid and blank.

"I give up."

"Then you've seen him?"

"On the threshold—guarding it."

"Guarding it?" She glowed over her fan. "Distinct?"

"Immense. But dim. Dark. Dreadful," said poor George Withermore.

She continued to wonder. "You didn't go in?"

The young man turned away. "He forbids!"

"You say I needn't," she went on after a moment. "Well then, need I?"

"See him?" George Withermore asked.

She waited an instant. "Give up."

"You must decide." For himself he could at last but drop upon the sofa with his bent face in his hands. He was not quite to know afterwards how long he had sat so; it was enough that what he did next know was that he was alone among her favourite objects. Just as he gained his feet, however, with this sense and that of the door standing open to the hall, he found himself afresh confronted, in the light, the warmth, the rosy space, with her big black perfumed presence. He saw at a glance, as she offered him a huger, bleaker stare over the mask of her fan, that she had been above; and so it was that, for the last time, they faced together their strange question. "You've seen him?" Withermore asked.

He was to infer later on from the extraordinary way she closed her eyes, and, as if to steady herself, held them tight and long, in silence, that beside the unutterable vision of Ashton Doyne's wife his own might rank as an escape. He knew before she spoke that all was over. "I give up."

Lady Ferry

Sarah Orne Jewett

We have an instinctive fear of death; yet we have a horror of a life prolonged far beyond the average limit: it is sorrowful; it is pitiful; it has no attractions.

This world is only a schoolroom for the larger life of the next. Some leave it early, and some late: some linger long after they seem to have learned all its lessons. This world is no heaven: its pleasures do not last even through our little lifetimes.

There are many fables of endless life, which in all ages have caught the attention of men; we are familiar with the stories of the old patriarchs who lived their hundreds of years: but one thinks of them wearily, and without envy.

•

When I was a child, it was necessary that my father and mother should take a long sea-voyage. I never had been separated from them before; but at this time they thought it best to leave me behind, as I was not strong, and the life on board ship did not suit me. When I was told of this decision, I was very sorry, and at once thought I should be miserable without my mother; besides, I pitied myself exceedingly for losing the sights I had hoped to see in the country which they were to visit. I had an uncontrollable dislike to being sent to school, having in some way been frightened by a maid of my mother's, who had put many ideas and aversions into my head which I was many years in outgrowing. Having dreaded this possibility, it was a great relief to know that I was not to be sent to school at all, but to be put under the charge of two elderly cousins of my father,—a gentleman and his wife whom I had once seen, and liked dearly. I knew that their home was at a fine old-fashioned country-place, far from town, and close beside a river, and I was pleased with this prospect, and at once began to make charming plans for the new life.

I had lived always with grown people, and seldom had had any thing to do with children. I was very small for my age, and a strange mixture of childishness and maturity; and, having the appearance of being absorbed in my own affairs, no one ever noticed me much, or seemed to think it better that I should not listen to the conversation. In spite of considerable curiosity, I followed an instinct which directed me never to ask questions at these times: so I often heard stray sentences which puzzled me, and which really would have been made simple and common-place at once, if I had only asked their meaning. I was, for the most of the time, in a world of my own. I had a great deal of imagination, and was always telling myself stories; and my mind was adrift in these so much, that my real absent-mindedness was mistaken for childish unconcern. Yet I was a thoroughly simple, unaffected child. My dreams and thoughtfulness gave me a certain tact and perception unusual in a child; but my pleasures were as deep in simple things as heart could wish.

It happened that our cousin Matthew was to come to the city on business the week that the ship was to sail, and that I could stay with my father and mother to the very last day, and then go home with him. This was much pleasanter than leaving sooner under the care of an utter stranger, as was at first planned. My cousin Agnes wrote a kind letter about my coming, which seemed to give her much pleasure. She remembered me very well, and sent me a message which made me feel of consequence; and I was delighted with the plan of making her so long a visit.

One evening I was reading a story-book, and I heard my father say in an undertone, "How long has madam been at the ferry this last time? Eight or ten years, has she not? I suppose she is there yet?"—"Oh, yes!" said my mother, "or Agnes would have told us. She spoke of her in the last letter you had, while we were in Sweden."

"I should think she would be glad to have a home at last, after her years of wandering about. Not that I should be surprised now to hear that she had disappeared again. When I was staying there while I was young, we thought she had drowned herself, and even had the men search for her along the shore of the river; but after a time cousin Matthew heard of her alive and well in Salem; and I believe she appeared again this last time as suddenly as she went away."

"I suppose she will never die," said my mother gravely. "She must be terribly old," said my father. "When I saw her last, she had scarcely changed at all from the way she looked when I was a boy. She is even more quiet and gentle than she used to be. There is no danger that the child will have any fear of her; do you think so?"—"Oh, no! but I think I will tell her that madam is a very old woman, and that I hope she will be very kind, and try not to annoy her; and that she must not be frightened at her strange notions. I doubt if she knows what craziness is."—"She would be wise if she could define it," said my father with a smile. "Perhaps we had better say nothing about the old lady. It is probable that she stays altogether in her own room, and that the child will rarely see her. I never have realized until lately the horror of such a long life as hers, living on and on, with one's friends gone long ago: such an endless life in this world!"

Then there was a mysterious old person living at the ferry, and there was a question whether I would not be "afraid" of her. She "had not changed" since my father was a boy: "it was horrible to have one's life endless in this world!"

The days went quickly by. My mother, who was somewhat of an invalid, grew sad as the time drew near for saying good-by to me, and was more tender and kind than ever before, and more indulgent of every wish and fancy of mine. We had been together all my life, and now it was to be long months before she could possibly see my face again, and perhaps she was leaving me forever. Her time was all spent, I believe, in thoughts for me, and in making arrangements for my comfort. I did see my mother again; but the tears fill my eyes when I think how dear we became to each other before that first parting, and with what a lingering, loving touch, she herself packed my boxes, and made sure, over and over again, that I had whatever I should need; and I remember how close she used to hold me when I sat in her lap in the evening, saying that she was afraid I should have grown too large to be held when she came back again. We had more to say to each other than ever before, and I think, until then, that my mother never had suspected how much I observed of life and of older people in a certain way; that I was something more than a little child who went from one interest to another carelessly. I have known since that my mother's childhood was much like mine. She, however, was timid, while I had inherited from my father his fearlessness, and lack of suspicion; and these qualities, like a fresh wind, swept away any cobwebs of nervous anticipation and sensitiveness. Every one was kind to me, partly, I think, because I interfered with no one. I was glad of the kindness, and, with my unsuspected dreaming and my happy childishness, I had gone through life with almost perfect contentment, until this pain of my first real loneliness came into my heart.

It was a day's journey to cousin Matthew's house, mostly by rail; though, toward the end, we had to travel a considerable distance by stage, and at last were left on the river-bank opposite my new home, and I saw a boat waiting to take us across. It was just at sunset, and I remember wondering if my father and mother were out of sight of land, and if they were watching the sky; if my father would remember that only the evening before we had gone out for a walk together, and there had been a sunset so much like this. It somehow seemed long ago. Cousin Matthew was busy talking with the ferry-man; and indeed he had found acquaintances at almost every part of the journey, and had not been much with me, though he was kind and attentive in his courteous, old-fashioned way, treating me with the same ceremonious politeness which he had shown my mother. He pointed out the house to me: it was but a little way from the edge of the river. It was very large and irregular, with great white chimneys; and, while the river was all in shadow, the upper windows of two high gables were catching the last red glow of the sun. On the opposite side of a green from the house were the farm-house and buildings; and the green sloped down to the water, where there was a wharf and an ancient-looking storehouse. There were some old boats and long sticks of timber lying on the shore; and I saw a flock of white geese march solemnly up toward the barns. From the open green I could see that a road went up the hill beyond. The trees in the garden and orchard were the richest green; their round tops were clustered thick together; and there were some royal great elms near the house. The fiery red faded from the high windows as we came near the shore, and cousin Agnes was ready to meet me; and when she put her arms round me as kindly as my mother would have done, and kissed me twice in my father's fashion, I was sure that I loved her, and would be contented. Her hair was very gray; but she did not look, after all, so very old. Her face was a grave one, as if she had had many cares; yet they had all made her stronger, and there had been some sweetness, and something to be glad about, and to thank God for, in every sorrow. I had a feeling always that she was my sure defence and guard. I was safe and comfortable with her: it was the same feeling which one learns to have toward God more and more, as one grows older.

We went in through a wide hall, and up stairs, through a long passage, to my room, which was in a corner of one of the gables. Two windows looked on the garden and the river: another looked across to the other gable, and into the square, grassy court between. It was a rambling, great house, and seemed like some English houses I had seen. It would be great fun to go into all the rooms some day soon.

"How much you are like your father!" said cousin Agnes, stooping to kiss me again, with her hand on my shoulder. I had a sudden consciousness of my bravery in having behaved so well all day; then I remembered that my father and mother were at every instant being carried farther and farther away. I could almost hear the waves dash about the ship; and I could not help crying a little. "Poor little girl!" said cousin Agnes: "I am very sorry." And she sat down, and took me in her lap for a few minutes. She was tall, and held me so comfortably, and I soon was almost happy again; for she hoped I would not be lonely with her, and that I would not think she was a stranger, for she had

known and loved my father so well; and it would make cousin
Matthew so disappointed and uneasy if I were discontented;
and would I like some bread and milk with my supper, in the
same blue china bowl, with the dragon on it, which my father
used to have when he was a boy? These arguments were by no
means lost upon me, and I was ready to smile presently; and
then we went down to the dining-room, which had some
solemn-looking portraits on the walls, and heavy, stiff furniture;
and there was an old-fashioned woman standing ready to wait,
whom cousin Agnes called Deborah, and who smiled at me
graciously.

Cousin Matthew talked with his wife for a time about what
had happened to him and to her during his absence; and then
he said, "And how is madam to-day? you have not spoken of
her."—"She is not so well as usual," said cousin Agnes. "She has
had one of her sorrowful times since you went away. I have sat
with her for several hours to-day; but she has hardly spoken to
me." And then cousin Matthew looked at me, and cousin Agnes
hesitated for a minute. Deborah had left the room.

"We speak of a member of our family whom you have not
seen, although you may have heard your father speak of her. She
is called Lady Ferry by most people who know of her; but you
may say madam when you speak to her. She is very old, and her
mind wanders, so that she has many strange fancies; but you
must not be afraid, for she is very gentle and harmless. She is
not used to children; but I know you will not annoy her, and I
dare say you can give her much pleasure." This was all that was
said; but I wished to know more. It seemed to me that there was
a reserve about this person, and the old house itself was the very
place for a mystery. As I went through some of the other rooms
with cousin Agnes in the summer twilight, I half expected to
meet Lady Ferry in every shadowy corner; but I did not dare to
ask a question. My father's words came to me,—"Such an endless life," and "living on and on." And why had he and my
mother never spoken to me afterward of my seeing her? They
had talked about it again, perhaps, and did not mean to tell me,
after all.

I saw something of the house that night, the great kitchen,

with its huge fireplace, and other rooms up stairs and down; and cousin Agnes told me, that by daylight I should go everywhere, except to Madam's rooms: I must wait for an invitation there.

The house had been built a hundred and fifty years before, by Colonel Haverford, an Englishman, whom no one knew much about, except that he lived like a prince, and would never tell his history. He and his sons died; and after the Revolution the house was used for a tavern for many years,—the Ferry Tavern,—and the place was busy enough. Then there was a bridge built down the river, and the old ferry fell into disuse; and the owner of the house died, and his family also died, or went away; and then the old place, for a long time, was either vacant, or in the hands of different owners. It was going to ruin at length, when cousin Matthew bought it, and came there from the city to live years before. He was a strange man; indeed, I know now that all the possessors of the Ferry farm must have been strange men. One often hears of the influence of climate upon character; there is a strong influence of place; and the inanimate things which surround us indoors and out make us follow out in our lives their own silent characteristics. We unconsciously catch the tone of every house in which we live, and of every view of the outward, material world which grows familiar to us, and we are influenced by surroundings nearer and closer still than the climate or the country which we inhabit. At the old Haverford house it was mystery which one felt when one entered the door; and when one came away, after cordiality, and days of sunshine and pleasant hospitality, it was still with a sense of this mystery, and of something unseen and unexplained. Not that there was any thing covered and hidden necessarily; but it was the quiet undertone in the house which had grown to be so old, and had known the magnificent living of Colonel Haverford's time, and afterward the struggles of poor gentlemen and women, who had hardly warmed its walls with their pitiful fires, and shivering, hungry lives; then the long procession of travellers who had been sheltered there in its old tavern days; finally, my cousin Matthew and his wife, who had made it their home, when, with all their fortune, they felt empty-handed, and as if their lives were ended, because their only son had died. Here they had learned to be happy again in a quiet sort of way, and had become older and serener, loving this lovable place by the river, and keepers of its secret—whatever that might be.

I was wide awake that first evening: I was afraid of being sent to bed, and, to show cousin Agnes that I was not sleepy, I chattered far more than usual. It was warm, and the windows of the parlor where we sat looked upon the garden. The moon had risen, and it was light out of doors. I caught every now and then the faint smell of honeysuckle, and presently I asked if I might go into the garden a while; and cousin Agnes gave me leave, adding that I must soon go to bed, else I would be very tired next day. She noticed that I looked grave, and said that I must not dread being alone in the strange room, for it was so near her own. This was a great consolation; and after I had been told that the tide was in, and I must be careful not to go too near the river wall, I went out through the tall glass door, and slowly down the wide garden-walk, from which now and then narrower walks branched off at right angles. It was the pride of the place, this garden; and the box-borders especially were kept with great care. They had partly been trimmed that day; and the evening dampness brought out the faint, solemn odor of the leaves, which I never have noticed since without thinking of that night. The roses were in bloom, and the snowball-bushes were startlingly white, and there was a long border filled with lilies-of-the-valley. The other flowers of the season were all there and in blossom; yet I could see none well but the white ones, which looked like bits of snow and ice in the summer shadows,—ghostly flowers which one could see at night.

It was still in the garden, except once I heard a bird twitter sleepily, and once or twice a breeze came across the river, rustling the leaves a little. The small-paned windows glistened in the moonlight, and seemed like the eyes of the house watching me, the unknown new-comer.

For a while I wandered about, exploring the different paths, some of which were arched over by the tall lilacs, or by arbors where the grape-leaves did not seem fully grown. I wondered if my mother would miss me. It seemed impossible that I should have seen her only that morning; and suddenly I had a consciousness that she was thinking of me, and she seemed so close to me, that it would not be strange if she could hear what I said. And I called her twice softly; but the sound of my unanswered voice frightened me. I saw some round white flowers at my feet, looking up mockingly. The smell of the earth and the new grass seemed to smother me. I was afraid to be there all alone in the wide open air; and all the tall bushes that were so still around me took strange shapes, and seemed to be alive. I was so terribly far away from the mother whom I had called; the pleasure of my journey, and my coming to cousin Agnes, faded from my mind, and that indescribable feeling of hopelessness and dread, and of having made an irreparable mistake, came in its place. The thorns of a straying slender branch of a rose-bush caught my sleeve maliciously as I turned to hurry away, and then I caught sight of a person in the path just before me. It was such a relief to see some one, that I was not frightened when I saw that it must be Lady Ferry.

She was bent, but very tall and slender, and was walking slowly with a cane. Her head was covered with a great hood or wrapping of some kind, which she pushed back when she saw me. Some faint whitish figures on her dress looked like frost in the moonlight; and the dress itself was made of some strange stiff silk, which rustled softly like dry rushes and grasses in the autumn,—a rustling noise that carries a chill with it. She came close to me, a sorrowful little figure very dreary at heart, standing still as the flowers themselves; and for several minutes she did not speak, but watched me, until I began to be afraid of her. Then she held out her hand, which trembled as if it were trying to shake off its rings. "My dear," said she "I bid you welcome: I have known your father. I was told of your coming. Perhaps you will walk with me? I did not think to find you here alone." There was a fascinating sweetness in Madam's voice, and I at once turned to walk beside her, holding her hand fast, and keeping pace with her feeble steps. "Then you are not afraid of me?" asked the old lady, with a strange quiver in her voice. "It is a long time since I have seen a child."—"No," said I, "I am not afraid of you. I was frightened before I saw you, because I was all alone, and I wished I could see my father and mother"; and I hung my head so that my new friend could not see the tears in my eyes, for she watched me curiously. "All alone: that is like me," said she to herself. "All alone? a child is not all alone, but there is no one like me. I am something alone: there is nothing else of my fashion, a creature who lives forever!" and Lady Ferry sighed pitifully. Did she mean that she never was going to die like other people? But she was silent, and I did not dare to ask for any explanation as we walked back and forward. Her fingers kept moving round my wrist, smoothing it as if she liked to feel it, and to keep my hand in hers. It seemed to give her pleasure to have me with her, and I felt quite at my ease presently, and began to talk a little, assuring her that I did not mind having taken the journey of that day. I had taken some long journeys: I had been to China once, and it took a great while to get there; but London was the nicest place I had ever seen; had Lady Ferry ever been in London? And I was surprised to hear her say drearily that she had been in London; she had been every-where.

"Did you go to Westminster Abbey?" I asked, going on with the conversation childishly. "And did you see where Queen Elizabeth and Mary Queen of Scots are buried? Mamma had told me all about them."

"Buried, did you say? Are they dead too?" asked Madam eagerly. "Yes, indeed!" said I: "they have been dead a long time."—"Ah! I had forgotten," answered my strange compan-ion. "Do you know of any one else who has died beside them? I have not heard of any one's dying and going home for so long! Once every one died but me—except some young people; and I do not know them."—"Why, every one must die," said I won-deringly. "There is a funeral somewhere every day, I suppose."—"Every one but me," Madam repeated sadly,—"every one but me, and I am alone."

Just now cousin Agnes came to the door, and called me. "Go in now, child," said Lady Ferry. "You may come and sit with me tomorrow if you choose." And I said goodnight, while she turned, and went down the walk with feeble, lingering steps. She paced to and fro, as I often saw her afterwards, on the flagstones; and some bats flew that way like ragged bits of darkness, holding somehow a spark of life. I watched her for a minute: she was like a ghost, I thought, but not a fearful ghost,—poor Lady Ferry!

"Have you had a pleasant walk?" asked cousin Matthew politely. "To-morrow I will give you a border for your own, and some plants for it, if you like gardening." I joyfully answered that I should like it very much, and so I began to feel already the pleasure of being in a real home, after the wandering life to which I had become used. I went close to cousin Agnes's chair to tell her confidentially that I had been walking with Madam in the garden, and she was very good to me, and asked me to come to sit with her the next day; but she said very odd things.

"You must not mind what she says," said cousin Agnes; "and I would never dispute with her, or even seem surprised, if I were you. It hurts and annoys her, and she soon forgets her strange fancies. I think you seem a very sensible little girl, and I have told you about this poor friend of ours as if you were older. But you understand, do you not?" And then she kissed me good-night, and I went up stairs, contented with her assurance that she would come to me before I went to sleep.

I found a pleasant-faced young girl busy putting away some of my clothing. I had seen her just after supper, and had fancied her very much, partly because she was not so old as the rest of the servants. We were friendly at once, and I found her very talkative; so finally I asked the question which was uppermost in my mind,—Did she know any thing about Madam?

"Lady Ferry, folks call her," said Martha, much interested. "I never have seen her close to, only from the other side of the garden, where she walks at night. She never goes out by day. Deborah waits upon her. I haven't been here long; but I have always heard about Madam, bless you! Folks tell all kinds of strange stories. She's fearful old, and there's many believes she never will die; and where she came from nobody knows. I've heard that her folks used to live here; but nobody can remember them, and she used to wander about; and once before she was here,—a good while ago; but this last time she come was nine years ago; one stormy night she came across the ferry, and scared them to death, looking in at the window like a ghost. She said she used to live here in Colonel Haverford's time. They saw she wasn't right in her head—the ferry-men did. But she came up to the house, and they let her in, and she went straight to the rooms in the north gable, and she never has gone away; it was in an awful storm she come, I've heard, and she looked just the same as she does now. There! I can't tell half the stories I've heard, and Deborah she most took my head off," said Martha, "because, when I first came, I was asking about her; and she said it was a sin to gossip about a harmless old creature whose mind was broke, but I guess most everybody thinks there's something mysterious. There's my grandmother—her mind is failing her; but she never had such ways! And then those clothes that my lady in the gable wears: they're unearthly looking; and I heard a woman say once, that they come out of a chest in the big garret, and they belonged to a Mistress Haverford who was hung for a witch, but there's no knowing that there is any truth in it." And Martha would have gone on with her stories, if just then we had not heard cousin Agnes's step on the stairway, and I hurried into bed.

But my bright eyes and excited look betrayed me. Cousin Agnes said she had hoped I would be asleep. And Martha said perhaps it was her fault; but I seemed wakeful, and she had talked with me a bit, to keep my spirits up, coming to a new, strange place. The apology was accepted, but Martha evidently had orders before I next saw her; for I never could get her to discuss Lady Ferry again; and she carefully told me that she should not have told those foolish stories, which were not true: but I knew that she still had her thoughts and suspicions as well as I. Once, when I asked her if Lady Ferry were Madam's real name, she answered with a guilty flush, "That's what the folks hereabout called her, because they didn't know any other at first." And this to me was another mystery. It was strongly impressed upon my mind that I must ask no questions, and that Madam was not to be discussed. No one distinctly forbade this; but I felt that it would not do. In every other way I was sure that I was allowed perfect liberty, so I soon ceased to puzzle myself or other people, and accepted Madam's presence as being perfectly explainable and natural,—just as the rest of the household did,—except once in a while something would set me at work romancing and wondering; and I read some stories in one of the books in the library,—of Peter Rugg the missing man, whom one may always meet riding from Salem to Boston in every storm, and of the Flying Dutchman and the Wandering Jew, and some terrible German stories of doomed people, and curses that were fulfilled. These made a great impression upon me; still I was not afraid, for all such things were far outside the boundaries of my safe little world; and I played by myself along the shore of the river and in the garden; and I had my lessons with cousin Agnes, and drives with cousin Matthew who was nearly always silent, but very kind to me. The house itself was an unfailing entertainment, with its many rooms, most of which were never occupied, and its quaint, sober furnishings, some of which were as old as the house itself. It was like a story-book; and no one minded my going where I pleased.

I missed my father and mother; but the only time I was really unhappy was the first morning after my arrival. Cousin Agnes was ill with a severe headache; cousin Matthew had ridden away to attend to some business; and, being left to myself, I had a most decided reaction from my unnaturally bright feelings of the day before. I began to write a letter to my mother; but unluckily I knew how many weeks must pass before she saw it, and it was useless to try to go on. I was lonely and homesick. The rain fell heavily, and the garden looked forlorn, and so unlike the enchanting moonlighted place where I had been in the evening! The walks were like little canals; and the rose-bushes looked wet and chilly, like some gay young lady who had been caught in the rain in party-dress. It was low-tide in the middle of the day, and the river-flats looked dismal. I fed cousin Agnes's flock of tame sparrows which came around the windows, and afterward some robins. I found some books and some candy which had come in my trunk, but my heart was very sad; and just after noon I was overjoyed when one of the servants told me that cousin Agnes would like to have me come to her room.

She was even kinder to me than she had been the night before; but she looked very ill, and at first I felt awkward, and did not know what to say. "I am afraid you have been very dull, dearie," said she, reaching out her hand to me. "I am sorry, and my headache hardly lets me think at all yet. But we will have better times to-morrow—both of us. You must ask for what you want; and you may come and spend this evening with me, for I shall be getting well then. It does me good to see your kind little face. Suppose you make Madam a call this afternoon. She told me last night that she wished for you, and I was so glad. Deborah will show you the way."

Deborah talked to me softly, out of deference to her mistress's headache, as we went along the crooked passages. "Don't you mind what Madam says, leastways don't you dispute her. She's got a funeral going on to-day"; and the grave woman smiled grimly at me. "It's curious she's taken to you so; for she never will see any strange folks. Nobody speaks to her about new folks lately," she added warningly, as she tapped at the door, and Madam asked, "Is it the child?" And Deborah lifted the latch. When I was fairly inside, my interest in life came back redoubled, and I was no longer sad, but looked round eagerly. Madam spoke to me, with her sweet old voice, in her courtly, quiet way, and stood looking out of the window.

There were two tall chests of drawers in the room, with shining brass handles and ornaments; and at one side, near the door, was a heavy mahogany table, on which I saw a large leather-covered Bible, a decanter of wine and some glasses, beside some cakes in a queer old tray. And there was no other furniture but a great number of chairs which seemed to have been collected from different parts of the house.

With these the room was almost filled, except an open space in the centre, toward which they all faced. One window was darkened; but Madam had pushed back the shutter of the other, and stood looking down at the garden. I waited for her to speak again after the first salutation, and presently she said I might be seated; and I took the nearest chair, and again waited her pleasure. It was gloomy enough, with the silence and the twilight in the room; and the rain and wind out of doors sounded louder than they had in cousin Agnes's room; but soon Lady Ferry came toward me.

"So you did not forget the old woman," said she, with a strange emphasis on the word old, as if that were her title and her chief characteristic. "And were not you afraid? I am glad it seemed worth while; for to-morrow would have been too late. You may like to remember by and by that you came. And my funeral is to be to-morrow, at last. You see the room is in readiness. You will care to be here, I hope. I would have ordered you some gloves if I had known; but these are all too large for your little hands. You shall have a ring; I will leave a command for that"; and Madam seated herself near me in a curious, high-backed chair. She was dressed that day in a maroon brocade, figured with bunches of dim pink flowers; and some of these flowers looked to me like wicked little faces. It was a mocking, silly creature that I saw at the side of every prim bouquet, and I looked at the faded little imps, until they seemed as much alive as Lady Ferry herself.

Her head nodded continually, as if it were keeping time to an inaudible tune, as she sat there stiffly erect. Her skin was pale and withered; and her cheeks were wrinkled in fine lines, like the crossings of a cobweb. Her eyes might once have been blue; but they had become nearly colorless, and, looking at her, one might easily imagine that she was blind. She had a singularly sweet smile, and a musical voice, which, though sad, had no trace of whining. If it had not been for her smile and her voice, I think madam would have been a terror to me. I noticed to-day, for the first time, a curious fragrance, which seemed to come from her old brocades and silks. It was very sweet, but unlike any thing I had ever known before; and it was by reason of this that afterward I often knew, with a little flutter at my heart, she had been in some other rooms of the great house beside her own. This perfume seemed to linger for a little while wherever she had been, and yet it was so faint! I used to go into the darkened chambers often, or even stay for a while by myself in the unoccupied lower rooms, and I would find this fragrance, and wonder if she were one of the oldtime fairies, who could vanish at their own will and pleasure, and wonder, too, why she had come to the room. But I never met her at all.

That first visit to her and the strange fancy she had about the funeral I have always remembered distinctly.

"I am glad you came," Madam repeated: "I was finding the day long. I am all ready, you see. I shall place a little chair which is in the next room, beside your cousin's seat for you. Mrs. Agnes is ill, I hear; but I think she will come to-morrow. Have you heard any one say if many guests are expected?"—"No, Madam," I answered, "no one has told me;" and just then the thought flitted through my head that she had said the evening before that all her friends were gone. Perhaps she expected their ghosts: that would not be stranger than all the rest.

The open space where Lady Ferry had left room for her coffin began to be a horror to me, and I wished Deborah would come back, or that my hostess would open the shutters; and it was a great relief when she rose and went into the adjoining room, bidding me follow her, and there opened a drawer containing some old jewelry; there were also some queer Chinese carvings, yellow with age—just the things a child would enjoy. I looked at them delightedly. This was coming back to more familiar life; and I soon felt more at ease, and chattered to Lady Ferry of my own possessions, and some coveted treasures of my mother's, which were to be mine when I grew older.

Madam stood beside me patiently, and listened with a half smile to my whispered admiration. In the clearer light I could see her better, and she seemed older,—so old, so old! and my father's words came to me again. She had not changed since he was a boy; living on and on, and 'the horror of an endless life in this world!' And I remembered what Martha had said to me, and the consciousness of this mystery was a great weight upon me of a sudden. Why was she living so long? and what had happened to her? and how long could it be since she was a child?

There was something in her manner which made me behave, even in my pleasure, as if her imagined funeral were there in reality, and as if, in spite of my being amused and tearless, the solemn company of funeral guests already sat in the next room to us with bowed heads, and all the shadows in the world had assembled there materialized into the tangible form of crape. I opened and closed the boxes gently, and, when I had seen every thing, I looked up with a sigh to think that such a pleasure was ended, and asked if I might see them again some day. But the look in her face made me recollect myself, and my own grew crimson, for it seemed at that moment as real to me as to Lady Ferry herself that this was her last day of mortal life. She walked away, but presently came back, while I was wondering if I might not go, and opened the drawer again. It creaked, and the brass handles clacked in a startling way, and she took out a little case, and said I might keep it to remember her by. It held a little vinaigrette,—a tiny silver box with a gold one inside, in which I found a bit of fine sponge, dark brown with age, and still giving a faint, musty perfume and spiciness. The outside was rudely chased, and was worn as if it had been carried for years in somebody's pocket. It had a spring, the secret of which Lady Ferry showed me. I was delighted, and instinctively lifted my face to kiss her. She bent over me, and waited an instant for me to kiss her again. "Oh!" said she softly, "it is so long since a child has kissed me! I pray God not to leave you lingering like me, apart from all your kindred, and your life so long that you forget you ever were a child."—"I will kiss you every day," said I, and then again remembered that there were to be no more days according to her plan; but she did not seem to notice my mistake.

And after this I used to go to see Madam often. For a time there was always the same gloom and hushed way of speaking, and the funeral services were to be on the morrow; but at last one day I found Deborah sedately putting the room in order, and Lady Ferry apologized for its being in such confusion; the idea of the funeral had utterly vanished, and I hurried to tell cousin Agnes with great satisfaction. I think that both she and cousin Matthew had a dislike for my being too much with Madam. I was kept out of doors as much as possible because it was much better for my health; and through the long summer days I strayed about wherever I chose. The country life was new and delightful to me. At home, Lady Ferry's vagaries were carelessly spoken of, and often smiled at; but I gained the idea that they disguised the truth, and were afraid of my being frightened. She often talked about persons who had been dead a very long time,—familiar characters in history, and, though cousin

Agnes had said that she used to be fond of reading, it seemed to me that Madam might have known these men and women after all.

Once a middle-aged gentleman, an acquaintance of cousin Matthew's, came to pass a day and night at the ferry, and something happened then which seemed wonderful to me. It was early in the evening after tea, and we were in the parlor; from my seat by cousin Agnes I could look out into the garden, and presently, with the gathering darkness, came Lady Ferry, silent as a shadow herself, to walk to and fro on the flagstones. The windows were all open, and the guest had a clear, loud voice, and pleasant, hearty laugh; and, as he talked earnestly with cousin Matthew, I noticed that Lady Ferry stood still, as if she were listening. Then I was attracted by some story which was being told, and forgot her, but afterward turned with a start, feeling that there was some one watching; and, to my astonishment, Madam had come to the long window by which one went out to the garden. She stood there a moment, looking puzzled and wild; then she smiled, and, entering, walked in most stately fashion down the long room, toward the gentlemen, before whom she courtesied with great elegance, while the stranger stopped speaking, and looked at her with amazement, as he rose, and returned her greeting.

"My dear Captain Jack McAllister!" said she; "what a surprise! and are you not home soon from your voyage? This is indeed a pleasure." And Lady Ferry seated herself, motioning to him to take the chair beside her. She looked younger than I had ever seen her; a bright color came into her cheeks; and she talked so gayly, in such a different manner from her usual mournful gentleness. She must have been a beautiful woman; indeed she was that still.

"And did the good ship Starlight make a prosperous voyage? and had you many perils?—do you bring much news to us from the Spanish Main? We have missed you sadly at the assemblies; but there must be a dance in your honor. And your wife; is she not overjoyed at the sight of you? I think you have grown old and sedate since you went away. You do not look the gay sailor, or seem so light-hearted."

"I do not understand you, madam," said the stranger. "I am certainly John McAllister; but I am no captain, neither have I been at sea. Good God! is it my grandfather whom you confuse me with?" cried he. "He was Jack McAllister, and was lost at sea more than seventy years ago, while my own father was a baby. I am told that I am wonderfully like his portrait; but he was a younger man than I when he died. This is some masquerade."

Lady Ferry looked at him intently, but the light in her face was fast fading out. "Lost at sea—lost at sea, were you, Jack McAllister, seventy years ago? I know nothing of years; one of my days is like another, and they are gray days, they creep away and hide, and sometimes one comes back to mock me. I have lived a thousand years; do you know it? Lost at sea—captain of the ship Starlight? Whom did you say?—Jack McAllister, yes, I knew him well—pardon me; good-evening"; and my lady rose, and with her head nodding and drooping, with a sorrowful, hunted look in her eyes, went out again into the shadows. She had had a flash of youth, the candle had blazed up brilliantly; but it went out again as suddenly, with flickering and smoke.

"I was startled when I saw her beside me," said Mr. McAllister. "Pray, who is she? she is like no one I have ever seen. I have been told that I am like my grandfather in looks and in voice; but it is years since I have seen any one who knew him well. And did you hear her speak of dancing? It is like seeing one who has risen from the dead. How old can she be?"—"I do not know," said cousin Matthew, "one can only guess at her age."—"Would not she come back? I should like to question her," asked the other. But cousin Matthew answered that she always refused to see strangers, and it would be no use to urge her, she would not answer him.

"Who is she? Is she any kin of yours?" asked Mr. McAllister.

"Oh, no!" said my cousin Agnes: "she has had no relatives since I have known her, and I think she has no friends now but ourselves. She has been with us a long time, and once before this house was her home for a time,—many years since. I suppose no one will ever know the whole history of her life; I wish often that she had power to tell it. We are glad to give shelter, and the little care she will accept, to the poor soul, God only knows where she has strayed and what she has seen. It is an enormous burden,—so long a life, and such a weight of memories; but I think it is seldom now that she feels its heaviness.— Go out to her, Marcia my dear, and see if she seems troubled. She always has a welcome for the child," cousin Agnes added, as I unwillingly went away.

I found Lady Ferry in the garden; I stole my hand into hers, and, after a few minutes of silence, I was not surprised to hear her say that they had killed the Queen of France, poor Marie Antoinette! She had known her well in her childhood, before she was a queen at all—"a sad fate, a sad fate," said Lady Ferry. We went far down the gardens and by the river-wall, and when we were again near the house, and could hear Mr. McAllister's voice as cheery as ever, madam took no notice of it. I had hoped she would go into the parlor again, and I wished over and over that I could have waited to hear the secrets which I was sure must have been told after cousin Agnes had sent me away.

One day I thought I had made a wonderful discovery. I was fond of reading, and found many books which interested me in cousin Matthew's fine library; but I took great pleasure also in hunting through a collection of old volumes which had been cast aside, either by him, or by some former owner of the house, and which were piled in a corner of the great garret. They were mostly yellow with age, and had dark brown leather or shabby paper bindings; the pictures in some were very amusing to me. I used often to find one which I appropriated and carried down stairs; and on this day I came upon a dusty, odd-shaped little book, for which I at once felt an affection. I looked at it a little. It seemed to be a journal, there were some stories of the Indians, and next I saw some reminiscences of the town of Boston, where, among other things, the author was told the marvellous story of one Mistress Honor Warburton, who was cursed, and doomed to live in this world forever. This was startling. I at once thought of Madam, and was reading on further to know the rest of the story, when some one called me, and I foolishly did not dare to carry my book with me. I was afraid I should not find it if I left it in sight; I saw an opening near me at the edge of the floor by the eaves, and I carefully laid my treasure inside. But, alas! I was not to be sure of its safe hiding-place in a way that I fancied, for the book fell down between the boarding of the thick walls, and I heard it knock as it fell, and knew by the sound that it must be out of reach. I grieved over this loss for a long time; and I felt that it had been most unkind-ly taken out of my hand. I wished heartily that I could know the rest of the story; and I tried to summon courage to ask Madam, when we were by ourselves, if she had heard of Honor Warburton, but something held me back.

There were two other events just at this time which made this strange old friend of mine seem stranger than ever to me. I had a dream one night, which I took for a vision and a reality at the time. I thought I looked out of my window in the night, and there was bright moonlight, and I could see the other gable plainly; and I looked in at the windows of an unoccupied parlor which I never had seen open before, under Lady Ferry's own rooms. The shutters were pushed back, and there were candles burning; and I heard voices, and presently some tinkling music, like that of a harpsichord I had once heard in a very old house where I had been in England with my mother. I saw several couples go through with a slow, stately dance; and, when they stopped and seated themselves, I could hear their voices; but they spoke low, these midnight guests. I watched until the door was opened which led into the garden, and the company came out and stood for a few minutes on the little lawn, making their adieus, bowing low, and behaving with astonishing courtesy and elegance: finally the last good-nights were said, and they went away. Lady Ferry stood under the pointed porch, looking after them, and I could see her plainly in her brocade gown, with the impish flowers, a tall quaint cap, and a high lace frill at her throat, whiter than any lace I had ever seen, with a glitter on it; and there was a glitter on her face too. One of the other ladies was dressed in velvet, and I thought she looked beautiful: their eyes were all like sparks of fire. The gentlemen wore cloaks and ruffs, and high-peaked hats with wide brims, such as I had seen in some very old pictures which hung on the walls of the long west room. These were not pilgrims or Puritans, but gay gentle-men; and soon I heard the noise of their boats on the pebbles as they pushed off shore, and the splash of the oars in the water. Lady Ferry waved her hand, and went in at the door; and I found myself standing by the window in the chilly, cloudy night: the opposite gable, the garden, and the river, were indistinguishable in the darkness. I stole back to bed in an agony of fear; for it had been very real, that dream. I surely was at the window, for my hand had been on the sill when I waked; and I heard a church-bell ring two o'clock in a town far up the river. I never had heard this solemn bell before, and it seemed frightful; but I knew afterward that in the silence of a misty night the sound of it came down along the water.

In the morning I found that there had been a gale in the night; and cousin Matthew said at breakfast time that the tide had risen so that it had carried off two old boats that had been left on the shore to go to pieces. I sprang to the window, and sure enough they had disappeared. I had played in one of them the day before. Should I tell cousin Matthew what I had seen or dreamed? But I was too sure that he would only laugh at me; and yet I was none the less sure that those boats had carried passengers.

When I went out to the garden, I hurried to the porch, and saw, to my disappointment, that there were great spiders' webs in the corners of the door, and around the latch, and that it had not been opened since I was there before. But I saw something shining in the grass, and found it was a silver knee-buckle. It must have belonged to one of the ghostly guests, and my faith in them came back for a while, in spite of the cobwebs. By and by I bravely carried it up to Madam, and asked if it were hers. Sometimes she would not answer for a long time, when one rudely broke in upon her reveries, and she hesitated now, looking at me with singular earnestness. Deborah was in the room; and, when she saw the buckle, she quietly said that it had been on the window-ledge the day before, and must have slipped out. "I found it down by the door-step in the grass," said I humbly; and then I offered Lady Ferry some strawberries which I had picked for her on a broad green leaf, and came away again.

A day or two after this, while my dream was still fresh in my mind, I went with Martha to her own home, which was a mile

or two distant,—a comfortable farmhouse for those days, where
I was always made welcome. The servants were all very kind to
me: as I recall it now, they seemed to have a pity for me, because
I was the only child perhaps. I was very happy, that is certain,
and I enjoyed my childish amusements as heartily as if there
were no unfathomable mysteries or perplexities or sorrows anywhere in the world.

I was sitting by the fireplace at Martha's, and her grandmother, who was very old, and who was fast losing her wits, had been
talking to me about Madam. I do not remember what she said,
at least, it made little impression; but her grandson, a worthless
fellow, sauntered in, and began to tell a story of his own, hearing
of whom we spoke. "I was coming home late last night," said he,
"and, as I was in that dark place along by the Noroway pines, old
Lady Ferry she went by me, and I was near scared to death. She
looked fearful tall—towered way up above me. Her face was all
lit up with blue light, and her feet didn't touch the ground. She
wasn't taking steps, she wasn't walking, but movin' along like a
sail-boat before the wind. I dodged behind some little birches,
and I was scared she'd see me; but she went right out o' sight up
the road. She ain't mortal."

"Don't scare the child with such foolishness," said his aunt
disdainfully. "You'll be seein' worse things a-dancin' before your
eyes than that poor, harmless old creatur' if you don't quit the
ways you've been following lately. If that was last night, you
were too drunk to see any thing"; and the fellow muttered, and
went out, banging the door. But the story had been told, and I
was stiffened and chilled with fright; and all the way home I was
in terror, looking fearfully behind me again and again.

When I saw cousin Agnes, I felt safer, and since cousin
Matthew was not at home, and we were alone, I could not resist
telling her what I had heard. She listened to me kindly, and
seemed so confident that my story was idle nonsense, that my
fears were quieted. She talked to me until I no longer was a
believer in there being any unhappy mystery or harmfulness;
but I could not get over the fright, and I dreaded my lonely
room, and I was glad enough when cousin Agnes, with her
unfailing thoughtfulness, asked if I would like to have her come

to sleep with me, and even went up stairs with me at my own early bedtime, saying that she should find it dull to sit all alone in the parlor. So I went to sleep, thinking of what I had heard, it is true, but no longer unhappy, because her dear arm was over me, and I was perfectly safe. I waked up for a little while in the night, and it was light in the room, so that I could see her face, fearless and sweet and sad, and I wondered, in my blessed sense of security, if she were ever afraid of any thing, and why I myself had been afraid of Lady Ferry.

I will not tell other stories: they are much alike, all my memories of those weeks and months at the ferry, and I have no wish to be wearisome. The last time I saw Madam she was standing in the garden door at dusk. I was going away before daylight in the morning. It was in the autumn: some dry leaves flittered about on the stone at her feet, and she was watching them. I said good-by again, and she did not answer me; but I think she knew I was going away, and I am sure she was sorry, for we had been a great deal together; and, child as I was, I thought to how many friends she must have had to say farewell.

Although I wished to see my father and mother, I cried as if my heart would break because I had to leave the ferry. The time spent there had been the happiest time of all my life, I think. I was old enough to enjoy, but not to suffer much, and there was singularly little to trouble one. I did not know that my life was ever to be different. I have learned, since those childish days, that one must battle against storms if one would reach the calm which is to follow them. I have learned also that anxiety, sorrow, and regret fall to the lot of every one, and that there is always underlying our lives, this mysterious and frightful element of existence; an uncertainty at times, though we do trust every thing to God. Under the best-loved and most beautiful face we know, there is hidden a skull as ghastly as that from which we turn aside with a shudder in the anatomist's cabinet. We smile, and are gay enough; God pity us! We try to forget our heartaches and remorse. We even call our lives commonplace, and, bearing our own heaviest burdens silently, we try to keep the commandment, and to bear one another's also. There is One who knows: we look forward, as he means we shall, and there is always a hand ready to help us, though we reach out for it doubtfully in the dark.

•

For many years after this summer was over, I lived in a distant, foreign country; at last my father and I were to go back to America. Cousin Agnes and cousin Matthew, and my mother, were all long since dead, and I rarely thought of my childhood, for in an eventful and hurried life the present claims one almost wholly. We were travelling in Europe, and it happened that one day I was in a bookshop in Amsterdam, waiting for an acquaintance whom I was to meet, and who was behind time.

The shop was a quaint place, and I amused myself by looking over an armful of old English books which a boy had thrown down near me, raising a cloud of dust which was plain evidence of their antiquity. I came to one, almost the last, which had a strangely familiar look, and I found that it was a copy of the same book which I had lost in the wall at the ferry. I bought it for a few coppers with the greatest satisfaction, and began at once to read it. It had been published in England early in the eighteenth century, and was written by one Mr. Thomas Highward of Chester,—a journal of his travels among some of the English colonists of North America, containing much curious and desirable knowledge, with some useful advice to those persons having intentions of emigrating. I looked at the prosy pages here and there, and finally found again those reminiscences of the town of Boston and the story of Mistress Honor Warburton, who was cursed, and doomed to live in this world to the end of time. She had lately been in Boston, but had disappeared again; she endeavored to disguise herself, and would not stay long in one place if she feared that her story was known, and that she was recognized. One Mr. Fleming, a man of good standing and repute, and an officer of Her Majesty Queen Anne, had sworn to Mr. Thomas Highward that his father, a person of great age, had once seen Mistress Warburton in his youth; that she then bore another name, but had the same appearance. "Not wishing to seem unduly credulous," said Mr. Highward, "I disputed this tale; but there was some considerable evidence in its favour, and at least this woman was of vast age, and was spoken of with extreme wonder by the town's folk."

I could not help thinking of my old childish suspicions of Lady Ferry, though I smiled at the folly of them and of this story more than once. I tried to remember if I had heard of her death; but I was still a child when my cousin Agnes had died. Had poor Lady Ferry survived her? and what could have become of her? I asked my father, but he could remember nothing, if indeed he ever had heard of her death at all. He spoke of our cousins' kindness to this forlorn soul, and that, learning her desolation and her piteous history (and being the more pitiful because of her shattered mind), when she had last wandered to their door, they had cared for the old gentlewoman to the end of her days— "for I do not think she can be living yet," said my father, with a merry twinkle in his eyes: "she must have been nearly a hundred years old when you saw her. She belonged to a fine old family which had gone to wreck and ruin. She strayed about for years, and it was a godsend to her to have found such a home in her last days."

•

That same summer we reached America, and for the first time since I had left it I went to the ferry. The house was still imposing, the prestige of the Haverford grandeur still lingered; but it looked forlorn and uncared for. It seemed very familiar; but the months I had spent there were so long ago, that they seemed almost to belong to another life. I sat alone on the doorstep for a long time, where I used often to watch for Lady Ferry; and forgotten thoughts and dreams of my childhood came back to me. The river was the only thing that seemed as young as ever. I looked in at some of the windows where the shutters were pushed back, and I walked about the garden, where I could hardly trace the walks, all overgrown with thick, short grass, though there were a few ragged lines of box, and some old rose-bushes; and I saw the very last of the flowers,—a bright red poppy, which had bloomed under a lilac-tree among the weeds.

Out beyond the garden, on a slope by the river, I saw the family burying-ground, and it was with a comfortable warmth at my heart that I stood inside the familiar old enclosure. There was my Lady Ferry's grave; there could be no mistake about it, and she was dead. I smiled at my satisfaction and at my foolish child-ish thoughts, and thanked God that there could be no truth in them, and that death comes surely,—say, rather, that the better life comes surely,—though it comes late.

The sad-looking, yellow-topped cypress, which only seems to feel quite at home in country burying-grounds, had kindly spread itself like a coverlet over the grave, which already looked like a very old grave; and the headstone was leaning a little, not to be out of the fashion of the rest. I traced again the words of old Colonel Haverford's pompous epitaph, and idly read some others. I remembered the old days so vividly there; I thought of my cousin Agnes, and wished that I could see her; and at last, as the daylight faded, I came away. When I crossed the river, the ferry-man looked at me wonderingly, for my eyes were filled with tears. Although we were in shadow on the water, the last red glow of the sun blazed on the high gable-windows, just as it did the first time I crossed over,—only a child then, with my life before me.

I asked the ferry-man some questions, but he could tell me nothing; he was a new-comer to that part of the country. He was sorry that the boat was not in better order; but there were almost never any passengers. The great house was out of repair: people would not live there, for they said it was haunted. Oh, yes! he had heard of Lady Ferry. She had lived to be very ancient; but she was dead.

"Yes," said I, "she is dead."

My Platonic Sweetheart

Mark Twain

I met her first when I was seventeen and she fifteen. It was in a dream. No, I did not meet her; I overtook her. It was in a Missourian village which I had never been in before, and was not in at that time, except dreamwise; in the flesh I was on the Atlantic seaboard ten or twelve hundred miles away. The thing was sudden, and without preparation—after the custom of dreams. There I was, crossing a wooden bridge that had a wooden rail and was untidy with scattered wisps of hay, and there she was, five steps in front of me; half a second previously neither of us was there. This was the exit of the village, which lay immediately behind us. Its last house was the blacksmith-shop; and the peaceful clinking of the hammers—a sound which nearly always seems remote, and is always touched with a spirit of loneliness and a feeling of soft regret for something, you don't know what—was wafted to my ear over my shoulder; in front of us was the winding country road, with woods on one side, and on the other a rail fence, with blackberry vines and hazel bushes crowding its angles; on an upper rail a bluebird, and scurrying toward him along the same rail a fox-squirrel with his tail bent high like a shepherd's crook; beyond the fence a rich field of grain, and far away a farmer in shirt-sleeves and straw hat wading knee-deep through it; no other representative of life, and no noise at all; everywhere a Sabbath stillness.

I remember it all—and the girl, too, and just how she walked, and how she was dressed. In the first moment I was five steps behind her; in the next one I was at her side—without either

101

stepping or gliding; it merely happened; the transfer ignored space. I noticed that, but not with any surprise; it seemed a natural process.

I was at her side. I put my arm around her waist and drew her close to me, for I loved her; and although I did not know her, my behavior seemed to me quite natural and right, and I had no misgivings about it. She showed no surprise, no distress, no displeasure, but put an arm around my waist, and turned up her face to mine with a happy welcome in it, and when I bent down to kiss her she received the kiss as if she was expecting it, and as if it was quite natural for me to offer it and her to take it and have pleasure in it. The affection which I felt for her and which she manifestly felt for me was a quite simple fact; but the quality of it was another matter. It was not the affection of brother and sister—it was closer than that, more clinging, more endearing, more reverent; and it was not the love of sweethearts, for there was no fire in it. It was somewhere between the two, and was finer than either, and more exquisite, more profoundly contenting. We often experience this strange and gracious thing in our dream-loves; and we remember it as a feature of our childhood-loves, too.

We strolled along, across the bridge and down the road, chatting like the oldest friends. She called me George, and that seemed natural and right, though it was not my name; and I called her Alice, and she did not correct me, though without doubt it was not her name. Everything that happened seemed just natural and to be expected. Once I said, "What a dear little hand it is!" and without any words she laid it gratefully in mine for me to examine it. I did it, remarking upon its littleness, its delicate beauty, and its satin skin, then kissed it; she put it up to her lips without saying anything and kissed it in the same place.

Around a curve of the road, at the end of half a mile, we came to a log house, and entered it and found the table set and everything on it steaming hot—a roast turkey, corn in the ear, butterbeans, and the rest of the usual things—and a cat curled up asleep in a splint-bottomed chair by the fireplace; but no people; just emptiness and silence. She said she would look in the next room if I would wait for her. So I sat down, and she passed through a door, which closed behind her with a click of the latch. I waited and waited. Then I got up and followed, for I could not any longer bear to have her out of my sight. I passed through the door, and found myself in a strange sort of cemetery, a city of innumerable tombs and monuments stretching far and wide on every hand, and flushed with pink and gold lights flung from the sinking sun. I turned around, and the log house was gone. I ran here and there and yonder down the lanes between the rows of tombs, calling Alice; and presently the night closed down, and I could not find my way. Then I woke, in deep distress over my loss, and was in my bed in Philadelphia. And I was not seventeen, now, but nineteen.

Ten years afterward, in another dream, I found her. I was seventeen again, and she was still fifteen. I was in a grassy place in the twilight deeps of a magnolia forest some miles above Natchez, Mississippi; the trees were snowed over with great blossoms, and the air was loaded with their rich and strenuous fragrance; the ground was high, and through a rift in the wood a burnished patch of the river was visible in the distance. I was sitting on the grass, absorbed in thinking, when an arm was laid around my neck, and there was Alice sitting by my side and looking into my face. A deep and satisfied happiness and an unwordable gratitude rose in me, but with it there was no feeling of surprise; and there was no sense of a time-lapse; the ten years amounted to hardly even a yesterday; indeed, to hardly even a noticeable fraction of it. We dropped in the tranquilest way into affectionate caressings and pettings, and chatted along without a reference to the separation; which was natural, for I think we did not know there had been any that one might measure with either clock or almanac. She called me Jack and I called her Helen, and those seemed the right and proper names, and perhaps neither of us suspected that we had ever borne others; or, if we did suspect it, it was probably not a matter of consequence.

She had been beautiful ten years before; she was just as beautiful still; girlishly young and sweet and innocent, and she was still that now. She had had blue eyes, a hair of flossy gold before; she had black hair now, and dark-brown eyes. I noted these differences, but they did not suggest change; to me she was the same girl she was before, absolutely. It never occurred to me to ask what became of the log house; I doubt if I even thought of it. We were living in a simple and natural and beautiful world where everything that happened was natural and right, and was not perplexed with the unexpected or with any forms of surprise, and so there was no occasion for explanations and no interest attaching to such things.

We had a dear and pleasant time together, and were like a couple of ignorant and contented children. Helen had a summer hat on. She took it off presently and said, "It was in the way; now you can kiss me better." It seemed to me merely a bit of courteous and considerate wisdom, nothing more; and a natural thing for her to think of and do. We went wandering through the woods, and came to a limpid and shallow stream a matter of three yards wide. She said:

"I must not get my feet wet, dear; carry me over."

I took her in my arms and gave her my hat to hold. This was to keep my own feet from getting wet. I did not know why this should have that effect; I merely knew it; and she knew it, too. I crossed the stream, and said I would go on carrying her, because it was so pleasant; and she said it was pleasant to her, too, and wished we had thought of it sooner. It seemed to me a pity that we should have walked so far, both of us on foot, when we could have been having this higher enjoyment; and I spoke of it regretfully, as a something lost which could never be got back. She was troubled about it, too, and said there must be some way to get it back; and she would think. After musing deeply a little while she looked up radiant and proud, and said she had found it.

"Carry me back and start over again."

I can see, now, that that was no solution, but at the time it seemed luminous with intelligence, and I believed that there was not another little head in the world that could have worked out that difficult problem with such swiftness and success. I told her that, and it pleased her; and she said she was glad it all hap-

pened, so that I could see how capable she was. After thinking
a moment she added that it was "quite atreous." The words
seemed to mean something, I do not know why: in fact, it
seemed to cover the whole ground and leave nothing more to
say; I admired the nice aptness and the flashing felicity of the
phrase, and was filled with respect for the marvelous mind that
had been able to engender it. I think less of it now. It is a noticeable fact that the intellectual coinage of Dreamland often passes
for more there than it would fetch here. Many a time in after
years my dream-sweetheart threw off golden sayings which
crumbled to ashes under my pencil when I was setting them
down in my note-book after breakfast.

I carried her back and started over again; and all the long
afternoon I bore her in my arms, miles upon miles, and it never
occurred to either of us that there was anything remarkable in a
youth like me being able to carry that sweet bundle around half
a day without some sense of fatigue or need of rest. There are
many dream-worlds, but none is so rightly and reasonably and
pleasantly arranged as that one.

After dark we reached a great plantation-house, and it was
her home. I carried her in, and the family knew me and I knew
them, although we had not met before; and the mother asked
me with ill-disguised anxiety how much twelve times fourteen
was, and I said a hundred and thirty-five, and she put it down on
a piece of paper, saying it was her habit in the process of per-
fecting her education not to trust important particulars to her
memory; and her husband was offering me a chair, but noticed
that Helen was asleep, so he said it would be best not to disturb
her; and he backed me softly against a wardrobe and said I could
stand more easily now; then a negro came in, bowing humbly,
with his slouch-hat in his hand, and asked me if I would have my
measure taken. The question did not surprise me, but it confused me and worried me, and I said I should like to have advice
about it. He started toward the door to call advisers; then he and
the family and the lights began to grow dim, and in a few
moments the place was pitch dark; but straightway there came
a flood of moonlight and a gust of cold wind, and I found myself
crossing a frozen lake, and my arms were empty. The wave of

grief that swept through me woke me up, and I was sitting at my desk in the newspaper office in San Francisco, and I noticed by the clock that I had been asleep less than two minutes. And what was of more consequence, I was twenty-nine years old.

That was 1864. The next year and the year after I had momentary glimpses of my dream-sweetheart, but nothing more. These are set down in my note-books under their proper dates, but with no talks nor other particulars added; which is sufficient evidence to me that there were none to add. In both of these instances there was the sudden meeting and recognition, the eager approach, then the instant disappearance, leaving the world empty and of no worth. I remember the two images quite well; in fact, I remember all the images of that spirit, and can bring them before me without help of my note-book. The habit of writing down my dreams of all sorts while they were fresh in my mind, and then studying them and rehearsing them and trying to find out what the source of dreams is, and which of the two or three separate persons inhabiting us is their architect, has given me a good dream-memory— a thing which is not usual with people, for few drill the dream-memory, and no memory can be kept strong without that.

I spent a few months in the Hawaiian Islands in 1866, and in October of that year I delivered my maiden lecture; it was in San Francisco. In the following January I arrived in New York, and had just completed my thirty-first year. In that year I saw my platonic dream-sweetheart again. In this dream I was again standing on the stage of the Opera House in San Francisco, ready to lecture, and with the audience vividly individualized before me in the strong light. I began, spoke a few words, and stopped, cold with fright; for I discovered that I had no subject, no text, nothing to talk about. I choked for a while, then got out a few words, a lame, poor attempt at humor. The house made no response. There was a miserable pause, then another attempt, and another failure. There were a few scornful laughs; otherwise the house was silent, unsmilingly austere, deeply offended. I was consuming with shame. In my distress I tried to work upon its pity. I began to make servile apologies, mixed with

gross and ill-timed flatteries, and to beg and plead for forgive-
ness; this was too much, and the people broke into insulting
cries, whistlings, hootings, and cat-calls, and in the midst of this
they rose and began to struggle in a confused mass toward the
door. I stood dazed and helpless, looking out over this spectacle,
and thinking how everybody would be talking about it next day,
and I could not show myself in the streets. When the house was
become wholly empty and still, I sat down on the only chair that
was on the stage and bent my head down on the reading-desk to
shut out the look of that place. Soon that familiar dream-voice
spoke my name, and swept all my troubles away:

"Robert!"

I answered:

"Agnes!"

The next moment we two were lounging up the blossomy
gorge called the Iao Valley, in the Hawaiian Islands. I recognized, without any explanations, that Robert was not my name,
but only a pet name, a common noun, and meant "dear"; and
both of us knew that Agnes was not a name, but only a pet name,
a common noun, whose spirit was affectionate, but not convey-
able with exactness in any but the dream-language. It was about
the equivalent of "dear," but the dream-vocabulary shaves
meanings finer and closer than do the world's day-time dictionaries. We did not know why those words should have those
meanings; we had used words which had no existence in any
known language, and had expected them to be understood, and
they were understood. In my note-books there are several letters from this dream-sweetheart, in some unknown tongue—
presumably dream-tongue—with translations added. I should
like to be master of that tongue, then I could talk in shorthand.
Here is one of those letters—the whole of it:

"Rax oha tal."

Translation: "When you receive this it will remind you that I
long to see your face and touch your hand, for the comfort of it
and the peace."

It is swifter than waking thought; for thought is not thought
at all, but only a vague and formless fog until it is articulated into
words.

We wandered far up the fairy gorge, gathering the beautiful flowers of the ginger-plant and talking affectionate things, and tying and retying each other's ribbons and cravats, which didn't need it; and finally sat down in the shade of a tree and climbed the vine-hung precipices with our eyes, up and up and up toward the sky to where the drifting scarfs of white mist clove them across and left the green summits floating pale and remote, like spectral islands wandering in the deeps of space; and then we descended to earth and talked again.

"How still it is—and soft, and balmy, and reposeful! I could never tire of it. You like it, don't you, Robert?"

"Yes, and I like the whole region—all the islands. Maui. It is a darling island. I have been here before. Have you?"

"Once, but it wasn't an island then."

"What was it?"

"It was a sufa."

I understood. It was the dream-word for "part of a continent."

"What were the people like?"

"They hadn't come yet. There weren't any."

"Do you know, Agnes—that is Haleakala, the dead volcano, over there across the valley; was it here in your friend's time?"

"Yes, but it was burning."

"Do you travel much?"

"I think so. Not here much, but in the stars a good deal."

"Is it pretty there?"

She used a couple of dream-words for "You will go with me some time and you will see." Non-committal, as one perceives now, but I did not notice it then.

A man-of-war-bird lit on her shoulder; I put out my hand and caught it. Its feathers began to fall out, and it turned into a kitten; then the kitten's body began to contract itself to a ball and put out hairy, long legs, and soon it was a tarantula; I was going to keep it, but it turned into a star-fish, and I threw it away. Agnes said it was not worth while to try to keep things; there was no stability about them. I suggested rocks; but she said a rock was like the rest; it wouldn't stay. She picked up a stone, and it turned into a bat and flew away. These curious matters interested me, but that was all; they did not stir my wonder.

While we were sitting there in the Iao gorge talking, a Kanaka came along who was wrinkled and bent and white-headed, and he stopped and talked to us in the native tongue, and we understood him without trouble and answered him in his own speech. He said he was a hundred and thirty years old, and he remembered Captain Cook well, and was present when he was murdered; saw it with his own eyes, and also helped. Then he showed us his gun, which was of strange make, and he said it was his own invention and was to shoot arrows with, though one loaded it with powder and it had a percussion lock. He said it would carry a hundred miles. It seemed a reasonable statement; I had no fault to find with it, and it did not in any way surprise me. He loaded it and fired an arrow aloft, and it darted into the sky and vanished. Then he went his way, saying that the arrow would fall near us in half an hour, and would go many yards into the earth, not minding the rocks.

I took the time, and we waited, reclining upon the mossy slant at the base of a tree, and gazing into the sky. By and by there was a hissing sound, followed by a dull impact, and Agnes uttered a groan. She said, in a series of fainting gasps:

"Take me to your arms—it passed through me—hold me to your heart—I am afraid to die—closer—closer. It is growing dark—I cannot see you. Don't leave me—where are you? You are not gone? You will not leave me? I would not leave you."

Then her spirit passed; she was clay in my arms.

The scene changed in an instant, and I was awake and crossing Bond Street in New York with a friend, and it was snowing hard. We had been talking, and there had been no observable gaps in the conversation. I doubt if I had made any more than two steps while I was asleep. I am satisfied that even the most elaborate and incident-crowded dream is seldom more than a few seconds in length. It would not cost me very much of a strain to believe in Mohammed's seventy-year dream, which began when he knocked his glass over, and ended in time for him to catch it before the water was spilled.

Within a quarter of an hour I was in my quarters, undressed, ready for bed, and was jotting down my dream in my note-

book. A striking thing happened now. I finished my notes, and
was just going to turn out the gas when I was caught with a
most strenuous gape, for it was very late and I was very
drowsy. I fell asleep and dreamed again. What now follows
occurred while I was asleep; and when I woke again the gape
had completed itself, but not long before, I think, for I was
still on my feet. I was in Athens—a city which I had not then
seen, but I recognized the Parthenon from the pictures,
although it had a fresh look and was in perfect repair. I passed
by it and climbed a grassy hill toward a palatial sort of mansion
which was built of red terra-cotta and had a spacious portico,
whose roof was supported by a rank of fluted columns with
Corinthian capitals. It was noonday, but I met no one. I passed
into the house and entered the first room. It was very large
and light, its walls were of polished and richly tinted and
veined onyx, and its floor was a pictured pattern in soft colors
laid in tiles. I noted the details of the furniture and the ornaments—a thing which I should not have been likely to do
when awake—and they took sharp hold and remained in my
memory; they are not really dim yet, and this was more than
thirty years ago.

There was a person present—Agnes. I was not surprised to
see her, but only glad. She was in the simple Greek costume,
and her hair and eyes were different as to color from those she
had had when she died in the Hawaiian Islands half an hour
before, but to me she was exactly her own beautiful little self as
I had always known her, and she was still fifteen, and I was seventeen once more. She was sitting on an ivory settee, crocheting
something or other, and had her crewels in a shallow willow
work-basket in her lap. I sat down by her and we began to chat
in the usual way. I remembered her death, but the pain and the
grief and the bitterness which had been so sharp and so desolat-
ing to me at the moment that it happened had wholly passed
from me now, and had left not a scar. I was grateful to have her
back, but there was no realizable sense that she had ever been
gone, and so it did not occur to me to speak about it, and she
made no reference to it herself. It may be that she had often
died before, and knew that there was nothing lasting about it,

and consequently nothing important enough in it to make conversation out of.

When I think of that house and its belongings, I recognize what a master in taste and drawing and color and arrangement is the dream-artist who resides in us. In my waking hours, when the inferior artist in me is in command, I cannot draw even the simplest picture with a pencil, nor do anything with a brush and colors; I cannot bring before my mind's eye the detailed image of any building known to me except my own house at home; of St. Paul's, St. Peter's, the Eiffel Tower, the Taj, the Capitol at Washington, I can reproduce only portions, partial glimpses; the same with Niagara Falls, the Matterhorn, and other familiar things in nature; I cannot bring before my mind's eye the face or figure of any human being known to me; I have seen my family at breakfast within the past two hours; I cannot bring their images before me, I do not know how they look; before me, as I write, I see a little grove of young trees in the garden; high above them projects the slender lance of a young pine, beyond it is a glimpse of the upper half of a dull-white chimney covered by an A-shaped little roof shingled with brown-red tiles, and half a mile away is a hill-top densely wooded, and the red is cloven by a curved, wide vacancy, which is smooth and grass-clad; I cannot shut my eyes and reproduce that picture as a whole at all, nor any single detail of it except the grassy curve, and that but vaguely and fleetingly.

But my dream-artist can draw anything, and do it perfectly; he can paint with all the colors and all the shades, and do it with delicacy and truth; he can place before me vivid images of palaces, cities, hamlets, hovels, mountains, valleys, lakes, skies, glowing in sunlight or moonlight, or veiled in driving gusts of snow or rain, and he can set before me people who are intensely alive, and who feel, and express their feelings in their faces, and who also talk and laugh, sing and swear. And when I wake I can shut my eyes and bring back those people, and the scenery and the buildings; and not only in general view, but often in nice detail. While Agnes and I sat talking in that grand Athens house, several stately Greeks entered from another part of it, disputing warmly about something or other, and passed us by with courteous recognition; and among them was Socrates. I recognized him by his nose. A moment later the house and Agnes and Athens vanished away, and I was in my quarters in New York again and reaching for my note-book.

In our dreams—I know it!—we do make the journeys we seem to make; we do see the things we seem to see; the people, the horses, the cats, the dogs, the birds, the whales, are real, not chimeras; they are living spirits, not shadows; and they are immortal and indestructible. They go whither they will; they visit all resorts, all points of interest, even the twinkling suns that wander in the wastes of space. That is where those strange mountains are which slide from under our feet while we walk, and where those vast caverns are whose bewildering avenues close behind us and in front when we are lost, and shut us in. We know this because there are no such things here, and they must be there, because there is no other place.

This tale is long enough, and I will close it now. In the forty-four years that I have known my Dreamland sweetheart, I have seen her once in two years on an average. Mainly these were glimpses, but she was always immediately recognizable, not-withstanding she was so given to repairing herself and getting up doubtful improvements in her hair and eyes. She was always fifteen, and looked it and acted it; and I was always seventeen, and never felt a day older. To me she is a real person, not a fiction, and her sweet and innocent society has been one of the prettiest and pleasantest experiences of my life. I know that to you her talk will not seem of the first intellectual order; but you should hear her in Dreamland—then you would see!

I saw her a week ago, just for a moment. Fifteen, as usual, and I seventeen, instead of going on sixty-three, as I was when I went to sleep. We were in India, and Bombay was in sight; also Windsor Castle, its towers and battlements veiled in a delicate haze, and from it the Thames flowed, curving and winding between its swarded banks, to our feet. I said:

"There is no question about it, England is the most beautiful of all the countries."

Her face lighted with approval, and she said, with that sweet and earnest irrelevance of hers:

"It is, because it is so marginal."

Then she disappeared. It was just as well; she could probably have added nothing to that rounded and perfect statement without damaging its symmetry.

This glimpse of her carries me back to Maui, and that time when I saw her gasp out her young life. That was a terrible thing to me at the time. It was preternaturally vivid; and the pain and the grief and the misery of it to me transcended many sufferings that I have known in waking life. For everything in a dream is more deep and strong and sharp and real than is ever its pale imitation in the unreal life which is ours when we go about awake and clothed with our artificial selves in this vague and dull-tinted artificial world. When we die we shall slough off this cheap intellect, perhaps, and go abroad into Dreamland clothed in our real selves, and aggrandized and enriched by the command over the mysterious mental magician who is here not our slave, but only our guest.

The Philosophy of Relative Existences

Frank R. Stockton

In a certain summer, not long gone, my friend Bentley and I
found ourselves in a little hamlet which overlooked a placid
valley, through which a river gently moved, winding its way
through green stretches until it turned the end of a line of low
hills and was lost to view. Beyond this river, far away, but visible
from the door of the cottage where we dwelt, there lay a city.
Through the mists which floated over the valley we could see
the outlines of steeples and tall roofs; and buildings of a character which indicated thrift and business stretched themselves
down to the opposite edge of the river. The more distant parts
of the city, evidently a small one, lost themselves in the hazy
summer atmosphere.

Bentley was young, fair-haired, and a poet; I was a philoso-
pher, or trying to be one. We were good friends, and had come
down into this peaceful region to work together. Although we
had fled from the bustle and distractions of the town, the
appearance in this rural region of a city, which, so far as we
could observe, exerted no influence on the quiet character of
the valley in which it lay, aroused our interest. No craft plied up
and down the river; there were no bridges from shore to shore;
there were none of those scattered and half-squalid habitations
which generally are found on the outskirts of a city; there came
to us no distant sound of bells; and not the smallest wreath of
smoke rose from any of the buildings.

In answer to our inquiries our landlord told us that the city
over the river had been built by one man, who was a visionary,

114

and who had a great deal more money than common sense. "It is not as big a town as you would think, sirs," he said, "because the general mistiness of things in this valley makes them look larger than they are. Those hills, for instance, when you get to them are not as high as they look to be from here. But the town is big enough, and a good deal too big; for it ruined its builder and owner, who when he came to die had not money enough left to put up a decent tombstone at the head of his grave. He had a queer idea that he would like to have his town all finished before anybody lived in it, and so he kept on working and spending money year after year and year after year until the city was done and he had not a cent left. During all the time that the place was building hundreds of people came to him to buy houses or to hire them, but he would not listen to anything of the kind. No one must live in his town until it was all done. Even his workmen were obliged to go away at night to lodge. It is a town, sirs, I am told, in which nobody has slept for even a night. There are streets there, and places of business, and churches, and public halls, and everything that a town full of inhabitants could need; but it is all empty and deserted, and has been so as far back as I can remember, and I came to this region when I was a little boy."

"And is there no one to guard the place?" we asked; "no one to protect it from wandering vagrants who might choose to take possession of the buildings?"

"There are not many vagrants in this part of the country," he said; "and if there were, they would not go over to that city. It is haunted."

"By what?" we asked.

"Well, sirs, I scarcely can tell you; queer beings that are not flesh and blood, and that is all I know about it. A good many people living hereabouts have visited that place once in their lives, but I know of no one who has gone there a second time."

"And travelers," I said; "are they not excited by curiosity to explore that strange uninhabited city?"

"Oh, yes," our host replied; "almost all visitors to the valley go over to that queer city—generally in small parties, for it is not a place in which one wishes to walk about alone. Sometimes they see things, and sometimes they don't. But I never knew any man or woman to show a fancy for living there, although it is a very good town."

This was said at supper-time, and, as it was the period of full moon, Bentley and I decided that we would visit the haunted city that evening. Our host endeavored to dissuade us, saying that no one ever went over there at night; but as we were not to be deterred, he told us where we would find his small boat tied to a stake on the river-bank. We soon crossed the river, and landed at a broad, but low, stone pier, at the land end of which a line of tall grasses waved in the gentle night wind as if they were sentinels warning us from entering the silent city. We pushed through these, and walked up a street fairly wide, and so well paved that we noticed none of the weeds and other growths which generally denote desertion or little use. By the bright light of the moon we could see that the architecture was simple, and of a character highly gratifying to the eye. All the buildings were of stone and of good size. We were greatly excited and interested, and proposed to continue our walks until the moon should set, and to return on the following morning—"to live here, perhaps," said Bentley. "What could be so romantic and yet so real? What could conduce better to the marriage of verse and philosophy?" But as he said this we saw around the corner of a cross-street some forms as of people hurrying away.

"The specters," said my companion, laying his hand on my arm.

"Vagrants, more likely," I answered, "who have taken advantage of the superstition of the region to appropriate this comfort and beauty to themselves."

"If that be so," said Bentley, "we must have a care for our lives."

We proceeded cautiously, and soon saw other forms fleeing before us and disappearing, as we supposed, around corners and into houses. And now suddenly finding ourselves upon the edge of a wide, open public square, we saw in the dim light—for a tall steeple obscured the moon—the forms of vehicles, horses, and men moving here and there. But before, in our astonishment, we could say a word one to the other, the moon moved past the steeple, and in its bright light we could see none of the signs of life and traffic which had just astonished us.

Timidly, with hearts beating fast, but with not one thought of turning back, nor any fear of vagrants,—for we were now sure that what we had seen was not flesh and blood, and therefore harmless,—we crossed the open space and entered a street down which the moon shone clearly. Here and there we saw dim figures, which quickly disappeared; but, approaching a low stone balcony in front of one of the houses, we were surprised to see, sitting thereon and leaning over a book which lay open upon the top of the carved parapet, the figure of a woman who did not appear to notice us.

"That is a real person," whispered Bentley, "and it does not see us."

"No," I replied; "it is like the others. Let us go near it."

We drew near to the balcony and stood before it. At this the figure raised its head and looked at us. It was beautiful, it was young; but its substance seemed to be of an ethereal quality which we had never seen or known of. With its full, soft eyes fixed upon us, it spoke:

"Why are you here?" it asked. "I have said to myself that the next time I saw any of you I would ask you why you come to trouble us. Cannot you live content in your own realms and spheres, knowing, as you must know, how timid we are, and how you frighten us and make us unhappy? In all this city there is, I believe, not one of us except myself who does not flee and hide from you whenever you cruelly come here. Even I would do that, had not I declared to myself that I would see you and speak to you, and endeavor to prevail upon you to leave us in peace."

The clear, frank tones of the speaker gave me courage. "We are two men," I answered, "strangers in this region, and living for the time in the beautiful country on the other side of the river. Having heard of this quiet city, we have come to see it for ourselves. We had supposed it to be uninhabited, but now that we find that this is not the case, we would assure you from our hearts that we do not wish to disturb or annoy any one who lives here. We simply came as honest travelers to view the city."

The figure now seated herself again, and as her countenance

was nearer to us, we could see that it was filled with pensive thought. For a moment she looked at us without speaking. "Men!" she said. "And so I have been right. For a long time I have believed that the beings who sometimes come here, filling us with dread and awe, are men."

"And you," I exclaimed—"who are you, and who are these forms that we have seen, these strange inhabitants of this city?"

She gently smiled as she answered: "We are the ghosts of the future. We are the people who are to live in this city generations hence. But all of us do not know that, principally because we do not think about it and study about it enough to know it. And it is generally believed that the men and women who sometimes come here are ghosts who haunt the place."

"And that is why you are terrified and flee from us?" I exclaimed. "You think we are ghosts from another world?"

"Yes," she replied; "that is what is thought, and what I used to think."

"And you," I asked, "are spirits of human beings yet to be?"

"Yes," she answered; "but not for a long time. Generations of men, I know not how many, must pass away before we are men and women."

"Heavens!" exclaimed Bentley, clasping his hands and raising his eyes to the sky, "I shall be a spirit before you are a woman."

"Perhaps," she said again, with a sweet smile upon her face, "you may live to be very, very old."

But Bentley shook his head. This did not console him. For some minutes I stood in contemplation, gazing upon the stone pavement beneath my feet. "And this," I ejaculated, "is a city inhabited by the ghosts of the future, who believe men and women to be phantoms and specters?"

She bowed her head.

"But how is it," I asked, "that you discovered that you are spirits and we mortal men?"

"There are so few of us who think of such things," she answered, "so few who study, ponder, and reflect. I am fond of study, and I love philosophy; and from the reading of many books I have learned much. From the book which I have here I have learned most; and from its teachings I have gradually come to the belief, which you tell me is the true one, that we are spirits and you men."

"And what book is that?" I asked.

"It is 'The Philosophy of Relative Existences,' by Rupert Vance."

"Ye gods!" I exclaimed, springing upon the balcony, "that is my book, and I am Rupert Vance." I stepped toward the volume to seize it, but she raised her hand.

"You cannot touch it," she said. "It is the ghost of a book. And did you write it?"

"Write it? No," I said; "I am writing it. It is not yet finished."

"But here it is," she said, turning over the last pages. "As a spirit book it is finished. It is very successful; it is held in high estimation by intelligent thinkers; it is a standard work."

I stood trembling with emotion. "High estimation!" I said. "A standard work!"

"Oh, yes," she replied with animation; "and it well deserves its great success, especially in its conclusion. I have read it twice."

"But let me see these concluding pages," I exclaimed. "Let me look upon what I am to write."

She smiled, and shook her head, and closed the book. "I would like to do that," she said, "but if you are really a man you must not know what you are going to do."

"Oh, tell me, tell me," cried Bentley from below, "do you know a book called 'Stellar Studies,' by Arthur Bentley? It is a book of poems."

The figure gazed at him. "No," it said presently; "I never heard of it."

I stood trembling. Had the youthful figure before me been flesh and blood, had the book been a real one, I would have torn it from her.

"O wise and lovely being!" I exclaimed, falling on my knees before her, "be also benign and generous. Let me but see the last page of my book. If I have been of benefit to your world; more than all, if I have been of benefit to you, let me see, I implore you—let me see how it is that I have done it."

She rose with the book in her hand. "You have only to wait until you have done it," she said, "and then you will know all that you could see here." I started to my feet, and stood alone upon the balcony.

"I am sorry," said Bentley, as we walked toward the pier where we had left our boat, "that we talked only to that ghost girl, and that the other spirits were all afraid of us. Persons whose souls are choked up with philosophy are not apt to care much for poetry; and even if my book is to be widely known, it is easy to see that she may not have heard of it."

I walked triumphant. The moon, almost touching the horizon, beamed like red gold. "My dear friend," said I, "I have always told you that you should put more philosophy into your poetry. That would make it live."

"And I have always told you," said he, "that you should not put so much poetry into your philosophy. It misleads people."

"It didn't mislead that ghost girl," said I.

"How do you know?" said he. "Perhaps she is wrong, and the other inhabitants of the city are right, and we may be the ghosts after all. Such things, you know, are only relative. Anyway," he continued, after a little pause, "I wish I knew that those ghosts were now reading the poem I am going to begin to-morrow."

The Upper Berth

F. Marion Crawford

Somebody asked for the cigars. We had talked long, and the conversation was beginning to languish; the tobacco smoke had got into the heavy curtains, the wine had got into those brains which were liable to become heavy, and it was already perfectly evident that, unless somebody did something to rouse our oppressed spirits, the meeting would soon come to its natural conclusion, and we, the guests, would speedily go home to bed, and most certainly to sleep. No one had said anything very remarkable; it may be that no one had anything very remarkable to say. Jones had given us every particular of his last hunting adventure in Yorkshire. Mr. Tompkins, of Boston, had explained at elaborate length those working principles, by the due and careful maintenance of which the Atchison, Topeka, and Santa Fé Railroad not only extended its territory, increased its departmental influence, and transported livestock without starving them to death before the day of actual delivery, but, also, had for years succeeded in deceiving those passengers who bought its tickets into the fallacious belief that the corporation aforesaid was really able to transport human life without destroying it. Signor Tombola had endeavoured to persuade us, by arguments which we took no trouble to oppose, that the unity of his country in no way resembled the average modern torpedo, carefully planned, constructed with all the skill of the greatest European arsenals, but, when constructed, destined to be directed by feeble hands into a region where it must undoubtedly explode, unseen, unfeared, and unheard, into the illimitable wastes of political chaos.

It is unnecessary to go into further details. The conversation had assumed proportions which would have bored Prometheus on his rock, which would have driven Tantalus to distraction, and which would have impelled Ixion to seek relaxation in the simple but instructive dialogues of Herr Ollendorff, rather than submit to the greater evil of listening to our talk. We had sat at table for hours; we were bored, we were tired, and nobody showed signs of moving.

Somebody called for cigars. We all instinctively looked towards the speaker. Brisbane was a man of five-and-thirty years of age, and remarkable for those gifts which chiefly attract the attention of men. He was a strong man. The external proportions of his figure presented nothing extraordinary to the common eye, though his size was above the average. He was a little over six feet in height, and moderately broad in the shoulder; he did not appear to be stout, but, on the other hand, he was certainly not thin; his small head was supported by a strong and sinewy neck; his broad, muscular hands appeared to possess a peculiar skill in breaking walnuts without the assistance of the ordinary cracker, and, seeing him in profile, one could not help remarking the extraordinary breadth of his sleeves, and the unusual thickness of his chest. He was one of those men who are commonly spoken of among men as deceptive; that is to say, that though he looked exceedingly strong he was in reality very much stronger than he looked. Of his features I need say little. His head is small, his hair is thin, his eyes are blue, his nose is large, he has a small moustache, and a square jaw. Everybody knows Brisbane, and when he asked for a cigar everybody looked at him.

"It is a very singular thing," said Brisbane.

Everybody stopped talking. Brisbane's voice was not loud, but possessed a peculiar quality of penetrating general conversation, and cutting it like a knife. Everybody listened. Brisbane, perceiving that he had attracted their general attention, lit his cigar with great equanimity.

"It is very singular," he continued, "that thing about ghosts. People are always asking whether anybody has seen a ghost. I have."

"Bosh! What, you? You don't mean to say so, Brisbane? Well, for a man of his intelligence!"

A chorus of exclamations greeted Brisbane's remarkable statement. Everybody called for cigars, and Stubbs, the butler, suddenly appeared from the depths of nowhere with a fresh bottle of dry champagne. The situation was saved; Brisbane was going to tell a story.

I am an old sailor, said Brisbane, and as I have to cross the Atlantic pretty often, I have my favourites. Most men have their favourites. I have seen a man wait in a Broadway bar for three-quarters of an hour for a particular car which he liked. I believe the bar-keeper made at least one-third of his living by that man's preference. I have a habit of waiting for certain ships when I am obliged to cross that duck-pond. It may be a prejudice, but I was never cheated out of a good passage but once in my life. I remember it very well; it was a warm morning in June, and the Custom House officials, who were hanging about waiting for a steamer already on her way up from the Quarantine, presented a peculiarly hazy and thoughtful appearance. I had not much luggage—I never have. I mingled with the crowd of passengers, porters, and officious individuals in blue coats and brass buttons, who seemed to spring up like mushrooms from the deck of a moored steamer to obtrude their unnecessary services upon the independent passenger. I have often noticed with a certain interest the spontaneous evolution of these fellows. They are not there when you arrive; five minutes after the pilot has called 'Go ahead!' they, or at least their blue coats and brass buttons, have disappeared from deck and gangway as completely as though they had been consigned to that locker which tradition unanimously ascribes to Davy Jones. But, at the moment of starting, they are there, clean shaved, blue coated, and ravenous for fees. I hastened on board. The *Kamtschatka* was one of my favourite ships. I say was, because she emphatically no longer is. I cannot conceive of any inducement which could entice me to make another voyage in her. Yes, I know what you are going to say. She is uncommonly clean in the run aft, she has enough bluffing off in the bows to keep her dry, and the lower berths are most of them double. She has a lot of advantages, but I won't cross in her again. Excuse the digression. I got on board. I hailed a steward, whose red nose and redder whiskers were equally familiar to me.

"One hundred and five, lower berth," said I, in the business-like tone peculiar to men who think no more of crossing the Atlantic than taking a whisky cocktail at down-town Delmonico's.

The steward took my portmanteau, great-coat, and rug. I shall never forget the expression of his face. Not that he turned pale. It is maintained by the most eminent divines that even miracles cannot change the course of nature. I have no hesitation in saying that he did not turn pale; but, from his expression, I judged that he was either about to shed tears, to sneeze, or to drop my portmanteau. As the latter contained two bottles of particularly fine old sherry presented to me for my voyage by my old friend Snigginson van Pickyns, I felt extremely nervous. But the steward did none of these things.

"Well, I'm d——d!" said he in a low voice, and led the way.

I supposed my Hermes, as he led me to the lower regions, had had a little grog, but I said nothing, and followed him. 105 was on the port side, well aft. There was nothing remarkable about the state-room. The lower berth, like most of those upon the *Kamtschatka,* was double. There was plenty of room; there was the usual washing apparatus, calculated to convey an idea of luxury to the mind of a North American Indian; there were the usual inefficient racks of brown wood, in which it is more easy to hang a large-sized umbrella than the common tooth-brush of commerce. Upon the uninviting mattresses were carefully folded together those blankets which a great modern humorist has aptly compared to cold buckwheat cakes. The question of towels was left entirely to the imagination. The glass decanters were filled with a transparent liquid faintly tinged with brown, but from which an odour less faint, but not more pleasing, ascended to the nostrils, like a far-off sea-sick reminiscence of oily machinery. Sad-coloured curtains half-closed the upper berth. The hazy June daylight shed a faint illumination upon the desolate little scene. Ugh! how I hate that state-room!

The steward deposited my traps and looked at me, as though

he wanted to get away—probably in search of more passengers and more fees. It is always a good plan to start in favour with those functionaries, and I accordingly gave him certain coins there and then.

"I'll try and make yer comfortable all I can," he remarked, as he put the coins in his pocket. Nevertheless, there was a doubtful intonation in his voice which surprised me. Possibly his scale of fees had gone up, and he was not satisfied; but on the whole I was inclined to think that, as he himself would have expressed it, he was "the better for a glass". I was wrong, however, and did the man injustice.

Nothing especially worthy of mention occurred during that day. We left the pier punctually, and it was very pleasant to be fairly under way, for the weather was warm and sultry, and the motion of the steamer produced a refreshing breeze. Everybody knows what the first day at sea is like. People pace the decks and stare at each other, and occasionally meet acquaintances whom they did not know to be on board. There is the usual uncertainty as to whether the food will be good, bad, or indifferent, until the first two meals have put the matter beyond a doubt; there is the usual uncertainty about the weather, until the ship is fairly off Fire Island. The tables are crowded at first, and then suddenly thinned. Pale-faced people spring from their seats and precipitate themselves towards the door, and each old sailor breathes more freely as his sea-sick neighbour rushes from his side, leaving him plenty of elbow-room and an unlimited command over the mustard.

One passage across the Atlantic is very much like another, and we who cross very often do not make the voyage for the sake of novelty. Whales and icebergs are indeed always objects of interest, but, after all, one whale is very much like another whale, and one rarely sees an iceberg at close quarters. To the majority of us the most delightful moment of the day on board an ocean steamer is when we have taken our last turn on deck, have smoked our last cigar, and having succeeded in tiring ourselves, feel at liberty to turn in with a clear conscience. On that first night of the voyage I felt particularly lazy, and went to bed in 105 rather earlier than I usually do. As I turned in, I was amazed to see that I was to have a companion. A portmanteau, very like my own, lay in the opposite corner, and in the upper berth had been deposited a neatly-folded rug, with a stick and umbrella. I had hoped to be alone, and I was disappointed; but I wondered who my room-mate was to be, and I determined to have a look at him.

Before I had been long in bed he entered. He was, as far as I could see, a very tall man, very thin, very pale, with sandy hair and whiskers and colourless grey eyes. He had about him, I thought, an air of rather dubious fashion; the sort of man you might see in Wall Street, without being able precisely to say what he was doing there—the sort of man who frequents the Café Anglais, who always seems to be alone and who drinks champagne; you might meet him on a racecourse, but he would never appear to be doing anything there either. A little over-dressed—a little odd. There are three or four of his kind on every ocean steamer. I made up my mind that I did not care to make his acquaintance, and I went to sleep saying to myself that I would study his habits in order to avoid him. If he rose early, I would rise late; if he went to bed late, I would go to bed early. I did not care to know him. If you once know people of that kind they are always turning up. Poor fellow! I need not have taken the trouble to come to so many decisions about him, for I never saw him again after that first night in 105.

I was sleeping soundly when I was suddenly waked by a loud noise. To judge from the sound, my room-mate must have sprung with a single leap from the upper berth to the floor. I heard him fumbling with the latch and bolt of the door, which opened almost immediately, and then I heard his footsteps as he ran at full speed down the passage, leaving the door open behind him. The ship was rolling a little, and I expected to hear him stumble or fall, but he ran as though he were running for his life. The door swung on its hinges with the motion of the vessel, and the sound annoyed me. I got up and shut it, and groped my way back to my berth in the darkness. I went to sleep again; but I have no idea how long I slept.

When I awoke it was still quite dark, but I felt a disagreeable sensation of cold, and it seemed to me that the air was damp. You know the peculiar smell of a cabin which has been wet with sea-water. I covered myself up as well as I could and dozed off again, framing complaints to be made the next day, and selecting the most powerful epithets in the language. I could hear my room-mate turn over in the upper berth. He had probably returned while I was asleep. Once I thought I heard him groan, and I argued that he was sea-sick. That is particularly unpleasant when one is below. Nevertheless I dozed off and slept till early daylight.

The ship was rolling heavily, much more than on the previous evening, and the grey light which came in through the porthole changed in tint with every movement according as the angle of the vessel's side turned the glass seawards or skywards. It was very cold—unaccountably so for the month of June. I turned my head and looked at the porthole, and I saw to my surprise that it was wide open and hooked back. I believe I swore audibly. Then I got up and shut it. As I turned back I glanced at the upper berth. The curtains were drawn close together; my companion had probably felt cold as well as I. It struck me that I had slept enough. The state-room was uncomfortable, though, strange to say, I could not smell the dampness which had annoyed me in the night. My room-mate was still asleep— excellent opportunity for avoiding him, so I dressed at once and went on deck. The day was warm and cloudy, with an oily smell on the water. It was seven o'clock as I came out—much later than I had imagined. I came across the doctor, who was taking his first sniff of the morning air. He was a young man from the West of Ireland—a tremendous fellow, with black hair and blue eyes, already inclined to be stout; he had a happy-go-lucky, healthy look about him which was rather attractive.

"Fine morning," I remarked, by way of introduction.

"Well," said he, eyeing me with an air of ready interest, "it's a fine morning and it's not a fine morning. I don't think it's much of a morning."

"Well, no—it is not so very fine," said I.

"It's just what I call fuggly weather," replied the doctor.

"It was very cold last night, I thought," I remarked. "However, when I looked about, I found that the porthole was wide open. I had not noticed it when I went to bed. And the state-room was damp, too."

"Damp!" said he. "Whereabouts are you?"

"One hundred and five—"

To my surprise the doctor started visibly, and stared at me.

"What is the matter?" I asked.

"Oh—nothing," he answered; "only everybody has complained of that state-room for the last three trips."

"I shall complain too," I said. "It has certainly not been properly aired. It is a shame!"

"I don't believe it can be helped," answered the doctor. "I believe there is something—well, it is not my business to frighten passengers."

"You need not be afraid of frightening me," I replied. "I can stand any amount of damp. If I should get a bad cold I will come to you."

I offered the doctor a cigar, which he took and examined very critically.

"It is not so much the damp," he remarked. "However, I dare say you will get on very well. Have you a room-mate?"

"Yes; a deuce of a fellow, who bolts out in the middle of the night, and leaves the door open."

Again the doctor glanced curiously at me. Then he lit the cigar and looked grave.

"Did he come back?" he asked presently.

"Yes. I was asleep, but I waked up, and heard him moving. Then I felt cold and went to sleep again. This morning I found the porthole open."

"Look here," said the doctor quietly, "I don't care much for this ship. I don't care a rap for her reputation. I tell you what I will do. I have a good-sized place up here. I will share it with you, though I don't know you from Adam."

I was very much surprised at the proposition. I could not imagine why he should take such a sudden interest in my welfare. However, his manner as he spoke of the ship was peculiar.

"You are very good, doctor," I said. "But, really, I believe even now the cabin could be aired, or cleaned out, or something. Why do you not care for the ship?"

"We are not superstitious in our profession, sir," replied the doctor, "but the sea makes people so. I don't want to prejudice you, and I don't want to frighten you, but if you will take my advice you will move in here. I would as soon see you overboard," he added earnestly, "as know that you or any other man was to sleep in 105."

"Good gracious! Why?" I asked.

"Just because on the last three trips the people who have slept there actually have gone overboard," he answered gravely.

The intelligence was startling and exceedingly unpleasant, I confess. I looked hard at the doctor to see whether he was making game of me, but he looked perfectly serious. I thanked him warmly for his offer, but told him I intended to be the exception to the rule by which every one who slept in that particular stateroom went overboard. He did not say much, but looked grave as ever, and hinted that, before we got across, I should probably reconsider his proposal. In the course of time we went to breakfast, at which only an inconsiderable number of passengers assembled. I noticed that one or two of the officers who breakfasted with us looked grave. After breakfast I went into my stateroom in order to get a book. The curtains of the upper berth were still closely drawn. Not a word was to be heard. My roommate was probably still asleep.

As I came out I met the steward whose business it was to look after me. He whispered that the captain wanted to see me, and then scuttled away down the passage as if very anxious to avoid any questions. I went toward the captain's cabin, and found him waiting for me.

"Sir," said he, "I want to ask a favour of you."

I answered that I would do anything to oblige him.

"Your room-mate has disappeared," he said. "He is known to have turned in early last night. Did you notice anything extraordinary in his manner?"

The question coming, as it did, in exact confirmation of the fears the doctor had expressed half an hour earlier, staggered me.

"You don't mean to say he has gone overboard?" I asked.

"I fear he has," answered the captain.

"This is the most extraordinary thing—" I began.

"Why?" he asked.

"He is the fourth, then?" I explained. In answer to another question from the captain, I explained, without mentioning the doctor, that I had heard the story concerning 105. He seemed very much annoyed at hearing that I knew of it. I told him what had occurred in the night.

"What you say," he replied, "coincides almost exactly with what was told me by the room-mates of two of the other three. They bolt out of bed and run down the passage. Two of them were seen to go overboard by the watch; we stopped and lowered boats, but they were not found. Nobody, however, saw or heard the man who was lost last night—if he is really lost. The steward, who is a superstitious fellow, perhaps, and expected something to go wrong, went to look for him this morning, and found his berth empty, but his clothes lying about, just as he had left them. The steward was the only man on board who knew him by sight, and he has been searching everywhere for him. He has disappeared! Now, sir, I want to beg you not to mention the circumstance to any of the passengers; I don't want the ship to get a bad name, and nothing hangs about an ocean-goer like stories of suicides. You shall have your choice of any one of the officers' cabins you like, including my own, for the rest of the passage. Is that a fair bargain?"

"Very," said I; "and I am much obliged to you. But since I am alone, and have the state-room to myself, I would rather not move. If the steward will take out that unfortunate man's things, I would as leif stay where I am. I will not say anything about the matter, and I think I can promise you that I will not follow my room-mate."

The captain tried to dissuade me from my intention, but I preferred having a state-room alone to being the chum of any officer on board. I do not know whether I acted foolishly, but if I had taken his advice I should have had nothing more to tell. There would have remained the disagreeable coincidence of several suicides occurring among men who had slept in the same cabin, but that would have been all.

That was not the end of the matter, however, by any means. I obstinately made up my mind that I would not be disturbed by such tales, and I even went so far as to argue the question with the captain. There was something wrong about the state-room, I said. It was rather damp. The porthole had been left open last night. My room-mate might have been ill when he came on board, and he might have become delirious after he went to bed. He might even now be hiding somewhere on board, and might be found later. The place ought to be aired and the fastening on the port looked to. If the captain would give me leave, I would see that what I thought necessary was done immediately.

"Of course you have a right to stay where you are if you please," he replied, rather petulantly; "but I wish you would turn out and let me lock the place up, and be done with it."

I did not see it in the same light, and left the captain, after promising to be silent concerning the disappearance of my companion. The latter had had no acquaintances on board, and was not missed in the course of the day. Towards evening I met the doctor again, and he asked me whether I had changed my mind. I told him I had not.

"Then you will before long," he said, very gravely.

We played whist in the evening, and I went to bed late. I will confess now that I felt a disagreeable sensation when I entered my state-room. I could not help thinking of the tall man I had seen on the previous night, who was now dead, drowned, tossing about in the long swell, two or three hundred miles astern. His face rose very distinctly before me as I undressed, and I even went so far as to draw back the curtains of the upper berth, as though to persuade myself that he was actually gone. I also bolted the door of the state-room. Suddenly I became aware that the porthole was open, and fastened back. This was more than I could stand. I hastily threw on my dressing-gown and went in search of Robert, the steward of my passage. I was very angry, I remember, and when I found him I dragged him roughly to the door of 105, and pushed him towards the open porthole.

"What the deuce do you mean, you scoundrel, by leaving that port open every night? Don't you know it is against the regulations? Don't you know that if the ship heeled and the water began to come in, ten men could not shut it? I will report you to the captain, you blackguard, for endangering the ship!"

I was exceedingly wroth. The man trembled and turned pale, and then began to shut the round glass plate with the heavy brass fittings.

"Why don't you answer me?" I said roughly.

"If you please, sir," faltered Robert, "there's nobody on board as can keep this 'ere port shut at night. You can try it yourself, sir. I ain't a-going to stop hany longer on board o' this vessel, sir; I ain't, indeed. But if I was you, sir, I'd just clear out and go and sleep with the surgeon, or something, I would. Look 'ere, sir, is that fastened what you may call securely, or not, sir? Try it, sir, see if it will move a hinch."

I tried the port, and found it perfectly tight.

"Well, sir," continued Robert triumphantly, "I wager my reputation as a A1 steward that in 'arf an hour it will be open again; fastened back, too, sir, that's the horful thing—fastened back!"

I examined the great screw and the looped nut that ran on it.

"If I find it open in the night, Robert, I will give you a sovereign. It is not possible. You may go."

"Soverin did you say, sir? Very good, sir. Thank ye, sir. Good night, sir. Pleasant reepose, sir, and all manner of hinchantin' dreams, sir."

Robert scuttled away, delighted at being released. Of course, I thought he was trying to account for his negligence by a silly story, intended to frighten me, and I disbelieved him. The consequence was that he got his sovereign, and I spent a very peculiarly unpleasant night.

I went to bed, and five minutes after I had rolled myself up in my blankets the inexorable Robert extinguished the light that burned steadily behind the ground-glass pane near the door. I lay quite still in the dark trying to go to sleep, but I soon found that impossible. It had been some satisfaction to be angry with the steward, and the diversion had banished that unpleasant sensation I had at first experienced when I thought of the drowned man who had been my chum; but I was no longer sleepy, and I lay awake for some time, occasionally glancing at the porthole, which I could just see from where I lay, and which, in the darkness, looked like a faintly-luminous soup-plate suspended in blackness. I believe I must have lain there for an hour, and, as I remember, I was just dozing into sleep when I was roused by a draught of cold air, and by distinctly feeling the spray of the sea blown upon my face. I started to my feet, and not having allowed in the dark for the motion of the ship, I was instantly thrown violently across the state-room upon the couch which was placed beneath the porthole. I recovered myself immediately, however, and climbed upon my knees. The porthole was again wide open and fastened back!

Now these things are facts. I was wide awake when I got up, and I should certainly have been waked by the fall had I still been dozing. Moreover, I bruised my elbows and knees badly, and the bruises were there on the following morning to testify to the fact, if I myself had doubted it. The porthole was wide open and fastened back—a thing so unaccountable that I remember very well feeling astonishment rather than fear when I discovered it. I at once closed the plate again, and screwed down the loop nut with all my strength. It was very dark in the state-room. I reflected that the port had certainly been opened within an hour after Robert had at first shut it in my presence, and I determined to watch it, and see whether it would open again. Those brass fittings are very heavy and by no means easy to move. I could not believe that the clump had been turned by the shaking of the screw. I stood peering out through the thick glass at the alternate white and grey streaks of the sea that foamed beneath the ship's side. I must have remained there a quarter of an hour.

Suddenly, as I stood, I distinctly heard something moving behind me in one of the berths, and a moment afterwards, just as I turned instinctively to look—though I could, of course, see nothing in the darkness—I heard a very faint groan. I sprang across the state-room, and tore the curtains of the upper berth aside, thrusting in my hands to discover if there were any one there. There was some one.

I remember that the sensation as I put my hands forward was as though I were plunging them into the air of a damp cellar, and from behind the curtains came a gust of wind that smelled horribly of stagnant sea-water. I laid hold of something that had the shape of a man's arm, but was smooth, and wet, and icy cold. But suddenly, as I pulled, the creature sprang violently forward against me, a clammy, oozy mass, as it seemed to me, heavy and wet, yet endowed with a sort of supernatural strength. I reeled across the state-room, and in an instant the door opened and the thing rushed out. I had not had time to be frightened, and quickly recovering myself, I sprang through the door and gave chase at the top of my speed, but I was too late. Ten yards before me I could see—I am sure I saw it—a dark shadow moving in the dimly lighted passage, quickly as the shadow of a fast horse thrown before a dog-cart by the lamp on a dark night. But in a moment it had disappeared, and I found myself holding on to the polished rail that ran along the bulkhead where the passage turned towards the companion. My hair stood on end, and the cold perspiration rolled down my face. I am not ashamed of it in the least: I was very badly frightened.

Still I doubted my senses, and pulled myself together. It was absurd, I thought. The Welsh rarebit I had eaten had disagreed with me. I had been in a nightmare. I made my way back to my state-room, and entered it with an effort. The whole place smelled of stagnant sea-water, as it had when I had waked on the previous evening. It required my utmost strength to go in, and grope among my things for a box of wax lights. As I lighted a railway reading lantern which I always carry in case I want to read after the lamps are out, I perceived that the porthole was again open, and a sort of creeping horror began to take possession of me which I never felt before, nor wish to feel again. But I got a light and proceeded to examine the upper berth, expecting to find it drenched with sea-water.

But I was disappointed. The bed had been slept in, and the smell of the sea was strong; but the bedding was as dry as a bone. I fancied that Robert had not had the courage to make the bed after the accident of the previous night—it had all been a hideous dream. I drew the curtains back as far as I could and examined the place very carefully. It was perfectly dry. But the porthole was open again. With a sort of dull bewilderment of horror I closed it and screwed it down, and thrusting my heavy stick through the brass loop, wrenched it with all my might, till the thick metal began to bend under the pressure. Then I hooked my reading lantern into the red velvet at the head of the couch, and sat down to recover my senses if I could. I sat there all night, unable to think of rest—hardly able to think at all. But the porthole remained closed, and I did not believe it would now open again without the application of a considerable force.

The morning dawned at last, and I dressed myself slowly, thinking over all that had happened in the night. It was a beautiful day and I went on deck, glad to get out into the early, pure sunshine, and to smell the breeze from the blue water, so different from the noisome, stagnant odour of my state-room. Instinctively I turned aft, towards the surgeon's cabin. There he stood, with a pipe in his mouth, taking his morning airing precisely as on the preceding day.

"Good morning," said he quietly, but looking at me with evident curiosity.

"Doctor, you were quite right," said I. "There is something wrong about that place."

"I thought you would change your mind," he answered, rather triumphantly. "You have had a bad night, eh? Shall I make you a pick-me-up? I have a capital recipe."

"No, thanks," I cried. "But I would like to tell you what happened."

I then tried to explain as clearly as possible precisely what had occurred, not omitting to state that I had been scared as I had never been scared in my whole life before. I dwelt particularly on the phenomenon of the porthole, which was a fact to which I could testify, even if the rest had been an illusion. I had closed it twice in the night, and the second time I had actually bent the brass in wrenching it with my stick. I believe I insisted a good deal on this point.

"You seem to think I am likely to doubt the story," said the doctor, smiling at the detailed account of the state of the port-hole. "I do not doubt it in the least. I renew my invitation to you. Bring your traps here, and take half my cabin."

"Come and take half of mine for one night," I said. "Help me to get at the bottom of this thing."

"You will get to the bottom of something else if you try," answered the doctor.

"What?" I asked.

"The bottom of the sea. I am going to leave this ship. It is not canny."

"Then you will not help me to find out—"

"Not I," said the doctor quickly. "It is my business to keep my wits about me—not to go fiddling about with ghosts and things."

"Do you really believe it is a ghost?" I inquired, rather con-temptuously. But as I spoke I remembered very well the horri-ble sensation of the supernatural which had got possession of me during the night. The doctor turned sharply on me.

"Have you any reasonable explanation of these things to offer?" he asked. "No; you have not. Well, you say you will find an explanation. I say that you won't, sir, simply because there is not any."

"But, my dear sir," I retorted, "do you, a man of science, mean to tell me that such things cannot be explained?"

"I do," he answered stoutly. "And, if they could, I would not be concerned in the explanation."

I did not care to spend another night alone in the state-room, and yet I was obstinately determined to get at the root of the disturbances. I do not believe there are many men who would have slept there alone, after passing two such nights. But I made up my mind to try it, if I could not get any one to share a watch with me. The doctor was evidently not inclined for such an experiment. He said he was a surgeon, and that in case any acci-dent occurred on board he must be always in readiness. He could not afford to have his nerves unsettled. Perhaps he was quite right, but I am inclined to think that his precaution was prompted by his inclination. On inquiry, he informed me that there was no one on board who would be likely to join me in my investigations, and after a little more conversation I left him. A little later I met the captain, and told him my story. I said that, if no one would spend the night with me, I would ask leave to have the light burning all night, and would try it alone.

"Look here," said he, "I will tell you what I will do. I will share your watch myself, and we will see what happens. It is my belief that we can find out between us. There may be some fellow skulking on board, who steals a passage by frightening the passengers. It is just possible that there may be something queer in the carpentering of that berth."

I suggested taking the ship's carpenter below and examining the place; but I was overjoyed at the captain's offer to spend the night with me. He accordingly sent for the workman and ordered him to do anything I required. We went below at once. I had all the bedding cleared out of the upper berth, and we examined the place thoroughly to see if there was a board loose anywhere, or a panel which could be opened or pushed aside. We tried the planks everywhere, tapped the flooring, unscrewed the fittings of the lower berth and took it to pieces—in short, there was not a square inch of the state-room which was not searched and tested. Everything was in perfect order, and we put everything back in its place. As we were finishing our work, Robert came to the door and looked in.

"Well, sir—find anything, sir?" he asked, with a ghastly grin.

"You were right about the porthole, Robert," I said, and I gave him the promised sovereign. The carpenter did his work silently and skilfully, following my directions. When he had done he spoke.

"I'm a plain man, sir," he said. "But it's my belief you had better just turn out your things, and let me run half a dozen four-inch screws through the door of this cabin. There's no good never came o' this cabin yet, sir, and that's all about it. There's been four lives lost out o' here to my own remembrance, and that in four trips. Better give it up, sir—better give it up!"

"I will try it for one night more," I said.

"Better give it up, sir—better give it up! It's a precious bad job," repeated the workman, putting his tools in his bag and leaving the cabin.

But my spirits had risen considerably at the prospect of having the captain's company, and I made up my mind not to be prevented from going to the end of this strange business. I abstained from Welsh rarebits and grog that evening, and did not even join in the customary game of whist. I wanted to be quite sure of my nerves, and my vanity made me anxious to make a good figure in the captain's eyes.

The captain was one of those splendidly tough and cheerful specimens of seafaring humanity whose combined courage, hardihood, and calmness in difficulty leads them naturally into high positions of trust. He was not the man to be led away by an idle tale, and the mere fact that he was willing to join me in the investigation was proof that he thought there was something seriously wrong, which could not be accounted for on ordinary theories, nor laughed down as a common superstition. To some extent, too, his reputation was at stake, as well as the reputation of the ship. It is no light thing to lose passengers overboard, and he knew it.

About ten o'clock that evening, as I was smoking a last cigar, he came up to me, and drew me aside from the beat of the other passengers who were patrolling the deck in the warm darkness.

"This is a serious matter, Mr. Brisbane," he said. "We must make up our minds either way—to be disappointed or to have a pretty rough time of it. You see I cannot afford to laugh at the affair, and I will ask you to sign your name to a statement of whatever occurs. If nothing happens tonight we will try it again tomorrow and the next day. Are you ready?"

So we went below, and entered the state-room. As we went in I could see Robert the steward, who stood a little further down the passage, watching us, with his usual grin, as though certain that something dreadful was about to happen. The captain closed the door behind us and bolted it.

"Supposing we put your portmanteau before the door," he

suggested. "One of us can sit on it. Nothing can get out then. Is the port screwed down?"

I found it as I had left it in the morning. Indeed, without using a lever, as I had done, no one could have opened it. I drew back the curtains of the upper berth so that I could see well into it. By the captain's advice I lighted my reading lantern, and placed it so that it shone upon the white sheets above. He insisted upon sitting on the portmanteau, declaring that he wished to be able to swear that he had sat before the door.

Then he requested me to search the state-room thoroughly, an operation very soon accomplished, as it consisted merely in looking beneath the lower berth and under the couch below the porthole. The spaces were quite empty.

"It is impossible for any human being to get in," I said, "or for any human being to open the port."

"Very good," said the captain calmly. "If we see anything now, it must be either imagination or something supernatural."

I sat down on the edge of the lower berth.

"The first time it happened," said the captain, crossing his legs and leaning back against the door, "was in March. The passenger who slept here, in the upper berth, turned out to have been a lunatic—at all events, he was known to have been a little touched, and he had taken his passage without the knowledge of his friends. He rushed out in the middle of the night, and threw himself overboard, before the officer who had the watch could stop him. We stopped and lowered a boat; it was a quiet night, just before that heavy weather came on; but we could not find him. Of course his suicide was afterwards accounted for on the ground of his insanity."

"I suppose that often happens?" I remarked, rather absently.

"Not often—no," said the captain; "never before in my experience, though I have heard of it happening on board of other ships. Well, as I was saying, that occurred in March. On the very next trip— What are you looking at?" he asked, stopping suddenly in his narration.

I believe I gave no answer. My eyes were riveted upon the porthole. It seemed to me that the brass loop-nut was beginning to turn very slowly upon the screw—so slowly, however, that I was not sure it moved at all. I watched it intently, fixing its position in my mind, and trying to ascertain whether it changed. Seeing where I was looking, the captain looked, too.

"It moves!" he exclaimed, in a tone of conviction. "No, it does not," he added, after a minute.

"If it were the jarring of the screw," said I, "it would have opened during the day; but I found it this evening jammed tight as I left it this morning."

I rose and tried the nut. It was certainly loosened, for by an effort I could move it with my hands.

"The queer thing," said the captain, "is that the second man who was lost is supposed to have got through that very port. We had a terrible time over it. It was in the middle of the night, and the weather was very heavy; there was an alarm that one of the ports was open and the sea running in. I came below and found everything flooded, the water pouring in every time she rolled, and the whole port swinging from the top bolts—not the port-hole in the middle. Well, we managed to shut it, but the water did some damage. Ever since that the place smells of sea-water from time to time. We supposed the passenger had thrown himself out, though the Lord only knows how he did it. The steward kept telling me that he cannot keep anything shut here. Upon my word—I can smell it now, cannot you?" he inquired, sniffing the air suspiciously.

"Yes—distinctly," I said, and I shuddered as that same odour of stagnant sea-water grew stronger in the cabin. "Now, to smell like this, the place must be damp," I continued, "and yet when I examined it with the carpenter this morning everything was perfectly dry. It is most extraordinary—hallo!"

My reading lantern, which had been placed in the upper berth, was suddenly extinguished. There was still a good deal of light from the pane of ground glass near the door, behind which loomed the regulation lamp. The ship rolled heavily, and the curtain of the upper berth swung far out into the state-room and back again. I rose quickly from my seat on the edge of the bed, and the captain at the same moment started to his feet with a loud cry of surprise. I had turned with the intention of taking down the lantern to examine it, when I heard his exclamation, and immediately afterwards his call for help. I sprang towards him. He was wrestling with all his might with the brass loop of the port. It seemed to turn against his hands in spite of all his efforts. I caught up my cane, a heavy oak stick I always used to carry, and thrust it through the ring and bore on it with all my strength. But the strong wood snapped suddenly and I fell upon the couch. When I rose again the port was wide open, and the captain was standing with his back against the door, pale to the lips.

"There is something in that berth!" he cried, in a strange voice, his eyes almost starting from his head. "Hold the door, while I look—it shall not escape us, whatever it is!"

But instead of taking his place, I sprang upon the lower bed, and seized something which lay in the upper berth.

It was something ghostly, horrible beyond words, and it moved in my grip. It was like the body of a man long drowned, and yet it moved, and had the strength of ten men living; but I gripped it with all my might—the slippery, oozy, horrible thing—the dead white eyes seemed to stare at me out of the dusk; the putrid odour of rank sea-water was about it, and its shiny hair hung in foul wet curls over its dead face. I wrestled with the dead thing; it thrust itself upon me and forced me back and nearly broke my arms; it wound its corpse's arms about my neck, the living death, and overpowered me, so that I, at last, cried aloud and fell, and left my hold.

As I fell the thing sprang across me, and seemed to throw itself upon the captain. When I last saw him on his feet his face was white and his lips set. It seemed to me that he struck a violent blow at the dead being, and then he, too, fell forward upon his face, with an inarticulate cry of horror.

The thing paused an instant, seeming to hover over his prostrate body, and I could have screamed again for very fright, but I had no voice left. The thing vanished sudddenly, and it seemed to my disturbed senses that it made its exit through the open port, though how that was possible, considering the smallness of the aperture, is more than any one can tell. I lay a long time on the floor, and the captain lay beside me. At last I partially recovered my senses and moved, and instantly I knew that my arm was broken—the small bone of my left forearm near the wrist.

I got upon my feet somehow, and with my remaining hand I tried to raise the captain. He groaned and moved, and at last came to himself. He was not hurt, but he seemed badly stunned.

Well, do you want to hear any more? There is nothing more. That is the end of my story. The carpenter carried out his scheme of running half a dozen four-inch screws through the door of 105; and if ever you take a passage in the *Kamtschatka,* you may ask for a berth in that state-room. You will be told that it is engaged—yes—it is engaged by that dead thing.

I finished the trip in the surgeon's cabin. He doctored my broken arm, and advised me not to "fiddle about with ghosts and things" any more. The captain was very silent, and never sailed again in that ship, though it is still running. And I will not sail in her either. It was a very disagreeable experience, and I was very badly frightened, which is a thing I do not like. That is all. That is how I saw a ghost—if it was a ghost. It was dead, anyhow.

An Itinerant House

Emma Frances Dawson

"Eternal longing with eternal pain,
Want without hope, and memory saddening all,
All congregated failure and despair
Shall wander there through some old maze of wrong."

"**H**is *wife?*" cried Felipa.

"Yes," I answered, unwillingly; for until the steamer brought Mrs. Anson I believed in this Mexican woman's right to that name. I felt sorry for the bright eyes and kind heart that had cheered Anson's lodgers through weary months of early days in San Francisco.

She burst into tears. None of us knew how to comfort her. Dering spoke first: "Beauty always wins friends."

Between her sobs she repeated one of the pithy sayings of her language: "It is as easy to find a lover as to keep a friend, but as hard to find a friend as to keep a lover."

"Yes," said Volz, "a new friendship is like a new string to your guitar—you are not sure what its tone may prove, nor how soon it may break."

"But at least its falsity is learned at once," she sobbed.

"Is it possible," I asked, "that you had no suspicion?"

"None. He told me—" She ended in a fresh gust of tears.

"The old story," muttered Dering. "Marryatt's skipper was right in thinking everything that once happened would come again somewhere."

Anson came. He had left the new-comer at the Niantic, on pretense of putting his house in order. Felipa turned on him before we could go.

"Is this true?" she cried.

Without reply he went to the window and stood looking out. She sprang toward him, with rage distorting her face.

"Coward!" she screamed, in fierce scorn.

Then she fell senseless. Two doctors were called. One said she was dead. The other, at first doubtful, vainly tried hot sealing-wax and other tests. After thirty-six hours her funeral was planned. Yet Dering, once medical student, had seen an electric current used in such a case in Vienna, and wanted to try it. That night, he, Volz, and I offered to watch. When all was still, Dering, who had smuggled in the simple things needed, began his weird work.

"Is it not too late? " I asked.

"Every corpse," said he, "can be thus excited soon after death, for a brief time only, and but once. If the body is not lifeless, the electric current has power at any time."

Volz, too nervous to stay near, stood in the door open to the dark hall. It was a dreadful sight. The dead woman's breast rose and fell; smiles and frowns flitted across her face.

"The body begins to react finely," cried Dering, making Volz open the windows, while I wrapped hot blankets round Felipa, and he instilled clear coffee and brandy.

"It seems like sacrilege! Let her alone!" I exclaimed. "Better dead than alive!"

"My God! say not that!" cried Volz; "the nerve which hears is last to die. She may know all we say."

"Musical bosh!" I muttered.

"Perhaps not," said Dering; "in magnetic sleep that nerve can be roused."

The night seemed endless. The room gained an uncanny look, the macaws on the gaudy, old-fashioned wall-paper seemed fluttering and changing places. Volz crouched in a heap near the door. Dering stood by Felipa, watching closely. I paced the shadowy room, looked at the gleam of the moon on the bay, listened to the soughing wind in the gum-trees mocking the sea, and tried to recall more cheerful scenes, but always bent under the weight of that fearful test going on beside me. Where was her soul? Beyond the stars, in the room with us, or "like trodden snowdrift melting in the dark?" Volz came behind, startling me by grasping my elbow.

"Shall I not play?" he whispered. "Familiar music is remembrance changed to sound—it brings the past as perfume does. Gypsy music in her ear would be like holding wild flowers to her nostrils."

"Ask Dering," I said; "he will know best."

I heard him urging Dering.

"She has gypsy blood," he said; "their music will rouse her."

Dering unwillingly agreed. "But nothing abrupt—begin low," said he.

Vaguely uneasy, I turned to object; but Volz had gone for his violin. Far off arose a soft, wavering, sleepy strain, like a wind blowing over a field of poppies. He passed, in slow, dramatic style, through the hall, playing on the way. As he came in, oddly sustained notes trembled like sighs and sobs; these were by degrees subdued, though with spasmodic outbursts, amid a grand movement as of phantom shapes through cloud-land. One heart-rending phrase recurring as of one of the shadowy host striving to break loose, but beaten back by impalpable throngs, numberless grace-notes trailing their sparks like fireworks. No music of our intervals and our rhythms, but perplexing in its charm like a draught that maddens. Time, space, our very identities, were consumed in this white heat of sound. I held my breath. I caught his arm.

"It is too bold and distracting," I cried. "It is enough to kill us! Do you expect to torment her back? How can it affect us so?"

"Because," he answered, laying down his violin and wiping his brow, "in the gypsy minor scale the fourth and seventh are augmented. The sixth is diminished. The frequent augmentation of the fourth makes that sense of unrest."

"Bah! Technical terms make it no plainer," I said, returning to the window.

He played a whispered, merry discordance, resolving into click of castanets, laugh, and dance of a gypsy camp. Out of the whirl of flying steps and tremolo of tambourines rose a tender voice, asking, denying, sighing, imploring, passing into an over-ruling, long-drawn call that vibrated in widening rings to reach the farthest horizon—nay, beyond land or sea, "east of the sun, west of the moon." With a rush returned the wild jollity of men's bass laughter, women's shrill reply, the stir of the gypsy camp. This dropped behind vague, rolling measures of clouds and chaos, where to and fro floated grotesque goblins of grace-notes like the fancies of a madman; struggling, rising, falling, vain-reaching strains; fierce cries like commands. The music seemed another vital essence thrilling us with its own emotion.

"No more, no more!" I cried, half gasping, and grasping Volz's arm. "What is it, Dering?"

He had staggered from the bed and was trying to see his watch. "It is just forty-four hours!" he said, pointing to Felipa.

Her eyes were open! We were alarmed as if doing wrong and silently watched her. Fifteen minutes later her lips formed one word:

"Idiots!"

Half an hour after she flung the violin from bed to floor, but would not speak. People began to stir about the house. The prosaic sounds jarred on our strained nerves. We felt brought from another sphere. Volz and I were going, but Felipa's upraised hand kept us. She sat up, looking a ghastly vision. Turning first toward me she quoted my words:

"'Better dead than alive!' True. You knew I would be glad to die. What right had you to bring me back? God's curses on you! I was dead. Then came agony. I heard your voices. I thought we were all in hell. Then I found how by your evil cunning I was to be forced to live. It was like an awful nightmare. I shall not for-get you, nor you me. These very walls shall remember—here, where I have been so tortured no one shall have peace! Fools! Leave me! Never come in this room again!"

We went, all talking at once, Dering angry at her mood; Volz, sorry he had not reached a soothing *pianissimo* passage; I, own-ing we had no right to make the test. We saw her but once more, when with a threatening nod toward us she left the house.

From that time a gloom settled over the place. Mrs. Anson

proved a hard-faced, cold-hearted, Cape Cod woman, a scold and drudge, who hated us as much as we disliked her. Homesick and unhappy, she soon went East and died. Within a year, Anson was found dead where he had gone hunting in the Saucelito woods, supposed a suicide; Dering was hung by the Vigilantes, and the rest were scattered on the four winds. Volz and I were last to go. The night before we sailed, he for Australia, I for New York, he said:

"I am sorry for those who come after us in this house."

"Not knowing of any tragedy here," I said, " they will not feel its influence."

"They must feel it," he insisted; "it is written in the Proverbs, 'Evil shall not depart from his house.'"

Some years later, I was among passengers embarking at New York for California, when there was a cry of "Man overboard!" In the confusion of his rescue, among heartless and pitiful talk, I overheard one man declare that the drowned might be revived.

"Oh, yes!" cried a well-known voice behind me. "But they might not thank you."

I turned—to find Volz! He was coming out with Wynne, the actor. Enjoying our comradeship on the voyage, on reaching San Francisco we took rooms together, on Bush Street, in an old house with a large garden. Volz became leader of the orchestra, and Wynne, leading man at the same theatre. Lest my folks, a Maine deacon's family, should think I was on the road to ruin, I told in letters home only of the city missionary in the house.

Volz was hard worked. Wynne was not much liked. My business went wrong. It rained for many weeks; to this we laid the discomfort that grew to weigh on us. Volz wreaked his sense of it on his violin, adding to the torment of Wynne and myself, for to lonesome anxious souls "the demon in music" shows horns and cloven foot in the trying sounds of practice. One Sunday Volz played the "Witches Dance," the "Dream," and "The long, long weary day."

"I can bear it no longer!" said Wynne. "I feel like the haunted Matthias in 'The Bells.' If I could feel so when acting such parts, it would make my fortune. But I feel it only here."

"I think," said Volz, "it is the *gloria fonda* bush near the window; the scent is too strong." He dashed off Strauss' fretful, conflicting "Hurry and Delay."

"There, there! It is too much," said I. "You express my feelings."

He looked doubtful. "Put it in words," said he.

"How can I?" I said. "When our firm sent me abroad, I went sight-seeing among old palaces, whose Gobelin tapestries framed in their walls were faded to gray phantoms of pictures, but out of some the thrilling eyes followed me till I could not stay in their range. My feeling here is the uneasy one of being watched."

"Ha!" said Volz. "You remind me of Heine, when he wrote from Livorno. He knew no Italian, but the old palaces whispered secrets unheard by day. The moon was interpreter, knew the lapidary style, translated to dialect of his heart."

"'Strange effects after the moon,'" mused Wynne. "That gives new meaning to Kent's threat: 'I'll make a sop o' the moonshine of you!'"

Volz went on: "Heine wrote: 'The stones here speak to me, and I know their mute language. Also, they seem deeply to feel what I think. So a broken column of the old Roman times, an old tower of Lombardy, a weather-beaten Gothic piece of a pillar understands me well. But I am a ruin myself, wandering among ruins.'"

"Perhaps, like Poe's hero," said I, "'I have imbibed shadows of fallen columns at Balbec, and Tadmor, and Persepolis, until my very soul has become a ruin.'"

"But I, too," said Wynne, "feel the unrest of Tannhauser:

> 'Alas! what seek I here, or anywhere,
> Whose way of life is like the crumbled stair
> That winds and winds about a ruined tower,
> And leads no whither.'"

"I am oppressed," Volz owned, "as if some one in my presence was suffering deeply."

"I feel," said Wynne, "as if the scene was not set right for the

performance now going on. There is a hitch and drag somewhere—scene-shifters on a strike. Happy are you poets and
musicians, who can express what is vague."

Volz laughed. "As in Liszt's oratorio of 'Christus,'" said he,
"where a sharp, ear-piercing *sostenuto* on the piccolo-flute
shows the shining of the star of Bethlehem." He turned to me.
"Schubert's 'Wanderer' always recalls to me a house you and I
know to be under a ban."

"Haunted?" asked Wynne. "Of all speculative theories, St.
Martin's sends the most cold thrills up one's back. He said none
of the dead come back, but some stay."

"What we Germans call *gebannt*—tied to one spot," said Volz.
"But this is no ghost, only a proof of what a German psychologist
holds, that the magnetic man is a spirit."

"Go on, 'and tell quaint lies'—I like them," said Wynne.

I told in brief outline, with no names, the tale Volz and I
knew, while we strolled to Telegraph Hill, passing five streets
blocked by the roving houses common to San Francisco.

Wynne said: "They seem to have minds of their own, with
their entrances and exits in a *moving* drama."

"Sort of 'Poor Jo's,'" said I.

"Castles in chess," said Volz.

"Io-like," said Wynne, "with a gad in their hearts that forever
drives them on."

A few foreign sailors lounged on the hill top, looking at the
view. The wind blew such a gale we did not stay. The steps we
had known, cut in the side, were gone. Where the old house
used to be, goats were browsing.

"Perchance we do inhabit it but now," mockingly cried
Wynne; "methinks it must be so."

"Then," said Volz, thoughtfully, "it might be what Germans
call 'far-working'—acted in distance—that affects us."

"What do you mean?" I asked. "Do you know anything of her
now?"

"I know she went to Mexico," said he; "that is all."

"What is 'far-working?'" asked Wynne. "If I could act in the
distance, and here too—'what larks!'"

"Yes—if," said I. "Think how all our lives turn on that pivot. Suppose Hawthorne's offer to join Wilkes' exploring expedition had been taken!"

"Only to wills that know no 'if' is 'far-working' possible," said Volz. "Substance or space can no more hinder this force than the one of mineral magnetism. Passavent joins it with pictures falling, or watches stopping at the time of a death. In sleep-walking, some kinds of illness, or nearness of death, the nervous ether is not so closely allied to its material conductors, the nerves, and may be loosened to act from afar, the surest where blood or feeling makes attraction or repulsion."

Wynne in the two voices of the play repeated:

> "Victor.—Where is the gentleman?
> Chispe.—As the old song says:
> > 'His body is in Segovia,
> > His soul is in Madrid.'"

We could learn about the house we were in only that five families had moved in and out during the last year. Wynne resolved to shake off the gloom that wrapped us. In struggles to defy it, he on the strength of a thousand-dollar benefit, made one payment on the house and began repairs.

On an off-night he was vainly trying to study a new part. Volz advised the relief to his nerves of reciting the dream scene from "The Bells," reminding him he had compared it with his rest-lessness there. Wynne denied it.

"Yes," said Volz, "where the mesmerizer forces Matthias to confess."

But Wynne refused, as if vexed, till Volz offered to show in music his own mood, and I agreed to read some rhymes about mine. Volz was long tuning his violin.

"I feel," he said, "as if the passers-by would hear a secret. Music is such a subtle expression of emotion—like flower-odor rolls far and affects the stranger. Hearken! In Heine's 'Reisebilder,' as the cross was thrown ringing on the banquet table of the gods, they grew dumb and pale, and even paler till they melted in mist. So shall you at the long-drawn wail of my violin grow breathless, and fade from each other's sight."

The music closed round us, and we waited in its deep solitude. One brief, sad phrase fell from airy heights to lowest depths into a sea of sound, whose harmonious eddies as they widened breathed of passion and pain, now swooning, now reviving, with odd pauses and sighs that rose to cries of despair, but the tormenting first strain recurring fainter and fainter, as if drowning, drowning, drowned—yet floating back for repeated last plaint, as if not to be quelled, and closing, as it began, the whole.

As I read the name of my verses, Volz murmured: "*Les Nuits Blanches*. No. 4. Stephen Heller."

SLEEPLESS NIGHTS.

Against the garden's mossy paling
    I lean, and wish the night away,
Whose faint, unequal shadows trailing
    Seem but a dream of those of day.

Sleep burdens blossom, bud, and leaf,
    My soul alone aspires, dilates,
Yearns to forget its care and grief—
    No bath of sleep its pain abates.

How dread these dreams of wide-eyed nights!
    What is, and is not, both I rue,
My wild thoughts fly like wand'ring kites,
    No peace falls with this balmy dew.

Through slumb'rous stillness, scarcely stirred
    By sudden trembles, as when shifts
O'er placid pool some skimming bird,
    Its Lethean bowl a poppy lifts.

If one deep draught my doubts could solve,
    The world might bubble down its brim,
Like Cleopatra's pearl dissolve,
    With all my dreams within its rim.

What should I know but calm repose?
    How feel, recalling this lost sphere?
Alas! the fabled poppy shows
    Upon its bleeding heart—a tear!

Wynne unwillingly began to recite: "'I fear nothing, but dreams are dreams—'"

He stammered, could not go on, and fell to the floor. We got him to bed. He never spoke sanely after. His wild fancies appalled us watching him all night.

"Avaunt Sathanas! That's not my cue," he muttered. "A full house to-night. How could Talma forget how the crowd looked, and fancy it a pack of skeletons? Tell Volz to keep the violins playing through this scene, it works me up as well as thrills the audience. Oh, what tiresome nights I have lately, always dreaming of scenes where rival women move, as in 'Court and Stage,' where, all masked, the king makes love to Frances Stewart before the queen's face! How do I try to cure it? 'And being thus frighted, swear a prayer or two and sleep again.' Madame, you're late; you've too little rouge; you'll look ghastly. We're not called yet; let's rehearse our scene. Now, then, I enter left, pass to the window. You cry 'is this true?' and faint. All crowd about. Quick curtain."

Volz and I looked at each other.

"Can our magnetism make his senses so sharp that he knows what is in our minds?" he asked me.

"Nonsense!" I said. "Memory, laudanum, and whisky."

"There," Wynne went on, "the orchestra is stopping. They've rung up the curtain. Don't hold me. The stage waits, yet how can I go outside my door to step on dead bodies? Street and sidewalk are knee-deep with them. They rise and curse me for disturbing them. I lift my cane to strike. It turns to a snake, whose slimy body writhes in my hand. Trying to hold it from biting me, my nails cut my palm till blood streams to drown the snake."

He awed us not alone from having no control of his thoughts, but because there came now and then a strange influx of emotion as if other souls passed in and out of his body.

"Is this hell?" he groaned. "What blank darkness! Where am I? What is that infernal music haunting me through all space? If I could only escape it I need not go back to earth—to that room where I feel choked, where the very wall paper frets me with its flaunting birds flying to and fro, mocking my fettered state.

'Here, here in the very den of the wolf!' Hallo, Benvolio, call-boy's hunting you. Romeo's gone on.

> 'See where he steals—
> Locked in some gloomy covert under key
> Of cautionary silence, with his arms
> Threaded, like these cross-boughs, in sorrow's knot.'

What is this dread that weighs like a nightmare? 'I do not fear; like Macbeth, I only inhabit trembling.' 'For one of them—she is in hell already, and burns, poor soul! For the other'—Ah! must I die here, alone in the woods, felled by a coward, Indian-like, from behind a tree? None of the boys will know. 'I just now come from a whole world of mad women that had almost—what, is she dead?' Poor Felipa!"

"Did you tell him her name?" I asked Volz.

"No," said he. "Can one man's madness be another's real life?"

"Blood was spilt—the avenger's wing hovered above my house," raved Wynne. "What are these lights, hundreds of them—serpent's eyes? Is it the audience—coiled, many-headed monster, following me round the world? Why do they hiss? I've played this part a hundred times. 'Taught by Rage, and Hunger, and Despair?' Do they, full-fed, well-clothed, light-hearted, know how to judge me? 'A plague on both your houses!' What is that flame? Fire that consumes my vitals—spon-ta-neous com-bustion! It is then possible. Water! water!"

The doctor said there had been some great strain on Wynne's mind. He sank fast, though we did all we could. Toward morning I turned to Volz with the words:

"He is dead."

The city missionary was passing the open door. He grimly muttered:

"Better dead than alive!"

"My God! say not that!" cried Volz. "The nerve which hears is last to die. He may know——"

He faltered. We stood aghast. The room grew suddenly famil-iar. I tore off a strip of the gray tint on the walls. Under it we found the old paper with its bright macaws.

"Ah, ha!" Volz said; "will you now deny my theory of 'far-working?'"

Dazed, I could barely murmur: "Then people *can* be affected by it!"

"Certainly," said he, "as rubbed glasses gain electric power."

Within a week we sailed—he for Brazil, I for New York.

Several years after, at Sacramento, Arne, an artist I had known abroad, found me on the overland train, and on reaching San Francisco urged me to go where he lodged.

"I am low-spirited here," he said; "I don't know why."

I stopped short on the crowded wharf. "Where do you live?" I asked.

"Far up Market Street,' said he.

"What sort of a house?" I insisted.

"Oh—nothing modern—over a store," he answered.

Reassured, I went with him. He lived in a jumble of easels, portfolios, paint, canvas, bits of statuary, casts, carvings, foils, red curtains, Chinese goatskins, woodcuts, photographs, sketches, and unfinished pictures. On the wall hung a scene from "The Wandering Jew," as we saw it at the Adelphi, in London, where in the Arctic regions he sees visions foreshadowing the future of his race. Under it was quoted:

> ———"All in my mind is confused, nor can I dissever
> The mould of the visible world from the shape of my
>   thought in me—
> The Inward and Outward are fused, and through them murmur
>   forever
> The sorrow whose sound is the wind and the roar of the
>   limitless sea."

"Do you remember," Arne asked, "when we saw that play? Both younger and more hopeful. How has the world used you? As for me, I have done nothing since I came here but that sketch, finished months ago. I have not lost ambition, but I feel fettered."

"Absinthe?—opium?—tobacco?" I hinted.

"Neither," he answered. "I try to work, but visions, widely different from what I will, crowd on me, as on the Jew in the play. Not the unconscious brain action all thinkers know, but a dictation from without. No rush of creative impulses, but a dragging sense of something else I ought to paint."

"Briefly," I said, "you are a 'Haunted Man.'"

"Haunted by a wilful design," said he. "I feel as if something had happened somewhere which I *must* show."

"What is it like?" I asked.

"I wish I could tell you," he replied. "But only odd bits change places, like looking in a kaleidoscope; yet all cluster around one centre."

One day, looking over his portfolios, I found an old *Temple Bar*, which he said he kept for this passage—which he read to me—from T. A. Trollope's "Artist's Tragedy":

> "The old walls and ceilings and floors must be saturated with the exhalations of human emotions! These lintels, doorways, and stairs have become, by long use and homeliness, dear to human hearts, and have become so intimately blended a portion of the mental furniture of human lives, that they have contributed their part to the formation of human characters. Such facts and considerations have gone to the fashioning of the mental habitudes of all of us. If all could have been recorded! If emotion had the property of photographing itself on the surfaces of the walls which had witnessed it! Even if only passion, when translated into acts, could have done so! Ah, what palimpsests! What deciphering of tangled records! What skilful separation of successive layers of 'passionography!'"

"I know a room," said Arne, "thronged with acts that elbow me from my work and fill me with unrest."

I looked at him in mute surprise.

"I suppose," he went on, "such things do not interest you."

"No—yes," I stammered. "I have marked in traveling how lonely houses change their expression as you come near, pass, and leave them. Some frown, others smile. The Bible buildings had life of their own and human diseases; the priests cursed or blessed them as men."

"Houses seem to remember," said he. "Some rooms oppress us with a sense of lives that have been lived in them."

"That," I said, "is like Draper's theory of shadows on walls always staying. He shows how after a breath passes over a coin or key, its spectral outline remains for months after the substance is removed. But can the mist of circumstance sweeping over us make our vacant places hold any trace of us?"

"Why not? Who can deny it? Why do you look at me so?" he asked.

I could not tell him the sad tale. I hesitated; then said: "I was thinking of Volz, a friend I had, who not only believed in what Bulwer calls 'a power akin to mesmerism and superior to it, once called Magic, and that it might reach over the dead, so far as their experience on earth' but also in animal magnetism from any distance."

Arne grew queerly excited. "If Time and Space exist but in our thoughts, why should it not be true?" said he. "Macdonald's lover cries, 'That which has been is, and the Past can never cease. She is mine, and I shall find her—what matters it when, or where, or how?'" He sighed. "In Acapulco, a year ago, I saw a woman who has been before me ever since—the centre of the circling, changing, crude fancies that trouble me."

"Did you know her?" I asked.

"No, nor anything about her, not even her name. It is like a spell. I must paint her before anything else, but I cannot yet decide how. I feel sure she has played a tragic part in some life-drama."

"Swinburne's queen of panthers," I hinted.

"Yes. But I was not in love. Love I must forego. I am not a man with an income."

"I know you are not a nincompoop!" I said, always trying to change such themes by a jest. I could not tell him I knew a place which had the influence he talked of. I could not re-visit that house.

Soon after he told me he had begun his picture, but would not show it. He complained that one figure kept its back toward him. He worked on it till he fell ill. Even then he hid it. "Only a layer of passionography," he said.

I grew restless. I thought his mood affected mine. It was a torment as well as a puzzle to me that his whole talk should be of the influence of houses, rooms, even personal property that had known other owners. Once I asked him if he had anything like the brown coat Sheridan swore drew ill-luck to him.

"Sometimes I think," he answered, "it is this special brown paint artists prize which affects me. It is made from the best asphaltum, and that can be got only from Egyptian mummy-cloths. Very likely dust of the mummies is ground in it. I ought to feel their ill-will."

One day I went to Saucelito. In the still woods I forgot my unrest till coming to the stream where, as I suddenly remembered, Anson was found dead, a dread took me which I tried to lose by putting into rhyme. Turning my pockets at night, I crumpled the page I had written on, and threw it on the floor.

In uneasy sleep I dreamed I was again in Paris, not where I liked to recall being, but at "Bullier's," and in war-time. The bald, spectacled leader of the orchestra, leaning back, shamming sleep, while a dancing, stamping, screaming crowd wave tri-colored flags, and call for the "Chant du Depart." Three thousand voices in a rushing roar that makes the twenty thousand lights waver, in spasmodic but steady chorus:

> "Les departs—parts—parts!
> Les departs—parts—parts!
> Les departs—parts—parts!"

Roused, I supposed by passing rioters, I did not try to sleep again, but rose to write a letter for the early mail. As I struck a light I saw, smoothed out on the table, the wrinkled page I had cast aside. The ink was yet wet on two lines added to each verse. A chill crept over me as I read:

FOREST MURMURS.

Across the woodland bridge I pass,
  And sway its three long, narrow planks,
To mark how gliding waters glass
  Bright blossoms doubled ranks on ranks;
And how through tangle of the ferns
Floats incense from veiled flower-urns,
What would the babbling brook reveal?
What may these trembling depths conceal?

Dread secret of the dense woods, held
With restless shudders horror-spelled!

How shift the shadows of the wood,
   As if it tossed in troubled sleep!
Strange whispers, vaguely understood,
   Above, below, around me creep;
While in the sombre-shadowed stream
Great scarlet splashes far down gleam,
The odd-reflected, stately shapes
Of cardinals in crimson capes;
Not those—but spectral pools of blood
That stain these sands through strongest flood!

Like blare of trumpets through black nights—
   Or sunset clouds before a storm—
Are these red phantom water-sprites
   That mock me with fantastic form;
With flitting of the last year's bird
Fled ripples that its low flight stirred—
How should these rushing waters learn
Aught but the bend of this year's fern?
The lonesome wood, with bated breath,
Hints of a hidden blow—and death!

I could not stay alone. I ran to Arne's room. As I knocked, the
falling of some light thing within made me think he was stirring.
I went in. He sat in the moonlight, back to me before his easel.
The picture on it might be the one he kept secret. I would not
look. I went to his side and touched him. He had been dead for
hours! I turned the unseen canvas to the wall.

Next day I packed and planned to go East. I paid the landlady
not to send Arne's body to the morgue, and watched it that
night, when a sudden memory swept over me like a tidal wave.
There was a likeness in the room to one where I had before
watched the dead. Yes—there were the windows, there the
doors—just here stood the bed, in the same spot I sat. What
wildness was in the air of San Francisco!

To put such crazy thoughts to flight I would look at Arne's last
work. Yet I wavered, and more than once turned away after lay-

ing my hand on it. At last I snatched it, placed it on the easel and lighted the nearest gas-burner before looking at it. Then—great heavens!

How had this vision come to Arne? It was the scene where Felipa cursed us. Every detail of the room reproduced, even the gay birds on the wall-paper, and her flower-pots. The figures and faces of Dering and Volz were true as hers, and in the figure with averted face which Arne had said kept its back to him, I knew—myself! What strange insight had he gained by looking at Felipa? It was like the man who trembled before the unknown portrait of the Marquise de Brinvilliers.

How long I gazed at the picture I do not know. I heard, without heeding, the door-bell ring and steps along the hall. Voices. Some one looking at rooms. The landlady, saying this room was to let, but unwilling to show it, forced to own its last tenant lay there dead. This seemed no shock to the stranger.

"Well," said her shrill tones, "poor as he was he's better dead than alive!"

The door opened as a well-known voice cried: "My God! say not that! The nerve which hears is last to die—"

Volz stood before me! Awe-struck, we looked at each other in silence. Then he waved his hand to and fro before his eyes.

"Is this a dream?" he said. "There," pointing to the bed; "you"—to me; "the same words—the very room! Is it our fate?"

I pointed to the picture and to Arne. "The last work of this man, who thought it a fancy sketch?"

While Volz stood dumb and motionless before it, the landlady spoke:

"Then you know the place. Can you tell what ails it? There have been suicides in this room. No one prospers in the house. My cousin, who is a house-mover, warned me against taking it. He says before the store was put under it here it stood on Bush Street, and before that on Telegraph Hill."

Volz clutched my arm. "It is 'The Flying Dutchman' of a house!" he cried, and drew me fast down stairs and out into a dense fog which made the world seem a tale that was told, blotting out all but our two slanting forms, bent as by what poor Wynne would have called "a blast from hell," hurrying blindly away. I heard the voice of Volz as if from afar: "The magnetic man *is* a spirit!"

The Moonlit Road

Ambrose Bierce

I. Statement of Joel Hetman, Jr.

I am the most unfortunate of men. Rich, respected, fairly well educated and of sound health—with many other advantages usually valued by those having them and coveted by those who have them not—I sometimes think that I should be less unhappy if they had been denied me, for then the contrast between my outer and my inner life would not be continually demanding a painful attention. In the stress of privation and the need of effort I might sometimes forget the somber secret ever baffling the conjecture that it compels.

I am the only child of Joel and Julia Hetman. The one was a well-to-do country gentleman, the other a beautiful and accomplished woman to whom he was passionately attached with what I now know to have been a jealous and exacting devotion. The family home was a few miles from Nashville, Tennessee, a large, irregularly built dwelling of no particular order of architecture, a little way off the road, in a park of trees and shrubbery.

At the time of which I write I was nineteen years old, a student at Yale. One day I received a telegram from my father of such urgency that in compliance with its unexplained demand I left at once for home. At the railway station in Nashville a distant relative awaited me to apprise me of the reason for my recall: my mother had been barbarously murdered—why and by whom none could conjecture, but the circumstances were these:

My father had gone to Nashville, intending to return the next afternoon. Something prevented his accomplishing the business in hand, so he returned on the same night, arriving just before the dawn. In his testimony before the coroner he explained that having no latchkey and not caring to disturb the sleeping servants, he had, with no clearly defined intention, gone round to the rear of the house. As he turned an angle of the building, he heard a sound as of a door gently closed, and saw in the darkness, indistinctly, the figure of a man, which instantly disappeared among the trees of the lawn. A hasty pursuit and brief search of the grounds in the belief that the trespasser was some one secretly visiting a servant proving fruitless, he entered at the unlocked door and mounted the stairs to my mother's chamber. Its door was open, and stepping into black darkness he fell headlong over some heavy object on the floor. I may spare myself the details; it was my poor mother, dead of strangulation by human hands!

Nothing had been taken from the house, the servants had heard no sound, and excepting those terrible finger-marks upon the dead woman's throat—dear God! that I might forget them!—no trace of the assassin was ever found.

I gave up my studies and remained with my father, who, naturally, was greatly changed. Always of a sedate, taciturn disposition, he now fell into so deep a dejection that nothing could hold his attention, yet anything—a footfall, the sudden closing of a door—aroused in him a fitful interest; one might have called it an apprehension. At any small surprise of the senses he would start visibly and sometimes turn pale, then relapse into a melancholy apathy deeper than before. I suppose he was what is called a "nervous wreck." As to me, I was younger then than now—there is much in that. Youth is Gilead, in which is balm for every wound. Ah, that I might again dwell in that enchanted land! Unacquainted with grief, I knew not how to appraise my bereavement; I could not rightly estimate the strength of the stroke.

One night, a few months after the dreadful event, my father and I walked home from the city. The full moon was about three hours above the eastern horizon; the entire countryside had the

solemn stillness of a summer night; our footfalls and the cease-
less song of the katydids were the only sound aloof. Black shadows of bordering trees lay athwart the road, which, in the short
reaches between, gleamed a ghostly white. As we approached
the gate to our dwelling, whose front was in shadow, and in
which no light shone, my father suddenly stopped and clutched
my arm, saying, hardly above his breath:

"God! God! what is that?"

"I hear nothing," I replied.

"But see—see!" he said, pointing along the road, directly
ahead.

I said: "Nothing is there. Come, father, let us go in—you are
ill."

He had released my arm and was standing rigid and motionless in the center of the illuminated roadway, staring like one
bereft of sense. His face in the moonlight showed a pallor and
fixity inexpressibly distressing. I pulled gently at his sleeve, but
he had forgotten my existence. Presently he began to retire
backward, step by step, never for an instant removing his eyes
from what he saw, or thought he saw. I turned half round to follow, but stood irresolute. I do not recall any feeling of fear, unless a sudden chill was its physical manifestation. It seemed as if
an icy wind had touched my face and enfolded my body from
head to foot; I could feel the stir of it in my hair.

At that moment my attention was drawn to a light that suddenly streamed from an upper window of the house: one of the
servants, awakened by what mysterious premonition of evil who
can say, and in obedience to an impulse that she was never able
to name, had lit a lamp. When I turned to look for my father he
was gone, and in all the years that have passed no whisper of his
fate has come across the borderland of conjecture from the
realm of the unknown.

II. Statement of Caspar Grattan

To-day I am said to live; to-morrow, here in this room, will lie
a senseless shape of clay that all too long was I. If anyone lift the

cloth from the face of that unpleasant thing it will be in gratifica-
tion of a mere morbid curiosity. Some, doubtless, will go further
and inquire, "Who was he?" In this writing I supply the only
answer that I am able to make—Caspar Grattan. Surely, that
should be enough. The name has served my small need for more
than twenty years of a life of unknown length. True, I gave it to
myself, but lacking another I had the right. In this world one
must have a name; it prevents confusion, even when it does not
establish identity. Some, though, are known by numbers, which
also seem inadequate distinctions.

One day, for illustration, I was passing along a street of a city,
far from here, when I met two men in uniform, one of whom,
half pausing and looking curiously into my face, said to his companion, "That man looks like 767." Something in the number
seemed familiar and horrible. Moved by an uncontrollable impulse, I sprang into a side street and ran until I fell exhausted in
a country lane.

I have never forgotten that number, and always it comes to
memory attended by gibbering obscenity, peals of joyless laughter, the clang of iron doors. So I say a name, even if self-
bestowed, is better than a number. In the register of the potter's
field I shall soon have both. What wealth!

Of him who shall find this paper I must beg a little consideration. It is not the history of my life; the knowledge to write that
is denied me. This is only a record of broken and apparently
unrelated memories, some of them as distinct and sequent as
brilliant beads upon a thread, others remote and strange, having
the character of crimson dreams with interspaces blank and
black—witch-fires glowing still and red in a great desolation.

Standing upon the shore of eternity, I turn for a last look
landward over the course by which I came. There are twenty
years of footprints fairly distinct, the impressions of bleeding
feet. They lead through poverty and pain, devious and unsure,
as of one staggering beneath a burden—

Remote, unfriended, melancholy, slow.

Ah, the poet's prophecy of Me—how admirable, how dread-
fully admirable!

Backward beyond the beginning of this *via dolorosa*—this epic of suffering with episodes of sin—I see nothing clearly; it comes out of a cloud. I know that it spans only twenty years, yet I am an old man.

One does not remember one's birth—one has to be told. But with me it was different; life came to me full-handed and dowered me with all my faculties and powers. Of a previous existence I know no more than others, for all have stammering intimations that may be memories and may be dreams. I know only that my first consciousness was of maturity in body and mind—a consciousness accepted without surprise or conjecture. I merely found myself walking in a forest, half-clad, footsore, unutterably weary and hungry. Seeing a farmhouse, I approached and asked for food, which was given me by one who inquired my name. I did not know, yet knew that all had names. Greatly embarrassed, I retreated, and night coming on, lay down in the forest and slept.

The next day I entered a large town which I shall not name. Nor shall I recount further incidents of the life that is now to end—a life of wandering, always and everywhere haunted by an overmastering sense of crime in punishment of wrong and of terror in punishment of crime. Let me see if I can reduce it to narrative.

I seem once to have lived near a great city, a prosperous planter, married to a woman whom I loved and distrusted. We had, it sometimes seems, one child, a youth of brilliant parts and promise. He is at all times a vague figure, never clearly drawn, frequently altogether out of the picture.

One luckless evening it occurred to me to test my wife's fidelity in a vulgar, commonplace way familiar to everyone who has acquaintance with the literature of fact and fiction. I went to the city, telling my wife that I should be absent until the following afternoon. But I returned before daybreak and went to the rear of the house, purposing to enter by a door with which I had secretly so tampered that it would seem to lock, yet not actually fasten. As I approached it, I heard it gently open and close, and saw a man steal away into the darkness. With murder in my heart, I sprang after him, but he had vanished without even the bad luck of identification. Sometimes now I cannot even persuade myself that it was a human being.

Crazed with jealousy and rage, blind and bestial with all the elemental passions of insulted manhood, I entered the house and sprang up the stairs to the door of my wife's chamber. It was closed, but having tampered with its lock also, I easily entered and despite the black darkness soon stood by the side of her bed. My groping hands told me that although disarranged it was unoccupied.

"She is below," I thought, "and terrified by my entrance has evaded me in the darkness of the hall."

With the purpose of seeking her I turned to leave the room, but took a wrong direction—the right one! My foot struck her, cowering in a corner of the room. Instantly my hands were at her throat, stifling a shriek, my knees were upon her struggling body; and there in the darkness, without a word of accusation or reproach, I strangled her till she died!

There ends the dream. I have related it in the past tense, but the present would be the fitter form, for again and again the somber tragedy reenacts itself in my consciousness— over and over I lay the plan, I suffer the confirmation, I redress the wrong. Then all is blank; and afterward the rains beat against the grimy window-panes, or the snows fall upon my scant attire, the wheels rattle in the squalid streets where my life lies in poverty and mean employment. If there is ever sunshine I do not recall it; if there are birds they do not sing.

There is another dream, another vision of the night. I stand among the shadows in a moonlit road. I am aware of another presence, but whose I cannot rightly determine. In the shadow of a great dwelling I catch the gleam of white garments; then the figure of a woman confronts me in the road—my murdered wife! There is death in the face; there are marks upon the throat. The eyes are fixed on mine with an infinite gravity which is not reproach, nor hate, nor menace, nor anything less terrible than recognition. Before this awful apparition I retreat in terror—a terror that is upon me as I write. I can no longer rightly shape the words. See! they—

Now I am calm, but truly there is no more to tell: the incident ends where it began—in darkness and in doubt.

Yes, I am again in control of myself: "the captain of my soul." But that is not respite; it is another stage and phase of expiation. My penance, constant in degree, is mutable in kind: one of its variants is tranquility. After all, it is only a life-sentence. "To Hell for life"—that is a foolish penalty: the culprit chooses the duration of his punishment. To-day my term expires.

To each and all, the peace that was not mine.

III. Statement of the Late Julia Hetman, Through the Medium Bayrolles

I had retired early and fallen almost immediately into a peaceful sleep, from which I awoke with that indefinable sense of peril which is, I think, a common experience in that other, earlier life. Of its unmeaning character, too, I was entirely persuaded, yet that did not banish it. My husband, Joel Hetman, was away from home; the servants slept in another part of the house. But these were familiar conditions; they had never before distressed me. Nevertheless, the strange terror grew so insupportable that conquering my reluctance to move I sat up and lit the lamp at my bedside. Contrary to my expectation this gave me no relief; the light seemed rather an added danger, for I reflected that it would shine out under the door, disclosing my presence to whatever evil thing might lurk outside. You that are still in the flesh, subject to horrors of the imagination, think what a monstrous fear that must be which seeks in darkness security from malevolent existences of the night. That is to spring to close quarters with an unseen enemy—the strategy of despair!

Extinguishing the lamp I pulled the bedclothing about my head and lay trembling and silent, unable to shriek, forgetful to pray. In this pitiable state I must have lain for what you call hours—with us there are no hours, there is no time.

At last it came—a soft, irregular sound of footfalls on the stairs! They were slow, hesitant, uncertain, as of something that did not see its way; to my disordered reason all the more terrifying for that, as the approach of some blind and mindless malevolence to which is no appeal. I even thought that I must have left the hall lamp burning and the groping of this creature proved it a monster of the night. This was foolish and inconsistent with my previous dread of the light, but what would you have? Fear has no brains; it is an idiot. The dismal witness that it bears and the cowardly counsel that it whispers are unrelated. We know this well, we who have passed into the Realm of Terror, who skulk in eternal dusk among the scenes of our former lives, invisible even to ourselves and one another, yet hiding forlorn in lonely places; yearning for speech with our loved ones, yet dumb, and as fearful of them as they of us. Sometimes the disability is removed, the law suspended: by the deathless power of love or hate we break the spell—we are seen by those whom we would warn, console, or punish. What form we seem to them to bear we know not; we know only that we terrify even those whom we most wish to comfort, and from whom we most crave tenderness and sympathy.

Forgive, I pray you, this inconsequent digression by what was once a woman. You who consult us in this imperfect way—you do not understand. You ask foolish questions about things unknown and things forbidden. Much that we know and could impart in our speech is meaningless in yours. We must communicate with you through a stammering intelligence in that small fraction of our language that you yourselves can speak. You think that we are of another world. No, we have knowledge of no world but yours, though for us it holds no sunlight, no warmth, no music, no laughter, no song of birds, nor any companionship. O God! what a thing it is to be a ghost, cowering and shivering in an altered world, a prey to apprehension and despair!

No, I did not die of fright: the Thing turned and went away. I heard it go down the stairs, hurriedly, I thought, as if itself in sudden fear. Then I rose to call for help. Hardly had my shaking hand found the doorknob when—merciful heaven!—I heard it returning. Its footfalls as it remounted the stairs were rapid, heavy and loud; they shook the house. I fled to an angle of the

wall and crouched upon the floor. I tried to pray. I tried to call
the name of my dear husband. Then I heard the door thrown
open. There was an interval of unconsciousness, and when I
revived I felt a strangling clutch upon my throat—felt my arms
feebly beating against something that bore me backward—felt
my tongue thrusting itself from between my teeth! And then I
passed into this life.

No, I have no knowledge of what it was. The sum of what we
knew at death is the measure of what we know afterward of all
that went before. Of this existence we know many things, but no
new light falls upon any page of that; in memory is written all of
it that we can read. Here are no heights of truth overlooking the
confused landscape of that dubitable domain. We still dwell in
the Valley of the Shadow, lurk in its desolate places, peering
from brambles and thickets at its mad, malign inhabitants. How
should we have new knowledge of that fading past?

What I am about to relate happened on a night. We know
when it is night, for then you retire to your houses and we can
venture from our places of concealment to move unafraid about
our old homes, to look in at the windows, even to enter and gaze
upon your faces as you sleep. I had lingered long near the dwelling where I had been so cruelly changed to what I am, as we do
while any that we love or hate remain. Vainly I had sought some
method of manifestation, some way to make my continued existence and my great love and poignant pity understood by my
husband and son. Always if they slept they would wake, or if in
my desperation I dared approach them when they were awake,
would turn toward me the terrible eyes of the living, frightening
me by the glances that I sought from the purpose that I held.

On this night I had searched for them without success, fear-
ing to find them; they were nowhere in the house, nor about the
moonlit lawn. For, although the sun is lost to us forever, the
moon, full-orbed or slender, remains to us. Sometimes it shines
by night, sometimes by day, but always it rises and sets, as in that
other life.

I left the lawn and moved in the white light and silence along
the road, aimless and sorrowing. Suddenly I heard the voice of
my poor husband in exclamations of astonishment, with that of

my son in reassurance and dissuasion; and there by the shadow
of a group of trees they stood—near, so near! Their faces were
toward me, the eyes of the elder man fixed upon mine. He saw
me—at last, at last, he saw me! In the consciousness of that, my
terror fled as a cruel dream. The death-spell was broken: Love
had conquered Law! Mad with exultation I shouted—I *must*
have shouted, "He sees, he sees: he will understand!" Then,
controlling myself, I moved forward, smiling and consciously
beautiful, to offer myself to his arms, to comfort him with en-
dearments, and, with my son's hand in mine, to speak words that
should restore the broken bonds between the living and the
dead.

Alas! alas! his face went white with fear, his eyes were as those
of a hunted animal. He backed away from me, as I advanced,
and at last turned and fled into the wood—whither, it is not
given to me to know.

To my poor boy, left doubly desolate, I have never been able
to impart a sense of my presence. Soon he, too, must pass to this
Life Invisible and be lost to me forever.

The Conquering Will

Harriet Prescott Spofford

There was no doubt that he was a masterful man. He ruled everyone on shore as he had ruled everyone at sea. His wife had never meant to marry him; but she did. When the fleet went into Asiatic waters she had declared she would not follow; but she did. When the child died she had wished to clothe herself in black; but she didn't. Wherever he was Captain Gilbert's will was the only will. Whenever she resisted him she felt like a wave shattering itself to foam against a rock in the mid-seas.

Sometimes she wondered if there were any hypnotic quality about him. Her mother had said she was possessed. But she really knew better. So far as she was concerned, she knew that the reason the Captain had his own way was simply because she loved him. And so far as everyone else was concerned, she was glad he did have his own way.

She had at first admired Captain Gilbert more than she loved him—admired his superb and stalwart figure of the large, heroic type; his Greek head, ringed over with short, yellow curls; his bold features, his eyes, that had in them the blue of the skies but also the glance of the eagle; his commanding air. And moreover, his manner, when he chose, had an inexpressible charm that carried all before it. No one dared contend with him—and then no one wished to do so. No wonder he was a masterful man. He was never resisted; and the habit had become nature.

Indeed, his wife hardly knew, after a while, when she had a wish other than her husband's. It is true she thought blue more becoming, but he liked to see her in pink, and she always went about like a lovely blush rose. It was also true that there had been a time when she cared about dancing; but Captain Gilbert would not endure the familiarity of the waltz, and so she never waltzed—when Captain Gilbert was looking. It is true she enjoyed the theatre; but Captain Gilbert prepared to go to church, and she went to church, and felt afterward very righteous and content.

But on the other hand, she loved riding; and the Captain kept her provided with a mount that was the envy of all the other women in the field. He himself rode like a centaur, and she never admired him more than in the saddle. She was fond of sea bathing, and he took for her every Summer a little place by the seaside, and none of the mer-people ever disported themselves with more sense of possession of the deep sea caves than they did. She would have enjoyed land travel; but Captain Gilbert preferred seafaring, so that she never saw any other world than the world of waters. She recovered from her seasickness after a few days, and then took the keenest pleasure in the bounding and soaring from billow to billow, as if she were a seagull sitting on the wave or flying over it. Alone, too, in the vast region of sunlit sky and sea, or when night carried space into dark infinity, or when they rode triumphant over storm, and every man on the yacht was a machine moved by the Captain's will, he seemed to her each time a more positive potency than before.

But if the Captain had his own way in the outside things of life his way was usually right. It was because he said that it simply should be done that the salary of Dr. Saintly was raised to living limit. It was he who, when the rest of the town where he lived when off duty frowned down an embezzling bank officer who had served his term in prison, insisted that the man should be helped to work and to respect again. It was he who brought home a forsaken woman of the place, and required civility for her so long as she did right. "If there is one thing certain," said the Captain, "it is that love is the best thing in the world. And I mean, Fanny, that you and I shall be as much at one with this great spirit filling the universe as holding the helpful hand to all can make us."

Perhaps, however, the Captain would not have carried things so before him if all his little world had not known of certain splendid achievements in the sea fights, giving him, in a measure, the right to his own way, giving him also the wounds that enforced his retirement and shortened his life. Wherever they were, people turned to look at him and to approve, and it gratified Mrs. Gilbert as much as when they turned to look at her— she was the woman whom this wonder among men had chosen out of all the women on the earth. But they always found it well worth their while to look at her. "The Lord may have thought He made the most beautiful thing possible when he made this rose," the Captain said to her once, stooping to a wayside bramble, "but I think He made the most beautiful thing when He made a woman. And you are a woman and a rose, too!"

"You make me blush," said Mrs. Gilbert; "and here, on the street!" They were going home from church across the fields. "Yes, I should wonder why I was given such a wife if it were not that she has such a husband," he added, laughing. And when Captain Gilbert laughed Mrs. Gilbert felt that the world went well, and she laughed, too. And she never looked prettier than when her red lips curved apart over the rice-pearl teeth, and disclosed ravishing little dimples in either velvet cheek.

But possibly Captain Gilbert could not have so completely dominated his wife if she had not felt in him a fine superiority to the small things of life and had not had a fearsome joy in sometimes following his thought out into what he called the Fourth Dimension. "This earth and its envelopings are beautiful," he said, "but when I remember that there are colors we cannot see, sounds too fine for our ears, I know we are only spelling the alphabet of all we shall find—out there. Nights when I have walked the deck, virtually alone, and have seen the stars sentinelling the great courts of space beyond space, I have felt sure they were made for no idleness—that there were reasons for their being; and in some form or other we shall tread their mazes and come out upon the reason for all things." She did not entirely understand him; but it may be that she admired him all the more on that account.

But there was one thing in which Captain Gilbert failed to

have his own way. One thing?—two things! He could not hinder men from staring at Mrs. Gilbert, and he could not hinder Mrs. Gilbert from showing—in the mildest mannered way—that she was conscious of the gaze and possibly not unpleased. "I am sure I can't help their looking at me," she pouted, turning away from the window.

"You can help making eyes at them!" he replied.

"Captain Gilbert! What language!"

"Suiting the word to the action."

"And as if I could help my eyes!" the tears making them like live jewels.

"I know they're beautiful eyes!" said the Captain, remorsefully. "But they're my eyes! They don't belong to every fool going by."

"I never knew such a tyrant! You're like the man in the 'Morte d'Arthur' who wanted his wife hideous before the court, but beautiful when alone with him."

"Precisely," said Captain Gilbert, laughing. "And I wish we had those days back—days when a man owned his wife, like any other precious thing, till a stronger took her——"

"It's always a stronger that takes her, one way or another."

"He'll be stronger than the laws of the universe if he takes you, that's all," said the Captain, lifting her in his arms and walking down the room with her as if she had been a child; "for by all the laws of the universe you are mine! And mine you will be forever, alive or dead!" And, to her troubled amazement, he was sobbing. "Fanny," he cried, "if you married another man after I died—after I died—if it were in the farthest star of the farthest heavens I should come back and punish him!"

"Oh!" cried Mrs. Gilbert. Then, through her own tears: "Why not leave that to me?"

Mrs. Gilbert was one of the women with whom this brigand-like way of making love is effective. And when, shortly afterward, Captain Gilbert betook himself to the farthest star and left her widowed, she missed the excitations and the raptures and the sense of being adored, even if tyrannised over; and she was not at all consoled by the fact that she looked charming in black, which there was no one now to forbid her.

But a little time works wonders. Mrs. Gilbert one day woke to the fact that she was free, with no one to say her nay; free as a bird in the air. At least, she would have been free if she had had any money to be free with. But Captain Gilbert's half-pay had stopped with his breath, and there was a delay about pension business and about other money, during which Mrs. Gilbert found herself so hard pressed as to be almost in despair about ways and means. And when Mr. Mercer proposed that she share a million with him, she was in more minds than one about accepting the idea, and she actually asked for time. Captain Gilbert, she reasoned, would never want her to be put about this way for money—her mourning was positively shabby. And she thought of it very seriously—it might do—Mr. Mercer was a gentleman. But when he called for his reply she came down, white to her lips, so white that she was ghastly, and said it was impossible.

It was the same way with Dr. Vaughn. It seemed so eminently respectable, so altogether what the gossips would have called too good a chance to lose, she would be so well cared for—and she was just on the point of yielding. But after a night's reflection she wrote that it was out of the question, her hand shaking so that her script looked like a field of wheat bowed in the wind.

And after that she went for a while so sedately, so demurely, so entirely as the fond and faithful widow should, that who but the rector should be acknowledging her fascination? And she knew in her heart that she would be a capital wife for a clergyman, that she might have the parish under her little thumb— she, a helpmeet better than the best! She said to herself it was a pity if she could not do as she pleased; she smiled on him; she came near giving him her hand to kiss in token of the ring it might wear presently. And then she sent him in his turn the hurried note that laid all hope low.

Captain Gilbert had been lost to the breathing world almost half a dozen years, and his wife was as much like a lovely blooming rose as ever, when John Mowbray crossed her path. And he not only crossed it, but he obstructed it. The years had passed quietly; her affairs had adjusted themselves; although she could have spent more, she was no longer in need of money. She had almost forgotten Mr. Mercer and his successors in misfortune. And John Mowbray was a man of an unfamiliar and engaging type. He loved music, the opera, Wagner; she had never had enough of music in her life. He was more or less of a student, acquainted with books, a haunter of libraries; it seemed to her that he held the gates open to a fair and inviting plaisance. Well born and well bred, he had the air, without having traveled much, of knowing men and manners and the world; but to travel was his intention—and she saw the gates open to a life of infinitely wider interest than this small daily round. He was on the sunny side, as she was; with a most agreeable personality, with a delightful courtesy, and as she began to suspect, with a sincere affection for herself.

He had come to see her, that snowy night, through all the storm, bringing her an armful of great red roses. There was something very pleasant about his coming in; it gave her a feeling of protection, emphasized the idea of shelter. She heaped the fire and presently the ruddy flames danced over the room and the flowers, and over the pretty woman disposing them in their bowls and jars, till it all seemed to John Mowbray, still warming his hands at the blaze, the ideal of a home. What a place to come to every night! What a place never to go away from! What a dream!

She knew what was coming very well. Some subtle instinct made her try to fortify herself against it. She sat down behind a table and leaned forward, rearranging with twinkling fingers the roses in the vase that nearly hid her face. And then in another moment he was half-kneeling beside her, and he was murmuring, "Fanny, Fanny! let it be real—this dream. I am dreaming! Tell me not to wake! Say, dear, say that you love me!" And before she knew it the strong arms were about her, and she was hiding her face on his shoulder.

What an evening of deep, serene happiness it was! Side by side they looked into the future, and its glow shed a light over them. "It is too much, too much happiness," she said, as they parted. "Something will hinder. I—I shall not be allowed——" And she grew very pale.

"Thank heaven, there is no one to allow or disallow," said John Mowbray. "You are not now the young girl to be dominated, but the woman whose beautiful nature has developed the power to choose, and I am crowned and blessed by your choice!"

"I am afraid—I am afraid——" she said, as he bade her goodnight.

"Of what, my love?" he asked her.

"Oh, of nothing, of nothing, so long as you are here!" she said, clinging to him more closely.

And "I am afraid!" she repeated again, as she went upstairs, though trembling with joy.

She had half a mind to sit up that night and not go to sleep at all. She dropped the curtain quickly as she saw the stars sparkling in the sky from which the snow clouds were already blowing away. The thought of that farthest star would come back and make her shiver. But she was tired out with emotion—with hope and joy and fear—and she fell asleep in the big armchair just as Captain Gilbert came into the room, strong, stalwart, mighty, and looking like the hero of some Viking legend.

The wind had blown a fine color into his face; his curls were sprayed with the melted snow, his eyes were as dazzlingly blue as a noonday sky. "I have come a long way to see you, my wife," he said, and the old familiar tone rang sweetly through all the chambers of her heart. "And I never saw you lovelier. How dear, how beautiful you are! How long we have belonged to each other! Do you remember the night by the gate under the honeysuckles, when you reached out your hand in the dark, uncertain if I was there, and suddenly I clasped it? Dear hand! I have never, never let it go! I never will! I saw a sapphire as blue as Lyra on my way here. I will have it for this little hand—only the hand is so slight, and the sapphire is so heavy. How quiet it is here—it is always quiet about you, my wife—you are so serene, and your husband is so stormy! Here is the smell of roses that always hovers about you—oh, how sweet, how sweet you are! Up, and let me sit down and hold you in my arms, you featherweight! There, rest the dear head. What makes you shiver so? It is warm. I am here—your husband. Warm? I am warm to my marrow, being with you, holding you, living again the delicious life we used to live. Oh, what life will be again with you, most perfect of women, most faithful of wives! I have been so cold, so far off, so longing for you! What ways I have traversed, what have I encountered, just for this hour! And it is worth it all. There are great things in store for us, little woman. Lean your cheek on mine—how velvet soft, how warm—you are mine, mine, mine——"

She heard, she remembered no more, but woke with the sun pouring into the window and streaming over her through the crimson warmth of the geraniums, and all her heart expanded with the old affection.

Suffused still with the mood of the night, she made her toilette and went down, thoughtless, reckless, almost gay—and met John Mowbray coming through the door, his sleigh-bells still jangling at the gate—he had come to take her sleighing. But at the first sight of his eager, expectant face she stopped. All her bloom fell away, she shook like a leaf; and he sprang forward, thinking she was about to fall. "No, no, no!" she cried. "Forget last night! Forget everything! It is impossible! It is out of the question. I am Captain Gilbert's wife still. Captain Gilbert—will not—will not allow it."

And then she dropped fainting into his arms.

She did not, however, lose consciousness entirely. She knew very well that John Mowbray was covering her face with kisses while carrying her to the sofa. The blood surged over her forehead in a conviction of guilt, and then she turned her face to the wall.

"What does this mean?" cried John Mowbray.

"He—he has been here," she faltered.

"Who has been here?" he demanded.

"Captain Gilbert."

"What—what is it you say?" he exclaimed, springing to his feet.

"He was here last night—I am not out of my head. Oh, no, I am not beside myself! He has been here before—the same way—whenever—— Oh, see how unworthy I am!"

And she covered her face with her hands.

He seated himself on the edge of the sofa and took down the two hands, holding them in his own.

"You mean you dreamed last night," he said.

"Oh, no, no! Dreamed? Oh, it was too real! Dreamed? I don't know—Do you suppose it could be just a dream? Always the same dream, only with differences? And he so all he used to be when he was best and tenderest, making me feel that he was my husband forever and ever, that I—— Oh, you see I love him still!"

"I should be ashamed of you if you didn't!" said John Mowbray, sternly. "But you love me, too! You know you do!"

"How can I love two men at once?" cried Fanny.

"You don't. One of us is an angel in heaven. I shall never have the least jealousy of your affection for him. You and I are on the earth. And when we are as angels in heaven we shall never marry or be given in marriage. Come, you need the air. Where is your thick cloak, your furs, a hood? Here is the sleigh at the gate. We will drive up the river. On the way we will stop at the rectory——"

"But—but——"

"Not a but about it. I shall have the right then to shield my wife in her dreams and from her dreams. And I don't believe anyone will come where I am to challenge him!" And Fanny Gilbert had found again the power that surrounded her like a fortress and the will that was perhaps as strong as Captain Gilbert's will.

It seemed that John Mowbray must have been right. After the sleigh ride and the brief ceremony at the rector's he took his wife away and into a round of gaieties that gave her no time to reflect. And then came the voyage overseas and the travel that should so fill thought and memory as to leave no room for the past. Under all the novelty and pleasure and excitement, and Mr. Mowbray's constant presence and care, she became a new creature. Blooming with fresh being, enlarged to the larger life, her prettiness became beauty, her liveliness sparkling, and her sweetness, to John Mowbray, enchanting. His pride in her was equal to his passion. It was with pleasure that he saw men's eyes follow her, and women's, too. When she rode, her trim grace and dauntless spirit hung afterward before his own eyes, as if he had seen Dian and her train pass by. At the opera, as she stood a moment, easy, gracious, dropping off her cloak and revealing a dazzle of jewels and gleaming tissues, of eyes like jewels, too, of roses, cream and blush, and of smiles, and when he saw her breathless, rapt in the music and the play, he felt a joy of possession that was like a pain; but with the emotion came a vague fear of its evanescence.

The premonition was not felt at once, however. There was a season of unassailed rapture before he noticed that Mrs. Mowbray had become very restless, seeking perpetually some new object, and so absent-minded that he sometimes spoke twice or thrice before she heard him. Glowing with colour and life and happiness in the evening, in the morning she would be as pale and sad and languid as if she had danced all night with witches, so that he wondered if she slept at all. She ate almost nothing, started at every sound, laughed nervously at nothing, and her eyes filled with tears likewise at nothing. She began to grow very thin. Suddenly he perceived that she was wasting away before his eyes.

Like Asa of old, Mr. Mowbray had recourse to the physicians, and that without loss of time. But as she persisted that nothing ailed her, and had no symptoms to present other than those they saw, they could do little beyond administering tonics, which were as idle as spring water.

"My dear one," he said to her at least, "tell me—what is it? There is something you hide from me. My precious one, my wife, tell me; are you unhappy?"

"Oh, yes, yes, yes!" she cried, lifting her hands passionately. "I am wretched! I am wretched!"

He turned as white as she. "Fanny!" he cried.

"Oh, not the way you think!" she cried. "But, oh! I cannot tell you!"

He sat down beside her and took her in his arms. "Whatever it is, you must tell me," he said gently. "You are my one thought in life. I can do nothing to serve you if I am in the dark."

"It is I!—It is I who am in the dark!" she wept.

"Tell me what you mean, my darling," he urged her.

"I—I don't know if I am your darling!" she exclaimed. "I don't know who I am!"

"Fanny, dearest, I don't understand. Be reasonable, my little wife, let me know."

"Am I your wife, or am I his?"

"Dearest?"

"I don't know. He comes—he has come every night——"

He clasped her convulsively in his arms. "I live a double life," she said, moving herself feebly yet resistingly. "All day I am yours. All night I am his!"

"Dear child! dear little one! You are ill. You are letting a dream——"

"It is not like any dream——"

"But, dream or not, it is when all your powers are submerged in sleep, when you are not fully yourself——"

"Oh, but in the daylight——"

"Yes, in the daylight, when you are you, then—then you are only mine!"

"I am afraid—I am afraid," she sighed. "Every night when I go to sleep—I don't know what may happen. Some night, some night, he will take me!" And her voice died to a whisper.

"Never!" he cried. "Never, while I am beside you."

At that moment, as she lay in his arms, they both were possessed by a great shuddering and fear. It was dark all about them, as if it were already night. A wind seemed to fill the room and then to hold its breath, a wind that might have been blowing from nowhere to nowhere, but hanging now still and chill.

"Hold me, hold me fast, John!" she murmured. "He has come for me!" Her arms fell, her head drooped nerveless over his arm. "Oh, John, I love——"

The lips, wide open, said no more. And in the instant of that last sigh John Mowbray knew, by some other than the sense of sight, that Captain Gilbert, masterful, laughing, debonair, towered like a shaft of sunlight before him.

"You are wronged of nothing," a voice that had no sound was ringing in his ears. "The bindweed falls that leans upon a straw. You would have made her happy if you might. But you could not conquer the unconquerable will. And I have come for my own!"

"As a destroying force—destroying joy, destroying life!" cried John Mowbray. "And I defy you! For though you carry her beyond your farthest star, she loves me best, and I will follow you!"

"Spirit to spirit, flesh to flesh, John Mowbray. She is mine!"

There was a flutter of the purple-veined eyelids in the face that had fallen from his arm, a tremor of the lips, a long, slow, bubbling sigh. Slipping, slipping from his grasp, a lifeless heap lay on the floor—and by all avenues through which the viewless thing may reach the soul, John Mowbray saw Captain Gilbert fading into an intenser light, his wife held close beside him. And then, though it was broad noonday, the world was black and still.

The Shadows on the Wall

Mary E. Wilkins Freeman

"Henry had words with Edward in the study the night before Edward died," said Caroline Glynn.

She was elderly, tall, and harshly thin, with a hard colourlessness of face. She spoke not with acrimony, but with grave severity. Rebecca Ann Glynn, younger, stouter and rosy of face between her crinkling puffs of gray hair, gasped, by way of assent. She sat in a wide flounce of black silk in the corner of the sofa, and rolled terrified eyes from her sister Caroline to her sister Mrs. Stephen Brigham, who had been Emma Glynn, the one beauty of the family. She was beautiful still, with a large, splendid, full-blown beauty; she filled a great rocking-chair with her superb bulk of femininity, and swayed gently back and forth, her black silks whispering and her black frills fluttering. Even the shock of death (for her brother Edward lay dead in the house,) could not disturb her outward serenity of demeanour. She was grieved over the loss of her brother: he had been the youngest, and she had been fond of him, but never had Emma Brigham lost sight of her own importance amidst the waters of tribulation. She was always awake to the consciousness of her own stability in the midst of vicissitudes and the splendour of her permanent bearing.

But even her expression of masterly placidity changed before her sister Caroline's announcement and her sister Rebecca Ann's gasp of terror and distress in response.

"I think Henry might have controlled his temper, when poor Edward was so near his end," said she with an asperity which disturbed slightly the roseate curves of her beautiful mouth.

"Of course he did not *know*," murmured Rebecca Ann in a faint tone strangely out of keeping with her appearance.

One involuntarily looked again to be sure that such a feeble pipe came from that full-swelling chest.

"Of course he did not know it," said Caroline quickly. She turned on her sister with a strange sharp look of suspicion. "How could he have known it?" said she. Then she shrank as if from the other's possible answer. "Of course you and I both know he could not," said she conclusively, but her pale face was paler than it had been before.

Rebecca gasped again. The married sister, Mrs. Emma Brigham, was now sitting up straight in her chair; she had ceased rocking, and was eyeing them both intently with a sudden accentuation of family likeness in her face. Given one common intensity of emotion and similar lines showed forth, and the three sisters of one race were evident.

"What do you mean?" said she impartially to them both. Then she, too, seemed to shrink before a possible answer. She even laughed an evasive sort of laugh. "I guess you don't mean anything," said she, but her face wore still the expression of shrinking horror.

"Nobody means anything," said Caroline firmly. She rose and crossed the room toward the door with grim decisiveness.

"Where are you going?" asked Mrs. Brigham.

"I have something to see to," replied Caroline, and the others at once knew by her tone that she had some solemn and sad duty to perform in the chamber of death.

"Oh," said Mrs. Brigham.

After the door had closed behind Caroline, she turned to Rebecca.

"Did Henry have many words with him?" she asked.

"They were talking very loud," replied Rebecca evasively, yet with an answering gleam of ready response to the other's curiosity in the quick lift of her soft blue eyes.

Mrs. Brigham looked at her. She had not resumed rocking. She still sat up straight with a slight knitting of intensity on her fair forehead, between the pretty rippling curves of her auburn hair.

"Did you—hear anything?" she asked in a low voice with a glance toward the door.

"I was just across the hall in the south parlour, and that door was open and this door ajar," replied Rebecca with a slight flush.

"Then you must have——"

"I couldn't help it."

"Everything?"

"Most of it."

"What was it?"

"The old story."

"I suppose Henry was mad, as he always was, because Edward was living on here for nothing, when he had wasted all the money father left him."

Rebecca nodded with a fearful glance at the door.

When Emma spoke again her voice was still more hushed. "I know how he felt," said she. "He had always been so prudent himself, and worked hard at his profession, and there Edward had never done anything but spend, and it must have looked to him as if Edward was living at his expense, but he wasn't."

"No, he wasn't."

"It was the way father left the property—that all the children should have a home here—and he left money enough to buy the food and all if we had all come home."

"Yes."

"And Edward had a right here according to the terms of father's will, and Henry ought to have remembered it."

"Yes, he ought."

"Did he say hard things?"

"Pretty hard from what I heard."

"What?"

"I heard him tell Edward that he had no business here at all, and he thought he had better go away."

"What did Edward say?"

"That he would stay here as long as he lived and afterward, too, if he was a mind to, and he would like to see Henry get him out; and then——"

"What?"

"Then he laughed."

"What did Henry say."

"I didn't hear him say anything, but——"

"But what?"

"I saw him when he came out of this room."

"He looked mad?"

"You've seen him when he looked so."

Emma nodded; the expression of horror on her face had deepened.

"Do you remember that time he killed the cat because she had scratched him?"

"Yes. Don't!"

Then Caroline re-entered the room. She went up to the stove in which a wood fire was burning—it was a cold, gloomy day of fall—and she warmed her hands, which were reddened from recent washing in cold water.

Mrs. Brigham looked at her and hesitated. She glanced at the door, which was still ajar, as it did not easily shut, being still swollen with the damp weather of the summer. She rose and pushed it together with a sharp thud which jarred the house. Rebecca started painfully with a half exclamation. Caroline looked at her disapprovingly.

"It is time you controlled your nerves, Rebecca," said she.

"I can't help it," replied Rebecca with almost a wail. "I am nervous. There's enough to make me so, the Lord knows."

"What do you mean by that?" asked Caroline with her old air of sharp suspicion, and something between challenge and dread of its being met.

Rebecca shrank.

"Nothing," said she.

"Then I wouldn't keep speaking in such a fashion."

Emma, returning from the closed door, said imperiously that it ought to be fixed, it shut so hard.

"It will shrink enough after we have had the fire a few days," replied Caroline. "If anything is done to it it will be too small; there will be a crack at the sill."

"I think Henry ought to be ashamed of himself for talking as he did to Edward," said Mrs. Brigham abruptly, but in an almost inaudible voice.

"Hush!" said Caroline, with a glance of actual fear at the closed door.

"Nobody can hear with the door shut."

"He must have heard it shut, and——"

"Well, I can say what I want to before he comes down, and I am not afraid of him."

"I don't know who is afraid of him! What reason is there for anybody to be afraid of Henry?" demanded Caroline.

Mrs. Brigham trembled before her sister's look. Rebecca gasped again. "There isn't any reason, of course. Why should there be?"

"I wouldn't speak so, then. Somebody might overhear you and think it was queer. Miranda Joy is in the south parlour sewing, you know."

"I thought she went upstairs to stitch on the machine."

"She did, but she has come down again."

"Well, she can't hear."

"I say again I think Henry ought to be ashamed of himself. I shouldn't think he'd ever get over it, having words with poor Edward the very night before he died. Edward was enough sight better disposition than Henry, with all his faults. I always thought a great deal of poor Edward, myself."

Mrs. Brigham passed a large fluff of handkerchief across her eyes; Rebecca sobbed outright.

"Rebecca," said Caroline admonishingly, keeping her mouth stiff and swallowing determinately.

"I never heard him speak a cross word, unless he spoke cross to Henry that last night. I don't know, but he did from what Rebecca overheard," said Emma.

"Not so much cross as sort of soft, and sweet, and aggravating," sniffled Rebecca.

"He never raised his voice," said Caroline; "but he had his way."

"He had a right to in this case."

"Yes, he did."

"He had as much of a right here as Henry," sobbed Rebecca, "and now he's gone, and he will never be in this home that poor father left him and the rest of us again."

"What do you really think ailed Edward?" asked Emma in hardly more than a whisper. She did not look at her sister.

Caroline sat down in a nearby armchair, and clutched the arms convulsively until her thin knuckles whitened.

"I told you," said she.

Rebecca held her handkerchief over her mouth, and looked at them above it with terrified, streaming eyes.

"I know you said that he had terrible pains in his stomach, and had spasms, but what do you think made him have them?"

"Henry called it gastric trouble. You know Edward has always had dyspepsia."

Mrs. Brigham hesitated a moment. "Was there any talk of an—examination?" said she.

Then Caroline turned on her fiercely.

"No," said she in a terrible voice. "No."

The three sisters' souls seemed to meet on one common ground of terrified understanding through their eyes. The old-fashioned latch of the door was heard to rattle, and a push from without made the door shake ineffectually. "It's Henry," Rebecca sighed rather than whispered. Mrs. Brigham settled herself after a noiseless rush across the floor into her rocking-chair again, and was swaying back and forth with her head comfortably leaning back, when the door at last yielded and Henry Glynn entered. He cast a covertly sharp, comprehensive glance at Mrs. Brigham with her elaborate calm; at Rebecca quietly huddled in the corner of the sofa with her handkerchief to her face and only one small reddened ear as attentive as a dog's uncovered and revealing her alertness for his presence; at Caroline sitting with a strained composure in her armchair by the stove. She met his eyes quite firmly with a look of inscrutable fear, and defiance of the fear and of him.

Henry Glynn looked more like this sister than the others. Both had the same hard delicacy of form and feature, both were tall and almost emaciated, both had a sparse growth of gray blond hair far back from high intellectual foreheads, both had an almost noble aquilinity of feature. They confronted each other with the pitiless immovability of two statues in whose marble lineaments emotions were fixed for all eternity.

Then Henry Glynn smiled and the smile transformed his face. He looked suddenly years younger, and an almost boyish reckless-ness and irresolution appeared in his face. He flung himself into a chair with a gesture which was bewildering from its incongruity with his general appearance. He leaned his head back, flung one leg over the other, and looked laughingly at Mrs. Brigham.

"I declare, Emma, you grow younger every year," he said.

She flushed a little, and her placid mouth widened at the corners. She was susceptible to praise.

"Our thoughts to-day ought to belong to the one of us who will *never* grow older," said Caroline in a hard voice.

Henry looked at her, still smiling. "Of course, we none of us forget that," said he, in a deep, gentle voice, "but we have to speak to the living, Caroline, and I have not seen Emma for a long time, and the living are as dear as the dead."

"Not to me," said Caroline.

She rose, and went abruptly out of the room again. Rebecca also rose and hurried after her, sobbing loudly.

Henry looked slowly after them.

"Caroline is completely unstrung," said he.

Mrs. Brigham rocked. A confidence in him inspired by his manner was stealing over her. Out of that confidence she spoke quite easily and naturally.

"His death was very sudden," said she.

Henry's eyelids quivered slightly but his gaze was unswerving.

"Yes," said he; "it was very sudden. He was sick only a few hours."

"What did you call it?"

"Gastric."

"You did not think of an examination?"

"There was no need. I am perfectly certain as to the cause of his death."

Suddenly Mrs. Brigham felt a creep as of some live horror over her very soul. Her flesh prickled with cold, before an inflection of his voice. She rose, tottering on weak knees.

"Where are you going?" asked Henry in a strange, breathless voice.

Mrs. Brigham said something incoherent about some sewing which she had to do, some black for the funeral, and was out of the room. She went up to the front chamber which she occupied. Caroline was there. She went close to her and took her hands, and the two sisters looked at each other.

"Don't speak, don't, I won't have it!" said Caroline finally in an awful whisper.

"I won't," replied Emma.

That afternoon the three sisters were in the study, the large front room on the ground floor across the hall from the south parlour, when the dusk deepened.

Mrs. Brigham was hemming some black material. She sat close to the west window for the waning light. At last she laid her work on her lap.

"It's no use, I cannot see to sew another stitch until we have a light," said she.

Caroline, who was writing some letters at the table, turned to Rebecca, in her usual place on the sofa.

"Rebecca, you had better get a lamp," she said.

Rebecca started up; even in the dusk her face showed her agitation.

"It doesn't seem to me that we need a lamp quite yet," she said in a piteous, pleading voice like a child's.

"Yes, we do," returned Mrs. Brigham peremptorily. "We must have a light. I must finish this to-night or I can't go to the funeral, and I can't see to sew another stitch."

"Caroline can see to write letters, and she is farther from the window than you are," said Rebecca.

"Are you trying to save kerosene or are you lazy, Rebecca Glynn?" cried Mrs. Brigham. "I can go and get the light myself, but I have this work all in my lap."

Caroline's pen stopped scratching.

"Rebecca, we must have the light," said she.

"Had we better have it in here?" asked Rebecca weakly.

"Of course! Why not?" cried Caroline sternly.

"I am sure I don't want to take my sewing into the other

room, when it is all cleaned up for to-morrow," said Mrs. Brigham.

"Why, I never heard such a to-do about lighting a lamp."

Rebecca rose and left the room. Presently she entered with a lamp—a large one with a white porcelain shade. She set it on a table, an old-fashioned card-table which was placed against the opposite wall from the window. That wall was clear of bookcases and books, which were only on three sides of the room. That opposite wall was taken up with three doors, the one small space being occupied by the table. Above the table on the old-fashioned paper, of a white satin gloss, traversed by an indeterminate green scroll, hung quite high a small gilt and black-framed ivory miniature taken in her girlhood of the mother of the family. When the lamp was set on the table beneath it, the tiny pretty face painted on the ivory seemed to gleam out with a look of intelligence.

"What have you put that lamp over there for?" asked Mrs. Brigham, with more of impatience than her voice usually revealed. "Why didn't you set it in the hall and have done with it. Neither Caroline nor I can see if it is on that table."

"I thought perhaps you would move," replied Rebecca hoarsely.

"If I do move, we can't both sit at that table. Caroline has her paper all spread around. Why don't you set the lamp on the study table in the middle of the room, then we can both see?"

Rebecca hesitated. Her face was very pale. She looked with an appeal that was fairly agonizing at her sister Caroline.

"Why don't you put the lamp on this table, as she says?" asked Caroline, almost fiercely. "Why do you act so, Rebecca?"

"I should think you *would* ask her that," said Mrs. Brigham. "She doesn't act like herself at all."

Rebecca took the lamp and set it on the table in the middle of the room without another word. Then she turned her back upon it quickly and seated herself on the sofa, and placed a hand over her eyes as if to shade them, and remained so.

"Does the light hurt your eyes, and is that the reason why you didn't want the lamp?" asked Mrs. Brigham kindly.

"I always like to sit in the dark," replied Rebecca chokingly.

Then she snatched her handkerchief hastily from her pocket and began to weep. Caroline continued to write, Mrs. Brigham to sew.

Suddenly Mrs. Brigham as she sewed glanced at the opposite wall. The glance became a steady stare. She looked intently, her work suspended in her hands. Then she looked away again and took a few more stitches, then she looked again, and again turned to her task. At last she laid her work in her lap and stared concentratedly. She looked from the wall around the room, taking note of the various objects; she looked at the wall long and intently. Then she turned to her sisters.

"What *is* that?" said she.

"What?" asked Caroline harshly; her pen scratched loudly across the paper.

Rebecca gave one of her convulsive gasps.

"That strange shadow on the wall," replied Mrs. Brigham.

Rebecca sat with her face hidden: Caroline dipped her pen in the inkstand.

"Why don't you turn around and look?" asked Mrs. Brigham in a wondering and somewhat aggrieved way.

"I am in a hurry to finish this letter, if Mrs. Wilson Ebbit is going to get word in time to come to the funeral," replied Caroline shortly.

Mrs. Brigham rose, her work slipping to the floor, and she began walking around the room, moving various articles of furniture, with her eyes on the shadow.

Then suddenly she shrieked out:

"Look at this awful shadow! What is it? Caroline, look, look! Rebecca, look! *What is it?*"

All Mrs. Brigham's triumphant placidity was gone. Her handsome face was livid with horror. She stood stiffly pointing at the shadow.

"Look!" said she, pointing her finger at it. "Look! What is it?"

Then Rebecca burst out in a wild wail after a shuddering glance at the wall:

"Oh, Caroline, there it is again! There it is again!"

"Caroline Glynn, you look!" said Mrs. Brigham. "Look! What is that dreadful shadow?"

Caroline rose, turned, and stood confronting the wall.

"How should I know?" she said.

"It has been there every night since he died," cried Rebecca.

"Every night?"

"Yes. He died Thursday and this is Saturday; that makes three nights," said Caroline rigidly. She stood as if holding herself calm with a vise of concentrated will.

"It—it looks like—like——" stammered Mrs. Brigham in a tone of intense horror.

"I know what it looks like well enough," said Caroline. "I've got eyes in my head."

"It looks like Edward," burst out Rebecca in a sort of frenzy of fear. "Only——"

"Yes, it does," assented Mrs. Brigham, whose horror-stricken tone matched her sister's, "only—— Oh, it is awful! What is it, Caroline?"

"I ask you again, how should I know?" replied Caroline. "I see it there like you. How should I know any more than you?"

"It *must* be something in the room," said Mrs. Brigham, staring wildly around.

"We moved everything in the room the first night it came," said Rebecca; "it is not anything in the room."

Caroline turned upon her with a sort of fury. "Of course it is something in the room," said she. "How you act! What do you mean by talking so? Of course it is something in the room."

"Of course, it is," agreed Mrs. Brigham, looking at Caroline suspiciously. "Of course it must be. It is only a coincidence. It just happens so. Perhaps it is that fold of the window curtain that makes it. It must be something in the room."

"It is not anything in the room," repeated Rebecca with obstinate horror.

The door opened suddenly and Henry Glynn entered. He began to speak, then his eyes followed the direction of the others'. He stood stock still staring at the shadow on the wall. It was life size and stretched across the white parallelogram of a door, half across the wall space on which the picture hung.

"What is that?" he demanded in a strange voice.

"It must be due to something in the room," Mrs. Brigham said faintly.

"It is not due to anything in the room," said Rebecca again with the shrill insistency of terror.

"How you act, Rebecca Glynn," said Caroline.

Henry Glynn stood and stared a moment longer. His face showed a gamut of emotions—horror, conviction, then furious incredulity. Suddenly he began hastening hither and thither about the room. He moved the furniture with fierce jerks, turning ever to see the effect upon the shadow on the wall. Not a line of its terrible outlines wavered.

"It must be something in the room!" he declared in a voice which seemed to snap like a lash.

His face changed. The inmost secrecy of his nature seemed evident until one almost lost sight of his lineaments. Rebecca stood close to her sofa, regarding him with woeful, fascinated eyes. Mrs. Brigham clutched Caroline's hand. They both stood in a corner out of his way. For a few moments he raged about the room like a caged wild animal. He moved every piece of furniture; when the moving of a piece did not affect the shadow, he flung it to the floor, the sisters watching.

Then suddenly he desisted. He laughed and began straightening the furniture which he had flung down.

"What an absurdity," he said easily. "Such a to-do about a shadow."

"That's so," assented Mrs. Brigham, in a scared voice which she tried to make natural. As she spoke she lifted a chair near her.

"I think you have broken the chair that Edward was so fond of," said Caroline.

Terror and wrath were struggling for expression on her face. Her mouth was set, her eyes shrinking. Henry lifted the chair with a show of anxiety.

"Just as good as ever," he said pleasantly. He laughed again, looking at his sisters. "Did I scare you?" he said. "I should think you might be used to me by this time. You know my way of wanting to leap to the bottom of a mystery, and that shadow does look—queer, like—and I thought if there was any way of accounting for it I would like to without any delay."

"You don't seem to have succeeded," remarked Caroline dryly, with a slight glance at the wall.

Henry's eyes followed hers and he quivered perceptibly.

"Oh, there is no accounting for shadows," he said, and he laughed again. "A man is a fool to try to account for shadows."

Then the supper bell rang, and they all left the room, but Henry kept his back to the wall, as did, indeed, the others.

Mrs. Brigham pressed close to Caroline as she crossed the hall. "He looked like a demon!" she breathed in her ear.

Henry led the way with an alert motion like a boy; Rebecca brought up the rear; she could scarcely walk, her knees trembled so.

"I can't sit in that room again this evening," she whispered to Caroline after supper.

"Very well, we will sit in the south room," replied Caroline. "I think we will sit in the south parlour," she said aloud; "it isn't as damp as the study, and I have a cold."

So they all sat in the south room with their sewing. Henry read the newspaper, his chair drawn close to the lamp on the table. About nine o'clock he rose abruptly and crossed the hall to the study. The three sisters looked at one another. Mrs. Brigham rose, folded her rustling skirts compactly around her, and began tiptoeing toward the door.

"What are you going to do?" inquired Rebecca agitatedly.

"I am going to see what he is about," replied Mrs. Brigham cautiously.

She pointed as she spoke to the study door across the hall; it was ajar. Henry had striven to pull it together behind him, but it had somehow swollen beyond the limit with curious speed. It was still ajar and a streak of light showed from top to bottom. The hall lamp was not lit.

"You had better stay where you are," said Caroline with guarded sharpness.

"I am going to see," repeated Mrs. Brigham firmly.

Then she folded her skirts so tightly that her bulk with its swelling curves was revealed in a black silk sheath, and she went with a slow toddle across the hall to the study door. She stood there, her eye at the crack.

In the south room Rebecca stopped sewing and sat watching with dilated eyes. Caroline sewed steadily. What Mrs. Brigham, standing at the crack in the study door, saw was this:

Henry Glynn, evidently reasoning that the source of the strange shadow must be between the table on which the lamp stood and the wall, was making systematic passes and thrusts all over and through the intervening space with an old sword which had belonged to his father. Not an inch was left unpierced. He seemed to have divided the space into mathematical sections. He brandished the sword with a sort of cold fury and calculation; the blade gave out flashes of light, the shadow remained unmoved. Mrs. Brigham, watching, felt herself cold with horror.

Finally Henry ceased and stood with the sword in hand and raised as if to strike, surveying the shadow on the wall threateningly. Mrs. Brigham toddled back across the hall and shut the south room door behind her before she related what she had seen.

"He looked like a demon!" she said again. "Have you got any of that old wine in the house, Caroline? I don't feel as if I could stand much more."

Indeed, she looked overcome. Her handsome placid face was worn and strained and pale.

"Yes, there's plenty," said Caroline; "you can have some when you go to bed."

"I think we had all better take some," said Mrs. Brigham. "Oh, my God, Caroline, what——"

"Don't ask and don't speak," said Caroline.

"No, I am not going to," replied Mrs. Brigham; "but——"

Rebecca moaned aloud.

"What are you doing that for?" asked Caroline harshly.

"Poor Edward," returned Rebecca.

"That is all you have to groan for," said Caroline. "There is nothing else."

"I am going to bed," said Mrs. Brigham. "I sha'n't be able to be at the funeral if I don't."

Soon the three sisters went to their chambers and the south parlour was deserted. Caroline called to Henry in the study to put out the light before he came upstairs. They had been gone about an hour when he came into the room bringing the lamp which had stood in the study. He set it on the table and waited a few minutes, pacing up and down. His face was terrible, his fair complexion showed livid; his blue eyes seemed dark blanks of awful reflections.

Then he took the lamp up and returned to the library. He set the lamp on the centre table, and the shadow sprang out on the wall. Again he studied the furniture and moved it about, but deliberately, with none of his former frenzy. Nothing affected the shadow. Then he returned to the south room with the lamp and again waited. Again he returned to the study and placed the lamp on the table, and the shadow sprang out upon the wall. It was midnight before he went upstairs. Mrs. Brigham and the other sisters, who could not sleep, heard him.

The next day was the funeral. That evening the family sat in the south room. Some relatives were with them. Nobody entered the study until Henry carried a lamp in there after the others had retired for the night. He saw again the shadow on the wall leap to an awful life before the light.

The next morning at breakfast Henry Glynn announced that he had to go to the city for three days. The sisters looked at him with surprise. He very seldom left home, and just now his practice had been neglected on account of Edward's death. He was a physician.

"How can you leave your patients now?" asked Mrs. Brigham wonderingly.

"I don't know how to, but there is no other way," replied Henry easily. "I have had a telegram from Doctor Mitford."

"Consultation?" inquired Mrs. Brigham.

"I have business," replied Henry.

Doctor Mitford was an old classmate of his who lived in a neighbouring city and who occasionally called upon him in the case of a consultation.

After he had gone Mrs. Brigham said to Caroline that after all

Henry had not said that he was going to consult with Doctor Mitford, and she thought it very strange.

"Everything is very strange," said Rebecca with a shudder.

"What do you mean?" inquired Caroline sharply.

"Nothing," replied Rebecca.

Nobody entered the library that day, nor the next, nor the next. The third day Henry was expected home, but he did not arrive and the last train from the city had come.

"I call it pretty queer work," said Mrs. Brigham. "The idea of a doctor leaving his patients for three days anyhow, at such a time as this, and I know he has some very sick ones; he said so. And the idea of a consultation lasting three days! There is no sense in it, and *now* he has not come. I don't understand it, for my part."

"I don't either," said Rebecca.

They were all in the south parlour. There was no light in the study opposite, and the door was ajar.

Presently Mrs. Brigham rose—she could not have told why; something seemed to impel her, some will outside her own. She went out of the room, again wrapping her rustling skirts around that she might pass noiselessly, and began pushing at the swollen door of the study.

"She has not got any lamp," said Rebecca in a shaking voice.

Caroline, who was writing letters, rose again, took a lamp (there were two in the room) and followed her sister. Rebecca had risen, but she stood trembling, not venturing to follow.

The doorbell rang, but the others did not hear it; it was on the south door on the other side of the house from the study. Rebecca, after hesitating until the bell rang the second time, went to the door; she remembered that the servant was out.

Caroline and her sister Emma entered the study. Caroline set the lamp on the table. They looked at the wall. "Oh, my God," gasped Mrs. Brigham, "there are—there are *two*—shadows." The sisters stood clutching each other, staring at the awful things on the wall. Then Rebecca came in, staggering, with a telegram in her hand. "Here is—a telegram," she gasped. "Henry is—dead."

The Eyes

Edith Wharton

I

We had been put in the mood for ghosts, that evening, after an excellent dinner at our old friend Culwin's, by a tale of Fred Murchard's—the narrative of a strange personal invitation.

Seen through the haze of our cigars, and by the drowsy gleam of a coal fire, Culwin's library, with its oak walls and dark old bindings, made a good setting for such evocations; and ghostly experiences at first hand being, after Murchard's opening, the only kind acceptable to us, we proceeded to take stock of our group and tax each member for a contribution. There were eight of us, and seven contrived, in a manner more or less adequate, to fulfil the condition imposed. It surprised us all to find that we could muster such a show of supernatural impressions, for none of us, excepting Murchard himself and young Phil Frenham— whose story was the slightest of the lot—had the habit of sending our souls into the invisible. So that, on the whole, we had every reason to be proud of our seven "exhibits," and none of us would have dreamed of expecting an eighth from our host.

Our old friend, Mr. Andrew Culwin, who had sat back in his armchair, listening and blinking through the smoke circles with the cheerful tolerance of a wise old idol, was not the kind of man likely to be favored with such contacts, though he had imagination enough to enjoy, without envying, the superior privileges of his guests. By age and by education he belonged to the stout Positivist tradition, and his habit of thought had been formed in

199

the days of the epic struggle between physics and metaphysics. But he had been, then and always, essentially a spectator, a humorous detached observer of the immense muddled variety show of life, slipping out of his seat now and then for a brief dip into the convivialities at the back of the house, but never, as far as one knew, showing the least desire to jump on the stage and do a "turn."

Among his contemporaries there lingered a vague tradition of his having, at a remote period, and in a romantic clime, been wounded in a duel; but his legend no more tallied with what we younger men knew of his character than my mother's assertion that he had once been "a charming little man with nice eyes" corresponded to any possible reconstitution of his physiognomy.

"He never can have looked like anything but a bundle of sticks," Murchard had once said of him. "Or a phosphorescent log, rather," some one else amended; and we recognized the happiness of this description of his small squat trunk, with the red blink of the eyes in a face like mottled bark. He had always been possessed of a leisure which he had nursed and protected, instead of squandering it in vain activities. His carefully guarded hours had been devoted to the cultivation of a fine intelligence and a few judiciously chosen habits; and none of the disturbances common to human experience seemed to have crossed his sky. Nevertheless, his dispassionate survey of the universe had not raised his opinion of that costly experiment, and his study of the human race seemed to have resulted in the conclusion that all men were superfluous, and women necessary only because someone had to do the cooking. On the importance of this point his convictions were absolute, and gastronomy was the only science which he revered as a dogma. It must be owned that his little dinners were a strong argument in favor of this view, besides being a reason—though not the main one—for the fidelity of his friends.

Mentally he exercised a hospitality less seductive but no less stimulating. His mind was like a forum, or some open meeting-place for the exchange of ideas: somewhat cold and drafty, but light, spacious and orderly—a kind of academic grove from which all the leaves have fallen. In this privileged area a dozen of us were wont to stretch our muscles and expand our lungs; and, as if to prolong as much as possible the tradition of what we felt to be a vanishing institution, one or two neophytes were now and then added to our band.

Young Phil Frenham was the last, and the most interesting, of these recruits, and a good example of Murchard's somewhat morbid assertion that our old friend "liked 'em juicy." It was indeed a fact that Culwin, for all his dryness, specially tasted the lyric qualities in youth. As he was far too good an Epicurean to nip the flowers of soul which he gathered for his garden, his friendship was not a disintegrating influence: on the contrary, it forced the young idea to robuster bloom. And in Phil Frenham he had a good subject for experimentation. The boy was really intelligent, and the soundness of his nature was like the pure paste under a fine glaze. Culwin had fished him out of a fog of family dullness, and pulled him up to a peak in Darien; and the adventure hadn't hurt him a bit. Indeed, the skill with which Culwin had contrived to stimulate his curiosities without robbing them of their bloom of awe seemed to me a sufficient answer to Murchard's ogreish metaphor. There was nothing hectic in Frenham's efflorescence, and his old friend had not laid even a finger tip on the sacred stupidities. One wanted no better proof of that than the fact that Frenham still reverenced them in Culwin.

"There's a side of him you fellows don't see. I believe that story about the duel!" he declared; and it was of the very essence of this belief that it should impel him—just as our little party was dispersing—to turn back to our host with the joking demand: "And now you've got to tell us about *your* ghost!"

The outer door had closed on Murchard and the others; only Frenham and I remained; and the devoted servant who presided over Culwin's destinies, having brought a fresh supply of soda water, had been laconically ordered to bed.

Culwin's sociability was a night-blooming flower, and we knew that he expected the nucleus of his group to tighten around him after midnight. But Frenham's appeal seemed to disconcert him comically, and he rose from the chair in which he had just reseated himself after his farewells in the hall.

"*My* ghost? Do you suppose I'm fool enough to go to the expense of keeping one of my own, when there are so many charming ones in my friends' closets? Take another cigar," he said, revolving toward me with a laugh.

Frenham laughed too, pulling up his slender height before the chimney piece as he turned to face his short bristling friend.

"Oh," he said, "you'd never be content to share if you met one you really liked."

Culwin had dropped back into his armchair, his shock head embedded in the hollow of worn leather, his little eyes glimmering over a fresh cigar.

"Liked—*liked?* Good Lord!" he growled.

"Ah, you *have*, then!" Frenham pounced on him in the same instant, with a side glance of victory at me; but Culwin cowered gnomelike among his cushions, dissembling himself in a protective cloud of smoke.

"What's the use of denying it? You've seen everything, so of course you've seen a ghost!" his young friend persisted, talking intrepidly into the cloud. "Or, if you haven't seen one, it's only because you've seen two!"

The form of the challenge seemed to strike our host. He shot his head out of the mist with a queer tortoise-like motion he sometimes had, and blinked approvingly at Frenham.

"That's it," he flung at us on a shrill jerk of laughter; "it's only because I've seen two!"

The words were so unexpected that they dropped down and down into a deep silence, while we continued to stare at each other over Culwin's head, and Culwin stared at his ghosts. At length Frenham, without speaking, threw himself into the chair on the other side of the hearth, and leaned forward with his listening smile. . . .

II

"Oh, of course they're not show ghosts—a collector wouldn't think anything of them . . . Don't let me raise your hopes . . . their one merit is their numerical strength: the exceptional fact of their being *two*. But, as against this, I'm bound to admit that at any moment I could probably have exorcised them both by asking my doctor for a prescription, or my oculist for a pair of spectacles. Only, as I never could make up my mind whether to go to the doctor or the oculist—whether I was afflicted by an optical or a digestive delusion—I left them to pursue their interesting double life, though at times they made mine exceedingly uncomfortable. . . .

"Yes—uncomfortable; and you know how I hate to be uncomfortable! But it was part of my stupid pride, when the thing began, not to admit that I could be disturbed by the trifling matter of seeing two.

"And then I'd no reason, really, to suppose I was ill. As far as I knew I was simply bored—horribly bored. But it was part of my boredom—I remember—that I was feeling so uncommonly well, and didn't know how on earth to work off my surplus energy. I had come back from a long journey—down in South America and Mexico—and had settled down for the winter near New York, with an old aunt who had known Washington Irving and corresponded with N. P. Willis. She lived, not far from Irvington, in a damp Gothic villa overhung by Norway spruces and looking exactly like a memorial emblem done in hair. Her personal appearance was in keeping with this image, and her own hair—of which there was little left—might have been sacrificed to the manufacture of the emblem.

"I had just reached the end of an agitated year, with considerable arrears to make up in money and emotion; and theoretically it seemed as though my aunt's mild hospitality would be as beneficial to my nerves as to my purse. But the deuce of it was that as soon as I felt myself safe and sheltered my energy began to revive; and how was I to work it off inside of a memorial emblem? I had, at that time, the illusion that sustained intellectual effort could engage a man's whole activity; and I decided to write a great book—I forget about what. My aunt, impressed by my plan, gave up to me her Gothic library, filled with classics bound in black cloth and daguerrotypes of faded celebrities; and I sat down at my desk to win myself a place among their number. And to facilitate my task she lent me a cousin to copy my manuscript.

"The cousin was a nice girl, and I had an idea that a nice girl was just what I needed to restore my faith in human nature, and principally in myself. She was neither beautiful nor intelligent—poor Alice Nowell!—but it interested me to see any woman content to be so uninteresting, and I wanted to find out the secret of her content. In doing this I handled it rather rashly, and put it out of joint—oh, just for a moment! There's no fatuity in telling you this, for the poor girl had never seen anyone but cousins. . . .

"Well, I was sorry for what I'd done, of course, and confoundedly bothered as to how I should put it straight. She was staying in the house, and one evening, after my aunt had gone to bed, she came down to the library to fetch a book she'd mislaid, like any artless heroine, on the shelves behind us. She was pink-nosed and flustered, and it suddenly occurred to me that her hair, though it was fairly thick and pretty, would look exactly like my aunt's when she grew older. I was glad I had noticed this, for it made it easier for me to decide to do what was right; and when I had found the book she hadn't lost I told her I was leaving for Europe that week.

"Europe was terribly far off in those days, and Alice knew at once what I meant. She didn't take it in the least as I'd expected—it would have been easier if she had. She held her book very tight, and turned away a moment to wind up the lamp on my desk—it had a ground-glass shade with vine leaves, and glass drops around the edge, I remember. Then she came back, held out her hand, and said: 'Good-bye.' And as she said it she looked straight at me and kissed me. I had never felt anything as fresh and shy and brave as her kiss. It was worse than any reproach, and it made me ashamed to deserve a reproach from her. I said to myself: 'I'll marry her, and when my aunt dies she'll leave us this house, and I'll sit here at the desk and go on with my book; and Alice will sit over there with her embroidery and look at me as she's looking now. And life will go on like that for any number of years.' The prospect frightened me a little, but at the time it didn't frighten me as much as doing anything to hurt her; and ten minutes later she had my seal ring on her finger, and my promise that when I went abroad she should go with me.

"You'll wonder why I'm enlarging on this incident. It's because the evening on which it took place was the very evening on which I first saw the queer sight I've spoken of. Being at that time an ardent believer in a necessary sequence between cause and effect, I naturally tried to trace some kind of link between what had just happened to me in my aunt's library, and what was to happen a few hours later on the same night; and so the coincidence between the two events always remained in my mind.

"I went up to bed with rather a heavy heart, for I was bowed under the weight of the first good action I had ever consciously committed; and young as I was, I saw the gravity of my situation. Don't imagine from this that I had hitherto been an instrument of destruction. I had been merely a harmless young man, who had followed his bent and declined all collaboration with Providence. Now I had suddenly undertaken to promote the moral order of the world, and I felt a good deal like the trustful spectator who has given his gold watch to the conjurer, and doesn't know in what shape he'll get it back when the trick is over. . . . Still, a glow of self-righteousness tempered my fears, and I said to myself as I undressed that when I'd got used to being good it probably wouldn't make me as nervous as it did at the start. And by the time I was in bed, and had blown out my candle, I felt that I really *was* getting used to it, and that, as far as I'd got, it was not unlike sinking down into one of my aunt's very softest wool mattresses.

"I closed my eyes on this image, and when I opened them it must have been a good deal later, for my room had grown cold, and intensely still. I was waked by the queer feeling we all know—the feeling that there was something in the room that hadn't been there when I fell asleep. I sat up and strained my eyes into the darkness. The room was pitch black, and at first I saw nothing; but gradually a vague glimmer at the foot of the bed turned into two eyes staring back at me. I couldn't distinguish the features attached to them, but as I looked the eyes grew more and more distinct: they gave out a light of their own.

"The sensation of being thus gazed at was far from pleasant, and you might suppose that my first impulse would have been to jump out of bed and hurl myself on the invisible figure attached to the eyes. But it wasn't—my impulse was simply to lie still. . . . I can't say whether this was due to an immediate sense of the uncanny nature of the apparition—to the certainty that if I did jump out of bed I should hurl myself on nothing—or merely to the benumbing effect of the eyes themselves. They were the very worst eyes I've ever seen: a man's eyes—but what a man! My first thought was that he must be frightfully old. The orbits were sunk, and the thick red-lined lids hung over the eyeballs like blinds of which the cords are broken. One lid drooped a little lower than the other, with the effect of a crooked leer; and between these folds of flesh, with their scant bristle of lashes, the eyes themselves, small glassy disks with an agate-like rim looked like sea pebbles in the grip of a starfish.

"But the age of the eyes was not the most unpleasant thing about them. What turned me sick was their expression of vicious security. I don't know how else to describe the fact that they seemed to belong to a man who had done a lot of harm in his life, but had always kept just inside the danger lines. They were not the eyes of a coward, but of someone much too clever to take risks; and my gorge rose at their look of base astuteness. Yet even that wasn't the worst; for as we continued to scan each other I saw in them a tinge of derision, and felt myself to be its object.

"At that I was seized by an impulse of rage that jerked me to my feet and pitched me straight at the unseen figure. But of course there wasn't any figure there, and my fists struck at emptiness. Ashamed and cold, I groped about for a match and lit the candles. The room looked just as usual—as I had known it would; and I crawled back to bed, and blew out the lights.

"As soon as the room was dark again the eyes reappeared; and I now applied myself to explaining them on scientific principles. At first I thought the illusion might have been caused by the glow of the last embers in the chimney; but the fireplace was on the other side of my bed, and so placed that the fire could not be reflected in my toilet glass, which was the only mirror in the room. Then it struck me that I might have been tricked by the reflection of the embers in some polished bit of wood or metal;

and though I couldn't discover any object of the sort in my line of vision, I got up again, groped my way to the hearth, and covered what was left of the fire. But as soon as I was back in bed the eyes were back at its foot.

"They were an hallucination, then: that was plain. But the fact that they were not due to any external dupery didn't make them a bit pleasanter. For if they were a projection of my inner consciousness, what the deuce was the matter with that organ? I had gone deeply enough into the mystery of morbid pathological states to picture the conditions under which an exploring mind might lay itself open to such a midnight admonition; but I couldn't fit it to my present case. I had never felt more normal, mentally and physically; and the only unusual fact in my situation—that of having assured the happiness of an amiable girl—did not seem of a kind to summon unclean spirits about my pillow. But there were the eyes still looking at me.

"I shut mine, and tried to evoke a vision of Alice Nowell's. They were not remarkable eyes, but they were as wholesome as fresh water, and if she had had more imagination—or longer lashes—their expression might have been interesting. As it was, they did not prove very efficacious, and in a few moments I perceived that they had mysteriously changed into the eyes at the foot of the bed. It exasperated me more to feel these glaring at me through my shut lids than to see them, and I opened my eyes again and looked straight into their hateful stare. . . .

"And so it went on all night. I can't tell you what that night was like, nor how long it lasted. Have you ever lain in bed, hopelessly wide awake, and tried to keep your eyes shut, knowing that if you opened 'em you'd see something you dreaded and loathed? It sounds easy, but it's devilishly hard. Those eyes hung there and drew me. I had the *vertige de l'abîme*,[1] and their red lids were the edge of my abyss. . . . I had known nervous hours before: hours when I'd felt the wind of danger in my neck; but never this kind of strain. It wasn't that the eyes were awful; they hadn't the majesty of the powers of darkness. But they had—how shall I say?—a physical effect that was the equivalent of a

---

[1]Vertigo.

bad smell: their look left a smear like a snail's. And I didn't see what business they had with me, anyhow—and I stared and stared, trying to find out.

"I don't know what effect they were trying to produce; but the effect they *did* produce was that of making me pack my portmanteau and bolt to town early the next morning. I left a note for my aunt, explaining that I was ill and had gone to see my doctor; and as a matter of fact I did feel uncommonly ill—the night seemed to have pumped all the blood out of me. But when I reached town I didn't go to the doctor's. I went to a friend's rooms, and threw myself on a bed, and slept for ten heavenly hours. When I woke it was the middle of the night, and I turned cold at the thought of what might be waiting for me. I sat up, shaking, and stared into the darkness; but there wasn't a break in its blessed surface, and when I saw that the eyes were not there I dropped back into another long sleep.

"I had left no word for Alice when I fled, because I meant to go back the next morning. But the next morning I was too exhausted to stir. As the day went on the exhaustion increased, instead of wearing off like the fatigue left by an ordinary night of insomnia: the effect of the eyes seemed to be cumulative, and the thought of seeing them again grew intolerable. For two days I fought my dread; and on the third evening I pulled myself together and decided to go back the next morning. I felt a good deal happier as soon as I'd decided, for I knew that my abrupt disappearance, and the strangeness of my not writing, must have been very distressing to poor Alice. I went to bed with an easy mind, and fell asleep at once; but in the middle of the night I woke, and there were the eyes. . . .

"Well, I simply couldn't face them; and instead of going back to my aunt's I bundled a few things into a trunk and jumped aboard the first steamer for England. I was so dead tired when I got on board that I crawled straight into my berth, and slept most of the way over; and I can't tell you the bliss it was to wake from those long dreamless stretches and look fearlessly into the dark, *knowing* that I shouldn't see the eyes. . . .

"I stayed abroad for a year, and then I stayed for another; and during that time I never had a glimpse of them. That was enough reason for prolonging my stay if I'd been on a desert island. Another was, of course, that I had perfectly come to see, on the voyage over, the complete impossibility of my marrying Alice Nowell. The fact that I had been so slow in making this discovery annoyed me, and made me want to avoid explanations. The bliss of escaping at one stroke from the eyes, and from this other embarrassment, gave my freedom an extraordinary zest; and the longer I savored it the better I liked its taste.

"The eyes had burned such a hole in my consciousness that for a long time I went on puzzling over the nature of the apparition, and wondering if it would ever come back. But as time passed I lost this dread, and retained only the precision of the image. Then that faded in its turn.

"The second year found me settled in Rome, where I was planning, I believe, to write another great book—a definitive work on Etruscan influences in Italian art. At any rate, I'd found some pretext of the kind for taking a sunny apartment in the Piazza di Spagna and dabbling about in the Forum; and there, one morning, a charming youth came to me. As he stood there in the warm light, slender and smooth and hyacinthine, he might have stepped from a ruined altar—one to Antinous, say; but he'd come instead from New York, with a letter from (of all people) Alice Nowell. The letter—the first I'd had from her since our break—was simply a line introducing her young cousin, Gilbert Noyes, and appealing to me to befriend him. It appeared, poor lad, that he 'had talent,' and 'wanted to write'; and, an obdurate family having insisted that his calligraphy should take the form of double entry, Alice had intervened to win him six months' respite, during which he was to travel abroad on a meager pittance, and somehow prove his ability to increase it by his pen. The quaint conditions of the test struck me first: it seemed about as conclusive as a medieval 'ordeal.' Then I was touched by her having sent him to me. I had always wanted to do her some service, to justify myself in my own eyes rather than hers; and here was a beautiful occasion.

"I imagine it's safe to lay down the general principle that predestined geniuses don't, as a rule, appear before one in the spring sunshine of the Forum looking like one of its banished gods. At any rate, poor Noyes wasn't a predestined genius. But he *was* beautiful to see, and charming as a comrade. It was only when he began to talk literature that my heart failed me. I knew all the symptoms so well—the things he had 'in him,' and the things outside him that impinged! There's the real test, after all. It was always—punctually, inevitably, with the inexorableness of a mechanical law—it was *always* the wrong thing that struck him. I grew to find a certain fascination in deciding in advance exactly which wrong thing he'd select; and I acquired an astonishing skill at the game. . . .

"The worst of it was that his *bêtise*[2] wasn't of the too obvious sort. Ladies who met him at picnics thought him intellectual; and even at dinners he passed for clever. I, who had him under the microscope, fancied now and then that he might develop some kind of a slim talent, something that he could make 'do' and be happy on; and wasn't that, after all, what I was concerned with? He was so charming—he continued to be so charming— that he called forth all my charity in support of this argument; and for the first few months I really believed there was a chance for him. . . .

"Those months were delightful. Noyes was constantly with me, and the more I saw of him, the better I liked him. His stupidity was a natural grace—it was as beautiful, really, as his eyelashes. And he was so gay, so affectionate, and so happy with me, that telling him the truth would have been about as pleasant as slitting the throat of some gentle animal. At first I used to wonder what had put into that radiant head the detestable delusion that it held a brain. Then I began to see that it was simply protective mimicry—an instinctive ruse to get away from family life and an office desk. Not that Gilbert didn't—dear lad!— believe in himself. There wasn't a trace of hypocrisy in him. He was sure that his 'call' was irresistible, while to me it was the saving grace of his situation that it *wasn't*, and that a little money, a little leisure, a little pleasure would have turned him into an inoffensive idler. Unluckily, however, there was no hope of money, and with the alternative of the office desk before him

---

[2]Stupidity, foolishness.

he couldn't postpone his attempt at literature. The stuff he turned out was deplorable, and I see now that I knew it from the first. Still, the absurdity of deciding a man's whole future on a first trial seemed to justify me in withholding my verdict, and perhaps even in encouraging him a little, on the ground that the human plant generally needs warmth to flower.

"At any rate, I proceeded on that principle, and carried it to the point of getting his term of probation extended. When I left Rome he went with me, and we idled away a delicious summer between Capri and Venice. I said to myself: 'If he has anything in him, it will come out now,' and it *did*. He was never more enchanting and enchanted. There were moments of our pilgrimage when beauty born of murmuring sound seemed actually to pass into his face—but only to issue forth in a flood of the palest ink. . . .

"Well, the time came to turn off the tap; and I knew there was no hand but mine to do it. We were back in Rome, and I had taken him to stay with me, not wanting him to be alone in his *pension* when he had to face the necessity of renouncing his ambition. I hadn't, of course, relied solely on my own judgment in deciding to advise him to drop literature. I had sent his stuff to various people—editors and critics—and they had always sent it back with the same chilling lack of comment. Really there was nothing on earth to say.

"I confess I never felt more shabby than I did when I decided to have it out with Gilbert. It was well enough to tell myself that it was my duty to knock the poor boy's hopes into splinters—but I'd like to know what act of gratuitous cruelty hasn't been justified on that plea? I've always shrunk from usurping the functions of Providence, and when I have to exercise them I decidedly prefer that it shouldn't be on an errand of destruction. Besides, in the last issue, who was I to decide, even after a year's trial, if poor Gilbert had it in him or not?

"The more I looked at the part I'd resolved to play, the less I liked it; and I liked it still less when Gilbert sat opposite me, with his head thrown back in the lamplight, just as Phil's is now. . . . I'd been going over his last manuscript, and he knew it, and he knew that his future hung on my verdict—we'd tacitly agreed to that. The manuscript lay between us, on my table—a novel, his first novel, if you please!—and he reached over and laid his hand on it, and looked up at me with all his life in the look.

"I stood up and cleared my throat, trying to keep my eyes away from his face and on the manuscript.

"'The fact is, my dear Gilbert,' I began—

"I saw him turn pale, but he was up and facing me in an instant.

"'Oh, look here, don't take on so, my dear fellow! I'm not so awfully cut up as all that!' His hands were on my shoulders, and he was laughing down on me from his full height, with a kind of mortally stricken gaiety that drove the knife into my side.

"He was too beautifully brave for me to keep up any humbug about my duty. And it came over me suddenly how I should hurt others in hurting him: myself first, since sending him home meant losing him; but more particularly poor Alice Nowell, to whom I had so longed to prove my good faith and my desire to serve her. It really seemed like failing her twice to fail Gilbert.

"But my intuition was like one of those lightning flashes that encircle the whole horizon, and in the same instant I saw what I might be letting myself in for if I didn't tell the truth. I said to myself: 'I shall have him for life'—and I'd never yet seen anyone, man or woman, whom I was quite sure of wanting on those terms. Well, this impulse of egotism decided me. I was ashamed of it, and to get away from it I took a leap that landed me straight in Gilbert's arms.

"'The thing's all right, and you're all wrong!' I shouted up at him; and as he hugged me, and I laughed and shook in his clutch, I had for a minute the sense of self-complacency that is supposed to attend the footsteps of the just. Hang it all, making people happy *has* its charms.

"Gilbert, of course, was for celebrating his emancipation in some spectacular manner; but I sent him away alone to explode his emotions, and went to bed to sleep off mine. As I undressed I began to wonder what their aftertaste would be—so many of the finest don't keep! Still, I wasn't sorry, and I meant to empty the bottle, even if it *did* turn a trifle flat.

"After I got into bed I lay for a long time smiling at the

memory of his eyes—his blissful eyes. . . . Then I fell asleep, and when I woke the room was deathly cold, and I sat up with a jerk—and there were *the other eyes*. . . .

"It was three years since I'd seen them, but I'd thought of them so often that I fancied they could never take me unawares again. Now, with their red sneer on me, I knew that I had never really believed they would come back, and that I was as defence-less as ever against them. . . . As before, it was the insane irrel-evance of their coming that made it so horrible. What the deuce were they after, to leap out at me at such a time? I had lived more or less carelessly in the years since I'd seen them, though my worst indiscretions were not dark enough to invite the searchings of their infernal glare; but at this particular moment I was really in what might have been called a state of grace; and I can't tell you how the fact added to their horror. . . .

"But it's not enough to say they were as bad as before: they were worse. Worse by just so much as I'd learned of life in the interval; by all the damnable implications my wider experience read into them. I saw now what I hadn't seen before: that they were eyes which had grown hideous gradually, which had built up their baseness coral-wise, bit by bit, out of a series of small turpitudes slowly accumulated through the industrious years. Yes—it came to me that what made them so bad was that they'd grown bad so slowly. . . .

"There they hung in the darkness, their swollen lids dropped across the little watery bulbs rolling loose in the orbits, and the puff of flesh making a muddy shadow underneath—and as their stare moved with my movements, there came over me a sense of their tacit complicity, of a deep hidden understanding between us that was worse than the first shock of their strange-ness. Not that I understood them; but that they made it so clear that someday I should. . . . Yes, that was the worst part of it, decidedly; and it was the feeling that became stronger each time they came back. . . .

"For they got into the damnable habit of coming back. They reminded me of vampires with a taste for young flesh, they seemed so to gloat over the taste of a good conscience. Every night for a month they came to claim their morsel of mine: since

I'd made Gilbert happy they simply wouldn't loosen their fangs. The coincidence almost made me hate him, poor lad, fortuitous as I felt it to be. I puzzled over it a good deal, but couldn't find any hint of an explanation except in the chance of his association with Alice Nowell. But then the eyes had let up on me the moment I had abandoned her, so they could hardly be the emissaries of a woman scorned, even if one could have pictured poor Alice charging such spirits to avenge her. That set me thinking, and I began to wonder if they would let up on me if I abandoned Gilbert. The temptation was insidious, and I had to stiffen myself against it; but really, dear boy! he was too charming to be sacrificed to such demons. And so, after all, I never found out what they wanted. . . ."

III

The fire crumbled, sending up a flash which threw into relief the narrator's gnarled face under its grey-black stubble. Pressed into the hollow of the chair back, it stood out an instant like an intaglio of yellowish red-veined stone, with spots of enamel for the eyes; then the fire sank and it became once more a dim Rembrandtish blur.

Phil Frenham, sitting in a low chair on the opposite side of the hearth, one long arm propped on the table behind him, one hand supporting his thrown-back head, and his eyes fixed on his old friend's face, had not moved since the tale began. He continued to maintain his silent immobility after Culwin had ceased to speak, and it was I who, with a vague sense of disappointment at the sudden drop of the story, finally asked: "But how long did you keep on seeing them?"

Culwin, so sunk into his chair that he seemed like a heap of his own empty clothes, stirred a little, as if in surprise at my question. He appeared to have half-forgotten what he had been telling us.

"How long? Oh, off and on all that winter. It was infernal. I never got used to them. I grew really ill."

Frenham shifted his attitude, and as he did so his elbow

struck against a small mirror in a bronze frame standing on the table behind him. He turned and changed its angle slightly; then he resumed his former attitude, his dark head thrown back on his lifted palm, his eyes intent on Culwin's face. Something in his silent gaze embarrassed me, and as if to divert attention from it I pressed on with another question:

"And you never tried sacrificing Noyes?"

"Oh, no. The fact is I didn't have to. He did it for me, poor boy!"

"Did it for you? How do you mean?"

"He wore me out—wore everybody out. He kept on pouring out his lamentable twaddle, and hawking it up and down the place till he became a thing of terror. I tried to wean him from writing—oh, ever so gently, you understand, by throwing him with agreeable people, giving him a chance to make himself felt, to come to a sense of what he *really* had to give. I'd foreseen this solution from the beginning—felt sure that, once the first ardour of authorship was quenched, he'd drop into his place as a charming parasitic thing, the kind of chronic Cherubino for whom, in old societies, there's always a seat at table, and a shelter behind the ladies' skirts. I saw him take his place as 'the poet': the poet who doesn't write. One knows the type in every drawing room. Living in that way doesn't cost much—I'd worked it all out in my mind, and felt sure that, with a little help, he could manage it for the next few years; and meanwhile he'd be sure to marry. I saw him married to a widow, rather older, with a good cook and a well-run house. And I actually had my eye on the widow. . . . Meanwhile I did everything to help the transition—lent him money to ease his conscience, introduced him to pretty women to make him forget his vows. But nothing would do him: he had but one idea in his beautiful obstinate head. He wanted the laurel and not the rose, and he kept on repeating Gautier's axiom, and battering and filing at his limp prose till he'd spread it out over Lord knows how many hundred pages. Now and then he would send a barrelful to a publisher, and of course it would always come back.

"At first it didn't matter—he thought he was 'misunderstood.' He took the attitudes of genius, and whenever an opus came home he wrote another to keep it company. Then he had a reaction of despair, and accused me of deceiving him, and Lord knows what. I got angry at that, and told him it was he who had deceived himself. He'd come to me determined to write, and I'd done my best to help him. That was the extent of my offence, and I'd done it for his cousin's sake, not his.

"That seemed to strike home, and he didn't answer for a minute. Then he said: 'My time's up and my money's up. What do you think I'd better do?'

"'I think you'd better not be an ass,' I said.

"What do you mean by being an ass?" he asked.

"I took a letter from my desk and held it out to him.

"'I mean refusing this offer of Mrs. Ellinger's: to be her secretary at a salary of five thousand dollars. There may be a lot more in it than that.'

"He flung out his hand with a violence that struck the letter from mine. 'Oh, I know well enough what's in it!' he said, red to the roots of his hair.

"'And what's the answer, if you know?' I asked.

"He made none at the minute, but turned away slowly to the door. There, with his hand on the threshold, he stopped to say, almost under his breath: 'Then you really think my stuff's no good?'

"I was tired and exasperated, and I laughed. I don't defend my laugh—it was in wretched taste. But I must plead in extenuation that the boy was a fool, and that I'd done my best for him—I really had.

"He went out of the room, shutting the door quietly after him. That afternoon I left for Frascati, where I'd promised to spend the Sunday with some friends. I was glad to escape from Gilbert, and by the same token, as I learned that night, I had also escaped from the eyes. I dropped into the same lethargic sleep that had come to me before when I left off seeing them; and when I woke the next morning in my peaceful room above the ilexes, I felt the utter weariness and deep relief that always followed on that sleep. I put in two blessed nights at Frascati, and when I got back to my rooms in Rome I found that Gilbert had gone. . . . Oh, nothing tragic had happened—the episode never rose to *that*. He'd simply packed his manuscripts and left for America—for his family and the Wall Street desk. He left a decent enough note to tell me of his decision, and behaved altogether, in the circumstances, as little like a fool as it's possible for a fool to behave. . . ."

IV

Culwin paused again, and Frenham still sat motionless, the dusky contour of his young head reflected in the mirror at his back.

"And what became of Noyes afterward?" I finally asked, still disquieted by a sense of incompleteness, by the need of some connecting thread between the parallel lines of the tale.

Culwin twitched his shoulders. "Oh, nothing became of him—because he became nothing. There could be no question of 'becoming' about it. He vegetated in an office, I believe, and finally got a clerkship in a consulate, and married drearily in China. I saw him once in Hong Kong, years afterward. He was fat and hadn't shaved. I was told he drank. He didn't recognize me."

"And the eyes?" I asked, after another pause which Frenham's continued silence made oppressive.

Culwin, stroking his chin, blinked at me meditatively through the shadows. "I never saw them after my last talk with Gilbert. Put two and two together if you can. For my part, I haven't found the link."

He rose, his hands in his pockets, and walked stiffly over to the table on which reviving drinks had been set out.

"You must be parched after this dry tale. Here, help yourself, my dear fellow. Here, Phil—" He turned back to the hearth.

Frenham made no rsponse to his host's hospitable summons. He still sat in his low chair without moving, but as Culwin advanced toward him, their eyes met in a long look; after which, the young man, turning suddenly, flung his arms across the table behind him, and dropped his face upon them.

Culwin, at the unexpected gesture, stopped short, a flush on his face.

"Phil—what the deuce? Why, have the eyes scared *you?* My dear boy—my dear fellow—I never had such a tribute to my literary ability, never!"

He broke into a chuckle at the thought, and halted on the hearthrug, his hands still in his pockets, gazing down at the youth's bowed head. Then, as Frenham still made no answer, he moved a step or two nearer.

"Cheer up, my dear Phil! It's years since I've seen them—apparently I've done nothing lately bad enough to call them out of chaos. Unless my present evocation of them has made *you* see them; which would be their worst stroke yet!"

His bantering appeal quivered off into an uneasy laugh, and he moved still nearer, bending over Frenham, and laying his gouty hands on the lad's shoulders.

"Phil, my dear boy, really—what's the matter? Why don't you answer? *Have* you seen the eyes?"

Frenham's face was still hidden, and from where I stood behind Culwin I saw the latter, as if under the rebuff of this unaccountable attitude, draw back slowly from his friend. As he did so, the light of the lamp on the table fell full on his congested face, and I caught its reflection in the mirror behind Frenham's head.

Culwin saw the reflection also. He paused, his face level with the mirror, as if scarcely recognizing the countenance in it as his own. But as he looked his expression gradually changed, and for an appreciable space of time he and the image in the glass confronted each other with a glare of slowly gathering hate. Then Culwin let go of Frenham's shoulders, and drew back a step. . . .

Frenham, his face still hidden, did not stir.

Consequences

Willa Cather

Henry Eastman, a lawyer, aged forty, was standing beside the Flatiron building in a driving November rainstorm, signaling frantically for a taxi. It was six-thirty, and everything on wheels was engaged. The streets were in confusion about him, the sky was in turmoil above him, and the Flatiron building, which seemed about to blow down, threw water like a mill-shoot. Suddenly, out of the brutal struggle of men and cars and machines and people tilting at each other with umbrellas, a quiet, well-mannered limousine paused before him, at the curb, and an agreeable, ruddy countenance confronted him through the open window of the car.

"Don't you want me to pick you up, Mr. Eastman? I'm running directly home now."

Eastman recognized Kier Cavenaugh, a young man of pleasure, who lived in the house on Central Park South, where he himself had an apartment.

"Don't I?" he exclaimed, bolting into the car. "I'll risk getting your cushions wet without compunction. I came up in a taxi, but I didn't hold it. Bad economy. I thought I saw your car down on Fourteenth Street about half an hour ago."

The owner of the car smiled. He had a pleasant, round face and round eyes, and a fringe of smooth, yellow hair showed under the rim of his soft felt hat. "With a lot of little broilers fluttering into it? You did. I know some girls who work in the cheap shops down there. I happened to be down-town and I stopped and took a load of them home. I do sometimes. Saves their poor little clothes, you know. Their shoes are never any good."

Eastman looked at his rescuer. "Aren't they notoriously afraid of cars and smooth young men?" he inquired.

Cavenaugh shook his head. "They know which cars are safe and which are chancy. They put each other wise. You have to take a bunch at a time, of course. The Italian girls can never come along; their men shoot. The girls understand, all right; but their fathers don't. One gets to see queer places, sometimes, taking them home."

Eastman laughed drily. "Every time I touch the circle of your acquaintance, Cavenaugh, it's a little wider. You must know New York pretty well by this time."

"Yes, but I'm on my good behavior below Twenty-third Street," the young man replied with simplicity. "My little friends down there would give me a good character. They're wise little girls. They have grand ways with each other, a romantic code of loyalty. You can find a good many of the lost virtues among them."

The car was standing still in a traffic block at Fortieth Street, when Cavenaugh suddenly drew his face away from the window and touched Eastman's arm. "Look, please. You see that hansom with the bony gray horse—driver has a broken hat and red flannel around his throat. Can you see who is inside?"

Eastman peered out. The hansom was just cutting across the line, and the driver was making a great fuss about it, bobbing his head and waving his whip. He jerked his dripping old horse into Fortieth Street and clattered off past the Public Library grounds toward Sixth Avenue. "No, I couldn't see the passenger. Someone you know?"

"Could you see whether there was a passenger?" Cavenaugh asked.

"Why, yes. A man, I think. I saw his elbow on the apron. No driver ever behaves like that unless he has a passenger."

"Yes, I may have been mistaken," Cavenaugh murmured absent-mindedly. Ten minutes or so later, after Cavenaugh's car had turned off Fifth Avenue into Fifty-eighth Street, Eastman exclaimed, "There's your same cabby, and his cart's empty. He's headed for a drink now, I suppose." The driver in the broken hat and the red flannel neck cloth was still brandishing the whip over his old gray. He was coming from the west now, and turned down Sixth Avenue, under the elevated.

Cavenaugh's car stopped at the bachelor apartment house between Sixth and Seventh Avenues where he and Eastman lived, and they went up in the elevator together. They were still talking when the lift stopped at Cavenaugh's floor, and Eastman stepped out with him and walked down the hall, finishing his sentence while Cavenaugh found his latch-key. When he opened the door, a wave of fresh cigarette smoke greeted them. Cavenaugh stopped short and stared into his hallway. "Now how in the devil—!" he exclaimed angrily.

"Someone waiting for you? Oh, no, thanks. I wasn't coming in. I have to work to-night. Thank you, but I couldn't." Eastman nodded and went up the two flights to his own rooms.

Though Eastman did not customarily keep a servant he had this winter a man who had been lent to him by a friend who was abroad. Rollins met him at the door and took his coat and hat.

"Put out my dinner clothes, Rollins, and then get out of here until ten o'clock. I've promised to go to a supper to-night. I shan't be dining. I've had a late tea and I'm going to work until ten. You may put out some kumiss and biscuit for me."

Rollins took himself off, and Eastman settled down at the big table in his sitting-room. He had to read a lot of letters submitted as evidence in a breach of contract case, and before he got very far he found that long paragraphs in some of the letters were written in German. He had a German dictionary at his office, but none here. Rollins had gone, and anyhow, the bookstores would be closed. He remembered having seen a row of dictionaries on the lower shelf of one of Cavenaugh's bookcases. Cavenaugh had a lot of books, though he never read anything but new stuff. Eastman prudently turned down his student's lamp very low—the thing had an evil habit of smoking—and went down two flights to Cavenaugh's door.

The young man himself answered Eastman's ring. He was freshly dressed for the evening, except for a brown smoking jacket, and his yellow hair had been brushed until it shone. He hesitated as he confronted his caller, still holding the door knob, and his round eyes and smooth forehead made their best imitation of a frown. When Eastman began to apologize, Cavenaugh's manner suddenly changed. He caught his arm and jerked him into the narrow hall. "Come in, come in. Right along!" he said excitedly. "Right along." he repeated as he pushed Eastman before him into his sitting-room. "Well I'll—" he stopped short at the door and looked about his own room with an air of complete mystification. The back window was wide open and a strong wind was blowing in. Cavenaugh walked over to the window and stuck out his head, looking up and down the fire escape. When he pulled his head in, he drew down the sash.

"I had a visitor I wanted you to see," he explained with a nervous smile. "At least I thought I had. He must have gone out that way," nodding toward the window.

"Call him back. I only came to borrow a German dictionary, if you have one. Can't stay. Call him back."

Cavenaugh shook his head despondently. "No use. He's beat it. Nowhere in sight."

"He must be active. Has he left something?" Eastman pointed to a very dirty white glove that lay on the floor under the window.

"Yes, that's his." Cavenaugh reached for his tongs, picked up the glove, and tossed it into the grate, where it quickly shriveled on the coals. Eastman felt that he had happened in upon something disagreeable, possibly something shady, and he wanted to get away at once. Cavenaugh stood staring at the fire and seemed stupid and dazed; so he repeated his request rather sternly, "I think I've seen a German dictionary down there among your books. May I have it?"

Cavenaugh blinked at him. "A German dictionary? Oh, possibly! Those were my father's. I scarcely know what there is." He put down the tongs and began to wipe his hands nervously with his handkerchief.

Eastman went over to the bookcase behind the Chesterfield, opened the door, swooped upon the book he wanted and stuck it under his arm. He felt perfectly certain now that something shady had been going on in Cavenaugh's rooms, and he saw no reason why he should come in for any hang-over. "Thanks. I'll send it back to-morrow," he said curtly as he made for the door.

Cavenaugh followed him. "Wait a moment. I wanted you to see him. You did see his glove," glancing at the grate.

Eastman laughed disagreeably. "I saw a glove. That's not evidence. Do your friends often use that means of exit? Somewhat inconvenient."

Cavenaugh gave him a startled glance. "Wouldn't you think so? For an old man, a very rickety old party? The ladders are steep, you know, and rusty." He approached the window again and put it up softly. In a moment he drew his head back with a jerk. He caught Eastman's arm and shoved him toward the window. "Hurry, please. Look! Down there." He pointed to the little patch of paved court four flights down.

The square of pavement was so small and the walls about it were so high, that it was a good deal like looking down a well. Four tall buildings backed upon the same court and made a kind of shaft, with flagstones at the bottom, and at the top a square of dark blue with some stars in it. At the bottom of the shaft Eastman saw a black figure, a man in a caped coat and a tall hat stealing cautiously around, not across the square of pavement, keeping close to the dark wall and avoiding the streak of light that fell on the flagstones from a window in the opposite house. Seen from that height he was of course fore-shortened and probably looked more shambling and decrepit than he was. He picked his way along with exaggerated care and looked like a silly old cat crossing a wet street. When he reached the gate that led into an alley way between two buildings, he felt about for the latch, opened the door a mere crack, and then shot out under the feeble lamp that burned in the brick arch over the gateway. The door closed after him.

"He'll get run in," Eastman remarked curtly, turning away from the window. "That door shouldn't be left unlocked. Any crook could come in. I'll speak to the janitor about it, if you don't mind," he added sarcastically.

"Wish you would." Cavenaugh stood brushing down the front of his jacket, first with his right hand and then with his left. "You saw him, didn't you?"

"Enough of him. Seems eccentric. I have to see a lot of buggy people. They don't take me in any more. But I'm keeping you and I'm in a hurry myself. Good night."

Cavenaugh put out his hand detainingly and started to say something; but Eastman rudely turned his back and went down the hall and out of the door. He had never felt anything shady about Cavenaugh before, and he was sorry he had gone down for the dictionary. In five minutes he was deep in his papers; but in the half hour when he was loafing before he dressed to go out, the young man's curious behavior came into his mind again.

Eastman had merely a neighborly acquaintance with Cavenaugh. He had been to a supper at the young man's rooms once, but he didn't particularly like Cavenaugh's friends; so the next time he was asked, he had another engagement. He liked Cavenaugh himself, if for nothing else than because he was so cheerful and trim and ruddy. A good complexion is always at a premium in New York, especially when it shines reassuringly on a man who does everything in the world to lose it. It encourages fellow mortals as to the inherent vigor of the human organism and the amount of bad treatment it will stand for. "Footprints that perhaps another," etc.

Cavenaugh, he knew, had plenty of money. He was the son of a Pennsylvania preacher, who died soon after he discovered that his ancestral acres were full of petroleum, and Kier had come to New York to burn some of the oil. He was thirty-two and was still at it; spent his life, literally, among the breakers. His motor hit the Park every morning as if it were the first time ever. He took people out to supper every night. He went from restaurant to restaurant, sometimes to half-a-dozen in an evening. The head waiters were his hosts and their cordiality made him happy. They made a life-line for him up Broadway and down Fifth Avenue. Cavenaugh was still fresh and smooth, round and plump, with a lustre to his hair and white teeth and a clear look in his round eyes. He seemed absolutely unwearied and unimpaired; never bored and never carried away.

Eastman always smiled when he met Cavenaugh in the entrance hall, serenely going forth to or returning from gladiatorial combats with joy, or when he saw him rolling smoothly up to the door in his car in the morning after a restful night in one of the remarkable new roadhouses he was always finding. Eastman had seen a good many young men disappear on Cavenaugh's route, and he admired this young man's endurance.

To-night, for the first time, he had got a whiff of something unwholesome about the fellow—bad nerves, bad company, something on hand that he was ashamed of, a visitor old and vicious, who must have had a key to Cavenaugh's apartment, for he was evidently there when Cavenaugh returned at seven o'clock. Probably it was the same man Cavenaugh had seen in the hansom. He must have been able to let himself in, for Cavenaugh kept no man but his chauffeur; or perhaps the janitor had been instructed to let him in. In either case, and whoever he was, it was clear enough that Cavenaugh was ashamed of him and was mixing up in questionable business of some kind.

Eastman sent Cavenaugh's book back by Rollins, and for the next few weeks he had no word with him beyond a casual greeting when they happened to meet in the hall or the elevator. One Sunday morning Cavenaugh telephoned up to him to ask if he could motor out to a roadhouse in Connecticut that afternoon and have supper; but when Eastman found there were to be other guests he declined.

On New Year's eve Eastman dined at the University Club at six o'clock and hurried home before the usual manifestations of insanity had begun in the streets. When Rollins brought his smoking coat, he asked him whether he wouldn't like to get off early.

"Yes, sir. But won't you be dressing, Mr. Eastman?" he inquired.

"Not to-night." Eastman handed him a bill. "Bring some change in the morning. There'll be fees."

Rollins lost no time in putting everything to rights for the night, and Eastman couldn't help wishing that he were in such a hurry to be off somewhere himself. When he heard the hall door close softly, he wondered if there were any place, after all, that he wanted to go. From his window he looked down at the long lines of motors and taxis waiting for a signal to cross Broadway. He thought of some of their probable destinations and decided that none of those places pulled him very hard. The night was warm and wet, the air was drizzly. Vapor hung in clouds about the *Times* Building, half hid the top of it, and made a luminous haze along Broadway. While he was looking down at the army of wet, black carriage-tops and their reflected head-lights and tail-lights, Eastman heard a ring at his door. He delib-erated. If it were a caller, the hall porter would have telephoned up. It must be the janitor. When he opened the door, there stood a rosy young man in a tuxedo, without a coat or hat.

"Pardon. Should I have telephoned? I half thought you wouldn't be in."

Eastman laughed. "Come in, Cavenaugh. You weren't sure whether you wanted company or not, eh, and you were trying to let chance decide it? That was exactly my state of mind. Let's accept the verdict." When they emerged from the narrow hall into his sitting-room, he pointed out a seat by the fire to his guest. He brought a tray of decanters and soda bottles and placed it on his writing table.

Cavenaugh hesitated, standing by the fire. "Sure you weren't starting for somewhere?"

"Do I look it? No, I was just making up my mind to stick it out alone when you rang. Have one?" he picked up a tall tumbler.

"Yes, thank you. I always do."

Eastman chuckled. "Lucky boy! So will I. I had a very early dinner. New York is the most arid place on holidays," he contin-ued as he rattled the ice in the glasses. "When one gets too old to hit the rapids down there, and tired of gobbling food to hea-thenish dance music, there is absolutely no place where you can get a chop and some milk toast in peace, unless you have strong ties of blood brotherhood on upper Fifth Avenue. But you, why aren't you starting for somewhere?"

The young man sipped his soda and shook his head as he replied:

"Oh, I couldn't get a chop, either. I know only flashy people, of course." He looked up at his host with such a grave and candid expression that Eastman decided there couldn't be anything very crooked about the fellow. His smooth cheeks were positively cherubic.

"Well, what's the matter with them? Aren't they flashing tonight?"

"Only the very new ones seem to flash on New Year's eve. The older ones fade away. Maybe they are hunting a chop, too."

"Well"—Eastman sat down—"holidays do dash one. I was just about to write a letter to a pair of maiden aunts in my old home town, up-state; old coasting hill, snow-covered pines, lights in the church windows. That's what you've saved me from."

Cavenaugh shook himself. "Oh, I'm sure that wouldn't have been good for you. Pardon me," he rose and took a photograph from the bookcase, a handsome man in shooting clothes. "Dudley, isn't it? Did you know him well?"

"Yes. An old friend. Terrible thing, wasn't it? I haven't got over the jolt yet."

"His suicide? Yes, terrible! Did you know his wife?"

"Slightly. Well enough to admire her very much. She must be terribly broken up. I wonder Dudley didn't think of that."

Cavenaugh replaced the photograph carefully, lit a cigarette, and standing before the fire began to smoke. "Would you mind telling me about him? I never met him, but of course I'd read a lot about him, and I can't help feeling interested. It was a queer thing."

Eastman took out his cigar case and leaned back in his deep chair. "In the days when I knew him best he hadn't any story, like the happy nations. Everything was properly arranged for him before he was born. He came into the world happy, healthy, clever, straight, with the right sort of connections and the right kind of fortune, neither too large nor too small. He helped to make the world an agreeable place to live in until he was twenty-six. Then he married as he should have married. His wife was a Californian, educated abroad. Beautiful. You have seen her picture?"

Cavenaugh nodded. "Oh, many of them."

"She was interesting, too. Though she was distinctly a person of the world, she had retained something, just enough of the large Western manner. She had the habit of authority, of calling out a special train if she needed it, of using all our ingenious mechanical contrivances lightly and easily, without over-rating them. She and Dudley knew how to live better than most people. Their house was the most charming one I have ever known in New York. You felt freedom there, and a zest of life, and safety—absolute sanctuary—from everything sordid or petty. A whole society like that would justify the creation of man and would make our planet shine with a soft, peculiar radiance among the constellations. You think I'm putting it on thick?"

The young man sighed gently. "Oh, no! One has always felt there must be people like that. I've never known any."

"They had two children, beautiful ones. After they had been married for eight years, Rosina met this Spaniard. He must have amounted to something. She wasn't a flighty woman. She came home and told Dudley how matters stood. He persuaded her to stay at home for six months and try to pull up. They were both fair-minded people, and I'm as sure as if I were the Almighty, that she did try. But at the end of the time, Rosina went quietly off to Spain, and Dudley went to hunt in the Canadian Rockies. I met his party out there. I didn't know his wife had left him and talked about her a good deal. I noticed that he never drank anything, and his light used to shine through the log chinks of his room until all hours, even after a hard day's hunting. When I got back to New York, rumors were creeping about. Dudley did not come back. He bought a ranch in Wyoming, built a big log house and kept splendid dogs and horses. One of his sisters went out to keep house for him, and the children were there when they were not in school. He had a great many visitors, and everyone who came back talked about how well Dudley kept things going.

"He put in two years out there. Then, last month, he had to come back on business. A trust fund had to be settled up, and he was administrator. I saw him at the club; same light, quick step, same gracious handshake. He was getting gray, and there was something softer in his manner; but he had a fine red tan on his face and said he found it delightful to be here in the season when everything is going hard. The Madison Avenue house had been closed since Rosina left it. He went there to get some things his sister wanted. That, of course, was the mistake. He went alone, in the afternoon, and didn't go out for dinner— found some sherry and tins of biscuit in the sideboard. He shot himself sometime that night. There were pistols in his smoking-room. They found burnt out candles beside him in the morning. The gas and electricity were shut off. I suppose there, in his own house, among his own things, it was too much for him. He left no letters."

Cavenaugh blinked and brushed the lapel of his coat. "I suppose," he said slowly, "that every suicide is logical and reasonable, if one knew all the facts."

Eastman roused himself. "No, I don't think so. I've known too many fellows who went off like that—more than I deserve, I think—and some of them were absolutely inexplicable. I can understand Dudley; but I can't see why healthy bachelors, with money enough, like ourselves, need such a device. It reminds me of what Dr. Johnson said, that the most discouraging thing about life is the number of fads and hobbies and fake religions it takes to put people through a few years of it."

"Dr. Johnson? The specialist? Oh, the old fellow!" said Cavenaugh imperturbably. "Yes, that's interesting. Still, I fancy if one knew the facts— Did you know about Wyatt?"

"I don't think so."

"You wouldn't, probably. He was just a fellow about town who spent money. He wasn't one of the *forestieri*, though. Had connections here and owned a fine old place over on Staten Island. He went in for botany, and had been all over, hunting things; rusts, I believe. He had a yacht and used to take a gay crowd down about the South Seas, botanizing. He really did botanize, I believe. I never knew such a spender—only not flashy. He helped a lot of fellows and he was awfully good to girls, the kind who come down here to get a little fun, who don't like to work and still aren't really tough, the kind you see talking hard for their dinner. Nobody knows what becomes of them, or what they get out of it, and there are hundreds of new ones every year. He helped dozens of 'em; it was he who got me curious about the little shop girls. Well, one afternoon when his tea was brought, he took prussic acid instead. He didn't leave any letters, either; people of any taste don't. They wouldn't leave any material reminder if they could help it. His lawyers found that he had just $314.72 above his debts when he died. He had planned to spend all his money, and then take his tea; he had worked it out carefully."

Eastman reached for his pipe and pushed his chair away from the fire. "That looks like a considered case, but I don't think philosophical suicides like that are common. I think they usually come from stress of feeling and are really, as the newspapers call them, desperate acts; done without a motive. You remember when Anna Karenina was under the wheels, she kept saying, 'Why am I here?'"

Cavenaugh rubbed his upper lip with his pink finger and made an effort to wrinkle his brows. "May I, please?" reaching for the whiskey. "But have you," he asked, blinking as the soda flew at him, "have you ever known, yourself, cases that were really inexplicable?"

"A few too many. I was in Washington just before Captain Jack Purden was married and I saw a good deal of him. Popular army man, fine record in the Philippines, married a charming girl with lots of money; mutual devotion. It was the gayest wedding of the winter, and they started for Japan. They stopped in San Francisco for a week and missed their boat because, as the bride wrote back to Washington, they were too happy to move. They took the next boat, were both good sailors, had exceptional weather. After they had been out for two weeks, Jack got up from his deck chair one afternoon, yawned, put down his book, and stood before his wife. 'Stop reading for a moment and look at me.' She laughed and asked him why. 'Because you happen to be good to look at.' He nodded to her, went back to the stern and was never seen again. Must have gone down to the lower deck and slipped overboard, behind the machinery. It was the luncheon hour, not many people about; steamer cutting through a soft green sea. That's one of the most baffling cases I know. His friends raked up his past, and it was as trim as a cottage garden. If he'd so much as dropped an ink spot on his fatigue uniform, they'd have found it. He wasn't emotional or moody; wasn't, indeed, very interesting; simply a good soldier, fond of all the pompous little formalities that make up a military man's life. What do you make of that, my boy?"

Cavenaugh stroked his chin. "It's very puzzling, I admit. Still, if one knew everything——"

"But we do know everything. His friends wanted to find something to help them out, to help the girl out, to help the case of the human creature."

"Oh, I don't mean things that people could unearth," said Cavenaugh uneasily. "But possibly there were things that couldn't be found out."

Eastman shrugged his shoulders. "It's my experience that when there are 'things' as you call them, they're very apt to be found. There is no such thing as a secret. To make any move at all one has to employ human agencies, employ at least one human agent. Even when the pirates killed the men who buried their gold for them, the bones told the story."

Cavenaugh rubbed his hands together and smiled his sunny smile.

"I like that idea. It's reassuring. If we can have no secrets, it means that we can't, after all, go so far afield as we might," he hesitated, "yes, as we might."

Eastman looked at him sourly. "Cavenaugh, when you've practised law in New York for twelve years, you find that people can't go far in any direction, except——" He thrust his forefinger sharply at the floor. "Even in that direction, few people can do anything out of the ordinary. Our range is limited. Skip a few baths, and we become personally objectionable. The slightest carelessness can rot a man's integrity or give him ptomaine poisoning. We keep up only by incessant cleansing operations, of mind and body. What we call character, is held together by all sorts of tacks and strings and glue."

Cavenaugh looked startled. "Come now, it's not so bad as that, is it? I've always thought that a serious man, like you, must know a lot of Launcelots." When Eastman only laughed, the younger man squirmed about in his chair. He spoke again hastily, as if he were embarrassed. "Your military friend may have had personal experiences, however, that his friends couldn't possibly get a line on. He may accidentally have come to a place where he saw himself in too unpleasant a light. I believe people can be chilled by a draft from outside, somewhere."

"Outside?" Eastman echoed. "Ah, you mean the far outside! Ghosts, delusions, eh?"

Cavenaugh winced. "That's putting it strong. Why not say tips from the outside? Delusions belong to a diseased mind, don't they? There are some of us who have no minds to speak of, who yet have had experiences. I've had a little something in that line myself and I don't look it, do I?"

Eastman looked at the bland countenance turned toward him. "Not exactly. What's your delusion?"

"It's not a delusion. It's a haunt."

The lawyer chuckled. "Soul of a lost Casino girl?"

"No; an old gentleman. A most unattractive old gentleman, who follows me about."

"Does he want money?"

Cavenaugh sat up straight. "No. I wish to God he wanted anything—but the pleasure of my society! I'd let him clean me out to be rid of him. He's a real article. You saw him yourself that night when you came to my rooms to borrow a dictionary, and he went down the fire-escape. You saw him down in the court."

"Well, I saw somebody down in the court, but I'm too cautious to take it for granted that I saw what you saw. Why, anyhow, should I see your haunt? If it was your friend I saw, he impressed me disagreeably. How did you pick him up?"

Cavenaugh looked gloomy. "That was queer, too. Charley Burke and I had motored out to Long Beach, about a year ago, sometime in October, I think. We had supper and stayed until late. When we were coming home, my car broke down. We had a lot of girls along who had to get back for morning rehearsals and things; so I sent them all into town in Charley's car, and he was to send a man back to tow me home. I was driving myself, and didn't want to leave my machine. We had not taken a direct road back; so I was stuck in a lonesome woody place, no houses about. I got chilly and made a fire, and was putting in the time comfortably enough, when this old party steps up. He was in shabby evening clothes and a top hat, and had on his usual white gloves. How he got there, at three o'clock in the morning, miles from any town or railway, I'll leave it to you to figure out. *He* surely had no car. When I saw him coming up to the fire, I disliked him. He had a silly, apologetic walk. His teeth were chattering, and I asked him to sit down. He got down like a clothes-horse folding up. I offered him a cigarette, and when he took off his gloves I couldn't help noticing how knotted and spotty his hands were. He was asthmatic, and took his breath with a wheeze. 'Haven't you got anything—refreshing in there?' he asked, nodding at the car. When I told him I hadn't, he sighed. 'Ah, you young fellows are greedy. You drink it all up. You drink it all up, all up—up!' he kept chewing it over."

Cavenaugh paused and looked embarrassed again. "The thing that was most unpleasant is difficult to explain. The old man sat there by the fire and leered at me with a silly sort of admiration that was—well, more than humiliating. 'Gay boy, gay dog!' he would mutter, and when he grinned he showed his teeth, worn and yellow—shells. I remembered that it was better to talk casually to insane people; so I remarked carelessly that I had been out with a party and got stuck.

"'Oh yes, I remember,' he said, 'Flora and Lottie and Maybelle and Marcelline, and poor Kate.'

"He had named them correctly; so I began to think I had been hitting the bright waters too hard.

"Things I drank never had seemed to make me woody; but you can never tell when trouble is going to hit you. I pulled my hat down and tried to look as uncommunicative as possible; but he kept croaking on from time to time, like this: 'Poor Kate! Splendid arms, but dope got her. She took up with Eastern religions after she had her hair dyed. Got to going to a Swami's joint, and smoking opium. Temple of the Lotus, it was called, and the police raided it.'

"This was nonsense, of course; the young woman was in the pink of condition. I let him rave, but I decided that if something didn't come out for me pretty soon, I'd foot it across Long

Island. There wasn't room enough for the two of us. I got up and took another try at my car. He hopped right after me.

"'Good car,' he wheezed, 'better than the little Ford.'

"I'd had a Ford before, but so has everybody; that was a safe guess.

"'Still,' he went on, 'that run in from Huntington Bay in the rain wasn't bad. Arrested for speeding, he-he.'

"It was true I had made such a run, under rather unusual circumstances, and had been arrested. When at last I heard my life-boat snorting up the road, my visitor got up, sighed, and stepped back into the shadow of the trees. I didn't wait to see what became of him, you may believe. That was visitation number one. What do you think of it?"

Cavenaugh looked at his host defiantly. Eastman smiled.

"I think you'd better change your mode of life, Cavenaugh. Had many returns?" he inquired.

"Too many, by far." The young man took a turn about the room and came back to the fire. Standing by the mantel he lit another cigarette before going on with his story:

"The second visitation happened in the street, early in the evening, about eight o'clock. I was held up in a traffic block before the Plaza. My chauffeur was driving. Old Nibbs steps up out of the crowd, opens the door of my car, gets in and sits down beside me. He had on wilted evening clothes, same as before, and there was some sort of heavy scent about him. Such an unpleasant old party! A thorough-going rotter; you knew it at once. This time he wasn't talkative, as he had been when I first saw him. He leaned back in the car as if he owned it, crossed his hands on his stick and looked out at the crowd—sort of hungrily.

"I own I really felt a loathing compassion for him. We got down the avenue slowly. I kept looking out at the mounted police. But what could I do? Have him pulled? I was afraid to. I was awfully afraid of getting him into the papers.

"'I'm going to the New Astor,' I said at last. 'Can I take you anywhere?'

"'No, thank you,' says he. 'I get out when you do. I'm due on West 44th. I'm dining to-night with Marcelline—all that is left of her!'

"He put his hand to his hat brim with a grewsome salute. Such a scandalous, foolish old face as he had! When we pulled up at the Astor, I stuck my hand in my pocket and asked him if he'd like a little loan.

"'No, thank you, but'—he leaned over and whispered, ugh!— 'but save a little, save a little. Forty years from now—a little— comes in handy. Save a little.'

"His eyes fairly glittered as he made his remark. I jumped out. I'd have jumped into the North River. When he tripped off, I asked my chauffeur if he'd noticed the man who got into the car with me. He said he knew someone was with me, but he hadn't noticed just when he got in. Want to hear any more?"

Cavenaugh dropped into his chair again. His plump cheeks were a trifle more flushed than usual, but he was perfectly calm. Eastman felt that the young man believed what he was telling him.

"Of course I do. It's very interesting. I don't see quite where you are coming out though."

Cavenaugh sniffed. "No more do I. I really feel that I've been put upon. I haven't deserved it any more than any other fellow of my kind. Doesn't it impress you disagreeably?"

"Well, rather so. Has anyone else seen your friend?"

"You saw him."

"We won't count that. As I said, there's no certainty that you and I saw the same person in the court that night. Has anyone else had a look in?"

"People sense him rather than see him. He usually crops up when I'm alone or in a crowd on the street. He never approaches me when I'm with people I know, though I've seen him hanging about the doors of theatres when I come out with a party; loafing around the stage exit, under a wall; or across the street, in a doorway. To be frank, I'm not anxious to introduce him. The third time, it was I who came upon him. In November my driver, Harry, had a sudden attack of appendicitis. I took him to the Presbyterian Hospital in the car, early in the evening. When I came home, I found the old villain in my rooms. I offered him a drink, and he sat down. It was the first time I had seen him in a steady light, with his hat off.

"His face is lined like a railway map, and as to color—Lord, what a liver! His scalp grows tight to his skull, and his hair is dyed until it's perfectly dead, like a piece of black cloth."

Cavenaugh ran his fingers through his own neatly trimmed thatch, and seemed to forget where he was for a moment.

"I had a twin brother, Brian, who died when we were sixteen. I have a photograph of him on my wall, an enlargement from a kodak of him, doing a high jump, rather good thing, full of action. It seemed to annoy the old gentleman. He kept looking at it and lifting his eyebrows, and finally he got up, tip-toed across the room, and turned the picture to the wall.

"'Poor Brian! Fine fellow, but died young,' says he.

"Next morning, there was the picture, still reversed."

"Did he stay long?" Eastman asked interestedly.

"Half an hour, by the clock."

"Did he talk?"

"Well, he rambled."

"What about?"

Cavenaugh rubbed his pale eyebrows before answering.

"About things that an old man ought to want to forget. His conversation is highly objectionable. Of course he knows me like a book; everything I've ever done or thought. But when he recalls them, he throws a bad light on them, somehow. Things that weren't much off color, look rotten. He doesn't leave one a shred of self-respect, he really doesn't. That's the amount of it." The young man whipped out his handkerchief and wiped his face.

"You mean he really talks about things that none of your friends know?"

"Oh, dear, yes! Recalls things that happened in school. Anything disagreeable. Funny thing, he always turns Brian's picture to the wall."

"Does he come often?"

"Yes, oftener, now. Of course I don't know how he gets in down-stairs. The hall boys never see him. But he has a key to my door. I don't know how he got it, but I can hear him turn it in the lock."

"Why don't you keep your driver with you, or telephone for me to come down?"

"He'd only grin and go down the fire escape as he did before. He's often done it when Harry's come in suddenly. Everybody has to be alone sometimes, you know. Besides, I don't want anybody to see him. He has me there."

"But why not? Why do you feel responsible for him?"

Cavenaugh smiled wearily. "That's rather the point, isn't it? Why do I? But I absolutely do. That identifies him, more than his knowing all about my life and my affairs."

Eastman looked at Cavenaugh thoughtfully. "Well, I should advise you to go in for something altogether different and new, and go in for it hard; business, engineering, metallurgy, something this old fellow wouldn't be interested in. See if you can make him remember logarithms."

Cavenaugh sighed. "No, he has me there, too. People never really change; they go on being themselves. But I would never make much trouble. Why can't they let me alone, damn it! I'd never hurt anybody, except, perhaps——"

"Except your old gentleman, eh?" Eastman laughed. "Seriously, Cavenaugh, if you want to shake him, I think a year on a ranch would do it. He would never be coaxed far from his favorite haunts. He would dread Montana."

Cavenaugh pursed up his lips. "So do I!"

"Oh, you think you do. Try it, and you'll find out. A gun and a horse beats all this sort of thing. Besides losing your haunt, you'd be putting ten years in the bank for yourself. I know a good ranch where they take people, if you want to try it."

"Thank you. I'll consider. Do you think I'm batty?"

"No, but I think you've been doing one sort of thing too long. You need big horizons. Get out of this."

Cavenaugh smiled meekly. He rose lazily and yawned behind his hand. "It's late, and I've taken your whole evening." He strolled over to the window and looked out. "Queer place, New York; rough on the little fellows. Don't you feel sorry for them, the girls especially? I do. What a fight they put up for a little fun! Why, even that old goat is sorry for them, the only decent thing he kept."

Eastman followed him to the door and stood in the hall, while Cavenaugh waited for the elevator. When the car came up Cavenaugh extended his pink, warm hand. "Good night."

The cage sank and his rosy countenance disappeared, his round-eyed smile being the last thing to go.

Weeks passed before Eastman saw Cavenaugh again. One morning, just as he was starting for Washington to argue a case before the Supreme Court, Cavenaugh telephoned him at his office to ask him about the Montana ranch he had recommended; said he meant to take his advice and go out there for the spring and summer.

When Eastman got back from Washington, he saw dusty trunks, just up from the trunk room, before Cavenaugh's door. Next morning, when he stopped to see what the young man was about, he found Cavenaugh in his shirt sleeves, packing.

"I'm really going; off to-morrow night. You didn't think it of me, did you?" he asked gaily.

"Oh, I've always had hopes of you!" Eastman declared. "But you are in a hurry, it seems to me."

"Yes, I am in a hurry." Cavenaugh shot a pair of leggings into one of the open trunks. "I telegraphed your ranch people, used your name, and they said it would be all right. By the way, some of my crowd are giving a little dinner for me at Rector's to-night. Couldn't you be persuaded, as it's a farewell occasion?" Cavenaugh looked at him hopefully.

Eastman laughed and shook his head. "Sorry, Cavenaugh, but that's too gay a world for me. I've got too much work lined up before me. I wish I had time to stop and look at your guns, though. You seem to know something about guns. You've more than you'll need, but nobody can have too many good ones." He put down one of the revolvers regretfully. "I'll drop in to see you in the morning, if you're up."

"I shall be up, all right. I've warned my crowd that I'll cut away before midnight."

"You won't, though," Eastman called back over his shoulder as he hurried downstairs.

The next morning, while Eastman was dressing, Rollins came in greatly excited.

"I'm a little late, sir. I was stopped by Harry, Mr. Cavenaugh's driver. Mr. Cavenaugh shot himself last night, sir."

Eastman dropped his vest and sat down on his shoe-box. "You're drunk, Rollins," he shouted. "He's going away to-day!"

"Yes, sir. Harry found him this morning. Ah, he's quite dead, sir. Harry's telephoned for the coroner. Harry don't know what to do with the ticket."

Eastman pulled on his coat and ran down the stairway. Cavenaugh's trunks were strapped and piled before the door. Harry was walking up and down the hall with a long green railroad ticket in his hand and a look of complete stupidity on his face.

"What shall I do about this ticket, Mr. Eastman?" he whispered. "And what about his trunks? He had me tell the transfer people to come early. They may be here any minute. Yes, sir. I brought him home in the car last night, before twelve, as cheerful as could be."

"Be quiet, Harry. Where is he?"

"In his bed, sir."

Eastman went into Cavenaugh's sleeping-room. When he came back to the sitting-room, he looked over the writing table; railway folders, time-tables, receipted bills, nothing else. He looked up for the photograph of Cavenaugh's twin brother. There it was, turned to the wall. Eastman took it down and looked at it; a boy in track clothes, half lying in the air, going over the string shoulders first, above the heads of a crowd of lads who were running and cheering. The face was somewhat blurred by the motion and the bright sunlight. Eastman put the picture back, as he found it. Had Cavenaugh entertained his visitor last night, and had the old man been more convincing than usual? "Well, at any rate, he's seen to it that the old man can't establish identity. What a soft lot they are, fellows like poor Cavenaugh!" Eastman thought of his office as a delightful place.

Call Me From the Valley

Manly Wade Wellman

Down it rained, on hill and hollow, the way you'd think the sky was too heavy to hold it back. It fell so thick and hard fish could have swum in it, all around where we sat holed up under the low wide porch of the country store—five of us. A leather-coated deputy sheriff with a pickup truck. A farmer, who'd sheltered his mule wagon in a shed behind. The old storekeeper, and us two strangers in that part of the hills, a quiet old gentleman and me with my silver-strung guitar.

The storekeeper hung a lantern to the porch rafters as it got dark. The farmer bought us all a bottle of soda, and the storekeeper broke us open a box of cookies. "Gentleman, you'll all be here for a spell, so sit comfortable," he said. "Friend," he said to me, "did I ask your name?"

"John," I named myself.

"Well, John, do you play that guitar you're a-toting?"

I played and sang for them, that old song about the hunter's true love:

> Oh, call me sweetheart, call me dear,
> Call me what you will,
> Call me from the valley low,
> Call me from the hill. . . .

Then there was talk about old things and thoughts. I recollect what some of them said:

Such as, you can't win solitaire by cheating just once, you've got to keep cheating; some animals are smarter than folks; who were the ancients who dug mine-holes in the Toe River country, and what were they after, and did they find it; nobody knows what makes the lights come and go like giant fireflies every night on Brown Mountain; you'll never see a man exactly six feet tall, because that was the height of the Lord Jesus.

And the farmer, who next to me was the youngest there, mentioned love and courting, and how when you true-love someone and need your eyes and thoughts clearest, they mist up and maybe make you trouble. That led to how you step down a mullein stalk toward your true love's house, and if it grows up again she loves you; and how the girls used to have dumb suppers, setting plates and knives and forks on the table at night and each girl standing behind a chair put ready, till at midnight the candles blew out and a girl saw, or she thought she saw, a ghosty-looking somebody in the chair before her, and that was the appearance of the somebody she'd marry.

"Knew of dumb suppers when I was just a chap," allowed the old storekeeper, "but most of the old folks then, they didn't relish the notion. Said it was a devil-made idea, and you might call in something better left outside."

"Ain't no such goings-on in this day and time," nodded the farmer. "I don't take stock in them crazy sayings and doings."

Back where I was born and raised, in the Drowning Creek country, I'd heard tell of dumb suppers but I'd never seen one, so I held my tongue. But the deputy grinned his teeth at the farmer.

"You plant by the moon, don't you?" he asked. "Above-ground things like corn at the full, and underground things like 'taters in the dark?"

"That ain't foolishness, that's the true way," the farmer said back. "Ask anybody's got a lick of sense about farming."

Then a big wiggling three-forked flash of lighting struck, it didn't seem more than arm's-length off, and the thunder was like the falling in of the hills.

"Law me," said the old gentleman, whose name seemed to be Mr. Jay. "That was a hooter."

"Sure God was," the farmer agreed him. "Old Forney Meechum wants us to remember he makes the rain around here."

My ears upped like a rabbit's. "I did hear this is the old Meechum-Donovant feud country," I said. "I've always been wanting to hear the true tale of that. And what about Forney Meechum making the rain—isn't he dead?"

"Deader than hell," the storekeeper told me. "Though folks never thought he could die, thought he'd just ugly away. But him and all the Meechum and Donovant men got killed. Both the names plumb died out, I reckon, yonder in the valley so low where you see the rain a-falling the lavishest. I used to hear about it when I was just a chap."

"Me, too," nodded the deputy. "Way I got it, Forney Meechum went somewheres west when he was young. Was with the James boys or the Younger boys, or maybe somebody not quite that respectable."

"And when he come back," took up the storekeeper again, "he could make it rain whenever it suited him."

"How?" I asked, and old Mr. Jay was listening, too.

"Ain't rightly certain how," said the farmer. "They tell he used to mix up mud in a hole, and sing a certain song. Ever hear such a song as that, John?"

I shook my head *no,* and he went on:

"Forney Meechum done scarier things than that. He witched wells dry. And he raised up dead ghosts to show him where treasure was hid. Even his own kinfolks was scared of him, and all the Meechums took orders from him. So when he fell out with Captain Sam Donovant over a property line, he made them break with all the Donovants."

"Fact," said the storekeeper, who wanted to tell part of the tale. "And them Meechums did what he told them, saving only his cousin's oldest girl, Miss Lute Meechum, and she'd swore eternal love with Captain Ben Donovant's second boy Jeremiah."

Another lighting flash, another thunder growl. Old Mr. Jay hunched his thin shoulders under his jeans coat, and allowed he'd pay for some cheese and crackers if the storekeeper'd fetch it out to us.

"Law me," said the farmer. "I ain't even now wanting to talk against Forney Meechum. But they tell he'd put his eye on Lute himself, and he'd quarreled with his own son Derwood about who'd have her. But next court day at the county seat, was a fight betwixt Jeremiah Donovant and Derwood Meechum, and Jeremiah stuck a knife in Derwood and killed him dead."

Mr. Jay leaned forward in the lantern light. It showed the gray stubble on his gentle old face. "Who drew the first knife?" he asked.

"I've heard tell Derwood drew the knife, and Jeremiah took it away and stuck it to him," said the farmer. "Anyway, Jeremiah Donovant had to run from the law, and down in the valley yonder the Meechums and the Donovants began a-shooting at each other."

"Fact," the storekeeper took it up again as he fetched out the cheese and crackers. "That was 50 years back, the last fight of all. Ary man on both sides was killed, down to boys of ten-twelve years. Old Forney called for rain, but somebody shot him just as he got it started."

"And it falls a right much to this day," said the farmer, gazing at the pour from the porch eaves. "That valley below us is so rainy it's a swamp like. And the widows and orphans that was left alive, both families, they was purely rained out and went other places to live."

"What about Miss Lute Meechum?" I asked next.

"I wondered about her, too," said Mr. Jay.

"Died," said the storekeeper. "Some folks say it was pure down grief killed her, that and lonesomeness for that run-off Jeremiah Donovant. I likewise heard tell old Forney shot her when she said for once and all she wouldn't have him."

The deputy sipped his soda. "All done and past now," he said. "Looks like we're rained in here for all night, gentlemen."

But we weren't. It slacked off while we ate our cheese, and then it was just a drip from the branches. The clouds shredded, and a moon poked through a moment, shy, like a girl at her first play-party. The deputy got up from the slab-bench where he'd been sitting.

"Hope my truck'll wallow up that muddy road to town," he said. "Who can I carry with me?"

"I got my mule," added the farmer. "I'll follow along and

snake you out when you get stuck in one of them mud holes. John, you better ride with me, you and Mr. Jay."

I shook my head. "I'm not going to town, thank you kindly. I'm going down that valley trail. Swore to an old friend I'd be at his family reunion, up in the hills on the yonder side, by supper time tomorrow."

Mr. Jay said he'd be going that way, too. The storekeeper offered to let us sleep in his feed shed, but I said I'd better start. "Coming, sir?" I asked old Mr. Jay.

"After while," he told me, so I went on alone. Three minutes down trail between those wet dark trees, and the lantern light under the porch was gone as if it had never shone.

Gentlemen, it was lonesome dark and damp going. I felt my muddy way along, with my brogan shoes squashy-full of water. And yet, sometimes, it wasn't as lonesome as you might call for. There were soft noises, like whispers or crawlings; and once there was a howl, not too far away, like a dog, or a man trying to sound like a dog, or maybe the neither of them. For my own comfort I began to pick the guitar and sing to myself; but the wrong tune had come unbidden:

> In the pines, in the pines,
> Where the sun never shines,
> And I shiver where the wind blows cold! . . .

I stopped when I got that far, it was too much the truth. And it came on to rain again.

I hauled off my old coat to wrap my guitar from it. Not much to see ahead, but I knew I kept going down slope and down slope, and no way of telling how far it went before it would start up to go to the hills where my friend's kinfolks would gather tomorrow. I told myself I was a gone gump not to stay at the store, the way I was so kindly bid. I hoped that that old Mr. Jay had the sense to stay under cover. But it was too far to go back. And I'd better find some place out of the wet, for my guitar more than me.

Must have been a bend to that trail, because I came all at once in view of the light in the cabin's glass window, before I notioned there was any living place around. The light looked warm yellow through the rain, and I hastened my wet feet. Close enough in, I could judge it was an old-made log house, the corners notch-locked and the logs clay-chinked, and the wide eaves with thick-split shakes on them, but I couldn't really see. "Hello, the house!" I yelled out.

No sound back. Maybe the rain was keeping them from hearing me. I felt my way to the flat door-stone and knocked. No stir inside.

Groping for a knob, I found none, only a leather latch string, old style. And, old style, it was out. In my grandsire's day, a latch string out meant come in. I pulled, and a wooden latch lifted inside and the door swung in before me.

The room was lit from a fireplace full of red coals, and from a candle stuck on a dish on a table middleway of the puncheon floor. That table took my eye as I stepped in. A cloth on it, and a plate of old white china with knife and fork at its sides, and a cup and saucer, yes and a folded napkin. But no food on the table, no coffee in the cup. A chair was set to the plate, and behind the chair, her hands crossed on its back, stood a woman, young and tall and proud-standing.

She didn't move. Nothing moved, except the candle flame in the stir of air from the open door. She might have been cut from wood and put up there to fool folks. I closed the door against the hard drum of the rain, and tracked wet marks on the puncheons as I came toward the table, I took off my old hat, and the water fell from it.

"Good evening, ma'am," I said.

Then her dark eyes moved in her pale face, her sweet, firm-jawed face. Her short, sad mouth opened, slow and shaky.

"You're not—" she started to mumble, half to herself. "I didn't mean—"

There was a copper light moving in her hair as she bent her head and looked down into the empty plate, and then I remembered that talk under the store porch.

"Dumb supper," I said. "I'm right sorry. The rain drove me in here. I reckon this is the only house around, and when nobody answered I walked in. I didn't mean to bother you."

And I couldn't help but look at how she'd set the dumb supper out. Knowing how such things weren't done any more, and hearing that very thing said that night, I was wondered to find it. Through my mind kept running how some scholar-men say it's a way of doing that came over from the Old Country, where dumb suppers were set clear back to the beginning of time. Things that old don't die easy after all, I reckoned.

"He'll still come and sit down," she said to me in her soft voice, like a low-playing flute heard far off. "I've called him and he'll come."

I hung my wet coat by the fireplace and she saw my guitar.

"Sing to help guide him," she said to me.

I looked at her, so proudly tall behind the chair. She wore a long green dress, and her eyes were darker than her copper hair, that was all in curly ringlets.

"Sing," she said again. "Tole him here."

I felt like doing whatever she told me. I swung the guitar in front of me, and began the song I'd given them at the store:

> Oh, call me sweetheart, call me dear,
> Call me what you will,
> Call me from the valley low,
> Call me from the hill.
>
> I hear you as the turtle dove
> That flies from bough to bough,
> And as she softly calls her mate,
> You call me softly now. . . .

One long hand waved me to stop, and I stopped with the silver strings still whispering to both of us. I felt my ears close up tight, they way they feel when you've climbed high, high on a mountain top.

"There's a power working here," I said.

"Yes," she barely made herself heard.

The fire, that had been just coals, found something to blaze up on. Smoke rose dark above the bright flames. The rain outside came barreling down, and there was a rising wind, too, with a whoop and a shove to it that made the lock-joints of the cabin's logs creak.

"Sounds like old Forney Meechum's hard at work." I tried to

make half a joke, but she didn't take it as such. Her dark-bright eyes lifted their lids to widen, and her hands, on the chair back again, took hold hard.

"Forney doesn't want me to do this," she told me, as if it was my ordinary business.

"He's dead," I reminded her, like to a child.

"No," she shook her copper head. "He's not dead, not all of him. And not all of me, either."

I wondered what she meant, and I stepped away from the fire that was burning bright and hot.

"Are you a Meechum or a Donovant?" I asked.

"A Meechum," she told me. "But my true love's a Donovant."

"Like Lute Meechum and Jeremiah Donovant?"

"You know about that." Her hands trembled a mite, for all they held so hard to the chair. "Who are you?"

"My name's John." I touched the strings to make them whisper again. "Yes, I know the tale about the feud. Old Forney Meechum, who could witch down the rain, said Lute Meechum mustn't have Jeremiah—"

"He's here!" she cried out, with all her loud voice at last.

The wind shook the cabin like a dice-box. The shakes on the roof must have ruffled worse than a hen's feathers. Up jumped the fire, and out winked the candle.

Jumpy myself, I was back against the logs of the wall, my free hand on a shelf-plank that was wedged there. The rain had wetted the clay chinking soft between the logs, and a muddy trickle fell on my fingers. I was watching the fire, and its dirty gray smoke stirred and swelled, and a fat-looking puff of it came crawling out like a live thing.

The smoke stayed in one bunch. It hung there, a sort of egg-shaped chunk of it, hanging above the stones of the hearth. I think the girl must have half fallen, then caught herself; for I heard the legs of the chair scrape on the puncheons. The smoke molded itself, in what light I could make out, and looked solid and shapy, as tall as me but thicker, and two streamy coils waving out in the air like arms.

"Don't!" the girl was begging something. "Don't let him—"

On that shelf at my hand stood a dish and an empty old bottle, the kind of bottle the old glassmakers blew a hundred years ago. I took up the dish in my right fist. I saw that smoke-shape drifting sort of slow and greedy, clear from the hearth, and between those two wavy streamy arm-coils rose up a lumpy thing like a head. There was enough firelight to see that this smoke was thicker than just smoke; it must have soot and ash-dust in it, solid enough to choke you. And in that lumpy head hung two dull sparks, for the eyes.

Gentlemen, more about it than that you'd not care to have me tell you.

I flung the dish, and it went singing through the room and it went straight for where I threw, but it didn't stop. It sailed right on past and into the fireplace, and I heard it smash to pieces on the stones. Where it had hit the smoke-shape, there showed a notchy hole all the way though, where the cheek would be on a living creature. And whatever it was I'd thrown at, it never stopped its slow drift over toward the table, gray and thick and horrible. And in the chimney the wind stomped up and down, like a dasher in a churn.

"No," the girl wailed again, and moved back, dragging the chair along with her.

Then at once I saw what was in whatever that thing had for a mind, and I ran at the table too, passing so close to one of the smoke-streamers that the wind I made fluttered it like a rag. Just as it slid in toward the chair, bending to sit down, I slapped my guitar across the seat with the silver strings up.

I'd figured right. It couldn't touch the silver, being an evil haunt. It moved behind the table, and its sparks flickered at us both. I felt a creeping hot smelly sense, like dirty smoke. It made me feel sick and shake-legged, but I made my eyes look back at those two glaring sparks.

"Are you Forney Meechum?" I asked at it. "Want to sit down at this dumb supper? Think it was laid out for you?"

It swayed back and forth, like a tree-branch, and outside the rain fell in its bucketfuls.

I moved quick around the table, with the guitar held toward it. I'd thought it moved slow, but it was across the room to the

other side the way a shadow flings itself when you move the
lamp. I ran after it, quick, and got to the door first.

"Not out this way," I yelled at it, and jabbed a finger into wet
clay chinking between logs. I quick marked a cross on the inside
of the door planks. Then the Forney Meechum thing was sliding
at the window.

"Not that way, either!" I shooed it back with the guitar, and
sketched a cross on the glass plane. Then the waving arm-streaks
and the lumpy cloud of head and body were sliding back toward
the table.

"Light that candle!" I hollered to the girl. "Light it!"

She heard, and she grabbed the candle up from the table. She
ran across the floor, the cloud hovering after her, and then she
was down on one knee, shoving the candle into the fireplace,
and that quick it lighted up.

And there wasn't any smoke-shape anywhere in the room we
now saw plain.

"Where did he go?" she asked me.

I looked around to see. He hadn't left by the door or the window, for I'd made my crosses there.

"He ran," I said. "Ran before us like a scared-out coward."

"But he was strong—" she started to say.

"He was bad," I put in, not very mannerly. "Badness thinks
it's strong, but it's scared—of lights and crosses, and silver."

Taking my guitar, I picked at the silver strings, and in the
music I made I walked around the room, and around again,
looking. For what was left of Forney Meechum must be somewhere, hiding. And we'd better find out where he hid, or he
might be out at us again when we weren't ready.

I glanced in the corners, up in the rafters. Then at the shelf.
Then I glanced at the shelf twice.

The old bottle that stood there, it was dark-looking, like
muddy water. Or like muddy water, and in the muddy water
maybe a hiding thing, like what can hide in such a place; a snake
or a worse thing than a snake, waiting its time.

I didn't want her to see then, so I made up something quick.

"Look over in the corner yonder," I said to her. "Take the
candle."

She moved to look, and I moved to follow her. Close against a wall, I scooped a lump of clay from the chinking, a wet gob as big as my thumb. I was within a long reach of the shelf.

"The corner," I said, pointing.

And, quick as I could make it, I jammed that clay down on top of the open bottle neck and shoved it in like a cork.

"What—" she began to say.

I picked up the bottle. It felt warm and tingly. In the candle-light we could see the thick dark boiling cloud inside, stirring and spinning and fighting every whichaway, with no way out. I took the candle and dripped wax on the clay, and in the wax I marked a cross with my thumb nail.

"Remember the Arabian nights book?" I asked.

She shook her head. "No. It's foreign, isn't it?"

"Has a thousand and one stories," I said, "and one of them tells how a haunt was tricked in a bottle like this and sealed away forever. Forney Meechum's safe in there."

She moved with the candle and put it on the table. She pushed the chair back into place and stood behind it in her green dress, straight and tall and proud, the way I'd first seen her.

"Now he can come," she said to me, very sure. "Jeremiah."

"Jeremiah Donovant?" I bubbled out.

"Who else?" she asked. "He's coming back to me, after all these years. I felt him coming."

"Then—" I said, but I didn't have to say it. I knew who she was by now.

"I told you I wasn't all dead," reminded Lute Meechum. "Forney shot me in the heart and flung me in a grave, but I couldn't all die. I just lay there till I knew Jeremiah was heading back for me."

I got my coat from beside the fireplace. It felt funny to be in that cabin, with one haunt inside the bottle and one standing behind the chair.

"Thank you for everything, John," she said, old-folksy man-nerly. "Thank you kindly. You can go now, it's all right."

The door squeaked open.

In out of the night came one of the wettest people you ever

could call for. His shoulders and pant legs were soaked, water dripped from his white hair and his old man's chin.

"Mr. Jay," I greeted hum.

"Jeremiah," Lute Meechum greeted him.

He walked across, paying me no mind. "I had to come," he said to her, and the candle went out again.

But I could see him sink down in the chair, and the light from the fireplace made his face look all of a sudden not old any more.

He put up his face, and she put hers down. He went all slack and limp. Restful.

I was outside, with the bottle and guitar. There was nary cloud in the sky, and the moon shone down like a ball of white fire.

The cabin was dark inside now, and I could see by the moon that it was a ruined wreck. The roof had fallen in, the window broken, the logs rotten—you'd swear nobody had set foot there for fifty years back. But inside, Jeremiah Donovant and Lute Meechum were together at last, and peaceful. So peaceful most folks would think they were dead and gone.

On along the trail that was now so clear, I found a tree that looked hollow. Down in its dark inside I put the bottle, and left it there.

It seemed to me I ought to be shaky and scared, but I wasn't. I felt right good. That dumb supper, now—the way I'd heard it said, sometimes a dumb supper calls up things that oughtn't be there; but now I'd seen a dead haunt, setting a dumb supper to tole a living man to her. And it wasn't bad. It wasn't wrong. They were happy about it, I knew that.

Walking in the bright moonlight, I began to strum my guitar, and, gentleman, the song I sang is really an old song:

> Beauty, strength, youth, are flowers and fading seen—
> Duty, faith, love, are roots and ever green. . . .

The Fire When It Comes

Parke Godwin

G ot to wake up soon.

I've been sick a long time, I mean really sick. Hard to remember why or how long, but it feels like that time I had hundred-and-three fever for a week. Sleep wasn't rest but endless, meaningless movement, and I'd wake up to change my sweaty nightdress for a clean one which would be soaked by sunup.

But this boring, weary dream has gone on for ages. I'm walking up and down the apartment trying to find the door. The furniture isn't mine. People come and go, replaced by others with even tackier sofas in colors loud enough to keep them awake, and I flutter around and past them on my own silly route as if I'd lost an earring and had to find it before I could get on with life. None of it's very real, murky as *cinema-verité* shot in a broom closet. I have to strain to recognize the apartment, and the sound track just mumbles. No feeling at all.

Just that it's gone on so long.

All right, enough of this. Lying around sick and fragile is romantic as hell, but I have to get it together, drop the needle on the world again and let it play. I'm—

Hell, I am out of it, can't even remember my name, but there's a twinge of pain in trying. Never mind, start with simple things. Move your hand, spider your fingers out from under the covers. Rub your face, open your eyes.

That hasn't worked the last thousand times. I can't wake up, and in a minute the stupid dream will start again with a new cast and no script, and I'll be loping up and down after that earring or the lost door. Hell, yes. Here it comes. Again.

No. It's different this time. I'd almost swear I was awake, standing near the balcony door with the whole long view of my apartment stretching out before me: living room, pullman kitchen, the bedroom, bathroom like an afterthought in the rear. It's clear daylight, and the apartment is bare. Sounds are painfully sharp. The door screams open and shuts like thunder.

A boy and a girl.

She's twenty-two at the outside, he's not much older. He looks sweet, happy and maybe a little scared. Nice face, the kind of sensitive expression you look at twice. The girl's mouth is firmer. Small and blonde and compact. I know that expression, tentative only for a moment before she begins to measure my apartment for possibilities, making it hers.

"Really a lot of room," she says. "I could do things with this place if we had the money."

My God, they're so *loud*. The boy drifts toward me while she bangs cupboard doors, checks out the bathroom, flushes the toilet.

"The john works. No plumbing problems."

"Al, come here. Look, a balcony."

"Wow, Lowen, is that for real?"

Of course it's real, love. Open the door, take a look and then get the hell out of my dreams.

"Let's look, Al." He invites the girl with one hand and opens the balcony door. He's in love with her and doesn't quite know how to handle it all yet. They wander out onto my tiny balcony and look down at 77th Street and out over the river where a garbage scow is gliding upstream. It's a lovely day. Jesus, how long since I've seen the sun? Kids are romping in the playground across Riverside Drive. Lowen and Al stand close together. When he pulls her to him, her hand slips up over his shoulder. The gold ring looks new.

"Can we afford it, Lowen?"

"We can if you want it."

"If? I never wanted anything so much in my life."

They hold each other and talk money as if it were a novelty, mentioning a rent way over what I pay. The frigging landlord would love to hang that price tag on this place. Lowen points to the drainpipe collar bedded in a patch of cement, monument stone to my epic battle with that bastard to clear the drain and anchor it so every rain didn't turn my balcony into a small lake. Lowen's pointing to letters scratched into the cement.

"GAYLA."

That's right, that's me. I remember now.

They look through the apartment again, excited now that they think they want it. Yes, if they're careful with their budget, if they get that cash wedding present from Aunt Somebody, they can work it. I feel very odd; something is funny here. They're too real. The dream is about them now.

Hey, wait a minute, you two.

The door bangs shut after them.

Hey, wait!

I run out onto the balcony and call to them in the street, and for the first time in this fever dream, I'm conscious of arms and legs that I still can't feel, and a fear growing out of a clearing memory.

Hey, hello. It's me, Gayla Damon.

Lowen turns and tilts his head as if he heard me, or perhaps for one more look at where he's going to live with Al-short-for-Alice. I can't tell from his smile, but I lean to it like a fire in winter, out over the low stone parapet—and then, oh Christ, I remember. For one terrible, sufficient flash, the memory flicks a light switch.

If I could cry or be sick, I'd do that. If I screamed loud enough to crack the asphalt on West End Avenue, nobody would hear. But I let it out anyway, and my scream fills the world as Lowen and Al stroll away toward Riverside Drive.

As if they could actually see me hunched over the balcony edge, head shaking back and forth in despair. They could will their real bodies to stop, real eyes to lift again to a real, vacant balcony.

Because they're real. I'm not. Not sick or dreaming, just not.

You died, Gayla baby. You're dead.

•

The last couple of days have been bad. Panic, running back and forth, scared to death or life, I don't know which, trying to find a way out without knowing where to go or why. I know I died, God, I am sure of that, but not how or how to get out.

There's no frigging door! Lowen and Al sail in and out unloading their junk, but when I try to find the door, it's Not, like me. I'm stuck here. I guess that's what fightens all of us because you can't imagine Not. I never bought the MGM version of heaven. For me, being dead was simply not being, zero, zilch, something you can't imagine. The closest you can come is when a dentist knocks you out with pentothol or how you felt two years before you were born.

No. I don't end, you say. Not me, not the center of the universe. And yet it's happened and I'm stuck with it, no way out, trying to hack the whole thing at once, skittering back and forth from the bedroom to the living room, through the kitchen with its new cream paint, crawling like cigarette smoke in the drapes, beating my nothing-fists against the wall sometimes, collapsing out of habit and exhaustion into a chair or bed I can't feel under me, wearing myself out with the only sensation left, exhaustion and terror.   ·

I'm not dead, I can't be dead, because if I am, why am I still here. Let me out!

To go where, honey?

There's a kind of time again. Al's pinned up a Japanese art calendar in the kitchen, very posh. This month it's a samurai warrior drawing his sword; either that or playing with himself. I can't see it that well, but the date is much too clear. 1981. No wonder the rent's gone up. Seven years since I—

No, that world is a downer. Exited is better. Just how is still a big fat blank wrapped in confusion. All I remember is my name and a few silly details about the apartment. No past, no memory to splice the little snippets of film that flash by too swiftly to catch. Not that it matters, but where's my body? Was I buried or burned, scattered or canned in memoriam in some mausoleum? Was there a husband, a lover? What kind of life did I have?

When I think hard, there's the phantom pain of someone gone, someone who hurt me. That memory is vaguely connected with another of crying into the phone, very drunk. I can't quite remember, just how it made me feel. Got to organize and think, I've worn myself out running scared, and still no answers. The only clear thought is an odd little thing; there must have been a lot of life in me to be kept so close to it.

Don't ask me about death. The rules are all new. I might be the first of the breed. It's still me, but unable to breathe or sleep or get hungry. Just energy that can still run down from overuse, and when that happens, Lowen and Al grow faint. That's all there is to me now, energy, and not much of that. I have to conserve, just float here by Al's painfully correct window drapes and think.

Does anyone know I'm here. I mean, Anyone?

A few more days. Al and Lowen are all moved in. Al's decor works very hard at being House Beautiful, an almost militant graciousness. Style with clenched teeth. And all her china matches—hell, yes, it would. But let's face it: whatever's happening to me is because of them. When they're close, I get a hint of solid objects around me, as if I could reach out and touch tables and chairs or Lowen, but touching life costs me energy. The degree of nearness determines how much of my pitiful little charge is spent. Like being alive in a way. Living costs. I learned that somewhere.

Just got the hell scared out of me. Al has a mirror in the bedroom, a big antique affair. Sometimes when she brushes her hair, I stand behind her, aching out of habit to get that brush into my own mop. Tonight as I watched, I saw myself behind her.

I actually jumped with fright, but Al just went on pumping away with the brush while I peered over her head at Gayla Damon. Thirty-three—I remember that now—and beginning to look it. Thank God that won't bother me any more. Yes, I was tall. Brownish-black hair not too well cut. Thin face, strong jaw, eyes large and expressive. They were my best feature, they broadcast every feeling I ever had. Lines starting around my mouth. Not a hard mouth but beginning to turn down around the edges, a little tired. Hardness would have helped, I guess. Some of Natalie Bond's brass balls.

Nattie Bond: a name, another memory.

No, it's gone, but there was a kind of pain with it. I stared at the mirror. Cruddy old black sweater and jeans: was I wearing them? You'd think I could check out in something better. Hey, brown eyes, how did they do you for the curtain call? Touch of pancake, I hope. You always looked dead without it. Oh, shit. . . .

A little crying helps. Even dry it's something.

I watch Lowen more and more, turning to him as a flower follows the sun, beginning to learn why I respond to him. Lowen's a listener and a watcher. He can be animated when he's feeling good or way down if he's not. Tired, depressed or angry, his brown eyes go almost black. Not terribly aggressive, but he does sense and respond to the life going on around him.

He likes the apartment and being quiet in it. He smokes, too, not much but enough to bother Al. They've worked out a compromise: anywhere but the bedroom. So, sometimes, I get a surprise visit in the living room when Lowen wakes up and wants a smoke. He sits for a few minutes in the dark, cigarette a bright arc from his mouth to the ashtray. I can't tell, but sometimes it seems he's listening to pure silence. He turns his head this way and that—toward me sometimes—and I feel weird; like he was sifting the molecules of silence, sensing a weight in them. Sometimes in the evening when he and Al are fixing dinner, Lowen will raise his head in that listening way.

It's a long-shot hope, but I wonder if he can feel *me*.

Why has he brought me back to time and space and caring? All these years there's been only blurred shadows and voices faint as a radio in the next room. Real light and sound and thought came only when he walked in. When Lowen's near, I perk up and glow; when he leaves, I fade to drift, disinterested, by the balcony door.

Lowen Sheppard: twenty-four at most, gentle, unconsciously graceful, awkward only when he tries to be more mature than he is. Don't work at it, lover, it'll come. Soft, straight brown hair that he forgets to cut until Al reminds him, which is often. She's great on detail, lives by it. Faces this apartment like a cage of lions to be tamed. Perhaps it's the best she ever had.

Lowen seems used to this much or maybe better. Mister nice guy, not my type at all, and yet I'm bound to him by a kind of fascination, bound without being able to touch his hair or speak to him. And it's no use wondering why, I'm learning that, too. Like that old Bergman flick where death comes to collect Max Von Sydow. Max says, "Tell me what eternity is like." And Death says, "Who knows? I just work here."

Don't call us. We'll call you.

Well, damnit, *someone* is going to know I'm here. If I can think, I can do, and I'm not going to sit here forever just around the corner from life. Lowen and Al are my world now, the only script left to work with. I'm a part of their lives like a wart on the thigh, somewhere between God and a voyeur.

Wait, a memory just . . . no. Gone too quick again.

If I could touch Lowen somehow. Let him know.

Lowen and Al are settled in, place for everything and everything in its place, and Al daring it to get out of line. Lowen works full time, and Al must do some part-time gig. She goes out in the early afternoon. The lights dim then. Just as well; I don't like what she's done with my apartment. Everything shrieks its price at you, but somehow Al's not comfortable with it. Maybe she never will be. That mouth is awful tight. She wanted to keep plastic covers over the sofa and chairs, the kind that go *crunkle* when you sit on them and make you feel like you're living in a commercial. But Lowen put his foot down on that.

"But, Al, they're to use, not just to look at."

"I know, but they're so nice and new."

"Look, I wear a rubber when we make love. I don't need them on my furniture."

She actually blushed. "Really, Lowen."

Son of a—she makes him—? Do guys still wear those things? Whatever happened to the sexual revolution?

It's indicative of their upbringing the way each eats, too. Al sits erect at the table and does the full choreography with her knife and fork, as if disapproving mama was watching her all the time. Cut the meat, lay the knife down, cross the fork to her right hand, spear, chew, swallow, and the whole thing over again. Left hand demurely on her lap.

Lowen leans slightly into his plate, what-the-hell elbows on the table. More often than not, he uses the fork in his left hand, placing things on it with his knife. The way he handles them both, he's definitely lived in England or Europe. Not born there, though. The fall of his speech has a hint of softness and mid-South nasal. Virginia or Maryland. Baltimore, maybe.

Perhaps it's just plain jealousy that puts me off Alice. She's alive. She can reach out and touch, hold, kiss what I can only look at. She's the strength in this marriage, the one who'll make it work. Lowen's softer, easier, with that careless assurance that comes from never having to worry about the rent or good clothes. He's been given to; Al's had to grab and fight. Now he's got a job and trying to cut it on his own for the first time. That's scary, but Al helps. She does a pretty fair job of supporting Lowen without letting him notice it too much.

She has her problems, but Lowen comes first. She gets home just before him, zips out to get fresh flowers for the table. A quick shower and a spritz of perfume, another swift agony at the mirror. And then Lowen is home and sitting down to dinner, telling her about the day. And Al listens, not so much to the words but the easy, charming sound, the quality she loves in him, as if she could learn it for herself. She's from New York, probably the Bronx. I remember the accent somehow. Petite and pretty, but she doesn't believe it no matter how much attention Lowen gives her. Spends a lot of time at the mirror when he's gone, not admiring but wondering. What does she really look like. What type is she, what kind of an image does she, should she, project; and can she do it? Lipstick: this shade or that? She fiddles and narrows her eyes, scrutinizing the goods, hopes for the advertised magic of Maybelline and ends up pretty much the same: more attractive than she thinks, not liking what she sees.

Except she doesn't see. She's carried it around all her life, too busy, too nervous and insecure to know what she's got. Stripped down for a bath, Al looks like she never had a pimple or a pound of fat in her life, but I swear she'll find something wrong, something not to like.

Don't slop that goo on your face, girl. You're great already. God, I only wish I had your skin. The crap I had to put on and take off every night, playing parts like—

Parts like. . . .

My God, I remember!

I was an actress. That's what I remember in quick flashes of hard light. The pictures whiz by like fast cars, but they're slowing down: stage sets, snatches of dialogue, dim faces in the front rows. Bill Wrenn giving me a piece of business to work out. Fragments of me like a painting on shattered glass. I grope for the pieces, fitting them together one by one.

Bill Wrenn: there's a warm feeling when I think of him, a trusting. Where did I meet him? Yes, it's coming back.

Bill directed that first season at Lexington Rep. Gentle and patient with a weariness that no longer expected any goodies from life, he always reminded me of a harried sheepdog with too many sheep to hustle. Forty years old, two marriages and struck out both times, not about to fall hard again.

But he did for me. I made it easy for him. We were out of the same mold, Bill and I. He sensed my insecurity as a woman and found ways to make it work for me onstage, found parts in me I'd never dream of playing. With most men, my whole thing began in bed and usually ended there. Bill and I didn't hurry; there was a love first. We enjoyed and respected each other's work, and theater was a church for us. We'd rehash each performance, sometimes staying up all night to put an extra smidge of polish on business or timing, to get a better laugh, to make something good just a hair better. We started with a love of something beyond us that grew toward each other, so that bed, when it came, was natural and easy as it was gorgeous.

I made him love me, my one genuine conquest. We even talked about getting married—carefully skirting around a lot of if's. I seem to remember him asking me one night in Lexington.

I *think* he asked then; there's a thick haze of vodka and grass over that night. Did I say yes? Not likely; by that time the old habits were setting in.

It was too good with Bill. That's not funny. Perfection, happiness, these are frightening things. Very few of us can live with them. After a while, I began to resent Bill. I mean, who the hell was he to take up so much of my life? I began to pick at him, finding things not to like, irritating habits like the nervous way he cleared his throat or dug in his ear when he was thinking out some stage problem; the way he picked his feet in bed and usually left the bathroom a mess. Just bitchiness. I even over reacted when he gave me notes after a performance. All bullshit and panic; just looking for a way out. How dare you love me, Bill Wrenn? Who asked you? Where did I get that way, where did it begin?

When Nick Charreau came into the company, he was tailor-made for me.

He was alone onstage the first time I saw him, a new cast replacement going through his blocking with the stage manager. Everything his predecessor did, Nick adjusted to show himself in a better light. He wasn't a better actor, but so completely, insolently sure of himself that he could pull off anything and make it look good, even a bad choice. Totally self-centered: if there were critics in the house, Nick lit up like a sign, otherwise it was just another working night in the sticks.

Nick was a lot better looking than Bill and eighteen years younger. Even-featured with a sharp, cool, detached expression. Eyes that looked right through you. He could tell me things wrong with myself that would earn Bill Wrenn a reaming out, but I took it from Nick. He didn't get close or involved all the way down. Perhaps that's why I chose him, out of cowardice. He wouldn't ever ask me to be a person.

When he finished the blocking session, I came down to lean on the stage apron. "You play that far back, you'll upstage everyone else in the scene."

"It's my scene. I'm beautifully lit up there." Nick's smile was friendly with just the right soupçon of cockiness. A little above us all, just enough to tickle my own self-doubt and make me want to take him on. I can handle you, mister. You're not so tough.

But he was. There was always part of Nick I couldn't reach or satisfy. I started out challenged, piqued, to cut him down to size in bed and ended up happy if he'd just smile at me.

Looking over Al's shoulder in the mirror, I know it's not what we're born but what we're made into. The game is called Hurt me, I haven't suffered enough. I needed a son of a bitch like Nick. You don't think I'd go around deserving someone like Bill, do you?

Call that weird, Alice? You're the same song, different verse. You have that wary, born-owing-money look yourself. You handle it better than I did—you knew a good man when you saw one—but you still feel like a loser.

The fights with Bill grew large, bitter and frequent. He knew what was happening and it hurt him. And one night we split.

"When will you grow up, Gayla?"

"Bill, don't make it harder than it has to be. Just wish me luck."

Dogged, tired, plopping fresh ice-cubes into his drink. "I care about you. About you, Gayla. That makes it hard. Nick's twenty-two and about an inch deep. He'll split in six months and you'll be out in the cold. When will you learn, Gay? It's not a game, it's not a great big candy store. It's people."

"I'm sorry, Bill."

"Honey," he sighed, "you sure are."

I still hovered, somehow needing his blessing. "Please? Wish me luck?"

Bill raised his glass, not looking up. "Sure, Gay. With Nick you'll need it."

"What's that mean?"

"Nothing, forget it."

"No, you don't just say things like that."

"Sorry, I'm all out of graciousness."

"What did you mean I'll need it."

Bill paused to take a swallow of his drink. "Come on, Gay. You're not blind."

"Other women? So what."

"Other anybody."

"Oh boy, you're—"

"Nick swings both ways."

"That's a lie!"

"He'd screw a light socket if it helped him to a part."

That was the nastiest thing Bill ever said about anyone. I felt angry and at the same time gratified that he made it easier to walk out mad. "Good-bye, Bill."

And then he looked up at me, showing what was hidden before. Bill Wrenn was crying. Crying for me, the only person in this fucking world who ever did. All the pain, anger, loss, welling up in those sad sheepdog eyes. I could have put my arms around him and stayed . . . no, wait, the picture's changing. I'm here in the apartment. *Get him out of here, Nick—*

No, it goes too fast or I will it to go. I can't, won't remember that yet because it hurts too much, and like a child I reach, cry out for the one thing I could always trust.

Bill-l-l—

Not a scream, just the memory of sound.

Lowen looks up from his book, puzzled. "Al? You call me?"

No answer. It's late, she's asleep.

Once more Lowen seems to listen, feeling the air and the silence, separating its texture with his senses. Searching. Then he goes back to his book, but he doesn't really try to read.

He heard me. He heard *me*. I can reach him.

Sooner or later, he'll know I'm here. Bust my hump or break my heart, I'll do it. Somehow. I've got to live, baby. Even dead, it's all I know how to do.

I've hit a new low, watched Lowen and Al make love. At first I avoided it, but gradually the prospect drew me as hunger draws you to a kitchen; hunger no longer a poignant memory but sharp need that grows with my strength.

I've never watched love-making before. Porn, yes, but that's for laughs, a nowhere fantasy. One of the character men in Lexington had a library of films we used to dig sometimes after a show, hooting at their ineptness. They could make you laugh or even horny now and then, but none of them ever dealt with reality. Porn removes you from the act, puts it at a safe distance.

Real sex is awkward, banal and somehow very touching to watch. It's all the things we are and want: involvement, commitment, warmth, passion, clumsiness, generosity or selfishness. Giving and receiving or holding back, all stained with the colors of openness or fear, lovely—and very vulnerable. All that, and yet the words are inadequate; you can't get any of that from watching. Like the man said, you had to be there.

Rogers and Astaire these two are not. It's all pretty straight missionary and more of an express than a local. Lowen does certain things and Al tries a few herself, sort of at arm's length and without much freedom. I don't think Lowen's had much experience, and Al, though she needs sex, probably learned somewhere that she oughtn't like it all that much. She's the new generation; she's heard it's her right and prerogative, but the no-no was bred in early. So she compromises by not enjoying it, by making it uphill for both of them. She inhibits Lowen without meaning to. He has to wait so long for her to relax and then work so hard to get her going. And of course at the best moment, like an insurance commercial in the middle of a cavalry charge, he has to stop and put on that stupid rubber. I wonder if Al's Catholic, she never heard of a diaphragm? Or maybe it's money. That's not so far out. Maybe she's uptight about getting pregnant because she remembers how it was to grow up poor. Maybe it's a lot of things adding up to this tentative ambivalence, wondering why the bells don't ring and the earth shake like she read in *Cosmopolitan*. I seem to remember that trip.

She doesn't give herself much time to relish it afterward, either. Kiss-kiss-bang-bang, then zip with the kleenex and pit-pat into the shower as if someone might catch them. Maybe that's the way it was before they married, a habit that set before either of them realized it.

But I've touched Lowen. God, yes, for one galvanized split-second I felt his body against me. I paid for it, but it had to be.

It was after they made love and Al did her sprint from bed through the shower and into her nightie-cocoon. Lowen went into the bathroom then. I heard the shower running and drifted in after him.

His body looked marvelous; smooth light olive against Al's blue flower-patterned bath curtains, the soap lather standing out sharp white against the last of his summer tan. Not too muscular; supple like Nick. It'll be a while before he has to worry about weight.

Lowen soaped and rinsed, and I enjoyed the shape of his chest and shoulders when he raised his arms over his head.

You're beautiful, Mr. Sheppard.

I had to do it then. I moved in and kissed him, *felt* his chest, stomach, his hardness against the memory of my pelvis. Only a second, a moment when I had to hold him.

The sensation that shivered through me was like a sudden electric shock. I pulled back, frightened and hurt, hovering in the shower curtain. Lowen jerked, grabbing for the towel rack, taut, scared as myself. Then, slowly, the fear faded and I saw that listening, probing attitude in the lift of his head before the instinctive fear returned. Lowen snapped the water off, stumbled out of the tub and just sat down on the john, dripping and shaking. He sat there for minutes, watching the water drying on his skin, runneling down the sides of the tub. Once he put a hand to his lips. They moved, forming a word I couldn't hear.

You felt me, damn you. You know I'm here. If I could just talk to you.

But the exhaustion and pain ebbed me. We slumped at opposite ends of the small bathroom, Lowen staring through me, not hearing the sob, the agony of the pictures that flashed into life. Touching him, I remember. After the shock of life comes the memory, filling me out by one more jagged fragment, measuring me in pain.

Al, Al, frowning at your mirror, wondering what magic you lack—I should have your problem. The guys probably lined up around the block when you were in school. Not for Gayla Damon; hell, that wasn't even my real name, not for a long, hard time. First there was big, fat Gail Danowski from the Bronx like you, and at seventeen what your men prayed for and likely never got, I couldn't give away.

Why do I have to remember that? Please, I tried so hard to get away from it. My father who worked for the city as a sand-hog, my dumpy mother with her permanent look of washed-out disgust, both of them fresh off the boat in 1938. My sister Sasha who got married at seventeen to get away from them. Big change: all Zosh did after that was have kids for that beer-drinking slob husband of hers. Jesus. Charlie disgusted me. Sunday afternoons he'd come over and watch football with my father, swill beer and stuff potato chips. Every once in a while he'd let out a huge belch, then sigh and pat his pot gut like he was so goddamn pleased with himself. For years, while Zosh's teeth went and her skin faded to chalk delivering five kids.

And me growing up in the middle of it, waiting for the big event of the day in the south Bronx, the Good Humor truck out on the street.

"Mommy, Mommy, the goojoomer's here! C'n I have a dime for the goojoomer?"

"Y'fadda din leave me no money."

Urgent jingling from the Good Humor, ready to leave and take excitement with it. "Mommy!"

"Geddouda here. I ain't got no dime, now shaddup."

I used to think about that a lot: a lousy dime. So little and so much to a kid. Go to hell, Momma. Not for the dime, but for a whole beauty you never had and never missed. You weren't going to keep me from it.

It wasn't much better in high school. I was embarrassed to undress for gym because of the holes in my underwear. And the stains sometimes because I had to use Momma's kotex and she didn't care if she ran out. I could have used tampax; virgin or not, I was a big, healthy ox like her and Zosh. I could have conceived an army. When Momma found the tampax I bought, she slapped me halfway across the room.

"What's this, hah? *Hah?* I ain't got enough trouble, you started already? You sneakin around, you little bitch?"

No such luck, Momma. They didn't want me. The closest I got to boys was talking about them. Sitting in a coffee shop over the debris of my cheap, starchy lunch, the table a garbage dump of bread crusts, spilled sugar and straw wrappers, shredding food bits and paper ends like our envious gossip dissected the girls we knew and the boys we wanted to know.

I never had any sense about men or myself. That happens when you're five foot seven in high school and still growing. A sequoia in a daisy bed, lumpy and lumbering, addicted to food, my refuge when I lost the courage for school dances. I fled home to the ice box and stayed there, eating myself out of my clothes, smearing my acne with Vis-o-Hex, or huddled for hours in a movie, seeing it twice over to pretend I was Hepburn or Bacall, slim, brittle and clever. Or Judith Anderson, tearing hell out of *Medea*. I read the play and practiced the lines at my mirror with stiff approximations of her gestures.

But it was *A Streetcar Named Desire* that changed my life. I hardly spoke for days after seeing it. The play stabbed me deep and sparked something that was going to be. I bought more plays and devoured them. Fewer trips to the movies now and more downtown to Broadway and the Village. Live theater, not unreeling on a spool, but happening the moment I saw it.

I was still a lump, still a hundred and fifty pounds of un-lusted-after virgin bohunk, and nobody was going to star Gail Danowski in anything but lunch. I walked alone with my dreams while the hungers grew.

You can go a little mad with loneliness, past caring. Virginity? I couldn't give it away, Momma; so I threw it away. No big Zanuck production, just a boy and a party I can't picture too clearly. We were drinking and wrestling, and I thought: all right, why not? Just once I'm gonna grab a little happiness even if it's just getting laid, what am I saving it for? But I had to get drunk before he fumbled at me. If there was pain or pleasure, I barely felt them, only knew that at last I tasted life where it sprang from the fountain. A meager cup, the cut version, the boy pulling at his clothes afterward, distant, disgusted.

"Shit, whyn't you tell me, Gail?"

Tell you what, lover? That I was a virgin, that by accident you were first? Is that a guilt trip? Whatever I lost, don't mourn it. Cry for the other things we lose in parked cars and motel beds because we're too drunk or there's too much guilt or fear for beauty. It was the beauty I missed. Be first any time, score up a hundred stiff, clumsy girls, say the silly words, break a hundred promises, brag about it afterwards. But leave something of yourself, something of beauty. Only that, and you part with a blessing.

He didn't.

The next morning, hung over and miserable, I looked at that frazzled thing in the mirror, had clean through and down to rock bottom, and knew from here on out I'd have to be me or just another Zosh. That day I started to build Gayla Damon.

I graduated an inch taller and thirty pounds lighter, did hard one-week stock as an apprentice. Seventeen hours a day of walk-ons, painting scenery, fencing and dance classes. Diction: practicing for hours with a cork between my teeth—

"Baby, the word is dance. DAAnce, hear the A? Not de-e-ance. Open your mouth and *use* it when you speak."

—Letting my hair grow and moving down to Manhattan, always running away from that lump in the mirror. I never outran her. She was always there, worrying out of my eyes at a thousand auditions, patting my stomach and thighs, searching a hundred dressing room mirrors, plastering pancake on imagined blemishes, grabbing any man's hand because it was there. The years just went, hurrying by like strangers on a street, trailing bits of memory like broken china from a dusty box: buses, planes, snatches of rehearsal, stock, repertory, old reviews.

> Miss Damon's talent is raw but unmistakable. When she's right, she *is* theater, vivid, filled with primordial energy that can burn or chill. If she can learn to control . . . she was superbly cast as. . . .

—A self-driven horse record-time sprinting from nowhere to noplace. Life? I lived it from eight to eleven o'clock every night and two matinees a week. For three hours each night, I loved, hated, sang, sorrowed enough for three lifetimes. Good houses, bad houses, they all got the best of me because my work had a love behind it. The rest was only fill, and who cared? Season after season of repertory, a dozen cities, a dozen summer towns barely glimpsed from opening night to closing, a blur of men and a lot of beds, flush or broke, it didn't matter.

Zosh caught a show once when I was playing in Westchester. Poor Zosh: pasty and fat as Momma by then, busting out of her dresses and her teeth shot. She came hesitantly into my dressing room, wondering if someone might throw her out. The first stage play she ever saw. She didn't know really what to make of it.

"Oh, it was great and all. You look good, Gail. God, you really got some figure now, what size you wear? I never knew about plays. You know me'n school, I always got my girlfriend to write my reports."

She barely sipped the scotch I poured her. "Charlie never buys nothin' but beer." I wanted to take her out for a good dinner, but, no, she had a sitter at home and it was expensive, and Charlie would yell if she came home too late when he was out bowling.

"Let the dumb ox yell. You're entitled once in a while."

"Hey, you really gettin'a mouth on you, Gail."

"Speaking of that, doesn't Charlie ever look at yours? Doesn't he know you need a dentist?"

"Well, you know how it is. The kids take it out of you."

I gave Zosh a hundred dollars to get her teeth fixed. She wrote that she spent it on the house and kids. *There was the gas bill and Christmas. You cant complain theres nobody on the other end of the phone. Ha-ha. My friends all want to know when your on TV.*

Are you still around, Zosh? Not that it matters. They buried you years ago. No one was going to do that to me.

And then suddenly I was thirty, that big, scary number. Working harder, running harder without knowing where, doing the where-did-it-all-go bit now and then (while the lights caught her best, most expressive angle). Where are you now, Bill? You must be pushing fifty. Did you find someone like me or just the opposite. I wouldn't blame you.

And how about you, Nick?

He'll split in six months. You'll be out in the cold.

When Bill said that, I remember thinking: hell, he's right. I'm thirty-two and after that comes thirty-three. Fourteen years, seven dollars in the bank, and where the hell am I?

But I was hung up on Nick's body and trying to please him. Perhaps there were other, unspoken things that have nothing to do with loving or sex. You get used very early to not liking yourself. You know you're a fraud, someday they'll all know. The Lump hiding inside your dieted figure and with-it clothes knows you haven't changed, no matter what. The Lump doesn't want to like you. How can she tolerate anyone who does? No, she'll sniff out someone who'll keep her in her lowly place.

Crimes and insanities. Hurting Bill was a very countable sin, but I knew what I needed. So it was Nick, not Bill, who moved in here with me.

And where are you this dark night, Nick? Did you make the big time? I hope so. You're almost thirty now. That's getting on for what you had to sell. Your kind of act has a short run.

My mind wanders like that when Lowen's not around.

Energy builds again, the lights dim up. I drift out onto the balcony, feeling that weight of depression it always brings. My sense of color is dimmed because the kids are asleep. 77th Street is a still shot in black and white. Not a soul, not even a late cab whispering up Riverside Drive.

Hey, look: there's a meteor, a falling star. Make a wish: be happy, Bill Wrenn.

And listen! A clock tower. Even with Lowen asleep, I can hear it. Two-three-four o'clock. Definitely, I'm getting stronger. More and more I can feel and sometimes see my legs when I walk, less like floating in a current. I move back through the apartment to hover over Lowen as he sleeps. Wanting. Wondering.

After all this time, why should it be Lowen who wakes me? Nothing's clear but that I can touch life again with him. If that's wrong, I didn't write the script. Name any form of life you want. A cold germ is just a bug trying to make a living in the only way it knows, in a place it doesn't understand, and it only takes a little out of the place trying. That's me, that's all of us. I'll take what I need to live. If there's air to breathe, don't tell me I can't. That's academic.

Al sleeps tiny and still beside Lowen, hardly a bump under

the covers. It must be wonderful to sleep like that. I could never stay out more than two hours at a time. No, wait: here she comes up out of it with a sigh and turnover that barely whispers the covers. She slides out of bed and pit-pats to the bathroom. Bladder the size of an acorn, up three times a night like I was.

When the john flushes, Lowen stirs and mumbles, flops over and sinks again. The bathroom door creaks, Al slips back in beside him. She doesn't settle down yet, but rests on one elbow, a momentary vigil over Lowen, a secret protecting. I'll bet he doesn't know she watches him like that. Then she slides under the covers very close, one arm over him, fingers spread lightly on his skin.

To lie beside Lowen like that, to touch him simply by willing it. If that were my hand resting on his skin. What wouldn't I give for that?

The idea is sudden and frightening. Why not?

If I could get inside Al, stretch out my arm inside hers, wear it like a glove; just for a moment move one real finger over Lowen's skin. It couldn't hurt her, and I need it so.

I wait for Al to fall asleep, scared of the whole notion. It could hurt. It hurt to touch Lowen before. Maybe it's against some natural law. They're flesh, I'm a memory. Lots of maybe's, but I have to try. Slow and scared, I drift down over Al and will what shape there is to me into the attitude of her body. There's no shock when I touch her, but a definite sensation like dipping into swift-running water. So weird, I pull away and have to build up my nerve to try again, settling like a sinking ship as the current of Al's healthy young life surges and tingles around me, and her chest rises and falls like a warm blanket over cozy sleep. My breasts nestle into hers, my arm stretching slowly to fill out the slim contour of her shoulder, elbow, wrist. It's hard and slow, like half-frozen syrup oozing through a hose. My fingers struggle one by one into hers.

So tired. Got to rest.

But I feel life, I *feel* it, humming and bubbling all around me. Jesus, I must have sounded like a steel mill inside, the way I drove myself. The power, such a wonder. Why did I waste so much time feeling miserable?

The electric clock glows at 5:03. More minutes pass while each finger tests itself in Al's, and then I try to move one on Lowen's skin.

The shock curdles me. I cringe away from it, shriveling back up Al's arm, all of me a shaky little ball in her middle. Just as in the shower, I felt skin against skin, even the tiny moisture of pores, but it drains me as if I've run five miles.

Rest and try again. Slow, so slow, so hard, but my fingers creep forward into Al's again. Same thing: the instant I let myself feel with Al's flesh, there's a bright shock and energy drains. If that's not enough, those delicate fingers weigh ten pounds each. I push, poop out, rest, try again, the hardest battle of my life, let alone death, and all in dogged silence broken only by their breathing and the muted *whir* of the clock.

6:32. The dark bedroom grays up to morning. I can see Lowen's face clearly now: very young, crumpled with sleep. He can't hear my soundless, exhausted panting like the heartbeat of a hummingbird.

6:48. Twelve minutes before the clock beeps the beginning of their day, one finger, one slender thread binding me to Lowen ... moves. Again. I go dizzy with the sensation but hang on, pouring the last strength into one huge effort. The small hand flexes all five fingers like a crab, sliding over the sparse hair on Lowen's chest. A flash-frame of Bill, of Nick, and a thrill of victory.

Hi, baby. I made it.

Then Al stirs, moves *don't, please, wait!* and flips over on her other side, unconcerned as a pancake. I let go, used up, drifting out to nowhere again, barely conscious of space or objects, too burned out even to feel frustrated after all that work.

But I did it. I know the way now. I'll be back.

Night after night I kept at it, fitting to Al's body, learning how to move her fingers without burning myself out. Stronger and surer, until I could move the whole hand and then the arm, and even if Lowen pressed the hand to his mouth or nestled his cheek against it, I could hold on.

And then I blew it, the story of my life. Klutz-woman strikes again. I tried to get in when they were making love.

I said before they're not too dexterous in the bedroom. Al gets uptight from the start, and I can see her lying there, eyes tight shut over Lowen's shoulder, hoping he'll come soon and get it over with. Not always; sometimes she wants it as much as him, but the old hangups are always there. She holds back, so he holds back. It's usually one-sided and finished soon.

But that evening everything seemed perfect. They had a light supper, several drinks rather than the usual one, and Lowen didn't spare the vodka. They just naturally segued to the bedroom, not rushed or nervous, undressing each other slowly, enjoyably, melting into each other's arms. Al brought in a candle from the supper table. Nice touch: Nick and I used to do that. They lie there caressing each other, murmuring drowsily. Lowen looks gorgeous in the soft glow, Al like a little Dresden doll. And me—poor, pathetic afterthought—watching it all and yearning.

Jesus, Al, act like you're alive. That's a man. Take hold of him.

Damn, it was too much. The hell with consequences. I draped myself over Al with the ease of practice, stretched my arms and legs along hers. Foolhardy, yes, but at last *my* arms went around Lowen, smoothing, then clawing down his back.

Love me, baby. Love all of me.

My mouth opened hungrily under his, licking his lips and then nipping at them. I writhed Al's slim body under his, pushed her hands to explore him from shoulders to thighs. I never had much trouble in bed. If the guy had anything going and didn't run through it like a fire drill, I could come half a dozen times, little ones and big ones, before he got there.

With Lowen it was like all the best orgasms I ever had. The moment before you start to go, you want to hold back, prolong it, but you can't. I was dependent on Al's chemistry now. Her body was strangely stiff as I hauled her over on top of Lowen. Something new for her. She went taut, resisting it.

"Lowen, wait."

He can't wait, though I'm the only one who sees the irony and the lie. Lowen is coming, I certainly want to, but Al is out of it. I want to *scream* at her, though I should have guessed it long before this. She always times her cries with his, as if they came together.

But it's a lie. She's faking it. She's learned that much.

My God, you're alive, the greatest gift anyone ever got. Does a past tense like me have to show you how?

With a strength like life itself, I churned her up and down on Lowen, hard, burning myself out to tear Al's careful controls from her emotions. She moaned, fighting me, afraid.

"Lowen, stop. Please stop."

You don't fake tonight, kid.

"Stop!"

No way. Go . . . *go!*

Lowen gripped her spasmodically, and I felt his hips tremble under mine/hers. He couldn't hold back any longer. With the last ounce of my will, I bent Al's body down over his, mouth to mouth.

"Now, Lowen. Now!"

Not Al's voice but mine, the first time I've heard it in seven years. Deeper, throatier than Al's. In the middle of coming, an alien bewilderment flooded Lowen's expression. Al stiffened like she was shot. With a cry of bleak terror, she tore herself loose and leaped clear off the bed, clawing for the lamp switch, big-eyed and terrified in the hard light.

"Oh, God. Oh, Jesus, what's happening?"

Confused, a little out of it himself now, Lowen sat up to stare back at her. "Al, what's the matter?"

She shuddered. "It's not me."

"What?"

"It's not *me.*" She snatched up her bathrobe like the last haven in the world. Lowen reached for her instinctively, comforting.

"It's all right, honey, it's—"

"No. It's like something hot inside me."

He went on soothing her, but he knew. I could see that in his eyes as he pulled Al down beside him. He knew: the last thing I saw, because the lights were going down for me, their last spill playing over memory-fragments before fading. A confused montage: Nick putting on his jacket, me fumbling for the phone, then pulling at the balcony door, and the darkness and the silence then were like dying again.

I've had some hangovers in my time, mornings of agony after a messy, screaming drunk. Coming back to queasy consciousness while the night's party repeats in your mind like a stupid film loop, and you wonder, in a foggy way, if you really spilled that drink on somebody, and—oh, no—you couldn't have said *that* to him, and if you're going to be sick right then or later.

Then the smog clears and you remember. Yeah. You spilled it and did it and you sure as hell said it, and the five best bloody mary's in the world won't help.

I blew it good this time, a real production number. Now they both know I'm here.

December 23. I know the date because Al's carefully crossed the days off her calendar where she never bothered before. I've been turned off for days. Almost Christmas, but you'd never know it around here. No holly, no tree, just a few cards opened and dropped on the little teakwood desk where they keep their bills. When Lowen brushes one aside, I can see a thin line of dust. Al hasn't been cleaning.

The kitchen is cluttered. The morning's dishes are still in the sink. Three cardboard boxes stand on the floor, each half full of wrapped dishes and utensils.

So that's it. They're moving. A moment of panic: where do I go from here, then? All right, it was my fault, but . . . don't go, Lowen. I'm not wild about this script myself, but don't ask me to turn out the lights and die again. Because I won't.

There's a miasma of oppression and apprehension all through the apartment. Al's mouth is tighter, her eyes frightened. Lowen comes out into the living room, reluctant and dutiful. Furtively, he tests the air as if to feel me in it. He sits down in his usual chair; 3:13 by the miniature grandfather clock on the book case. The lights and sound come up slowly with Lowen's nearness. He's home early this afternoon.

Al brings out the Waterford sherry set and puts it on the coffee table. She sits down, waiting with Lowen. The whole scene reminds me of actors taking places before the curtain rises; Al poised tensely on the sofa, revolving her sherry glass in white fingers; Lowen distant, into his own thoughts. The sound is still lousy.

". . . feel silly," Lowen ventures. ". . . all this way . . . time off from . . . just to . . ."

"No! . . . live here like this, not with . . ." Al is really shook; takes a cigarette from Lowen's pack on the coffee table and smokes it in quick, inexpert puffs. "You say you can feel her?"

Lowen nods, unhappy. He doesn't like any of this. "I loved this place from the first day."

"Lowen, answer me. Please."

"Yes."

"Where?"

"Somewhere close. Always to me."

Al stubs out the cigarette. "And we sure know it's *she,* don't we?"

"Al—"

"Oh, hell! I loved this place too, but this is crazy. I'm *scared,* Lowen. How long have you known?"

"Almost from the start."

"And you never told me."

"Why?" Lowen looks up at her. "I'm not a medium; nothing like this ever happened before. It was weird at first, but then I began to feel that she was just *here*—"

"What!"

"—and part of things . . . like the walls. I didn't even know it was a woman at first."

"Until that time in the shower," Al finishes for him. "Bitch."

Thanks a lot, kid. At least I know what to do with him.

"Look, Al, I can't tell you how I know, but I don't think she means any harm."

Al gulps down her sherry and fills the glass. "The—hell—she—doesn't. I'm not into church anymore. Even if I were, I wouldn't go running for the holy water every time a floor creaked, but don't tell me she doesn't mean anything, Lowen. You know what I'm talking about." Her hands dry-wash each other jerkily. "I mean that night, the way we made love. I—always wanted to make love to you like that. That . . . free."

The best you ever had, love.

Al gets up and paces, nervous. "All right, I've got these god-damned problems. You get taught certain things are wrong. If it's not for babies, it's wrong. It's wrong to use contraceptives, but we can't afford a baby, and—I don't know, Lowen. The world is crazy. But that night, it wasn't me. Not even my voice."

"No, it wasn't."

Lowen must be way down, depressed, because my energy is wavering with his, and sound fades in and out. There's a muffled knock at the door. Lowen opens it to a bald little man like a wizened guru in a heavy, fur-collared overcoat.

Wait, I know this guy. It's that little weasel, Hirajian, from Riverside Realty. He rented me this place. Hirajian settles him-self in a chair, briefcase on his knee, declining the sherry Al offers. He doesn't look too happy about being here, but the self-satisfied little bastard doesn't miss Al's legs, which make mine look bush league in retrospect.

I can't catch everything, but Hirajian's puzzled by something Al's saying. No problem about the lease, he allows, apartments rent in two days now, but she's apparently thrown him a curve.

Al now: ". . . not exactly our wish, but . . ."

"Unusual request . . . never anything. . . ."

Now Al is flat and clear: "Did you find out?"

Hirajian opens his briefcase and brings out a sheet of paper while I strain at his through-the-wall mumble.

"Don't know why . . . however . . . before you. . . ." He runs through a string of names until I make the connection. The ten-ants who came after me, all those damned extras who wandered through my dreams before Lowen.

Lowen stops him suddenly. He's not as depressed as Al; there's an eagerness in the question. "Did anyone die here?"

"Die?"

"It's very important." Al says.

Hirajian looks like an undertaker's assistant now, all profes-sional solemnity and reluctance. "As a matter of fact, yes. I was getting to that. In 1974, a Miss Danowski."

Lowen's head snaps up. "First name?"

"Gail."

"Anyone named Gayla? Someone cut the name Gayla in the cement on the balcony."

"That was the Danowski woman. Gayla Damon was her stage name. She was an actress. I remember because she put that name on the lease and had to do it again with her legal signature."

"Gayla."

"You knew her, Mr. Sheppard?"

"Gayla Damon. I should, it's awfully familiar, but—"

"Single?" Al asks. "What sort of person was she?"

Hirajian cracks his prim little smile like a housewife leaning over a back fence to gossip. "Yes and no, you know show people. Her boyfriend moved in with her. I know it's the fashion nowadays, but *we*," evidently Riverside and God, "don't approve of it."

There's enough energy to laugh, and I wish you could hear me, you little second-string satyr. You made a pass when you showed me this place. I remember: I was wearing that new tan suit from Bergdorf's, and I couldn't split fast enough. But it was the best place yet for the money, so I took it.

Damn it, how did I die? What happened. Don't fade out, weasel. Project, let me hear you.

Al sets down her sherry glass. "We just can't stay here. It's impossible."

Don't go, Lowen. You're all I have, all there is. I won't touch Al, I promise never again. But don't go.

Of course there were promises, Nick. There's always a promise. No one has to spell it out.

I said that once. I'm starting to remember.

While Hirajian patters on, Lowen's lost in some thought. There's something in his eyes I've never seen before. A concern, a caring.

"You mean he didn't come back even when he heard Gayla was dead?"

I love the way he says my name. Like a song, new strength.

"No end of legal trouble," Hirajian clucks. "We couldn't locate him or any family at first. A Mister . . . yes, a Mister

Wrenn came and made all the arrangements. An old boyfriend, I suppose."

You did that for me, Bill? You came back and helped me out. Boy, what I had and threw away. Sand through my fingers.

"Gayla. Gayla Damon." I grow stronger as Lowen repeats my name, stronger yet as he rises and takes a step toward the balcony door. I could touch him, but I don't dare now. "Yes. Just the name I forgot. It's hard to believe, Al, but it's the only thing I can believe."

Such a queer, tender look. Al reads it too. "What, Lowen?"

He strides quickly away to the bedroom, and the lights dim a little. Then he's back with a folded paper, so lost in some thought that Al just stares at him and Hirajian is completely lost.

"The things we learn about life," Lowen says. "An English professor of mine said once that life is too coincidental for art; that's why art is structured. Mr. Hirajian, you said no one else ever complained of disturbances in this apartment. I'm not a medium, can't even predict the weather. But I'm, beginning to understand a little of this."

Will you tell me, for Christ's sake?

He hands the paper to Al. It looks like an old theater program. "You see, Mister Hirajian, she's still here."

He has to say it again, delicately as possible. Hirajian poohpoohs the whole notion. "Oh really, now, you can't be sure of something like that."

"We know," Al says in a hard voice. "We haven't told you everything. She, it, something's here, and it's destructive."

"No, I don't think so." Lowen nods to the program. I can't see it too well. "Eagle Lake Playhouse, 1974. I saw her work."

You couldn't have. You were only—

"She played Gwendolyn in *Becket*. That's her autograph by her name."

Where the hell is Eagle Lake? Wait a minute. Wait—a—minute. I'm remembering.

"My father was taking me back to school. I spent my whole life in boarding schools all the way through college. Dad thought for our last night together, he'd take me to an uplifting play and

save himself making conversation. My parents were very effi-
cient that way.

"Gayla only had one scene, but she was so open, so completely translucent that I couldn't take my eyes off her."

I did play Eagle Lake, and there's a faint memory of some
double-breasted country-club type coming back for an autograph for his kid.

"I still remember, she had a line that went: 'My lord cares
for nothing in this world, does he?' She turned to Becket then,
and you could see a *line* in that turn, a power that reached
the other actor and came out to the audience. The other actors
were good, but Gayla lit up the stage with something—unbear-
ably human."

Damn right, love. I was gangbusters in that role. And you saw
me? I could almost believe in God now, though He hasn't called
lately.

"I was sixteen, and I thought I was the only one in the world
who could be so lonely. She showed me we're all alike in that.
All our feelings touch. Next day I hitchhiked all the way back to
the theater from school. . . ." Lowen trails off, looking at Al and
the apartment. "And this was her place. She wasn't very old.
How did she die?"

"Depressing," Hirajian admits. "Very ugly and depressing,
but then suicide always is."

What!

"But as regards your moving out just because—"

The hell I did, no *way*, mister. No. No. NO! I won't listen to
any more. Don't believe him, Lowen.

Lowen's on his feet, head tilted in that listening attitude. Al
puts down her glass, pale and tense. "What is it?"

"She's here now. She's angry."

"How do you know?"

"Don't ask me how, damn it. I know. She's here."

No, Lowen. On the worst, weakest day of my life, I couldn't
do that. Listen. Hear me. Please.

Then Al's up, frightened and desperate. "Go away, whoever
you are. For the love of God, go away."

I barely hear her, flinging myself away from them out onto

the balcony, silent mouth screaming at the frustration and stupid injustice of it. A lie, a lie, and Lowen is leaving, sending me back to nothing and darkness. But the strength is growing, born of rage and terror. Lowen. Lowen. Lowen. Hear me. I didn't. *Hear me.*

"Lowen, don't!"

I hear Al's voice, then the sudden, sharp sound of the balcony door wrenching open. And as I turn to Lowen, the whole, uncut film starts to roll. And, oh Jesus, I remember.

Eagle Lake. That's where it ended, Lowen. Not here, no matter what they tell you. That's where all the years, parts, buses, beds, the whole game came to an end. When I found that, no matter what, none of it worked any more. Maybe I was growing up a little at last, looking for the *me* in all of it.

Funny: I wasn't even going to audition for stock that summer, Bill called me to do a couple of roles at Eagle Lake, and Nick urged me to go. It was a good season, closing with *A Streetcar Named Desire*. The owner, Ermise Stour, jobbed in Natalie Bond for Blanche DuBois, and I was to be her understudy. Nattie's name wasn't smash movie box office any more, but still big enough for stock and star-package houses. She'd be Erm's insurance to make up whatever they lost on the rest of the season.

Erm, you tough old bag. You were going to sell that broken-down theater after every season. I'll bet you're still there, chain-smoking over a bottle of Chivas and babying that ratty poodle.

Ermise lived in a rambing ex-hotel with a huge fireplace in the lounge. We had all our opening-night parties there with a big blaze going because Eagle Lake never warmed up or dried out even in August.

At the opening party for *Becket*, all of us were too keyed up to get drunk, running on adrenaline from the show, slopping drinks and stuffing sandwiches, fending off the local reviewers, horny boy scouts with a course in journalism.

Dinner? No thanks. I've got a horrible week coming up, and it's all I can do to shower and fall into bed. Bill, let's get *out* of here. Thanks, you're a jewel, I needed a refill. Gimme your sweater. Jesus, doesn't it ever get warm in this place? You could age beef in our dressing room.

Nick was down for a few days the week before. Bill rather pointedly made himself scarce. He was still in love with me. That must have hurt, working with me day after day, keeping it inside, and I didn't help matters by dragging Nick everywhere like a prize bull: hey, look what I got! Smart girl, Gayla. With a year's study, you could be an idiot.

But Nick was gone, and we'd managed to get *Becket* open despite failing energy, colds, frayed nerves and lousy weather. It was good just to stand with Bill against the porch railing, watching moths bat themselves silly against the overhead light. Bill was always guarded when we were alone now. I kept it light and friendly, asked about his preparations for *Streetcar*. He sighed with an Old Testament flavor of doom.

"Don't ask. Erm had to cut the set budget, first read-through is tomorrow morning, and Nattie's plane won't get in until one. I'm going to be up all night and I'll still only be about five pages ahead of you people on blocking."

"Why's she late?"

"Who the hell knows? Business with her agent or something. You'll have to read in for her."

Good. One more precious rehearsal on my Blanche, one more time to read those beautiful words and perhaps find one more color in them before Natalie Bond froze it all in star glitter. That was all I had to look forward to now. The fatigue, the wet summer, lousy houses, all of it accumulated to a desolation I couldn't shrug off. I had a small part in *Streetcar*, but understudying Natalie Bond meant watching her do my role, never to touch the magic myself. Maybe her plane could crash—just a little—but even then, what? Somehow even the thought of Nick depressed me. Back in New York he'd get in to see the right agents where I couldn't, landing commercials, lining up this, grabbing that, always smarter at business than me.

That night before the party, I sat on my bed, staring glumly at the yellow-green wallpaper and my battered Samsonite luggage, and thought: *I'm tired of you. Something's gone. There's gotta be more than this.* And I curled up in my old gray bathrobe, wal-

lowing in self-pity. Nick, you want to get married? Bring me the
towel and wash my back? Baby me a little when I feel rotten,
like now? There's a big empty place in me wants to be pregnant
with more than a part. Tired, negative, I knew Nick would never
marry me; I was kidding myself.

So it was good to have Bill there on the porch for a minute. I
leaned against him and he put an arm around me. We should
have gone to bed and let it be beautiful one more time. It would
have been the last.

"Tired, Gay?"

"I want to go home."

Except I never in my whole life found where it was.

Natalie Bond came and conquered. She knew her lines pretty
well going in and crammed the rest with me in her room or the
restaurant down our street. No one recognized her at first with
her hair done just the right shade of fading dishwater blonde for
Blanche, most of her thin face hidden behind a huge pair of
prescription sunglasses.

She was near-sighted to blindness; some of her intensity on
film must have come from trying to feel out the blocking by
Braille. But a pro she was. She soaked up Bill's direction, drove
herself and us, and I saw the ruthless energy that made Nattie a
star.

I saw other things, too. Nattie hadn't been on a live stage for
a lot of years. She missed values left and right in Blanche and
didn't have time to pick them up on a two-week stock schedule.
Film is a director's medium. He can put your attention where
he wants with the camera. Stage work takes a whole different set
of muscles, and hers were flabby, unused to sustaining an action
or mood for two and a half hours.

But for the first time that season, we were nearly sold out at
the box office. Erm was impressed. Bill wasn't.

"They're coming to see a star. She could fart her way through
Blanche and they'll still say she's wonderful."

Maybe, but life wasn't all skittles for Nattie. She had two children in expensive schools and got endless phone calls from her
manager in California about taxes.

"I gotta work, honey," she told me over black coffee and dry toast. "The wolf's got my ass in his chops already."

She meant it. Another phone call, and that same afternoon between lunch and rehearsal call, Nattie Bond was gone, and I was sitting in Ermise's living room again while Erm swore back and forth across the worn carpet, waving her drink like a weapon, and Bill tried to look bereaved. He always wanted me for Blanche. He had me now.

"Screwed me from the word go." Ermise sprayed ashes over the rug and her poodle. "She knew this when she signed and never said a goddamn word."

The facts filtered through my rosy haze. Natalie's agent had a picture deal on the coast so close to signing that it was worth it to let Ermise sue. They'd just buy up her contract—if she could be in Los Angeles tomorrow.

Ermise hurled her cigarette into the trash-filled fireplace, gulped the last of her drink and turned a mental page. Nattie was one problem, the show another. "You ready to go, Gayla?"

"In my sleep, love."

I was already readjusting the role to the Blanche in my ear and not as sorry for the box office as Erm. Screw 'em all, they were going to see ten times the Blanche Nattie Bond could give them on the best day she ever worked.

"Bill wants me to give you a raise," Ermise said. "Wish I could, Gay, but things are tight."

I pulled the worn script out of my jeans, grinning like a fool back at Bill, who couldn't hide his glee any more. "Just pay on time, Erm. Keep out of my hair and don't clutter up my stage. Bill, let's go to work."

From my first rehearsal, the play convulsed and became a different animal. The whole cast had to shift gears for me, but no longer suffused by Nattie's hard light they began to find themselves and glimmer with life. I ate and slept with the script while Blanche came sure and clear. Hell, I'd been rehearsing her for fourteen years. It wasn't hard to identify: the hunger for love half appeased in bed-hopping and sexual junk food, and what that does to a woman. The blurred, darkening picture of a girl waiting in her best dress to go to the dance of life with someone who never came.

Then, just as it seemed to be coming together, it went flat, deader than I am now. But out of that death came a beautiful, risky answer.

Blanche DuBois is a bitch of a role and demands a powerhouse actress. That's the problem. Like the aura that surrounds Hamlet, the role accumulates a lot of star-shtick, and something very subtle can get lost. I determined to strip away the layers of gloss and find what was there to begin with.

"The part's a trap, Bill. All those fluttery, curlicued lines reach out and beg you to *act* them. And you wind up with dazzle again, a concert performance."

"Cadenzas," he agreed with me. "The old Williams poetry."

"Right! Cadenzas, scales. No, by God. I've played the Deep South. There's a smothered quality to those women that gets lost that way. The script describes her as a moth. Moths don't dazzle. They don't glitter."

"Remember that night on the porch," Bill said thoughtfully. "They don't glitter, but they do need the light."

And that was it. Blanche aspired to the things she painted with foolish words. A dream of glitter seen by a near-sighted person by a failing candle. The lines are ornate, but just possibly, Blanche is not quite as intelligent as she's been played.

A long artistic chance, but they're the only ones worth taking. If you don't have the guts to be wrong, take up accounting.

So my Blanche emerged a very pathetic woman, a little grotesque as such women are, not only desperate for love but logical in her hopes for Mitch. For all Belle Reeve and the inbred magnolias, she's not that far above him. Bill gave me my head, knowing that by finding my own Blanche, even being wrong for a while, I'd find the play's as well. On my terms and with my own reality.

I had three lovely labor-pained days of seeing her come alive. On the third day, I was sitting in a corner of the stage with coffee and a sandwich, digging at the script while the others lunched. When Sally Kent walked in, I snapped at her.

"Where's the rest. It's two o'clock. Let's go."

"They want you over at the office, Gay."

"What the hell for? I don't have time. Where's Bill?"

"At the office," Sally admitted reluctantly. "Natalie Bond is here. She's back in the show."

The kiss of death. Even as I shook my head, no, Erm wouldn't do this to me, I knew she would.

Ermise hunched in a chair by the fireplace, bitter with what she had to do, trying not to antagonize Bill any further. He poised on the sofa, seething like a malevolent cat.

"Nattie will do the show after all," Ermise said. "I have to put her back in, Gay."

I couldn't speak at first; sick, quivering on my feet with that horrible end-of-the-rope hollowness in my stomach. No place to go from here. No place. . . .

"When we pulled her name off the advertising, we lost more than a third of our reservations." Erm snorted. "I don't like it. I don't like her right now, but she's the only thing'll keep my theater open."

Bill's comment cut with the hard edge of disgust. "You know what this does to the cast, don't you? They've readjusted once. Now they have to do it again and open in two days. They were an ensemble with Gayla. Now they're the tail of a star vehicle."

Bill knew it was already lost, but he was doing this for me.

Ermise shook her head. "Gay, honey, I can't afford it, but I'm gonna raise you retroactive to the first week of your contract." Her hands fluttered in an uncharacteristically helpless gesture. "I owe you that. And you'll go back in as Eunice. But next season—"

I found my voice. It was strange, old. "Don't do this to me. This role, it's mine, I earned it. She'll ruin it."

"Don't look at me," Bill snapped to Ermise. "She's right."

Ermise went defensive. "I don't care who's right. You're all for Gay. Fine, but I can't run a theater that way. Lucky to break even as it is. Nattie's back, she plays, and that's the end of it. Gay's contract reads 'as cast.' She's Eunice. What else can I say?"

I showed her what else. I ripped the *Streetcar* script in four parts and threw them in the fireplace. "You can say good-by, Ermise. Then you can take your raise and shove it." I was already lurching toward the door, voice breaking. "Then you can put someone in my roles, because I'm leaving."

I meant it. Without Blanche, there was no reason to stay another minute. Finished. Done.

Except for Natalie Bond. I found her in her hotel room, already dressed for rehearsal and running over the script.

"Come on in, Gayla. Drink?"

"No."

She read my tension as I crouched with my back against the door. "All right, hon. Get it off your chest."

"I will."

I told the bitch what I felt and what I thought and didn't leave anything out. It was quite a speech for no rehearsal, beginning with my teens when I first knew I had to play Blanche, and the years and hard work that made me worthy of it. There wasn't a rep company in the east I hadn't worked, or a major role from Rosalind to Saint Joan I hadn't played. To walk out on the show like she did was pure shit. To crawl back was worse.

"Right," said Nattie. She faced me all through it, let me get it all out. I was crying when I finished. I sank down on a chair, grabbing for one of her kleenex.

"Now do you want a drink?"

"Yes, what the hell."

She wasn't all rat, Nattie. She could have put me down with the star routine, but she fixed me a stiff gin and soda without a word. I remember her fixing that drink: thick glasses and no make up, gristly thin. She had endless trouble with her uterus, infection after painful infecction and a work schedule that never allowed her to heal properly. A hysterectomy ended the whole thing. Nattie's face was thinner than mine, all the softness gone, mouth and cheeks drawn tight. No matter how sincere, the smile couldn't unclench.

And this, I thought, is what I want to be? Help me, Nick. Take me home. There's gotta be a home somewhere, a little rest.

"Know what we're like?" Nattie mused. "A little fish swim-

ming away from a big, hungry fish who's just about to be eaten
by a bigger fish. That's us, honey. And that's me in the middle."

She screwed Ermise, but someone shafted her too. The picture deal was a big fat fake. The producer wanted someone a
little bigger and hustled Nattie very plausibly to scare the lady
into reaching for a pen.

"I'm broke, Gayla. I owe forty thousand in back taxes, my
house is on a second mortgage, and my kids' tuition is overdue.
Those kids are all I have. I don't know where the hell to go from
here, but Ermise needs me and I sure as hell need the job."

While I huddled over my drink, unable to speak, Nattie
scribbled something on a memo pad.

"You're too good to waste, you're not commercial, and you'll
probably die broke. But I saw your rehearsal this morning."

I looked up at her in weepy surprise. The smile wasn't quite
so hard just then.

"If I can do it half that well, Gay. Half."

She shoved the paper into my hand. "That's my agent in New
York. He's with William Morris. If he can't get you work, no one
can. I'll call him myself." She glanced at her dressing table
clock. "Time, gotta run."

Nattie divined the finality in my shoulders as I sagged toward
the door. "You going to play Eunice?"

"No. I'm leaving."

Pinning her hair, she shot me a swift, unsmiling appraisal
through the mirror. "Good for you. You got a man in New
York?"

"Yeah."

"Get married," she mumbled through a mouthful of pins. "It's
not worth it." As the door closed, she raised her voice. "But call
my agent."

My bags were packed, but I hadn't bothered to change clothes.
That's why my permanent costume, I suppose. Who knew then
I'd get very tired of black. Bill insisted on driving me to the airport. When he came for me, I must have looked pathetic, curled
up on the bed in one more temporary, damp summer room just

waiting to eject me. No love lost; I got damned sick of yellow-green wallpaper.

Bill sat on the edge of the bed. "Ready, love?"

I didn't move or answer. Done, finished. Bill put aside the old hurt and lay down beside me, bringing me into his arms. I guess something in him had to open inspite of his defenses. He opened my heart gently as a baby's hand clutched around something that might harm it, letting me cry the last of it out against his shoulder. The light faded in the room while we lay together.

We kissed good-by like lovers at the departure gate. Bill was too much a part of me for anything less. Maybe he knew better than I how little was waiting for me.

"Be good, Gay."

"You too." I fiddled with his collar. "Don't forget to take your vitamins, you need them. Call me when you get back."

He hugged me one last time. "Why don't you marry me some-time?"

For a lot of reasons, Bill. Because I was a fool and something of a coward. The stunting begins in the seed when we learn not to like ourselves. The sad thing about life is that we usually get what we really want. Let it be.

Funny, though: that was my first and last proposal, and I kissed him goodby, walked out of his life, and four hours later I was dead.

There was time on the plane to get some of it together. Natalie was a star, at the top where I wanted to be, and look at her: most of the woman cut out of her, flogged to work not by ambition but need. Driven and used. She reminded me of a leg-less circus freak propelling herself on huge, overdeveloped arms, the rest of her a pitiful afterthought cared for by an expensive gynecologist. I thought: at least when I get home there'll be Nick. Don't call him from the airport; let it be a surprise. We'll get some coffee and coldcuts, make love and talk half the night. I needed to talk, to see us plain.

Get married, Nattie said. It isn't worth it.

Maybe not the way I chased it for fourteen years. I'd call her agent, keep working, but more New York jobs with time left

over to be with Nick, to sit on my balcony and just breathe or
read. To make a few friends outside of theater. To see a doctor
and find out how tough I really am, and if everything in the baby
box is working right, so that maybe—

Like she said, so maybe get married and have kids while I can.
A little commitment, Nick, a little tomorrow. If the word sounds
strange, I just learned it. Give me this, Nick. I need it.

The light was on in our living room as I hauled my suitcase
out of the cab and started up. Hell, I won't even buzz, just turn
the key in the lock and reach for him.

I did that.

There was—yes, I remember—one blessed moment of
breathing the good, safe air of my own living room as I set down
the luggage. I heard a faint stirring from the bedroom. Good,
I've surprised him. If Nick was just waking from a nap, we'd
have that much more time to touch each other.

"It's me, baby."

I crossed to the bedroom door, groping inside for the light
switch. "I'm home."

I didn't need the switch. There was enough light to see them
frozen on the torn-up bed. The other one was older, a little
flabby. He muttered something to Nick. I stood there, absurd
myself, and choked: "Excuse me."

Then, as if someone punched me in the stomach, I stumbled
to the bathroom, pushed the door shut and fell back against it.

"Get him out of here, Nick!"

The last word strangled off as I doubled over the john and
vomited all the horrible day out of me, with two hours left to
live, retching and sobbing, not wanting to hear whatever was
said beyond the door. After a short time, the front door closed.
I washed my face, dried it with the stiff, clumsy movements of
exhaustion, and got out to the living room somehow, past the
bed where Nick was smoking a cigarette, the sheet pulled up
over his lean thighs.

I remember pouring a drink. That was foolish on an empty
stomach, the worst thing anyone could have done. I sat on the
sofa, waiting.

"Nick." The silence from the bedroom was the only thing I could feel in my shock. "Nick, please come out. I want to talk to you."

I heard him rustle into his clothes. In a moment Nick came out, bleak and sullen.

"Why are you back so early?"

"No, they—" My reactions were still disjointed, coming out of shock, but the anger was building. "They put Nattie Bond back in the show. I walked out."

That seemed to concern him more than anything else. "You just walked out? They'll get Equity on you."

"Never mind about Equity, what are *we* gonna do?"

"What do you mean?" he asked calmly.

"Oh, man, are you for real?" I pointed at the door. "What was that?"

"That may be a Broadway job." He turned away into the kitchen. "Now get off my back."

"The hell I—"

"Hey look, Gayla. I haven't made any promises to you. You wanted me to move in. Okay, I moved in. We've had it good."

I began to shake. "Promises? Of course there were promises. There's always a promise, nobody has to spell it out. I could have gone to bed with Bill Wrenn plenty of times this summer, but I didn't."

He only shrugged. "So whose fault is that? Not mine."

"You bastard!" I threw my glass at him. He ducked, the thing went a mile wide, then Nick was sopping up whisky and bits of glass while I shook myself apart on the couch, teeth chattering so hard I had to clamp my mouth tight shut. It was all hitting me at once, and I couldn't handle half of it. Nick finished cleaning up without a word, but I could see even then the tight line of his mouth and the angry droop of his eyelids. He had guts of a kind, Nick. He could face anything because it didn't matter. All the important things were outside, to be reached for. Inside I think he was dead.

"The meanest thing Bill ever said to me," I stuttered. "When I left him for you, h-he said you played both sides of the fence.

And I c-called him a god-damn liar. I couldn't believe he'd be small enough to—Nick, I'm falling apart. They took my show, and I came home to you because I don't know what to do."

Nick came over, sat down and held me in his arms. "I'm not, Gayla."

"Not what?"

"What Bill said."

"Then w-what was this?"

He didn't answer, just kissed me. I clung to Nick like a lost child.

Why do we always try to rewrite what's happened? Even now I see myself pointing to the door and kissing him off with a real Bette Davis sizzler for a curtain. Bullshit. I needed Nick. The accounting department was already toting up the cost of what I wanted and saying: *I'll change him. It's worth it.*

I only cried wearily in his arms while Nick soothed and stroked me. "I'm not that," he said again. "Just that so many guys are hung up on role-playing and all that shit. Oh, it's been said about me."

I twisted in his lap to look at him. "Nick, why did you come to me?"

The question gave him more trouble than it should. "I like you. You're the greatest girl I ever met."

Something didn't add up. Nothing ever bugged Nick before; he could always handle it, but he was finding this hard.

"That's not enough," I persisted. "Not tonight."

Nick disengaged himself with a bored sigh. "Look, I have to go out."

"Go out? Now?" I couldn't believe he'd leave me like this. "Why?"

He walked away toward the bedroom. I felt the anger grow cold with something I'd never faced before, answers to questions that gnawed at the back of my mind from our first night. "Why, Nick? Is it him? Did that fat queer tell you to come over after you ditched the hag?"

Nick turned on me, lowering. "I don't like that word."

"Queer."

"I said—"

"Queer."

"All right." He kicked viciously at the bedroom door with all the force he wanted to spend stopping my mouth. "It's a fact in this business. That's why I get in places you don't. It's a business, cut and dried, not an *aht fawm* like you're always preaching."

"Come off it, Nick." I stood up, ready for him and wanting the fight. "That casting couch bit went out with Harlow. Is that how you get jobs? That, and the cheap, scene-stealing tricks you use when you know and I know I played you against the wall in Lexington, you hypocritical son of a bitch."

Nick threw up a warning hand. "Hey, wait just one damn minute, Bernhardt. I never said I was or ever could be as good as you. But I'll tell you one thing." Nick opened the closet and snaked his jacket off a hanger. "I'll be around and working when nobody remembers you, because I know the business. You've been around fourteen years and still don't know the score. You won't make rounds, you don't want to be bothered waiting for an agent to see you. You're a goddamn *ahtist*. You won't wait in New York for something to develop, hell no. You'll take any show going out to Noplaceville, and who the hell ever sees you but some jerkoff writing for a newspaper no one reads. Integrity? Bullshit, lady. You are *afraid* of New York, afraid to take a chance on it."

Nick subsided a little. "That guy who was here, he produces. He's got a big voice where it counts." Again he looked away with that odd, inconsistent embarrassment. "He didn't want to sleep with me, really. He's basically straight."

That was too absurd for anger. "Basically?"

"He only wanted a little affection."

"And you, Nick. Which way do you go basically. I mean was it his idea or yours?"

That was the first totally vulnerable moment I ever saw in Nick. He turned away, leaning against the sink. I could barely hear him. "I don't know. It's never made much difference. So what's the harm? I don't lose anything, and I may gain."

He started for the door, but I stopped him. "Nick, I need you. What's happened to me today, I'm almost sick. Please don't do this to me."

"Do what? Look." He held me a moment without warmth or conviction. "I'll only be gone a little while. We'll talk tomorrow, okay?"

"Don't go, Nick."

He straightened his collar carefully with a sidelong glance at the mirror. "We can't talk when you're like this. There's no point."

I dogged him desperately, needing something to hang onto. "Please don't go. I'm sorry for what I said. Nick, we can work it out, but don't leave me alone."

"I have to." His hand was already on the door, cutting me off like a thread hanging from his sleeve.

"Why!" It ripped up out of the bottom, out of the hate without which we never love or possess anything. "Because that fat faggot with his job means more than I do, right? How low do you crawl to make a buck in this business? Or is it all business? Jesus, you make me sick."

Nick couldn't be insulted. Even at the end, he didn't have that to spare me. Just a look from those cool blue eyes I tried so hard to please, telling me he was a winner in a game he knew, and I just didn't make it.

"It's your apartment. I'll move."

"Nick, don't go."

The door closed.

What did I do then? I should remember, they were the last minutes of my life. The door closed. I heard Nick thumping down the carpeted stairs, and thank God for cold comfort I didn't run after him. I poured a straight shot and finished it in one pull.

A hollow, eye-of-the-storm calm settled on me and then a depression so heavy it was a physical pain. I wandered through the apartment drinking too much and too fast, talking to Nick, to Bill, to Nattie, until I collapsed, clumsy, hiccuping drunk on the floor with half an hour to live.

Another drink. Get blind, drunk enough to reach . . . something, to blot out the Lump. Yeah, she's still with you, the goddamn little loser. Don't you ever learn, loser? No, she won't ever learn. Yesterday did this day's madness prepare. What play was that and who cares?

I tried to think but nothing came together. My life was a scattered tinkertoy, all joints and pieces without meaning or order. A sum of apples and oranges: parts played, meals eaten, clothes worn, he said and I said, old tickets, old programs, newspaper reviews yellowed and fragile as Blanche's love letters. Apples and oranges. Where did I leave anything of myself, who did I love, what did I have? No one. Nothing.

Only Bill Wrenn.

"Christ, Bill, help me!"

I clawed for the phone with the room spinning and managed to call the theater. One of the girl apprentices answered. I struggled to make myself understood with a thickening tongue. "Yeah, Bill Wrenn, 'simportant. Gayla Damon. Yeah, hi, honey. He's not? Goddamnit, he's gotta be. I *need* him. When'll he be back? Yeah . . . yeah. Tell'm call Gayla, please. Please. Yeah, trouble. Real trouble. I need him."

That's how it happened. I dropped the phone in the general vicinity of the hook and staggered to the pitching sink to make one more huge, suicidal drink, crying and laughing, part drunk, part hysteria. But Bill was going to bail me out like he always had, and, boy, ol' Gay had learned her lesson. I was a fool to leave him. He loved me. Bill loved me and I was afraid of that. Afraid to be loved. How dumb can you get?

"How dumb?" I raged mushily at the Lump in the mirror. "You with the great, soulful eyes. You never knew shit, baby."

I was sweating. The wool sweater oppressed my clammy skin. Some sober molecule said take it off, but no. It's cooler out on my balcony. I will go out on my beautiful, nighted balcony and present my case to the yet unknowing world.

I half fell through the door. The balcony had a low railing, lower than I judged as I stumbled and heaved my drunken weight behind the hand flung out to steady myself and—

Fell. No more time.

That's it, finished. Now I've remembered. It was that sudden, painless, meaningless. No fade out, no end title music resolving the conflict themes, only torn film fluttering past the projector light, leaving a white screen.

There's a few answers anyway. I could get a lump in my throat, if I had one, thinking how Bill came and checked me out. God, let's hope they kept me covered. I must have looked awful. Poor Bill; maybe I gave you such a rotten time because I knew you could take it and still hang in. That's one of the faces of love, Mister Wrenn.

But I'd never have guessed about Lowen. Just imagine: he saw me that long ago and remembered all these years because I showed him he wasn't alone. I still can't add it up. Apples and oranges.

Unless, just maybe. . . .

"Lowen!"

The sound track again, the needle dropped on time. The balcony door thunders open and slams shut. Al calls again, but Lowen ignores her, leaning against the door, holding it closed.

"Gayla?"

His eyes move searchingly over the balcony in the darkening winter afternoon. From my name etched in the cement, around the railing, Lowen's whole concentrated being probes the gray light and air, full of purpose and need.

"Gayla, I know you're here."

As he says my name, sound and vision and my own strength treble. I turn to him, wondering if through the sheer power of his need he can see me yet.

Lowen, can you hear me?

"I think I know what this means."

I stretch out my hand, open up, let it touch his face, and as I tingle and hurt with it, Lowen turns his cheek into the caress.

"Yes, I feel you close."

Talk to me, love.

"Isn't it strange, Gayla?"

Not strange at all, not us.

"When I saw you that night, I wanted to reach out and

touch you, but I was just too shy. Couldn't even ask for my own autograph."

Why not? I could have used a little touching.

"But I hitched all the way from school next day just to catch a glimpse of you. Hid in the back of the theater and watched you rehearse."

That was Blanche. You saw that?

"It was the same thing all over again. You had something that reached out and showed me how we're all alike. I never saw a lonelier person than you on that stage. Or more beautiful. I cried."

You saw Blanche. She did have a beauty.

"Oh, Gayla, the letters I wrote you and never sent. Forgive me. I forgot the name but not the lesson. If you hear me: you were the first woman I ever loved, and you taught me right. It's a giving."

I can hear Al's urgent knock on the other side of the door. "Lowen, what is it? Are you all right?"

He turns his head and smiles. God, he's beautiful. "Fine, Al. She loves this place, Gayla. Don't drive her away."

I won't, but don't go. Now when I'm beginning to understand so much.

He shakes his head. "This is our first house. We're new, all kinds of problems. Parents, religion, everything."

Can you *hear* me?

"We were never loved by anyone before, either of us. That's new, too. You pray for it—"

Like a fire:

"—like a fire to warm yourself."

You do hear me.

"But it's scary. What do you do with the fire when it comes?" Lowen's hands reach out, pleading. "Don't take this away from her. Don't hurt my Al. You're stronger than us. You can manage."

I stretch my hand to touch his. With all my will, I press the answer through the contact.

Promise, Lowen.

"Don't make me shut you out, I don't know if I could. Go away and keep our secret? Take a big piece of love with you?"

Yes. Just that I was reaching for something, like you, and I had it all the time. So do you, Lowen. You're a—

I feel again as I did when the star fell across the sky, joyful and new and big as all creation without needing a reason, as Lowen's real fingers close around the memory of mine.

You're a *mensche*, love. Like me.

Lowen murmurs: "I feel your hand. I don't care what anyone says. Your kind of woman doesn't kill herself. I'll never believe it."

Bet on it. And thank you.

So it was a hell of a lot more than apples and oranges. It was a giving, a love. Hear that, Bill? Nattie? What I called life was just the love, the giving, like kisses on the wind, thrown to the audience, to my work, to the casual men, to whom it may concern. I was a giver, and if the little takers like Nick couldn't dig that, tough. That's the way it went down. All the miserable, self-cheating years, something heard music and went on singing. If Nattie could do it half as well. If she was half as alive as me, she meant. I loved all my life, because they're the same thing. Man, I was beautiful.

That's the part of you that woke me, Lowen. You're green, but you won't go through life like a tourist. You're going to get hurt and do some hurting yourself, but maybe someday. . . .

That's it, Lowen. That's the plot. You said it: we all touch, and the touching continues us. All those nights, throwing all of myself at life, and who's to say I did it alone?

So when you're full up with life, maybe you'll wake like me to spill it over into some poor, scared guy or girl. You're full of life like me, Lowen. It's a beautiful, rare gift.

It's dark enough now to see stars and the fingernail sliver of moon. A lovely moment for Lowen and me, like a night with Bill a moment before we made love for the first time. Lowen and I holding hands in the evening. Understanding. His eyes move slowly from my hand up, up toward my face.

"Gayla, I can see you."

Can you, honest?

"Very clear. You're wearing a sweater and jeans. And you're smiling."

Am I ever!

"And very beautiful."

Bet your ass, love. I feel great, like I finally got it together.

One last painful, lovely current of life as Lowen squeezes my hand. "Good-by, Gayla."

So long, love.

Lowen yanks open the door. "Al, Mister Hirajian? Come on out. It's a lovely evening."

Alice peeks out to see Lowen leaning over the railing, enjoying the river and the early stars. His chest swells; he's laughing and he looks marvelous, inviting Al into his arms the way he did on their first day here. She comes unsurely to nestle in beside him, one arm around his waist. "Who were you talking to?"

"She's gone, Al. You've got nothing to be afraid of. Except being afraid."

"Lowen, I'm not going to—"

"This is our house, and nobody's going to take it away from us." He turns Al to him and kisses her. "Nobody wants to, that's a promise. So don't run away from it or yourself."

She shivers a little, still uncertain. "Do you really think we can stay. I can't—"

"Hey, love." Lowen leans into her, cocky and charming, but meaning it. "Don't tell a *mensche* what you can't. Hey, Hirajian."

When the little prune pokes his head out the door, Lowen sweeps his arm out over the river and the whole lit-up West Side. "Sorry for all the trouble, but we've changed our minds. I mean, look at it! Who could give up a balcony with a view like this?"

He's the last thing I see before the lights change: Lowen holding Al and grinning out at the world. I thought the lights were dimming, but it's something else, another cue coming up. The lights cross-fade up, up, more pink and amber, until—my God, it's gorgeous!

I'm not dead, not gone. I feel more alive than ever. I'm Gail and Gayla and Lowen and Bill and Al and all of them magnified, heightened, fully realized, flowing together like bright, silver streams into—

Will you look at that *set*. Fantastic. Who's on the lights?

So that's what You look like. Ri-i-ght. I'm with it now, and I love You too. Give me a follow-spot, Baby.

I'm on.